The German Heiress

The German Heiress

A Novel

Anika Scott

HARPER LARGE PRINT

An Imprint of HarperCollinsPublishers

FIRST HARPER LARGE PRINT EDITION

ISBN: 978-0-06-297897-4

Library of Congress Cataloging-in-Publication Data is available upon request.

20 21 22 23 24 LSC 10 9 8 7 6 5 4 3 2 1

To my daughters, Olivia and Amelia

1

Everybody stole. Organized, they called it.

They organized coal off moving trains. They organized cars left alone in the streets. They organized pipes from houses where unexploded bombs nested on the roofs. Mostly, they organized food. Dug up fields and slaughtered cows. Hijacked trucks and robbed stores. Just that morning, Clara had read about a man who brained his friend for a slice of bread. The news sent the faintest prickle down her neck, and then she got on with her plans. Everybody organized one way or another.

Instead of sitting near the oil lamp like the other women, Clara lounged against the wall as far from the light as she could get. After sundown when the Allies restored power, the overhead lights would frost them all, highlighting eye color and birthmarks and all the other details she'd rather nobody concern themselves with. She touched the identity card in her pocket, testing the paper, the cheap card stock, then the smooth surface of the photo. The card was almost legal, issued by the town with signature and stamps.

According to the card, her name was Margarete Müller.

It was too dim to read in the waiting room, so the women sized each other up in silence. They were mostly mothers, gray-faced and younger than her, their children on their laps. As Margarete Müller, Clara did her best to blend in. Her coat was the same patched wool as the other women, her stockings mended just like theirs. A small hole she hadn't gotten around to repairing was below the hem at her left knee. Still, the women stared. At the heels she'd chosen to wear despite the frost. At the hem of her skirt, slightly too high to be proper. At the dark red on her lips, makeup salvaged from the war. She knew what the women were thinking. Horrible, inappropriate, scandalous thoughts just because she was showing a little knee. Mothers could be so hurtful.

She tried to ignore them and watched the consulting-room door, still firmly closed, made of a thick oak that kept out the sound from the other side. When it opened and Herr Doctor Blum's voice floated out, the women sat straighter, patting their hair and pinching color into their cheeks. He came out with a mother and daughter, the girl in dirty plaits, her skin as sickly pale as Clara's not so long ago. His gaze passed over the waiting room, counting the patients, Clara guessed, calculating time, the amount of energy he'd have to expend to see them all. Since she started consulting him six months ago, he'd grown thinner, and now the bones in his face seemed to ripple under the skin.

He stooped in front of the girl, got right down to her eye level like no doctor Clara had ever seen—they were, as a rule, too arrogant for that—and he held his fist to the side of her head. Everyone in the room strained to watch as he gasped and seemed to find in the girl's ear a sweets wrapper. Empty. Frowning like a clown, he let it flutter to the floor. Then he tried again, the fist at her ear, the gasp . . . and out came a peppermint in silver paper. The girl snatched it and bolted for the door, her mother batting her lashes at the doctor on the way out. Clara knew Dr. Blum well enough to know he'd try to ration his mysterious supply of sweets. Whenever he found some on the black market, he vowed to give them out slowly over a week or more so the sick children had something to look forward to. But he couldn't bear it. His jar would be empty by the end of the day. Everyone in the surgery knew that.

When he once more turned his attention to the women, they coughed into their handkerchiefs and held thin hands to their foreheads. The children were pinched and poked, and a little boy burst out crying. Clara thought this a cruel way to get the doctor's attention. She took a moment to examine the hole in her stocking, bending enough for the hem to rise that bit more up her thigh.

Voice neutral, Dr. Blum said, "Fräulein Müller."

As she limped past him—she hadn't limped coming in; it had only occurred to her now to begin—the women's coughs grew hostile behind her.

Once they were alone, Dr. Blum scooped her up and sat her on the examining table. "You're early, my sweet. We were supposed to meet at five."

"I have to cancel. Oh, don't look at me like that. So puppyish."

She cupped his ears, soft and fragile, and kissed his wonderfully unremarkable face, one sharp cheek, then the other, and finally his chapped lips. He was a small man, shorter than she liked; they would be almost the same height if she stood with the posture she'd had in the war. Back then, the Allies had claimed an iron rod was fused to her spine. They had called her unnatural, part human, part machine. *Punch* did a caricature of her eating coal and drinking oil, with cogs for joints.

She had framed it and hung it next to her office chair to remind herself of what she'd become to the outside world.

Dr. Blum knew nothing about all that.

"Darling," she said, stroking his cheek, "I'm going to Essen for a few days."

"You said you were going at the end of the month, for Christmas."

"The weather is turning so fast. I thought I'd better go now for a short visit before the trains freeze to the tracks. I don't want to get stranded somewhere."

He looked skeptical, and it surprised her. He'd always been so understanding, so ready to listen. She'd first come to him complaining of weakness, a sudden darkness in her head, a weight pressing down on her so hard that she had to sit before she fainted. He prescribed pills that tasted of sugar, and foul concoctions that left an oily film in her throat. She'd had a touch of anemia, he told her. By then she knew the real diagnosis. Hunger, the national disease. For the first time in her life, she had gone hungry long enough for it to change her body down to the blood.

"Margarete, there's something wrong. You're very pale. I can tell by the shadows around your eyes that you haven't been sleeping."

She looked down at their hands, their fingers intertwined. "I'm just worried. Not about us, about my friend in Essen. I told you about Elisa, remember?"

"No, I'm not sure you did."

"She hasn't answered my letter. It's been bothering me for weeks. I must go and see that she's okay."

"It can't wait until Christmas? We have plans tonight."

She explained again about the weather, and the days off work she'd negotiated with her employer, a cement factory where the management was astonished at her knowledge of production and logistics. She seemed too young, they told her, to know so much. She smiled modestly at that and mumbled about the valuable work experience she'd had—in Essen.

"I'll be back before you know it," she said. "We'll be able to spend Christmas together."

Dr. Blum pulled away, ruffling his hair on the way to his desk. He yanked open the drawer, reached inside, and went back to her holding out his fists knuckles down. "Pick one."

"Is it a peppermint?" She brightened. "A chocolate?"

He raised one eyebrow, a cockeyed look that made her smile. He wasn't one for boyish humor, and she appreciated this side of him she hadn't known was there. She tapped his left fist. He opened it finger by finger.

"Oh," she said. "Oh my."

In the lamplight, the ring in his palm shimmered darkly like old gold. It was a simple band without stones, and her hands went clammy when she looked at it.

"I wanted to do this tonight," he said. "I'd gotten up the nerve—" He cleared his throat, began again. "Dear Margarete, I'm not a wealthy man." From there, he outlined his finances, the expenses of the surgery, the reality of living in the rooms upstairs, how the war had wiped out his savings. "But you won't go hungry," he said. "I swear you won't. We'll manage to live honestly. We won't be thieves or beggars like the rest."

She was still looking at the ring. They'd known each other such a short time, most of it as doctor and patient. She wanted to ask him why the rush? But he was blushing and making so many promises about their life together, she didn't have the heart to interrupt him.

"And I thought perhaps you could take over the bookkeeping," he said. "You have a good head for that. The paperwork and the charts are a bit of a mess. I've been drowning since I lost my assistant."

"Aha. You want the cheap labor?"

"Of course not." He pressed her to his chest. "Although . . ."

She thumped him on the arm, more nervous than she let on. Marriage had been a delicate topic in her family and she was still uncomfortable with it. She tried to imagine Dr. Blum meeting her father. She was sure Papa would like him, this steady, reliable, generous man. She imagined them shaking hands for the first time, Dr. Blum's respectful bow, Papa's gesture to stop the formalities. They were family, and these were new times, he would say. A chance for a new life.

Doctor Blum. Herr Doctor Adolf Blum. His first name still made her squirm, but maybe she could call him . . . Adi. In every other way, he was perfect. A quiet man leading a quiet life in this little corner of Germany. He had no family or close friends. He avoided social engagements, as she did. He never read the papers, which had seemed strange at first, but then, hadn't they all had enough of politics? When the radio announced news, he turned the dial to music. Polkas were his favorite. She had nothing to fear from a man who loved the polka.

She looked at the water stain on the ceiling, the cracked paint on the windowsill. She had never been in the rooms upstairs but could imagine them, dark and low and narrow. This house wasn't much, but she began to imagine it with a fresh coat of paint, better furniture, a little care. She could fix it up, make it a place her father could stand to live in after he was released. A peaceful, comfortable place for him to recover out of the public eye. He was going to need that. It would be especially useful to have a doctor in the family. She imagined Papa moving in, having to hold his arm as he limped up the stairs, and she blinked at Dr. Blum to make the image go away.

"May I set a condition?" she asked.

Dr. Blum took off his spectacles. His eyes were watercolor blue. "Really?"

"Really."

His kiss tasted like a warm sweet in her mouth. It was hard to pull away. "I don't want any fuss about the wedding," she said. "No announcements in the papers. A small ceremony, only witnesses."

"Of course, whatever you like."

Only one witness mattered, and that was Elisa. Clara wasn't about to marry without her oldest friend there to weave her a bridal crown out of chewing gum wrappers, or give her advice about men. Two months ago, Clara had finally judged it was safe enough to send her a letter, but had heard nothing in return. It was likely the post was being as unreliable as everything these days. Or perhaps Elisa hadn't wanted to write back, a real possibility considering Clara had left Essen at the end of the war without saying good-bye. At the time, she had thought it best if no one knew her plans. Elisa would not have had to lie under questioning, if it had come to that. But the silence over the past months was awful.

Clara had begun to stock up on food and check almost daily on the train-line repairs that would allow her to get back to Essen. Just for a short trip. To see how Elisa and her son were doing, to apologize for leaving them so abruptly. Once she explained, Clara was sure Elisa would forgive her. And she could deliver her wedding invitation in person.

She turned the ring in her palm. When she married, she would make her home here in Hamelin, not in Essen. The thought felt strange. So final. But perhaps it was safer in the long run. "Oh, darling, there's one other thing. There should be a photograph only for us. Nothing for friends or acquaintances."

She expected Dr. Blum to demand an explanation. Instead he slid the ring onto her finger. Slowly. Pregnant with suggestion. "That suits me perfectly."

They hugged, Clara not quite believing she was to be married. She hadn't slept last night, and she feared she wasn't thinking as clearly as she should. But it was warm in his arms, and she wanted the warmth to last a little longer. She hooked a finger in the waistband of his trousers. The shock on his face passed quickly, and then he pressed her hard against the table, urgent, almost desperate. She responded in kind, wanting him just as intensely. It had been years since she was with a man, and how dull that time had been. But then he ripped her stockings, a long tear she felt as a cold draft down her leg. She bit back a cry of surprise and indignation. Max would never have done that to her. She ground her teeth until her jaw ached, wanting Max gone—out of her mind. He shouldn't ruin this moment. But he was still her standard by which all other men were measured. He had known how to blaze through her and leave her as groomed as when they began. Dr. Blum didn't realize or care that she was going to have to walk out of the surgery looking like a tart who couldn't keep her hosiery in one piece.

Looking pleased with himself, he gave her one last kiss, poured schnapps from his desk drawer into two mugs, and toasted their future as Herr and Frau Doctor Adolf Blum. "I'm so glad we've sorted this out," he said. "Now we can drop the pretense."

The electricity flashed on. Around the consulting room, overhead lights glinted on the scale, the tap, the instruments on the cart. Clara blinked the sparks out of her eyes, but they didn't clear. They were in her head, insistent as an alarm.

"Don't worry, I'll be a good wife," she said cautiously. "Old maids are motivated to learn."

"Now, now, I'm serious." He caught her hands in

his, tighter than was comfortable. "We're going to be married. Don't you think we should talk? Be honest with each other?"

"Yes, of course." She glanced at the door. "But you have patients . . ."

"They can wait. My dear, I've been bothered by . . . well, not doubts. I don't doubt you. But I have questions. I hope you'll answer them right now. Then we'll start a new life, closer than we were before. Isn't that what you want?"

Maybe this wasn't going to be so bad. She had spoken very little of herself. Wasn't it natural for a groom to want to know something about his bride? "Tell me what's bothering you. We'll clear it all up."

He kissed her fingers. "These are complicated times. One must be careful, as you well know. When I decided to propose, I took the precaution of asking around about you."

She freed her hands from his. "Spying? You were spying on me?"

"Learning about you, especially what you were like before we met. You took lodgings at the Hermann house soon after the war. Frau Hermann said you always wore a scarf over your hair."

Frau Hermann, the old busybody.

"Once, by chance, she glimpsed you without it. Your

hair"—he touched the strands at her temple —"had just begun to grow back. It had been shaved."

"I had lice, I'm afraid." A lie. "I don't like to remember those times." The truth.

"Before you found work, you paid your rent on time without fail and never lacked for money. Where did you get it?"

"My family never believed in banks. We kept Reichsmarks under the mattress. When the war was ending—"

"Your family, yes. An important point." Dr. Blum folded his stethoscope into his pocket. "You never speak of your family. Frau Hermann said you get no post from anyone named Müller and no visits at all."

"The war, the Collapse, you know how hard it is to find people—"

"My dear, be honest. Are your parents alive?"

This was dangerous territory. It would be easier to say they were dead, but the thought alone opened up a vast well inside her.

"They're all right. I think. I haven't seen them since the war."

"You quarreled with them?"

"No. No, not really."

"Well, what then?"

She tried to think of an explanation he would believe.

It was taking her too long, and his face grew grim. "Did they emigrate?"

"No, it's not that. It's more . . . they're hard to reach."

"If we're to marry, I really should speak to your father."

She searched his face for an ulterior motive and saw only the earnest wrinkle of his brow. Of course the bridegroom wanted to meet the father of the bride. But Dr. Blum was treading too closely to the very problem that had kept her up all night. She had lied to him; she had seen her father since the war: yesterday evening in a British newsmagazine she'd been surprised to find in her land-lady's parlor. He was standing in front of what looked like a barracks, staring out of the photograph across two Allied zones directly at her.

She had smuggled the magazine up to her room and thrown herself onto her narrow bed before she had had the strength to examine the picture more closely. His coat billowed from his body as if he'd shrunk. Weren't the Americans feeding him in their blasted internment camp? On his chin was the shadow of a beard. It was unheard of, this lack of grooming. The dome of his forehead was starred with light, sweating as the photograph was taken. It appalled her. Papa did not sweat. More deeply shocking was the puffiness of his face and the slight prominence of his eyelids. She had seen this swelling in Grandfather before his heart failed. Now she saw it in Papa.

She had read the article below the picture, picked out words—incitement to war, support of a criminal regime, crimes against humanity—and they seemed to slap her awake after a long sleep. She couldn't grasp the vast scale of the charges against him. They painted him as inhumane. Cruel. Brutal. She would be the first to admit she didn't always understand her father, his motives, the face he showed the world. But just as she was not the machine-woman the Allies had thought her to be, he was not a monster who had rushed to war, eager to serve the Nazis, crushing thousands of lives in his fist. The war was never that simple for either of them. In his study at home, he would often talk with her about the decisions it had been necessary to make as head of the family and the family businesses. The leather arms of his favorite chair had worn down over the years from his rubbing them as he talked. She had been honored to be his confidante, privileged to see his anxiety and dilemmas, his conscience. These were deep, private aspects of him, to which the Allies had no access. To her knowledge, he had kept no journals, had left no record of his motivations for others to present in a courtroom. Only his public face and actions mattered, and those were clearly as damaging to him as Clara's were to her.

What the world knew wasn't the whole truth about either of them. Odd memories from her childhood had flooded her all night, like the time Papa had let her sit on his desk as he worked. He had sketched a bird for her, and laughed as she chirped beside him and flew the bird around his head.

Dr. Blum took her hands. "Margarete . . . ?"

"I'm sorry, you asked about my father. I'm afraid it's not possible to speak to him. At the moment."

"What does he do?"

"He's . . . he used to run a . . . small factory."

"Margarete, in the spirit of honesty, I must confess I know who you really are."

She brushed past him and cupped her hands under the tap. The water tasted like rust but it stopped the room from spinning. She had known this would happen eventually, but assumed it wouldn't be until much later, a year from now, two, five, when she was sure of him.

"Who do you think I am?"

"I'm sorry, my dear, but it's clear you're a Jew."

She thought she must have heard incorrectly, but there he was, Dr. Blum looking anxious, as if worried he had offended her. Curious, she asked, "How did you come to that conclusion?"

"There's something about you. Something different.

I sensed it the moment we met. Once I hit on the truth, it was obvious. You're attractive in a dark, smutty way. You're intelligent and hardworking, positive aspects of the more educated Jew, as we all know. You also seem to have a wonderful gift for secrecy and deception." He smiled with gentle encouragement. "My dear, I know how hard it is to admit the truth. Don't be ashamed."

He was looking at her with such warmth, and she didn't understand why. Why would he want to marry her if he thought such things, and mistook her as Jewish? Was his conscience eating away at him? Had photographs from the concentration camps driven him to this decision, a desire to make things right in his small way? She could accept that. Barely. As his wife, she would help him change his ugly views further. She had never held anything against anyone based on the happenstance of their birth, and she had never understood such prejudice against groups of people as a whole. The Allied newsmen didn't believe this, of course, but they didn't know her as well as they thought.

For now, she didn't correct Dr. Blum's false assumption. It was safer than the truth.

"Did you tell anyone about this?" she asked.

"Not yet. It's no one's business but ours. But you must tell me your real name."

At the cart, she picked up the hammer he used to

test reflexes. She wanted to bang it against her temple, clear her mind of the fog. "Please, don't ask me that."

"You'll have to tell me one day. It's only fair. We've got to keep faith with each other. We've got to. Don't you see? I don't care who you are. It's the world. The terrible people out there who judge us all."

She thought of the men who would sit in judgment of her father at Nuremberg, and the feelings from last night flooded her again—fear, dismay, even anger. They didn't know him, they couldn't possibly judge him fairly, accounting for all the things he truly was. They had made up their minds about him—and her. The article she'd read last night had mentioned Clara too. The missing daughter, wanted for questioning, which she knew to be a polite way of saying they would prosecute her as soon as they found her. That would mean internment, conviction, prison. For years.

She went back to Dr. Blum, her dear, misguided fiancé. She shouldn't judge him when he'd been honest with her. He was absurdly wrong, but she didn't have to enlighten him yet. The truth might scare him away exactly when she needed him. They could make a fresh start together. Live a new life. Be different people.

"I want to marry you," she said. "Nothing else matters."

"I'm so relieved." Dr. Blum stroked her cheek with his knuckles. "If the Allies give me any trouble, you— my loving wife—will testify to my generosity in this matter."

His hand felt like ice on her skin. She didn't like his smile, the smugness underneath, the sense of triumph. There was something in him she hadn't seen before. "Trouble?"

"Don't worry, my dear. It's nothing."

"It doesn't sound like nothing. Adi, what trouble?"

"One day people might come asking questions, that's all. I've been unfairly handled in the papers—"

She touched the cold table behind her. She read every newspaper she could get her hands on and had never seen his name.

"Your name isn't Blum?"

"All you need to know is that I did what was right no matter what some malicious people might say."

"What might they say?"

"The details don't—"

"The details matter. Tell me what you've done. Now."

He stiffened. Her old tone of command had slipped out. She had suppressed it since the war. It wouldn't do for people to think she was the kind of woman who was used to giving orders and having them obeyed. "Darling," she went on, "we're being honest with each other, remember? You can tell me anything."

"It's complicated." He sighed. "When the war started, I left my doctor's practice in Bremen to work at Ravensbrück."

"The concentration camp. For women."

"Our work has been completely maligned in the press," he said. "The Allies don't understand what the medical staff were trying to do. It was an act of self-defense. A kind of immunization of the people. We worked to protect the healthy Volk from the sick and corruptive influence of the Reich's natural enemies. For the record, I always thought the Party wasted too much energy on the Jew. The real danger through sheer numbers comes from the Slav. But duty was duty."

"What exactly did you do"—she was staring at the ring, the tiny reflection of herself deep in the gold—"at the camp?" Scratches crisscrossed the surface of the ring. On the inside were initials. Not hers, not his. Whose then? She wanted to believe he had gotten it on the black market, but her hand felt burned, as if dipped in acid.

"I worked with children."

"Were they ill?"

"The individual mattered less than protecting the whole, my sweet. For the general good, if a few needed to be sterilized . . ."

She couldn't listen to the rest. She let him talk while she maintained an understanding, attentive look on her face. A wisp of a memory curled into her mind: a thin Ukrainian girl in a checkered head scarf pouring her a cup of tea. Her eyes had met Clara's with a warmth Clara would never have expected because of who she was, because of who the girl was. Clara closed her eyes and the memory blew away, leaving her here and now with Dr. Blum. Or whoever he really was.

After a light kiss and a final good-bye, he accompanied her back into the waiting room. The women still sat with their children. They stared at her ripped stocking with hostility and envy. She had very little time to warn them about the creature that held her arm. All she could do was look at each woman as she passed, showing the depth of her disgust as it rose from her stomach and up her throat and settled, hard and clear, in her eyes. By the time she had buttoned her coat, the first of the women were fetching hats and mittens and herding their children out of the door.

2

On the way home, Clara stomped down the lane of half-timbered houses, a dusting of frost on the windowsills, a glow of weak light behind the panes. It was late afternoon and already dark. People were lining up at the grocer's next to her boardinghouse. They waited in silence, holding their empty buckets and sagging bags, the women in the back straining to see to the front of the line. At any moment, the grocer might come out and declare the shelves empty. Children built stone towers nearby and leap-frogged in the lane. Clara watched them play, saw the exhaustion and anxiety of their mothers in the line, and she thought of Blum and his doctor's tools. She'd seen no conscience in him, no remorse. And he'd expected her to understand him—

out of desperation, out of love? She'd been stupid, blind, and far too close to becoming the wife of that swine. A tiny part of her wondered if she was being unfair, judging him as harshly as others would judge her and her father, but she overruled that quickly enough. She wanted to shout at herself for not seeing what Blum was capable of.

"Excuse me, miss," said a British soldier, "are you all right?"

She started back from him, though he was looking at her with concern. Perhaps he'd noticed her distress, her torn stocking. He seemed very young, far younger than her, his nose red as though he'd just had a drink. His cigarette was half smoked, and several butts were scattered at his feet. His presence on the pavement confused her. Why was he standing so close to her door?

Her head bowed, she stuttered an answer in German peppered with easy English words. She was quite all right, thank you. She was only very cold, and hungry too. The soldier searched his pocket and gave her a sweet. It upset her and she didn't know why until she remembered Blum and his peppermints. She thanked him, pushed open the boardinghouse door and closed it quickly behind her. She hadn't exchanged casual words with a soldier in months, but every time it happened, it left her shaking. He couldn't possibly have any idea of who she was. Surely he was nothing more than a soldier being kind.

She tore the wool cap from her hair and dashed up the steps, dying to change her clothes and scrub herself with a soapy brush that would leave her raw and clean. She would finish packing for the trip to Essen, head to the station, wait on the platform as long as it took for a train to come.

The sharp singsong of her landlady came from the dining room. "Is that you, Fräulein Müller?"

Clara halted, too late to creep the rest of the way upstairs. Frau Hermann loomed in the foyer below, a teapot in her hand. She was a widow of the old type, in fake pearls and black skirts trimmed with dreary black lace.

"You're pale as death, my dear. What's happened?"

Clara held on to the banister. Her anger at Blum and the stronger anger at herself was exhausting. She'd had a close call, like dodging a car in the street, and she wanted to tell someone about it. But that was impossible. Blum still believed she would marry him, and if she told her landlady even a part of the truth, Frau Hermann would no doubt tell him that his bride was having second thoughts.

"I'm fine, Frau Hermann. Really."

"My dear, but you're shivering. Come and warm up."

Clara looked at her glove. As hard as she willed it, her hand wouldn't stop trembling. She still felt the burn of the wedding band. She'd left it with Blum until they could get it refitted. Except that she had no intention of marrying him. While she was away, she would consider how to break the engagement quietly, without drawing attention to herself.

Suddenly tea seemed like a wonderful idea, a moment to collect herself before making her escape. Frau Hermann was a gossip and had spied for Blum, but Clara didn't think her landlady knew what he was. She probably thought she was playing a part in the romance between her lodger and the local doctor, a welcome change from running the boardinghouse.

"I'll come in," Clara said, "for a moment."

In the dining room, the other lodgers were arranged around the table as if they were dolls Frau Hermann had placed for a tea party. They were a shabby lot: journeymen in dusty black waistcoats; young women who earned their money in mysterious ways. They greeted Clara without much interest. She sat next to one of the girls she shared her room with, a blonde who claimed she worked in a shop but who slept until noon and only went out at night. She was still in her dressing gown.

"Late shift again?" Clara asked.

The girl shrugged and didn't bother to look up from the July 1946 issue of *Die Frau* that the women of the boardinghouse had been passing around to each other for months. Clara had studied it like an instruction manual on how to be a normal woman who could conjure up a meal out of rationed food or alter old clothing into something new and lovely. Growing up, she'd never learned such useful things.

"Come, child, tell us what's upset you," Frau Hermann said as she poured the tea. She hovered next to Clara like a hungry raven. "You can tell us everything." She gestured at the table. "We're family."

As the boarders turned to look at her, Clara warmed her hands on her cup and thought of her real family gathered around the table for a meal long before the war. At first, the children behaved as their mother wished, but with each dish the servants brought, the composure of Clara and her brothers slipped. Feet pounded each other under the table, elbows poked, peas careered across the tablecloth until the children were laughing and Papa announced with his secret smile that that was quite enough. Clara behaved for the rest of the meal even if her brothers didn't. She would never do anything to be sent from the table.

A wave of sadness hit her, and she focused back on the other boarders. She had worked hard to avoid being noticed, and now their attention was on her for perhaps the first time since she had moved into Frau Hermann's house. She had thought she didn't want them interested in her—it was safer for her if they weren't—but now she wanted to tell them something, to coax them into caring at least a little about what she'd just gone through with Blum, even if she couldn't tell the whole truth.

"I've become engaged." Her voice sounded strange to her. Breathless and anxious.

Frau Hermann pressed a hand to her heart. "Oh, fräulein. I knew it. Oh, my dear. Congratulations." Her lips felt like a cold feather on Clara's cheek. She spun away, informing the table about Adolf Blum, a good, fine doctor. She opened the cupboard and, to Clara's surprise, pulled out a bottle of schnapps.

Clara's roommate touched her arm. "A doctor. Lucky you. Congratulations."

"Yes. Yes, thank you." The touch surprised her, made her want to get up and shake everyone's hand, or hug them, as if this really was a special occasion and the lodgers her friends.

Her mood deflated. She fidgeted with the napkin in her lap while Frau Hermann circled the table pouring the schnapps, talking all the while about how wonderful marriage was, especially in these hard times. It was a sign of renewal. A triumph of decency over the dark past.

"To new beginnings," Frau Hermann said, raising her glass.

Clara forced a smile. "To new beginnings."

The lodgers clinked glasses and drank and began talking of other things. Clara didn't join in. For a few minutes at the surgery, she had thought she would start her new life with Blum. Yet that was out of the question now. She had no desire to see him ever again. Even if he accepted her refusal to marry him, he might not feel safe now that she knew his secret. The last thing she needed was another potential enemy. It would be prudent to leave Hamelin for good.

But what was she supposed to do then? How was she supposed to live? And where? Her father was in the internment camp. Her mother had never been there for her when she needed the support. Her brothers were gone. Max was . . . somewhere, maybe still in Essen, but she didn't want to see him, or to indulge in the slither of anger and disappointment she felt at the mere idea of that man. She thought uneasily about the soldier outside, the hard realities of being in hiding, how reserved she'd been with everyone she knew here, the lies she'd told them, the careful construction of Margarete Müller in the eighteen months since the end of the war. Living like this drained her more than she had realized. How long could she possibly keep it up? The rest of her life?

It seemed impossible now. Part of her must have known that. The risk of a letter to Elisa, carefully worded so that only her friend would know who wrote it, the plan to go back to Essen for a visit—they were signs of how much she yearned for home. To walk the streets, smell the familiar smoky tang in the air, talk with someone who knew and loved the real her. She would still have to be careful. But surely no one would recognize her now? She smoothed her skirt over her thighs, far thinner than they used to be, her face transformed, she thought, by hunger and the strain of living with shortages and want. She would go home, yes, and—she promised herself—she would keep the visit short. She would take shelter with Elisa, who would help her decide where to go next.

She finished her tea, shoved a wedge of bread into her mouth, and stood up. Elisa wouldn't turn her away after all they'd been through. Yet the unanswered letter was troubling her again. It suddenly felt imperative that she get to Essen tonight, no matter how late.

"Where are you going, dear?" Frau Hermann asked.

"Oh, I forgot to tell you, I'll be going away for a few days."

"Where to?"

"I'll be back Sunday." She was turning away, and Frau Hermann caught her elbow and led her back to the table.

"Wait a moment, dear, no need to run away from us. I have something special for the new bride."

"That's so kind, but I really have to pack for the train—"

But her landlady pressed her firmly into her seat, then hurried into the kitchen, where she murmured something to her granddaughter, a stocky girl who tossed a worried glance into the dining room and then vanished. That look. What errand could Frau Hermann be sending the girl on with such urgency? The kitchen door slammed, and then Frau Hermann swept back into the dining room. With great satisfaction, she was brandishing a packet of Player's, offering each lodger one cigarette. "To smoke," she said, "not to hoard. We're celebrating Fräulein Müller's good fortune."

Clara didn't smoke. Frau Hermann knew this, yet she lit Clara's cigarette first, an odd look—of cunning? triumph?—in her eyes.

Uneasy, Clara puffed at the cigarette until it was low enough to set aside without offense. British cigarettes were selling for about four marks a stick, making Frau Hermann's gift a generous one. Too generous—as if she had plenty more. Where in the world had she gotten them from? And the bottle of schnapps? The black market? Allied soldiers? The boardinghouse had nothing those soldiers would want to buy, and Frau Hermann was too prim to sell her body. She wondered what else Frau Hermann could have sold for British favors.

Clara made her excuses and pounded up the stairs. In her room, she washed quickly in the basin and then dressed in as many layers of clothing as possible. The more she wore, the less she would have to carry. She pulled her bed away from the wall and peeled back the loose wallpaper, exposing the hole she had discovered soon after she moved in. Stacked inside were the tins of food she'd been saving for the trip to Essen. After packing these away in her backpack, she reached deeper into the hole, pawing the cold, loose mortar and cringing at the possibility of spiders. Finally, her fingers closed around the envelope. She opened it and took out the ring first. Far grander than Blum's, it was a one-carat diamond in a gold band, which she polished now and then when she was feeling homesick. Clara's grandfather had bought it for her grandmother on the occasion of an audience with Kaiser Wilhelm II in Berlin. Clara had never cared about kaisers, but had loved Grandmother Sophia, who took up tennis at age sixty and once tried to break the racket over her knee when she lost. Sophia had given her everything her mother hadn't provided: the warm body to lean against, the protective arm when there was strife with her brothers, an honest word of advice when she was anxious about her feet growing so fast or the hair sprouting under her arms. Clara slid the ring onto her finger. It fit perfectly.

The only other thing in the envelope was a photograph. Her family in the winter garden at Falkenhorst, her childhood home. Seeing it sparked a rush of love and sorrow. It had been taken late in 1940, the last time they were photographed all together, her parents, her brothers, and her. Grandmother Sophia formed the center, upright in her wheelchair, immaculate and frail. Papa stood behind her, his beloved mother, his hands on the back of her chair. The war hadn't aged him yet. His face was slim and sharp and he had a full head of pale gleaming hair. Yet even now, years later, Clara saw the hint of anxiety in his face. He had news for the family, but kept it quiet until after the photographer left.

Anne, Clara's mother, already knew. In the photograph, she stood to Papa's right, her lovely face pinched and anxious. This was so unusual for her, especially when cameras were around, that Clara had kept turning to look at her, and then at Papa, which had driven the photographer mad. In the final shot, her face was half turned to Papa, her hand nervously clutching the arm of Grandmother's wheelchair. Clara was twenty-four years old, hair tousled, wearing a harlequin-printed skirt Elisa had sewn for her because the colors cheered them both.

After the photographer left, dear Friedrich, dashing in his Luftwaffe uniform, had poured drinks for everyone. Grandmother Sophia first, of course, then Papa, Mother, the older sons Heinrich, in a suit, and Otto, in uniform. Next, himself, the youngest son. Only then did he carry a cognac over to Clara, the baby of the family. He raised an eyebrow at her. What's going on? She shrugged and was glad when he sat beside her on the divan.

Papa called the nurse to wheel Grandmother out, and Sophia said, "Just because I'm dying doesn't mean I'm blind, Theo. What's bothering you?"

He nursed his glass, his other hand balled in his pocket. His face was unusually pale, a trick of the daylight, Clara hoped, the cold, white sky penetrating the glass walls. "You're all aware I've been maintaining a line of communication with Fritz Thyssen in France," he said.

Thyssen was a fellow Catholic industrialist Papa had known all his life. After years of supporting Hitler, Thyssen had begun openly protesting the war. Hitler, he said, was driving Germany to ruin. As far as Clara was concerned, this was true, and though she'd never liked Thyssen's previous political views, she had been shocked when his industrial holdings were confiscated and his family driven into exile in Vichy France by the very party he'd once endorsed. Most recently, Germany had been demanding his extradition.

"I've just had word," Papa said, "that Fritz and his wife have been turned over to the Gestapo and brought back to Germany."

The heavy silence in the room made Clara lean against Frie-drich, who put his arm around her. He could usually see the good side of any situation, but even he looked grim.

Grandmother asked, "Where are they now?"

"Apparently they've been committed to some kind of a . . ." As Papa took another drink, he mumbled into his glass, ". . . sanatorium."

All around them, a draft rustled the palm trees her mother loved, the broad-leafed bushes, and the vines that would flower in summer.

"We'll do what we can for them," Papa said.

Anne put her hand on his arm, a warning look, but he ignored her. "The war is going well. It shouldn't last much longer. Until it's over, we will continue to serve our country and that is all."

He was looking at Clara, and she held his gaze as long as she could, but then she lowered her eyes, always the first to give in, and angry at herself for it. In the past, she had told him how much she disliked Thyssen, who had supported the Nazis when they were following his political agenda. But he had turned against the war, and now it wasn't so easy to paint him as blackly as she once did. As long as he was one of "them," she had been able to draw a clear line separating people like him from her father, who was not a true believer. She certainly wasn't either; she couldn't stand how the Reich sought to control how people lived, worked, and thought, or the hatred and violence of their ideology. Papa felt the same, but he considered himself a pragmatist. "Hold your nose, open your wallet, and shake their hands." That was his method of getting on with the regime. It galled her when he spoke at Party functions or chatted with Hitler and Mussolini when they visited Essen before the war, but she understood why he did it, from his perspective at least. In his study, he admitted to her how he despised some of the things he had to do to keep the government pacified. A little playacting on his part, he said, was necessary to protect the mines and factories, her and her brothers, her mother and grandmother too, and the reputation of the family. His primary duty was to preserve this legacy for the next generation. When he said that, he had put his hand on hers, and there was an electric shock as if he was transferring this duty to her.

His playacting was a sensible survival tactic, given the circumstances, even if the hint of cowardice left a bad taste in her mouth. But at least it was better than being a Nazi disciple, fawning over the little men in their uniforms, awed by the führer, eager to die in some twisted idea of glory. In private, she was quite bold about telling her father that a strong and just society had a free press and no political prisoners. He agreed with her with a wave of his hand. "But this is the world we live in." He tapped the arm of his chair. "This world, here and now. It's only temporary anyway. The kaiser was still around when you were a baby. He went. Weimar came and went. Now the Nazis are here. In a few years, they'll be gone too. Don't put your faith in this or that society. Put it in the only thing that endures."

The family, of course. It was a good family on the days she could avoid her mother, and she knew that it had sheltered her from the storms that had shaken Germany her whole life. But was there a point at which her father would say or do what he truly believed, despite the risk? Would she? Thyssen had spoken out and was taking the consequences, and now she knew—they all knew—no family was truly safe.

She had longed to talk more to Papa about all of this, but the topic seemed to irritate him lately. He made it clear that Thyssen's views were not the issue at all. The consequences of dissent were. Exile, confiscations, arrest. Ruin. Papa would not let that happen to this family. Did she understand?

In her attic room, she put the family photograph inside the woodstove. Then she added the magazine's picture of Papa in the internment camp. She lit the match and let it burn. If her brothers had lived, so much in her life would have been different. If she'd gone into exile. If there hadn't been a war. If, if, if. Like her father, she had playacted for years to preserve the family, and they had lost everything regardless. Did he see the irony the way she did?

She touched the flame to the paper and watched it consume her family and herself.

On the train station platform, Clara waited with the crowd sitting on their suitcases and bags, an hour when a train was supposed to come and didn't, another hour when she and many others got up to walk around and keep warm while maneuvering their way to the edge of the tracks. The closer she was, the better chance she had of getting a seat on the train. If it came at all.

When it finally arrived, the Reichsbahn men whistled and pushed the people on the platform back until the passengers had disembarked. Another whistle, and there was a surge forward, Clara kicking and boxing her way to a seat by the window, glassed by some miracle, but useless now because it was dark. People packed the rest of the car, pressing her to the wall, pinning her at the thigh, jamming her knees, stepping on her feet. Passengers hugged suitcases and sacks and backpacks like her own, except theirs looked empty. She guessed some of them were heading to the countryside to scrounge in the fields for a forgotten potato or an edible stalk. They had the blank stares of the hungry and smelled soiled. Out of nowhere, a bout of nausea hit her. She pressed her handkerchief to her nose and mouth and remembered the transports arriving at the family iron works from the occupied territories behind the Eastern Front. The doors of the freight cars rolling open, releasing the concentrated stench of the people inside, Russians perhaps, Ukrainians, thin, gray, frightened, peering out at her . . .

The train began to move, and she pulled her scarf in front of her face and breathed in deeply, her smell at least, no one else's. Think of now, not then. She was on her way. That was what she should dwell on. The thrill, the power of all this steel carrying her home. She tried to imagine what it was going to be like, which streets had been cleared of rubble, which buildings had been salvaged, which knocked down. She wondered if a single chestnut had been left standing on the Huyssenallee and, if so, would it ever sprout leaves again? She wondered about her family home, if it had survived. The iron works too, though she had seen aerial photographs of it in an Allied magazine. Kilometers of destruction, the same desert she had fled at the end of the war.

Her mood darkened again, and she struggled to pull her mind back to something that would soothe her. Elisa opening her door, not angry, not accusing her of abandonment, just a scream of surprise and delight. She would drag Clara into the house, crying, "God, God in heaven," over and over, though she didn't believe in anything of the sort. There would be long, emotional hugs. Tears, maybe. The time apart wouldn't matter. They had known one another for so long.

They had first met fifteen years ago at a café overlooking the Ruhr. The hills had unfolded below as Clara leaned on the terrace railing, gazing all the way down to the water. It was a warm spring day but the winds were strong, rattling the white tablecloths. People held down their hats, and some went inside. That was out of the question for her, because of the fresh air—there were so few places in the city where the air was this sweet—and because her mother had ordered her to stay with Elisa, the office girl.

Elisa, in a white hat, her curls wrestled to the back of her neck in an unfashionable bun. Her hands in her white gloves were fiddling with the porcelain. Her costume was the soft white of eggshells. She chewed her bottom lip and looked anxiously around her, reminding Clara somehow of a rabbit. It was the first time Clara had ever seen her, or, at least, had noticed her. Anne had said Elisa was seventeen and worked in the legal department at the Works. The poor thing needed a friend, and Clara did too. Anne wouldn't say why an office girl was suddenly deemed a fitting companion for her daughter, and Clara assumed it was a slight for something she herself had done, for the trouble she'd been in at school, or the times she'd walked in the garden barefoot like a heathen, as Anne would say. "You're becoming common, darling," Anne had told her not so long ago. And here was Elisa, a common girl to show Clara what she was in danger of being.

The whole situation was strange, but then Clara was accustomed to her mother's manipulative tendencies. People were indulgent with Anne because she was English and rich, and she suffered no fools. She shimmered in gray silk at a nearby table, pretending to read the newspaper, and somehow—Clara never knew how

she did it—observing everything through sulkily lowered eyelids. For a moment, Anne looked directly at
Clara at the railing, and ice chilled Clara's spine. She
returned to sit across from Elisa, not sure what to say to
this girl all in white. She looked nice. Maybe it was her
freckles.

"I think it's awful too," Elisa said quietly, the wind
taking her words out and over the hills.

"What is?"

"Making you come here. And me. It's humiliating."

Fidgeting with her napkin, Clara grasped for a topic
of conversation. "Well, what does your father do?"
This said half of what one needed to know about a
person.

"He died years ago." Elisa said this with a relief
Clara couldn't begin to understand.

The waitress brought the coffee and cake. Elisa took
a sip, drawing her lips back with a hiss. Then she tried
the cake, scooping a swirl of cream onto her fork and
licking it off like a cat. She held it in her mouth for
a moment, and Clara saw the pallor spreading around
her freckles.

"Is something wrong?"

"I just . . . have a delicate stomach."

"You're going to be sick." Clara got up, searching
for more napkins. What was she supposed to do with

this flimsy girl who couldn't stomach coffee and cream cake? "Are you going to faint?"

Something steely came into Elisa's eyes. "I don't faint."

"Well, you look like you're going to. Why did you come if you're not feeling well?"

"You should sit down. Your mother's watching."

Clara dropped back into her chair. "I have an aspirin. Will that help?"

Elisa began to cluck in her throat, and Clara thought this girl was going to be sick after all. But then Elisa's laughter erupted, so loudly the people at the other tables turned to stare. "No, an aspirin won't help."

"Is it catching?"

"No. You'll probably get it one day, though." The mirth drained from Elisa's face. "Don't tell your mother I said that. Please. We're laughing about . . . tell her it was about a film."

The fear in Elisa's face intrigued Clara. She forgot the question of illness, pulled her chair closer, and asked softly, "Why did my mother tell you to meet with me? She told me you needed a friend."

"I suppose I do." Elisa's lips parted, and a tingle ran up Clara's arms. Elisa was about to tell her something important. A secret.

But then the wind gusted over the terrace, shaking the tables and rattling the porcelain. The tablecloth whipped in Clara's face. As she batted it away, her hat dislodged itself from her hair. With a yelp, she ran after it to the edge of the terrace and jumped up, reaching out because her mother would be furious: a perfectly good hat flying into the river. Her feet were off the ground; she was teetering on the railing. Then she felt arms around her, Elisa pulling her back, light brown curls flying around her face.

"I saved your life," she said.

"Not my hat, though." They smiled shyly at each other. Fear seemed to sit deep in the flecks in Elisa's pale blue irises. When Clara saw that, she wanted to protect her, though she didn't know why or from what.

They returned to their table. Elisa walked stiffly as if her joints hurt. She lowered herself awkwardly into her chair and, with a sigh, pressed her hand to her stomach. Clara's stomach ached in sympathy, and she met Elisa's gaze.

Neither of them said anything about a baby. Not until a couple of months later when Elisa couldn't hide it anymore. By then, they were spending as much time with each other as Clara could get away with. Lounging on towels in the park, ogling boys at the cinema, or talking as they strolled under shady trees. She had never talked so much in her life. About fashion, politics, poetry, aeronautics, kittens. It was as though Elisa had uncorked her and all sorts of ideas bubbled out. Within the year, she entrusted Elisa with her deepest, darkest secrets. Like the scare she'd had with Max when Clara wept with fright in Elisa's bathroom because her cycle was late. Elisa had gone through this already, all of the same confusion and panic, and Clara was so grateful to have a friend who knew how it felt and didn't judge. When it turned out to be a false alarm, Elisa gave her some well-worn pamphlets that explained how to prevent such an issue in future. No one else in Clara's life would have done such a thing for her. Elisa was the sister she had always wanted, and if her mother regretted introducing her to this so-called commoner, too bad.

On the train, Clara longed to stretch her stiff legs, but there was no room in the cramped car. Out of the window was nothing but blackness, and it was hard to know how far the train had gone. By the ache in her backside, she'd been sitting on the hard bench at least an hour, maybe more. The woman opposite began reading Goethe's *Faust I* out loud by the glow of her flashlight. She murmured the verses, the only voice behind the roar and creak of the train.

"In the currents of life, in action's storm,
I float and I wave
With billowy—"

The brakes suddenly shrieked on the rails, and Clara was lifted off her seat. Everyone pitched forward with the momentum of the train as it slowed and rolled to a halt.

Passengers stooped to recover their bags and belongings scattered on the floor. The reader dusted off her Goethe. People whispered about the possibility of the boiler failing or the coal running out. They could be here for hours. To steady her nerves, Clara nibbled a small piece of bread.

Outside, lights strafed the train and were gone. Far off, someone whistled, and farther along the train, doors banged open. Clara turned with everyone else to look at the end of the carriage. A man climbed on board, backlit by the glare outside. His silhouette revealed his uniform, like a nightmare that had haunted her since the end of the war.

"Please stay calm, this is a routine search," he said in

German with a heavy English accent. The bread stuck in her throat.

Soldiers were crowding in behind him, their lights whirling over the passengers. Here and there, they examined someone's papers. Women only.

She pressed the ends of her scarf to her mouth. They couldn't be looking for her. If by chance they were, she was still safe. They would be expecting a proud-faced, curvy platinum blonde. Her old name was famous, her old face. She wouldn't have dared go back to Essen if she doubted what a year and a half of defeat had done to her body.

"Fräulein?" The soldier had a ginger mustache and cold eyes set deep into his skull. He seemed, somehow, like the soldier who had spoken to her outside her boardinghouse. She'd been too upset about Blum to look at him closely, and couldn't tell if she was imagining a resemblance.

Her temples pounded. "Yes, sir?"

"Your papers, please."

She clutched the identity card in her palm. She was Margarete Müller. Without the card, how would anyone know who she was supposed to be?

"Fräulein."

She let him examine it, her breaths puffing in the

light of his flashlight. "Is there something wrong?" she asked, so quietly he didn't seem to hear.

He reached for her elbow. "Come along."

"But why?"

The other passengers drew away from Clara as she was pulled upward. She tripped over feet and bags down the aisle and out into the cold night. The soldier led her across a strip of dead grass to the road where several army vehicles were parked.

"There's been a mistake," she said, turning to the train.

More soldiers blocked her, forced her back toward the road. In the glare of the headlights was a folding table. Standing next to it, a British officer.

He was very still, his hands deep in his pockets. She knew he was an officer because he didn't come to her; she was forced by the soldiers to stumble up the dirt road to him. He said something in German she couldn't hear over the rumble of the idling vehicles. He repeated himself.

"Look at me, please."

"Sir?" She tried to calm her voice. "There's been a mix-up."

He lifted her chin, a soft pressure she barely felt. He angled her face toward the light, this way and that. In the glare she could make out only the curve of his lips and the precise line of his mustache.

"You've changed," he said with a hint of regret. "Except . . ." Gently, he traced his thumbs around her eyes.

3

The British officer introduced himself as Thomas Fenshaw and then paused as if giving Clara time to recognize the name. She didn't. His rank came next—captain—mumbled as if it embarrassed him. She couldn't decide if he was attempting to set her at ease by reminding her that a civilian existed deep inside his uniform, or whether he expected her to introduce herself in return. Say her real name. Just like that. She was off balance, she was shivering with cold and fright, but she was not going to give herself away that easily.

They were on the edge of a barren field somewhere in Westphalia. She sensed the wide, flat land in the darkness all around her. With a gallant flourish, Fenshaw led her to a stool at his folding table. "Reynolds," he said to the ginger soldier who had taken her off the train. "Get the fräulein a tea. Black. She doesn't like it sweet."

"Oh, sir, but I do." It was important to contradict him right away, to show him he had the wrong woman any way she could. "It would be so wonderful to have real, sweet tea again."

Captain Fenshaw gave her an amused look, and said nothing else until Reynolds brought her a steaming thermos cup. The man had sugared it so heavily she felt the grit in her teeth.

"Good?" Fenshaw asked.

"Yes, sir. Thank you, sir." As the meek Margarete Müller, she added, "You're very kind, sir."

His lips twitched, and he turned to the light to examine her identity card. He rubbed it between thumb and index finger like a tailor might to judge the quality of his fabric.

"Margarete Müller."

"Yes, sir."

"Where are you going tonight?"

"Essen, sir. I have a ticket . . ." She searched her pockets, but it was hard to make her fingers do what she wanted.

"Why are you traveling to Essen?"

"Just visiting, sir."

"Anyone in particular?"

"Oh no, sir, I don't know anyone there anymore. I want to go to the gardens."

It was the first lie that came to mind, and she rushed to embroider it. "I'm not sure if you know Essen, sir. The Grugapark? I used to go to the gardens every season. To see how everything had changed. I wanted to go in autumn to see the leaves, but the trains are so unreliable. I thought I'd try now. The gardens are beautiful in the frost."

"Do you see that field over there?"

He pointed. The far edges of the field were invisible in the dark, but in the beams of the headlamps from the road, she could see footprints all over the furrows, random piles of dirt, holes in the ground. She imagined people from the city had been over it like locusts digging up whatever they could eat.

"That," Fenshaw said, "is what the gardens in Essen have looked like since the war."

He held her gaze a long moment, then he bent her identity card in his hand and continued to ask questions. Her birth date, how old she was, where she was born, her current address. This was on the card; he was testing her. He branched out into things like her current employer and the number on her ration card. She didn't know it by heart and reached into her coat to take it out. She had to concentrate to keep her hand steady as she passed it to him. Her knees, though, were trembling.

"While you're at it," he said, "please empty your pockets."

It was humiliating to stand by and do nothing while he pawed and poked her things: the coin purse emptied, the slips of paper read. He turned his attention to her backpack, piling everything on top of the files that already filled the table. He examined each can of food, opened her matchbox, sniffed her toothpaste. At least she'd burned her family photograph. Captain Thomas Fenshaw would not get his hands on that.

"Is there something you're looking for, sir?"

He gave her a brief smile, and continued with her clothes, shaking out each item, reading the label if it had one, then folding it carefully and moving on to the next. When he touched her underclothes, she bit her cheek to keep herself from saying something she would regret. She wound her arms around her waist, holding herself together. She was Margarete Müller. She couldn't let him shake her out of that certainty.

He finished putting her belongings back into the rucksack. "Why do you think I stopped your train, fräulein?"

Half a dozen soldiers were posted between the road and the carriages behind her. They were smallish men with the wiry build she'd seen in many British soldiers since the war. She could imagine them working long hours in the factories in their hometowns, twelve hours sweated out of them, but returning again and again because they needed to eat; they needed a job. They were tougher than they looked.

Carefully, she said, "You must be looking for a dangerous person, sir. Very . . . violent."

"There are many ways to be dangerous."

"I don't know anyone like that, sir. You've confused me with someone else. Please let me back on the train. It's so cold."

Fenshaw tapped a file. "Do you know what this is?" There were six files, all of them thick, their spines worn. "This is you, fräulein. Your entire life. Go on and have a look. Aren't you curious? I would be if I were you."

So many files just for her. She didn't seem old enough or important enough to warrant so much paper. As curious as she was, she didn't touch any of it.

Fenshaw opened a file in the middle. "This one is about that school you attended in Switzerland. Old classmates said you were the odd one out. Standoffish. Didn't really fit in. Good at math and languages, though." He was languidly peeling through the pages, not reading them, but summarizing from memory. "They said you

were expelled because of a sordid little incident with"—
he gave her a disappointed look—"the French master?"

Rubbish. The thing with the French master—that
was a lie. She couldn't say it to Fenshaw, and she flushed
with the indignity of having that old slander used
against her now. She hadn't been expelled. Not exactly.
Truth was she hadn't cared a fig about that mausoleum
of a school or the girls she had been forced to live with.
Their posturing, their shifting allegiances, their small
cruelties. She had three brothers. What did she need
with those girls? But that was her mistake. Not needing
them. They had invented the incident with the French
master, a circle of them testifying they had seen Clara
slipping into his room at night.

And worse, her mother had sided with the school,
refusing to defend her or even listen to what she had
to say. "A scandal," Anne called it, blaming Clara for
being involved in such unpleasantness in the first place.
Back at home, she lectured Clara about her station, her
reputation. Papa had thought the whole thing was a
coordinated intrigue against his beloved daughter and
sent stern protests to the school. But her mother . . .
She couldn't be trusted. That was what the incident had
taught Clara.

"I'm sorry, sir, but I've never been to Switzerland—

or anywhere else, really. I'd like to travel, but it wasn't possible—"

"You've never been to London?"

"No, but I'd like to. I've heard it's very nice."

He dug to the bottom of the files, opened one that seemed older than the rest, worn at the edges, stained with what looked like splashes of tea and the finger-prints of someone who had been eating chocolates. As he turned the crackling pages, she had the feeling he was excavating some ancient manuscript. How long had he been watching her? Years, it seemed. "You were in London regularly up to the war, but let's take one visit," he said, "in 1936. Your mother took you to a rally of the British Union of Fascists."

Ten years, then. She could hardly believe it, that the file might be that old and showing its age, one-third of her life. Why would Fenshaw have a file on her so early? Back then she had been nothing special; at least, nothing of interest to the British. A twenty-year-old heiress might rate the society pages, but was surely be-neath a government's notice.

"You didn't seem to be enjoying yourself up onstage," Fenshaw went on. "You kept picking at your fingernails during the speeches. Yawning behind your hand. Count-ing the light fixtures. Eventually you slipped out to have a nip from your flask in the cloakroom. Remember that foul little room? Smelled of mold and wet dog."

She didn't like how he told it, as if it was his own memory, not information gleaned from talking to people who had actually been there. She tried to remember if she had, indeed, seen him before, but that rally had been one of many, and she used to drink cognac, quite a lot, to get through all that pompous political talk. On her visits to Britain, she had been dismayed at the marches of the Blackshirts of the BUF, how eagerly they copied what was happening in Germany and Italy, their leader, Mosley, saluting from his moving car, men and women marching in lockstep, people on the streets raising their arms. Back then, Fascism was a disease that was spreading everywhere.

She looked past Fenshaw, past the soldiers to the train. It was still and quiet. She sensed the people inside, invisible in the dark, blaming her for the delay. He had not let the train move on yet. She still had a chance.

"Sir, please, I really don't know what you're talking about. I haven't done anything wrong. I don't know what I can tell you to make you see."

A sigh of disappointment. To the ginger soldier, he said, "She has an English head and a German soul, Reynolds. She assumes the government fouls things up. That's her English side. Comes from her mother."

"What about the German side, sir?" Reynolds asked.

Fenshaw tossed the file onto the stack. "Denial to the bitter end."

"My name is Margarete Müller, sir. I live in Hamelin. I got engaged today." She took off her glove and showed him her grandmother's ring, reversed on her finger so he wouldn't see the diamond. He shouldn't look at her and think of wealth. "My fiancé, he's . . . he's a . . ." A monster she hoped to see again only as a photograph in the papers under the label *Convicted*. "This is all a mix-up, sir. Nobody has questioned me before. I've never been in trouble with the authorities. Please, let me back on that train."

"I'll give you one thing, fräulein. Once you bite into a lie, you don't let go."

"I don't know what you mean, sir."

"Right. Let's play a little longer if it makes you feel better. What did you do during the war?"

"I was a secretary, sir."

"Where?"

"Krupp's."

"Reynolds, get me the female wartime employee list for the Krupp Steel Works in Essen."

She watched Fenshaw examine it, dismayed he had it there at all.

"There we are." Fenshaw tapped the list. "Worked at Krupp headquarters."

"Yes, sir."

"It says here the Margarete Müller in question—so *you*—died of injuries sustained in an air raid in October 1944." The papers fluttered back into place. "I have to say, you're the loveliest corpse I've ever seen."

"The records near the end of the war were so unreliable, sir. Someone must have made a mistake—"

"Do you remember who Clara Falkenberg is?"

The wind gusted around her, sweeping off the field and bringing the smells of damp ground, rotting leaves, and the hint of smoke from a fire lit nearby and not so long ago.

"Of course I've heard of her, sir. She was quite famous. In Essen."

"In all of Germany, I hear. The Reich's rather mysterious heiress. The last living child of the Falkenbergs. The last head of the family iron works. Do you know what they used to call her?"

Clärchen. Theodor's daughter. The Falkenberg. That bitch.

"The Iron Fräulein," he said. "Goebbels thought that one up himself. What did you think of it?"

She nearly corrected him. Goebbels didn't think of it, Himmler did. At least, that was the story her mother had told her. Clara had hated that Wagnerian nickname and all it represented. The Nazis had labeled her, used her name and image, and there had been little she could do to stop them.

"I always thought the fräulein must be proud of that name," she said. "It implied she was a strong person."

"She was. Strong, sensible, a mind of her own."

The praise surprised her so much, she didn't know what to say. How could he talk as if he knew her?

"Do you agree?" he asked. "Do you think Fräulein Falkenberg was a strong person?"

She had no idea what Fenshaw was getting at, couldn't guard herself, prepare her answers in her head. "Well, yes, sir."

"Why?"

"She . . . she ran those factories all alone. It's not work for a woman."

"Remind me again what she built?"

Her cheeks warmed despite the icy wind. "If I recall, she was involved in iron production and the manufacture of vehicle parts."

"And the assembly of vehicles, wasn't it? Such as . . ."

She coughed a little to buy time to think, but there was no use lying about things he obviously knew. "Airplanes."

"And?"

"Some armored vehicles."

"Tanks, you mean."

"I believe so. Like I said, it was no work for a woman."

"Fräulein Falkenberg should have spent the war knitting scarves for the boys on the Eastern Front, is that what you're saying?"

"Everyone did their bit." She couldn't keep the flint out of her voice. He was making fun of her. Captain Thomas Fenshaw presumed to make fun of her. Who did he think he was? Not some distant cousin on her mother's side, she hoped. For generations, her English kin had produced armies of lovely daughters who married into every family fool enough to take them.

Fenshaw patted his files into a tidy stack. "I've been tracking you for a very long time. It wasn't easy. You really did vanish in a puff of smoke until . . ." From another file, he revealed a thin blue paper folded into an envelope. It was the letter she'd written to Elisa two months ago. She nearly lunged for it, and it was everything she could do to restrain herself, to pretend the letter meant nothing.

"This led me to Hamelin, where I had the pleasure of meeting your very cooperative landlady, and now we're here." Fenshaw tapped the letter against his knee. "Things will go easier on you if you stop this performance. I'm not mistaken about you. This is not a mix-up. You are not the dead secretary Margarete Müller. You're the very alive, no longer missing, war criminal Clara Falkenberg."

A weight descended on her head, and a darkness, and she bent over slightly, trying to breathe. It was as if the anemia had returned. "It's not true. It's nonsense. Surely you're not being serious."

"Hear that, Reynolds? Good, clean upper class."

She couldn't remember speaking English, and why would that part of her creep out now? Margarete Müller had spoken passable English, but Clara couldn't risk it with Fenshaw. She was too fluent. German. She had to speak German. "The Falkenberg was blond, sir. Everybody knows that."

"Not a natural blond, I'm afraid." He tucked the letter away and pulled two photographs out of a file. Clara at ten, black-haired and frowning at the camera. Clara at twenty, in the blond wave she'd thought made her look more like her father and brothers. It was a trick of fate that she was the black sheep, so to speak, born with her mother's dark hair.

"I suppose," Fenshaw said, "your natural coloring wasn't fashionable after 1933."

"There's a resemblance, sir. People always pointed it out. But I'm not her."

"Yet you want me to believe you're *her*."

He held up the picture Clara had hoped he didn't have. In the war, the real Margarete Müller had been a drab and virginal girl, competent at her job, awed by Clara and their resemblance. They had chatted sometimes when Clara had business at Krupp's. It paid to have a friendly face embedded with the competition. When Clara heard Fräulein Müller had died, she had thought: How sad. And then: What if I get her papers?

Fenshaw tapped his fingers on the files, far too pleased with himself. He was too intelligent to fool with arguments, and besides, the facts were on his side, stacked up on his table. He was an officer, so she might appeal to his vanity, his pride, or his status. She had done this a little already, and it only seemed to amuse him. She didn't get a sense he wanted her sexually. Even when he'd touched her, she hadn't felt that kind of desire in him. It was something else, something more intense and threatening than the common attraction between a German woman and an Allied soldier.

She was left with his nationality. She had spent many summers in England enduring her mother's family, enough time to know how the English liked to see themselves. Decent. Tolerant. Fair. She decided to appeal to Fenshaw's decency. She opened her eyes wider so that the light from the army vehicles could sparkle in them. He would see inside her to a beating heart and a clean soul. He would see she had nothing to hide. She was an innocent young woman shivering in the cold. He had made a mistake and it would be less than gentlemanlike, it would be downright cruel, to detain her one more moment.

Slowly, he smiled at her, an indulgent smile as if he knew all her faults but didn't hold them against her. And then he lifted his hand.

Reynolds shouted, and there was a series of bellows in return, one soldier to another all the way across the grassy field to the train. Someone blew a whistle. The train answered, and soon it began to roll, its horn sounding like a final good-bye.

"You know, I hated school too," Fenshaw said, lighting a cigarette. "We were at the mercy of the system. The bastards."

The train's whistle echoed across the fields. She couldn't believe it was gone. She feared she'd never find her way home again, not as a free woman. "We're always at the mercy of the system we live in," she said.

"Some people thrive in their environment more than others."

"I didn't thrive."

"But you did. For a brief period in the war, you were

the most powerful woman your family ever produced. You managed an industrial empire."

She shook her head.

"No? How would you describe the work you did? Please don't say secretarial. We've been through that."

She tried out the alternatives in her head. Personnel. Logistics. Production. All pieces of the job she'd done at a desk of nearly black wood, the telephone and marble inkstand before her, the window reaching from her elbow to the ceiling. And all of that on the eighth floor of headquarters. Before the bombardments, she had loved the view of the factories below, a small city of fire and smoke that belonged to her family.

"I don't know what you want to hear, sir."

"We can start with the system of forced labor you established at the Falkenberg Iron Works."

"I didn't—" She bit her tongue.

"Didn't . . . import men and women from across Europe to work for you? Didn't keep them in labor camps under guard or behind barbed wire?" Fenshaw rested his elbow on his files. "You didn't starve them?"

No. She wanted to say she had never done these things. At least, not willingly. Not . . . with the intent to do harm. And he didn't tell the whole story. How the government controlled the labor system in the war. Most of the foreign workers had been forced to come to her, yes, but she had tried to avoid it, to fill her vacancies any other way she could. She could inform him about the recruitment drives in France, Belgium, the Netherlands, the wages she had promised and *paid*, the workers free to rent flats like a German anywhere in the city. Men did come voluntarily. That had existed too, she wanted to tell Fenshaw. Though as the war went on, if a highly skilled man asked to leave . . .

She folded her hands in her lap, ashamed of the trick played on some of the workers, their voluntary contracts changed to forced ones by the government. All she had been able to do was quietly warn them it was about to happen. She had planned to seek out each man herself, as head of the Labor Office, to give him any outstanding wages and the advice to not come to work the next day. But when she told Elisa, by now one of her assistants, the plan, Elisa had said it was nonsense. Fräulein Falkenberg couldn't do such a thing in person. "Leave it to me," she'd said, a twinkle of mischief in her eyes. Clara had reminded her friend that this wasn't a game. By helping workers escape, they were undermining the war effort.

She was trembling more violently now. "Sir, why are you doing this?" She showed Fenshaw her hands, how stiff the fingers were. "Why are we sitting out here in the cold?"

"You're uncomfortable?"

"Aren't you?"

"Answer my questions and I'll take you somewhere warm."

He'd said it in a friendly fashion, but his words sent a shiver of warning through her. This roadside inter- rogation—it was part of his calculations, a way to wear her down.

"I've been cooperating as best I can, sir."

"Tell me." He was fingering his files again as if look- ing for some fact he had lost. "Those poor sods you shipped in from Poland and the Soviet Union—did you see them as humans at all?"

Of course. She was so outraged, she nearly got up from her stool, ready to walk away from him. But when she moved, Fenshaw did too, close enough to catch her by the arm. Behind her, she sensed the soldiers clos- ing in.

"You have nothing to say?" Fenshaw asked. "About the transports, the hunger, the deaths?"

It was true, there had been—she touched a throbbing ache that had developed in her eye—casualties. Illness, injury, starvation. She had desperately appealed to the authorities for more rations. She had sent Max and Elisa to find any sources of food they could—nearly impos- sible with supplies vanishing all over the city as the war went on. Now and then, they risked buying from shady men who hoarded food or sold it on the wartime black market. But it wasn't enough. Clara couldn't supplement the rations of thousands of people out of her own pocket, even if there had been food to buy. And so people had sickened under the double weight of hunger and hard work. Some had died in her care. Did he think she had forgotten that?

"I don't know what you want me to say, sir."

Fenshaw rested his fist on the table and, for a moment, she thought he would lose his composure. "At the end of the war, why did you run?"

She curled her fingers in her gloves. She couldn't feel them any longer. She thought of the Ukrainian girl in the kerchief breaking into a smile, her third upper tooth on the left missing, giving her whole round face a kind of dogged, childlike hope. Clara closed her eyes. Oh, Galina.

"Are you so afraid of prison?" Fenshaw asked.

She nearly snapped at him: You don't know me. All your files, and you still don't know me.

"You were always a private person," he said. "Are you afraid of the attention? The press hounding you. The trial. Is that what you're scared of? The exposure?"

In the distance, the lights of a farmhouse or a village sparkled. Without the train, she felt the emptiness of the countryside and how completely she was trapped. Fenshaw was watching her through his cigarette smoke. Her whole life she had been watched one way or another, but never in such a sharp, probing way. The hairs on the back of her neck stood taut, as if he was pulling them slowly one at a time.

"Or are you doing this," he said, "because of your father?"

Moisture was collecting at her nostrils. She wanted to wipe it away, but she didn't dare move.

"The case against him is coming together, you know. He'll be charged with crimes against humanity, among other things. You read the papers, I'm sure."

She put her handkerchief to her nose after all, a gesture she knew made her look upset, but she couldn't stand the thought of him seeing her nose running.

"He thinks you're dead," Fenshaw said.

She began to shake her head; then she caught herself, because she had known this. It was the logical conclusion after she disappeared in the war. Logical, but not true. Deep down, she had held the girlish belief that Papa would know she was alive. He would just know.

"I tried to tell him you're only missing, but he wouldn't have it," Fenshaw said. "He's a bit of a fatalist. Understandably. From his perspective, the war took everything. His home and work, his status, his freedom.

All four of his children. He's given himself up to self-pity and grief."

She pressed her hands between her knees to stop them shaking. She had so many questions. Do the Americans know he's ill? What exactly has he said? Is he eating enough? And she couldn't ask any of it. She couldn't snatch up the files and see for herself.

"He doesn't look well," he said gently. "The Americans feed him, but I'm told he's getting thinner all the time. He's being treated for a heart condition."

So they did know. She wanted to demand Fenshaw tell her why her father was still being tried if the Allies knew they were killing him in their camp and would finish the job in prison.

"Fräulein"—Fenshaw leaned closer to her—"if we could tell him his last child is alive, his condition would improve. We could arrange for you to meet."

She could almost see it. A room in Papa's internment camp, an American guard at the door. Papa waiting for her, his elbow on a scuffed table and a half-smoked cigarette, a gift of mercy from the guard, pinched in his fingers. The shock of him in person, looking a decade older than he had two years ago. His wince as he got up from his chair to greet her, a thick sheen in his eyes. Not knowing if they should hug each other with an American in the room. She would try hard to keep herself together because if she cried, it would embarrass her father, and then maybe he wouldn't be able to keep himself together either.

"You are your father's child," Fenshaw said. "Everyone I've spoken to has said that. You don't want to turn your back on him now when he needs you most? Not after all you did for him?"

Her eyes felt stung and swollen, and she turned away to compose herself. It would be a short visit, she assumed. The Americans wouldn't allow a long reunion. And then, once she was gone, he'd be alone again and burdened by a new set of worries. His daughter was alive, yes, but caught. A prisoner like him.

There was another way. Elisa could tell Papa. He would get the news that Clara was alive in a letter, maybe, or indirectly via one of his lawyers. His condition would improve when he heard that his daughter, his last living child, was not only alive—but free.

"Captain, as I've said, I'm afraid you have the wrong woman. I can understand the mix-up, sir. It happened once or twice in Essen. I'm flattered you mistake me for her. She was very impressive. But surely you can see the difference."

He took off his cap and ran a hand through his hair. He looked about forty and had the studied blandness she had seen in many men on her summers in England.

She imagined him at a party, wearing tweeds, the type of man who would have dared speak to her only after several drinks, and even then only if they happened to be alone. A man who could not bear public embarrassment or rejection. His uniform gave him the confidence to talk to her as he was doing now. That and the defeat. It was easy to be on the winning side.

"What do you think is going to happen now?" he asked.

"I was hoping you'd drive me to the station in the next town, sir."

"Why would I do that?"

"Because it's the right thing to do, sir. I haven't done anything wrong."

"You're committed, then." He flicked away his cigarette. "Right. This way, please."

He took her arm as if escorting her at a dance and led her past the army vehicles to a covered truck. Soldiers pulled aside the canvas to reveal a steel locker lashed upright on the bed. The locker was the kind soldiers used to store their gear. It had other less innocent uses, she had heard, but she had never condoned that sort of punishment of foreign workers; nor had her father, no matter what the newspapers said.

Reynolds undid the padlock and trained his flashlight on the scratched interior of the locker.

"We found this at Krupp's," Fenshaw said. "I hear Falkenberg had one just like it."

She bristled at the lie. "I don't know what you're talking about, sir."

"You might remember that two men can squeeze into that locker. If they're forced. The lads tried it out. A tight fit. Had some neck pain afterward. Trouble breathing."

Her lungs fluttered for air.

"Miss Falkenberg, you're caught. It's over. If you can't admit it now, maybe you will after a spell in there."

"You can't do this. You wouldn't."

"You're giving me no choice. Admit who you are and we can get on with things. I'll take you with me in the car."

"Where would you take me?"

"For questioning. You'll be comfortable. Warm. Well fed. Don't be frightened."

"You're threatening me with that locker and you don't think I should be frightened?"

"I've been more than fair with you." He softened his voice. "All this fuss isn't necessary. You know we'll get at the truth one way or another. Someone in Essen will identify you if you don't admit it yourself. Be sensible."

That's exactly what she was. If she gave in, she knew what would happen, what would really happen. Fenshaw would hand her over to other soldiers. They would drag her to the interrogation prison no one spoke of but everyone knew existed. It was in Bad Nenndorf, not far from Hamelin. She had heard what happened to prisoners there.

Ignoring the outstretched hands of Fenshaw's man, she climbed onto the back of the truck herself.

Rock

The boy sat up in his field bed. He wasn't sure if it was night or day, but anyway, it didn't much matter. He slept when he felt like sleeping. He got up when he felt like getting up. He pulled on his boots, loving the moment when his foot slid into the leather. His foot stuck a bit and he had to tug. His feet had grown and he would have to find new boots, but he'd put off searching in the supplies. He loved the ones he had. Then came his tunic, his arms sliding into the sleeves, the firm fit, as if the tunic held him together. He licked his thumb and polished each button until they shone.

He stood up slowly and, once he was upright, he tilted his head. The black rock ceiling hung lower than it should for his height—or rather for the height he seemed to be acquiring faster than he thought possible. In one of the other tunnels, where he had always walked easily, he'd smashed his head against one of the beams that shored up the ceiling. That was why he'd gone to bed. Now he remembered.

He touched his skull—still tender—and then went to the crate he used as a table. Here was his favorite part of the uniform. He lifted the steel helmet, the cool metal soothing in his hands. He lowered it onto his head and immediately felt safe. When he patrolled the tunnel wearing this, he wouldn't have to worry about the low clearance.

Since it was chilly, he put on his coat, and since he was about to go on patrol, he buckled on his belt. His coat was getting a little musty, so he dabbed it with a few drops of the cologne he kept in his locker. He checked his sidearm and said, "Hold the fort, Gertrud." His canary fluttered in the nest he'd made for her out of twigs and leaves and paper. Then he stepped out into the main tunnel where the draft flowed through the ventilation shafts. Water dripped in hidden passageways beneath his feet. He didn't need a light to move through the tunnels anymore. He had learned to listen to the rock throbbing all around him. And so, as he always did when he began his patrol, he moved in the dark to the beginning of this place, where the rock opened to the outside world.

4

The ginger soldier Reynolds was shouting over the truck's motor. "How're you getting on? Still breathing in there?"

Clara opened her eyes to the thick, complete dark of the steel locker, and quickly shut them again. She didn't waste her breath answering him. She could breathe in a smokestack. She could breathe in a forge. She grew up in the haze of smog that seeped into the walls of Falkenhorst when she was a girl. Years ago, when the iron works were at full production and the wind blew just right, soot fell in the garden like flakes of black snow.

She didn't know how long she'd been in the locker. She measured time with the pains in her muscles and joints. An hour? More? When she angled her head toward the holes in the roof, pain shot down her spine, drilled a hole in her back, and crackled down her legs. Her feet had gone dead, and she moved them slowly, gasping.

The dark was worse. As a girl, she used to have nightmares in which she'd been unable to open her eyes. Without wanting to, she took the darkness of the locker and deepened it into the same dark as when she was eight years old and slept with the lamp on. If she didn't, if she closed her eyes without the red glow of light behind her lids, she feared she would never open them again. She used to thrash in her sleep, trying to wrestle her eyes open. She used to dream of picking at the threads sealing her lids. In the locker, she felt the same cold insertion of the needle into the tender skin, the tug as the needle slid through. Her eyes ached and were sticky and when she opened them—were they really open?—all she saw was the blackness and her papa, who had given her these nightmares, and cured them too.

He had summoned her via a servant to a room she had never before been allowed to enter. There were many at Falkenhorst, many locked doors. Her skin buzzed with anxiety as this one was opened for her. She stepped into a dim room with only one source of light: the lamp on the table next to her father.

"It's all right," he said, "come closer." There was a strange rustling sound, and she halted in the center of the room. She noticed the thick glove on Papa's left hand, and the towel bundled on his lap. She couldn't see what he held there.

He pulled aside a corner of the towel and cooed in a voice she rarely heard anymore. "Calm down, little bird."

Her heart surged with happiness—he hadn't called her that since she was small—but then she realized he wasn't talking to her at all. Out of the towel came the head of a young falcon, its beak snapping the air. It struggled and made high sounds she knew were screams of fright. A man hurried out of the shadows— she was so startled that she scampered out of his way and to the wall—and he knelt beside Papa and took hold of the bird so that its feet were pressed close to its body and its head held still. From a silver tablet on the table, Papa selected a fine needle, the thread reminding her of a strand of hair. He held the needle close to the falcon's eye.

"Papa, what are you doing?"

"Just watch."

She pressed her fists over her eyes. "No."

"Clara."

His tone made her shiver. She had told her father no. That was forbidden. After he made it clear she was not to hide her eyes again, he turned back to the bird. Tenderly he inserted the needle into the lower eyelid, drawing the thread outward. Clara bit back her tears and kept watching. The cries of the bird cut into her heart. Worse was the moment when it stopped protesting and endured the procedure on the first eye, then the second.

She didn't know how long he took. By the end of it, when the falcon's eyelids were stitched, and the threads tied and tucked under the feathers of its head, she wanted to scream and run. How could her father do something so cruel?

He set aside his needle and gestured for her to come closer. She obeyed, staring at the bird with disgust and pity. She wanted to pet it and knew she couldn't. It was blind, but she was sure it would snap at her hand.

"It doesn't look nice, I know," Papa said. "But this was a humane thing to do. It's a traditional technique, over a thousand years old, for taming a falcon." He patiently explained about the medieval Emperor Frederick II's book on falconry. She pretended to listen while she agonized over why he had not put a hood on the poor bird as others did. "Can you guess why we do this to her eyes?" he asked.

Her voice was stuck in her throat, wrapped in a fury and fear she was trying to ball up and contain as she had been taught. He shouldn't see the rebellious feelings inside her.

"If she can't see," he said, "she won't be so terrified of the strange new world around her. She will get used to my touch and my voice." With great tenderness, he stroked a finger over the bird's head, and it jerked to the side. "You see? She doesn't trust me yet."

Clara thought: Of course not. You just sewed her eyes shut.

"When she learns to trust me," he said, "I'll give her back her sight. She will be ready to see the world she's going to have to live in from now on. Do you understand why I wanted you to watch this?"

She nodded, though it was a lie. She had no idea what he was trying to teach her. That night, the nightmares began and continued for weeks. She wandered around Falkenhorst shattered, her eyes bruised from lack of sleep. When Grandmother Sophia asked her what was wrong (her mother never did), she said she didn't know. The family doctor gave her a tonic she spat out when no one was looking.

This was long before she met Elisa. Friedrich was the only one she could talk to. Home from school at last, Clara had jumped into his arms and made him carry her, laughing, out into the garden. She asked him if Papa had ever shown him such terrible things. Why had he done this to that poor bird, and to her?

Almost twelve at the time, Friedrich had thought deeply and said, "He was trying to toughen you up."

"Why?"

"You're a girl, dummkopf. He was making sure you didn't run away screaming and crying."

"I didn't scream or cry," she said with a trace of pride.

"Once he made me go down into one of our coal mines." Frie-drich fumbled the binoculars around his neck. Back then, he always wore them, ready for bird-watching in the family forest, where he spent hours under the trees and the sky. Clara was horrified at the thought of him going down into a hole in the ground. It was against his nature.

"Why would he do that to you?" she asked.

"I think he wanted to know if I would actually do it. If I really trusted him, you know?"

Friedrich had given her a clue about what made Papa tick. From then on, Clara watched their father as he stroked the falcon on its perch and spoke to it as gently as he'd once spoken to her. She saw this noble creature begin to eat out of his hand. Her nightmares faded. What did she have to fear? Her father had the subtle, awesome power to tame what was wild and dark in the world. This certainty remained for years. It shattered the first time she saw him raise his arm to a regime they both despised.

Reynolds was still calling to her from outside the locker. "Do you have enough air?"

Clara opened her eyes. Her lips were cracked and tasted of blood. Her tongue felt thick and prickly, as if it had grown hooks.

"You're all right, aren't you?" An edge of worry in Reynolds's voice. Maybe Fenshaw had told him to make sure she didn't suffocate. "Miss Falkenberg, say something."

She didn't answer to that name anymore, and anyway, she was not about to give him the reassurance of a response. Soon he was cursing, and the padlock clanged, and then, in a rush of fresh air, the doors swung open. She fell out reaching for water, and drank the canteen dry. On the bench, she stretched her legs until the needles and aches faded. Moving, breathing, she felt alive with energy, more than she had in a long time. Maybe the men who had endured the locker in the war felt like this. They came out stronger because the damned thing hadn't beaten them.

The canvas over the back of the truck was lashed to one side, and in the moonlight, the jagged remains of buildings sped by. "Essen?" she asked as Reynolds secured the locker doors. The truck took a quick turn, and he keeled over and caught the chain that held up the locker. His shoulder slammed against it, a hollow boom.

"Are you all right?" she asked.

He sat next to her on the bench and held out a cigarette. She took it out of politeness, surprised at his offer. "Think nothing of it," he said. "I'd give a cigarette to my worst enemy."

He was much younger than Fenshaw and maybe a decade younger than her. Early twenties, she guessed. It was possible he hadn't seen much of the war, or none at all, only the aftermath. Sometimes those boys were worse than the men who had been in combat. More zealous, regretting they'd missed all the "good" stuff. "Where did you fight, sir?" she asked in the careful, heavily accented English of Margarete Müller.

"I was in school." He sat stiffly and took quick puffs of his cigarette. He kept rubbing his bare hand on his knee. "What's it like?" he asked.

"Sorry, sir?"

"Being a war criminal."

She decided he was trying to be clever. "I'm not."

"Captain says you are."

"The captain is wrong."

"He's never wrong." Said with the total faith of a schoolboy.

She didn't know what to do with him. Normally she could count on appealing to a young soldier's lust or greed. Not with Reynolds. She sensed that he wouldn't do anything to jeopardize the trust Fenshaw seemed to put in him. But then, he had let her out of the locker. She doubted Fenshaw had wanted that.

"Why was I pulled off the train, sir? You could have arrested me in Hamelin."

"Captain wanted to keep things quiet."

"Why? Where is he taking me?"

"I'll tell you if you're straight with me. I've been nice, haven't I? I let you out. It's not right, locking up a human being like that, even knowing the things you did."

"I was a secretary, sir. I typed. I made telephone calls and took dictation. Hardly crimes."

"Don't you get tired of lying all the time?"

She was talking to a child. She lied, yes, she lied about her name, her past, her life, but the motive, the reason she did it . . . that was the important point. That was what the schoolboy Reynolds couldn't or wouldn't understand. He would think the same as Fenshaw, that she was the Iron Fräulein, the machine-woman the Nazis had supposedly loved and the Allies loathed. But this was nonsense, an image, a piece of propaganda that all of them used for their own ends. Why would the Allies try to understand that there was a difference between the real her and the woman they thought she was? This was why she lied.

"Just admit who you are and things'll go much easier for you," Reynolds said. "The captain doesn't go for those shabby prisons. He'll make sure you're treated well. Comfortable, just like he said." Reynolds was close to her, his breath a warm cloud of tobacco against her cheek. "You can tell me, fräulein. It only takes a start. You'll feel better telling the truth."

"I have to know where we're going."

He considered it a moment, then stubbed his cigarette out on the bench. "Captain wants some old boyfriend of yours in Essen to identify you. Maybe convince you to cooperate."

Max—they were taking her to Max. The truck rumbled over a pothole, and she gripped the bench. She didn't want to see him. Nothing he could say would convince her to collaborate with Fenshaw.

On the other side of the canvas, the landscape had changed. They were going through the sad and dark remains of a working-class neighborhood. Some of the black houses looked intact but most were heaps of rubble. It was impossible to know if this was Essen or one of the other industrial cities nearby, one dreary, identical block of brick and stone after another. Between the train and the truck, it felt as though she'd been traveling long enough to be close to home.

"What do you say?" Reynolds's voice was taut with anxiety and hope. She had no doubt he was trying to raise his value in his superior's eyes. The boy was ambitious. She wondered what he would do if he got what he wanted.

"If I talk to you, I don't want to be put back in that locker."

"You won't be. That's a promise. You are Clara Falkenberg, aren't you?"

Outside the truck, the anonymous, ruined city. If she was home, it would be easier to admit who she really was. A simple yes would be good enough for Reynolds, but there was so much more. She was the daughter of Theodor, in prison, and Anne, presumably in the empty, rambling halls of their family home. She was the sister of Heinrich, Otto, and Friedrich, taken in the war. She was the youngest child and the only one to survive. Reynolds couldn't possibly know what that meant, what it was like to see the pillars of her life crumble around her and find, in the end, that she was the only one left standing.

Still gazing out at the passing buildings, she said quietly, "You caught me, sir. Congratulations."

With a shout of triumph, Reynolds sprang to his feet. The truck careered around another corner, and the force threw him off balance. His head knocked with a deep bang into the locker doors. He stumbled, grasping at the tarp. In a moment, Clara had seized her bag and was over the truck's tailgate. The pavement was rushing away below her, there was no time to think, assess risk, be scared. She jumped, landing on her backpack, then her shoulder and hip. She was spinning in the street, and then she was on her feet, heading for the dark and silent ruins.

5

Jakob came to on his stomach, awakened by sharp pains tattooing his back. His body—yes, he still had a body, he knew that because it hurt—was sprawled in the bed of wet moss and leaves that had broken his fall. He opened his eyes to the inky dark of the valley. He sensed the rock looming behind him, the cliff face whose folds he now knew intimately, since he'd rolled down each and every one of them. High up there was the village, and the farmhouses, and the voices still laughing and mocking him.

Hello, cripple. Still alive?

The pain in his back stopped, and then it started up again. It felt as though somebody was tapping Morse code on his spine. Jab—jab—short pause—jab—long pause—*jab.*

"You can stop now," Jakob said, moaning, "I'm not a pincushion."

The jabs stopped. He thought he heard labored breathing behind him, but that couldn't be. The voices were still high up on the cliff. He fought to stay conscious, stay alert, ready to fight again if he had to. But his mind was clouding, drawn to sleep in order to forget the pain. He couldn't let himself be dragged under. Sleep meant freezing to death. During the long marches in Russia, when men fell in the road, Jakob had kept one foot moving in front of the other, through the white wastes and the biting wind. His feet ached. Tomorrow, he would look for a freshly dead Russian and steal his boots.

Where are you, cripple?

He shook awake again. Not Russia. He was not in Russia anymore. He was in the valley below Heisingen, part of Essen, his home. Those bastards up on the cliff had called him a—

Groaning, he rolled over and patted his left leg. His skin was slimy and prickled with goose bumps, and that's how he remembered they had stolen his trousers for the fun of it. He touched the sutured skin on his left knee. Four years since the amputation and sometimes it still came as a shock. In his head, Jakob was a whole man. He could run and kick, duck and dodge. In his head.

We're coming to get you, cripple.

Light flared in his eyes, and he threw his arm over his face. "So you found me, you miserable shits. What you going to do now, huh? Steal my underpants too?"

Whoever held the light hiccoughed when he breathed, but Jakob couldn't see him behind the glare.

"Well?"

No answer, only the hiccoughs. Jakob used the light to check his body for damage. Right leg—stiff but functioning. Head—worse than a hangover on the South Sea Club's illegal schnapps. Right arm—check. Left arm—*ow.* He worked the elbow, the shoulder. Nothing broken, but the arm felt like a bruise that went to the bone. He looked for his portable lamp or his prosthesis, but they weren't inside the pool of light or the weeds he pawed outside it.

"You just going to stand there or are you going to get this over with?"

The light vanished. He heard the familiar ring of nail-soled shoes retreating a few steps in the dark. Army boots?

"Wait. You're not with them, are you?" Jakob patted the ground, found a stone, then a thick branch. After several tries, he pulled himself onto the only foot he had left. The branch held, the world didn't. His head spun and he was falling.

The stranger caught him, gasped at his weight, buckled and then stabilized. His smell hurtled Jakob back to days he didn't want to remember. It was the smell of the front, of damp wool and oiled leather, of bergamot and citrus eau de cologne that didn't quite cover the stink of a soldier's fear. Whoever it was, he was thin, and he was shaking, and for the few moments Jakob had his arms around him, he felt the stranger's wildly beating heart.

He propped the branch under Jakob's arm, and dashed up the slope, his light bobbing until it vanished into what looked like a crevice in the cliff. Jakob staggered toward it, blind in the dark again. He fell onto his bare knee and pitched chin-first into the brambles. The ground turned to paste under his hands. Behind tangled vines, he found the crevice in the rock. He climbed through and landed, shaken, in a cave. His hand brushed something on the ground beside him, and he felt the cold, familiar shape of his portable lamp. It puzzled him for a moment until he realized the stranger must have dropped it here. He clipped it to his coat and switched it on.

Brick and timber walls around him, timber beams overhead. He rubbed the black paste on his hands. A coal mine. His father used to talk about coal as the black fortune under Essen, the whole Ruhr region. Here in the south, by the river, old mines dotted the cliffs. The coal veins were a scratch under the surface compared to the deep shafts up north. But they were getting coal out of the south before they knew what deep mining was. This mine could be hundreds of years old.

"*Glück auf,*" Jakob said. Nobody returned the traditional miner's greeting.

He knew what Papa would say in that ghost-story voice he got when he talked about his work. *A mine is a living thing. It'll kill you if you let it.* Jakob tapped the wood fittings. Dry, in good condition. Yet the ceiling sagged, the cliff's weight pressing on the tunnel. Close to collapse? He couldn't tell. He crawled to the dead end, Papa in his brain now. *One false move, one misstep and you'll drown in black waters or hurtle deep into the earth.*

Jakob eased himself beside a locker full of mining junk—rusted pick, leather hat, blasting caps. He found a shovel long enough to prop under his arm, a sturdier support than the branch. He held his breath, mindful of any explosives he may have missed, until he lifted the shovel clear of the locker.

Upright, he oriented himself. To the left, a brick archway, blasted and tidied. On the right, a proper doorway with iron fittings. He chose the tunnel to the right. The concrete walls and floor reminded him of an air-raid bunker. Wires and pipes ran along the ceiling, and there were faded labels on a few of the doors: *Communications, Command Center.*

He called, "Thanks for leading me in here, friend."

He told the invisible stranger what the shit-faced farmer's sons outside had done to him before they rolled him down the rock hill as if he were a bowling ball. They had thrown away his trousers and his wooden leg and worst of all—and wasn't this a sign of the times?—they had stolen his backpack. With the pork. Which he had organized fair and square after months of negotiation at a nearby farm. After the slaughter—illegal, but nobody had to tell the black-market squad, right?—he'd chopped up the pig himself in the farm's steaming washhouse. He'd dreamed of roasts, sausages, stews thick with bacon, half of it funneled directly into the bellies of his poor sisters, one pregnant—a mistake, but he couldn't blame her for lack of judgment. He had inherited most of the sense in the family. Anyway, for that pork, he'd traded his dead brother's shoes, his dead sister's communion dress, and his dead mother's gold chain.

"That's what the world has come to," Jakob said. "The dead have to pay to feed the living. Rotten world, eh?" He directed his light into the first open doorway he came to, and gasped. "Jesus, Maria, and Joseph."

Boxes. Wall-to-wall, unlabeled boxes as far as he could see, stacked in perfect geometric towers. He counted fifty-six, but maybe there were more where his light couldn't reach. He didn't know what was inside them, but he did know this was a dream. The bump on his head was making him see what he most needed: a roomful of something he might sell or trade or keep for himself. His fingertips tingled with anticipation as he touched the cardboard. Real enough. He tore it open. Tins gleamed in perfect circles like little mirrors. He groped for the opener that usually came in such boxes, and used it to bend back one lid. The rich smell of black bread drilled a direct line to his stomach. He shoved a fistful into his mouth. How much was here? Twenty tins times fifty-six boxes . . .

He plunged into the next room. More boxes, full of packages this time, crispy zwieback good for years if well packed. He reeled into the next room. Sacks of noodles and rice. In the next, tubs of Linz marmalade and ersatz honey. He nearly wept for joy in the room full of cigarettes, the new money, the hardest currency in Germany. They were Luz brand, worth two or three marks a stick. He couldn't believe his luck as he stuffed his pockets. This was a black-market warehouse, no doubt about it. Maybe the cologne-soaked stranger from outside was a racketeer.

"Hey, friend, you still here? Look, I know people. Can unload this food for you no problem. Profits in the stars, I'm telling you. Naturally we'd keep enough for ourselves. I mean, you can't sell all of it. Too hard to transport, and besides, winter is here. Remember last winter? If I ever see a turnip again, I'll bludgeon somebody with it. But this place . . ." Jakob passed the open doors and wished he had his backpack, a wheelbarrow, a truck that could haul these glorious calories home to his family. "This place will save us. We'll stuff our families all winter. You got a family?"

A low voice said, "Hands up, thief."

The hairs on Jakob's neck tingled. The voice came from out of nowhere, the empty tunnels. "Seen that film too, friend. Gangster shoot-out. Bang, bang." He bit open a pack of cigarettes and tipped one into his mouth. He wasn't dumb enough to light it in a coal mine, but the feel of it soothed him. "Why don't you come out and let me shake your hand? You helped me outside. I appreciate that. We got a lot to talk about."

Wherever the stranger was, he kept out of the beam of Jakob's lamp. "You're not *that* crippled."

"I love it when people tell me that. You going to show yourself?"

The stranger's voice had rust on the edges like a machine that needed oiling. "I said hands up."

"Can't. I'd fall over. War wound."

"Where?"

"You're looking at it. Left leg."

"I meant where were you when you got wounded?"

"Stalingrad. Look, you going to come out?"

"Nobody got out of Stalingrad. The German Army died a heroic death fighting for the Reich."

"A few of us got out, a few surrendered, and the rest died eating shit. You going to come out so I can see who I'm talking to?"

The stranger stepped into the tunnel. He held a fistful of darkness Jakob knew was a pistol. And he wore a tunic, field gray, the eagle and swastika over the breast pocket. For the first time in his life, Jakob let a cigarette fall unsmoked from his lips. Field gray was forbidden. The swastika was forbidden. "Dressed for a party, are you? Brits'll lock you up if they see you like that."

The stranger tilted his head away from Jakob's light. The miner's tilt, as Papa had always had even in the open air. "Name, rank, and unit."

"What?"

"Name, rank, and unit." The soldier's voice wavered, deep one moment, cracking the next.

"Wait a minute. How old are you?"

The soldier extended his arm.

"All right, I'll play along. Jakob Relling. Was a corporal. Twenty-Ninth Infantry, motorized. Wiped out in Stalingrad, and if you call that heroic, I'll split your lip."

The soldier straightened his back, parade-ground stiff. "Corporal Relling, in the name of the führer, I arrest you for stealing from the German Army."

"Listen, kid, any adults around here I can talk to? Who owns this stash you're sitting on?"

"You're my prisoner. Quiet." The soldier gestured with his gun at the tunnel behind him. "Move." He stepped backward without looking where he was going. In the face of that gun, Jakob's pains flooded back, all the places he hurt, all the places that would hurt if the boy pulled the trigger.

"Be reasonable, kid. We can talk—"

"Quiet. Move."

They went down new tunnels, passing new rooms, new vistas of food and supplies. Jakob spotted packets of dried pudding and tins of coffee-flavored chocolate. He thought he heard the soft whir of a machine. A pump? Electricity?

The soldier called for a halt. "In there."

"What's behind that curtain?"

The boy stared at him from under his steel helmet. Jakob drew back the curtain himself. Beyond was the dark of places he wanted to forget he ever knew. Cracks in the earth where tanks buried men. Bullet-riddled rooms and rat holes. Tunnels strung with wire. This was the dark of the sewer and the bunker. War dark.

"Hey, how long you going to keep me in there?"

Inside, something rustled. Like wings.

"Until the war ends."

6

Clara finally crept out of the freezing hovel where she'd spent her second night on the run. Only then did she see it was a pigeon coop, a miniature wooden house with a dusty red curtain in the window space. Whoever owned this luxury enclosure had loved his pigeons. They were gone now, only feathers scattered on the floor over splatters and stains. She brushed her coat of dried droppings and then limped, holding her hip, out of the yard and into the street.

Here was a solid block of brick houses dark with soot and grime, so anonymous, so much a part of every industrial city in the region, she couldn't be certain where she was. Before the war, she would have thought the street ugly, but not now. The houses were still standing, one after the other, down the entire row. This was the best she could hope for after the bombardments—an intact street. She hadn't seen many since jumping out of Fenshaw's truck. That night, she'd ducked in and out of the ruined buildings of what she later learned was Gelsenkirchen, on Essen's northeast border. She'd had to be fast and silent, avoiding the lights of Fenshaw's men as they searched. In the end, she had burrowed into a mountain of debris right in the street and stayed completely still until the men dispersed. From there, she had headed west, she'd hoped, slowed by pathways blocked with rubble, hiding in the ruins when she heard the rumble of a vehicle in the road. By dusk, she had climbed into the pigeon coop out of exhaustion, and slept until daylight. She'd seen no signs that signaled she had reached Essen. For all she knew, she had wandered in circles.

The few people outdoors, mostly women, led their children toward the end of the row where a large gate and a pit tower rose out of the light fog. Clara hesitated to speak to them, but then realized she looked torn and dirty enough that no one would recognize her. She stopped a woman in a flowered scarf. "I know this is a crazy question, but I need to know if this is Essen or Gelsenkirchen or—"

"Got hit in the head a little hard, eh?" the woman

said, without much interest. Her boy was tugging at her hand.

Clara touched her forehead and winced at the bruise. "I fell off a streetcar."

"Uh-huh. Well, it's Essen all right."

Clara forgot her bruises and pains. She was home. This was a street in her city. She was home, and now she had an advantage. Captain Fenshaw had every other advantage—guns, men, transport—but this was her place. Hers, from the smokestacks over her head to the mining tunnels under her feet.

She walked the street slowly, getting to know it, letting it sink in. There were no signs, no nameplates on the walls. She didn't know what district she was in, but she assumed she was in the north where most of the working-class neighborhoods had been built near the steel mills and factories and mines. At the end of the street was a junction. The view stopped her short.

A field of frost-covered rubble. It made her dizzy, the vast emptiness, the mind-boggling randomness of the destruction. The intact street behind her, the seemingly intact mine in front of her. And then, no-man's-land. Maybe a factory had once been here, but also houses, shops, a school perhaps, all leveled in the bombardments. In this city, there was no separating industry from life, and the Allies knew it. She had heard on the news that they were thinking of letting Essen die as a lesson to the world, to show what happened to war-mongering industrial cities.

Turning away from the ruins, she felt the same sorrow as she had when looking at her family photograph.

She continued toward the gates of what she knew by the familiar smell to be a coal mine. No one sat in the gatehouse to check who came and went, so she joined the people flowing into the paved yard, women and children mostly, buckets and pitchers in their fists, the children a gaggle of tiny legs and missing teeth. She felt keenly how she belonged to no one, while everyone else belonged to someone. Men in the plain coats and drab caps of miners threaded through the crowd looking for their women, picking up their children slowly with aching backs. She smelled potato soup coming from the open double doors of the canteen in the distance, and she suddenly felt light-headed and drained. She hoped this mine wasn't far from Elisa's house. But which one was it of the many across the city?

Again, there were no signs on the gatehouse, the canteen, or the other buildings surrounding the yard, so she wandered to the pithead and watched the wheel turn. It felt good to be back on familiar ground, in a living mine. Eleven years ago she had started her first job in one of the family's own, light secretarial work at first. She'd taken it as a lark, to annoy her mother. Elisa was a great help, teaching her the finer workings of an office, its systems and rhythms, all the little ways to increase efficiency. And Clara had been surprised by how much she liked it, earning her own money, acquiring responsibility. Papa was amused by what he teasingly called her "unbridled ambition," but he began taking her to meetings, introducing her to people who mattered. Her mother tolerated it all as long as Clara reported every detail about every meeting, every bit of office gossip, every contract or important document that crossed her desk.

She lined up with the women outside the canteen and listened to their chatter, expecting them to talk about her escape, whatever news the Allies had put out there about the events of two nights ago. Dangerous woman escaped from British custody, rewards for her capture. But the women had more important things to discuss. The shop allegedly selling ham. How to scrape together a Christmas dinner. The shortage of rat poison. She wished she could join in as she'd done at her first job. Now and then she had taken a meal at one of the canteen's long wooden tables, and the miners and their families had crowded the benches around her, everyone wanting a chance to sit with Fräulein Falkenberg. They were curious, and asked all sorts of questions. What was it like to drive a Mercedes? What did champagne taste like? Were the bath fixtures at Falkenhorst made of gold? She had turned the tables, just as interested in them. What did they do on Sundays? What songs were they rehearsing in the local choir? What books were they reading? And then: What worried them?

When they told her that medical supplies were low or the food subpar, she talked to the officers of the mine, who made changes based on her wishes alone. They assumed she spoke for her father.

Finally, she interrupted the women in the line. "I'm a bit turned around today. Which mine is this?" At the odd looks the women gave her, she took a guess. "Is this the Sophia shaft?" A Falkenberg mine named after her grandmother.

"Hope you gave him as good as he gave you," one of the women said, gesturing at Clara's face.

Clara touched the bruise on her left cheek, a dull pain under her glove. "A soldier roughed me up. A Tommy." She added a harder edge to her accent to show she was a local. "Think they can do whatever they want with us girls."

"Serves you right for going with one of them."

"I wasn't going anywhere with him. That's what got me into trouble. Which mine is this?"

"You almost got it right. It's Heinrich shaft two."

Clara smiled her thanks. This was excellent news. A Falkenberg mine, named after her grandfather, who was rumored to have been buried in an iron coffin. It was one of the ghoulish family stories Clara had loved as a girl. As she left the mine, she filled in where she was on her mental map of the city. Nearby she would find Falkenbergstrasse, the main artery of the city as she knew it, the northeast axis where goods and people flowed south to the city center and the southern rail lines and back up to the northern districts, ending at the family iron works. She guessed she was about twenty minutes from Elisa's house, a villa in the Sophienhof housing estate. Her grandmother had begun building the estate for Falkenberg workers forty years ago. After she died, the workers claimed she was the reason not a single bomb had dropped on Sophienhof all through the war. Grandmother held a protective hand over the homes she had built. The family was a power to be reckoned with even in death.

She left Falkenbergstrasse at a stone arch, the entrance to Sophienhof. Chimneys were smoking in some of the semidetached cottages. There was even glass in some of the windows, lace curtains, carved shutters, swept doorsteps, everything as she remembered. Just as it should be.

The fog was lifting. On the horizon, a vertical line pierced the sky like a black spear thrust into the clouds. That was Hans—Tall Hans—the tallest smokestack in the city and the heart of the iron works. He was always part of the horizon at Sophienhof, enduring as a mountain.

"Hello, Hans," she said, not feeling at all foolish to be talking to a smokestack. When she was little, Papa used to point up and say things like, "Hans is coughing a lot today," or "Hans needs a wash." As a girl she'd been sure the factories, power plants, and machines in the Works had lives. Had souls. The Works itself had been a great, humming, living creature. At the end of the war, it was silent, devastated by the bombs, but Hans defied them. He was still standing tall, towering over the cottages her family had built. The war hadn't taken that.

At a curve in the road, she detected a new scent in the air: the smell of old smoke and soot. The houses she could see were intact, curtained, groomed, yet there was that smell, a deep memory of the bombardments. She quickened her step, passing through the wood that separated the cottages from the villas for the higher employees. There used to be linden trees here, but now it was a forest of mossy stumps.

Her hip and shoulder were flaring with pain, her hands and feet numb with cold. She needed a hot oven and warm food. It was finally hitting her how profoundly Captain Fenshaw had changed her situation. She wasn't just in hiding anymore, she was on the run. She was homeless. She had no identity card, which meant in this world, she didn't exist. She couldn't check into a hotel, yet she couldn't spend her nights in pigeon houses, not when the air was growing sharper and the temperature dropping.

She needed to shelter with Elisa, to rest and heal and think about what to do next. But she worried she would pose a risk to her friend and to Elisa's son, Willy, if Captain Fenshaw discovered Clara in their house. She didn't know what he would do to them. Separate them, perhaps, Elisa in his custody, her son alone. He would be a teenager now but still, Clara couldn't allow that to happen. For a moment, she even considered finding her mother. Clara didn't think Anne would betray her to Fenshaw, but there was a chance she might use her daughter to gain something from her fellow Brits just as she'd done at those Fascist rallies and marches in England years ago. Clara hadn't trusted her mother since that incident at boarding school—her reaction, her treachery. No, she wouldn't go to her now. She had to take the risk with Elisa, but cautiously.

At the end of the wood, she saw what was left of the villas, and gasped in dismay.

The first house on the street, Elisa's house, was a ruin, smashed as if a great fist had pounded it from the sky. Two floors, brick and stone and glass, shattered. The roof had collapsed; the walls were fragments of what they used to be. The villa had been a wedding gift to Elisa from the Falkenbergs. Elisa had told her the house keys had appeared in an anonymous silver box as if delivered by elves. Clara had brushed off her thanks, as her mother advised. A house was nothing. The family had so much. Why not give to an employee who was so loyal?

And now it was gone. House after house was nothing more than a mound of rubble all along the street. She couldn't believe what she was seeing. It wasn't supposed to be like this.

A broken piece of Elisa's scorched front door lay in the dead grass as if the house had been nothing, not a place Clara's grandmother had built, her family had paid for, and Elisa had made her home. Clara lifted a side of the door so that it leaned against the stump of a tree. Its bright Mediterranean blue had survived, painted by Elisa for her son, though the color violated the neighborhood ordinances. When he was five, Willy had played in the woods by himself, and then wandered Sophienhof trying to find his way home. He had ended up in a neighbor's kitchen where the maid found him drinking milk straight out of the bottle. Elisa had painted the door, showed it to Willy, and said, "Look, this is home." He painted a small piece of wood the same shade and carried it around for years. When Clara had reported this to her mother, Anne had sniffed and said, "What a strange little creature."

Clara backed away from the door, from bits of the house scattered around the yard, appalling things that didn't belong in the open air—a cracked sink covered in mold, a stained toilet enthroned on the lawn. She circled the house to the back, and was relieved to see the orderly furrows in the vegetable garden Elisa had tended in the war. The garden was a sign that she was still here. In the cellar, maybe. It had to have survived the bombs. Clara descended a short flight of concrete steps set within the ground.

"Elisa?" Clara banged her fist on the cellar door. "Elisa, it's me. Open up." She spat on the hem of her scarf and rubbed her face. She was still rubbing away the dirt when the door opened a crack and a voice rumbled from within.

"What do you want?"

Not Elisa's voice. Or maybe Clara had forgotten how it sounded.

"It's me."

"Who?"

She almost said her real name, but her heart pounded a warning. "I'm looking for Elisabeth Sieland. Do you know where she is?"

The door opened wider. The woman looking up at her, squinting in the daylight, had the creased face of a squashed cabbage. Frizzing hair straggled out from under her head scarf. "You're hurt, fräulein. Your face."

"It's nothing. Is Elisabeth Sieland here? This is her house."

"Sieland? The *Rabenmutter*?"

Clara bristled at the old term. Because Elisa had worked outside the home even when her son was small, she had been called a neglectful raven mother often enough, sometimes to her face. It had wounded her deeply.

"Is she here or not?" Clara said.

The woman mounted the steps outside, looking with suspicion at the garden and the path that led around the house to the front. "Come back down, fräulein. Watch your step there. If you don't hold on, it's a long way to fall."

As the woman led her into the cellar, she apologized for her caution. The world had gone mad. There were gangs of youths on the streets; there were thieves and murderers about. Even here. "This used to be a good neighborhood, fräulein," she said. "Didn't have to lock our doors. And now? Leave a bucket outside with a hole in it and somebody'll steal it."

At the bottom of the steps, Clara rubbed her hip and caught her breath. Inside the cellar, miner's lamps hung from the walls as they had in the war. Here and there, net sacks containing turnips or a loaf of bread dangled from hooks in the ceiling. The trunks of oak trees shored up the cellar like pillars. She touched the bark. This had been Willy's idea. He'd probably been almost eleven, small for his age but looking oddly mature in his Jungvolk uniform. His *oma*, Elisa's mother, had died in a bombardment, and from then on, he had pored over air-raid leaflets, his finger following the words as he read in a whisper. After the oaks were installed, he took Clara on a tour, explaining the technical advantages, forgetting his shyness. "It looks like a forest underground, growing in the dark, right, fräulein?" Now Clara circled the trees, suddenly troubled. Something was missing, something that had been here in the war.

She could see half a dozen people, including children, in the bunks that Willy had insisted on building to army specifications. At a pinch, the children could squeeze three to one bed, one adult with one child in the lower bunk. There was one narrow bed at the back wall. Barely room for this family to sleep, and none at all for Elisa and Willy.

The woman introduced herself as Frau Berger and pointed to an old man she said was her father-in-law. He dabbed his lip with a handkerchief and watched Clara with suspicion.

"What are you doing here?" Clara asked. "This is Elisabeth Sieland's house."

"Sit here, fräulein"—Frau Berger pulled a chair from the table—"by the fire." She added in a whisper, "You're the one they're looking for, aren't you? The British were here."

"When?"

"Late last night and again this morning. Turned everything upside down, grand as you like. Had a poke about in the ruins of the house. I had to tell that officer not to collapse the roof on our heads." She gestured at the ceiling. "They came down here searching our things. Pulled the children out of bed too, like you were hiding under the blankets with them."

"Did he tell you who I am?"

"He showed us your identity card." She paused. "Fräulein Müller."

Clara waited for more. She wasn't sure of these people. They were squatters, that was clear, whether Elisa still lived here or not. She couldn't yet tell if it was to her advantage to say who she really was, if her identity would impress them. It might come down to whether they had worked for Krupp or Falkenberg. That was the division that had mattered, the sides everyone in the city used to take one way or another.

But now there was another side, a sense of self-preservation that trumped all the old loyalties. If she announced herself to these people like some exiled princess come home, they might turn her in for British cigarettes. Maybe Fenshaw had bribed them to work for him as he had done with her landlady in Hamelin.

Frau Berger was staring at her, and Clara realized why the woman had seated her here, the firelight in Clara's face, the lantern overhead. This was the brightest spot in the cellar. Well, then. Clara took off her hat. If Frau Berger wanted to see her, let her see.

The old man came closer, examining her from this angle, from that, his left foot dragging as he limped around her. He lowered his handkerchief. The left side of his mouth sagged, and when he spoke, his words slurred as if his tongue was too thick for him. "Clärchen," he said, and his eyes moistened. "It is you, Clärchen."

Her old nickname, Little Clara, echoed inside of her, filled her with a warmth she hadn't felt in a long time. The Falkenberg workers had given her the name when she was a girl and her father paraded her around the Works like a mascot. From then on, Papa had called her Clärchen too.

"You're sure?" Frau Berger asked.

The old man was dribbling again. He pressed his handkerchief to his mouth with a look of apology and embarrassment. "I worked for your grandfather. Your father too."

"He was an accountant," Frau Berger said, "for forty years."

"Your father used to bring you to headquarters and you'd stand behind his desk during meetings. He'd do the same for his sons, but it was different with you. He was a better man when you were watching. Fairer, more patient. Do you remember that?"

Clara was nodding, and by the time she realized, it was too late. Frau Berger gasped, her hand over her mouth. In the bunk bed, the children raised their heads, their necks thin as baby birds'.

The mistake was made. There was nothing else to be done.

Clara stood up, back straight—that iron rod which was supposedly in her spine—and faced Herr Berger the way her father had taught her. Direct, with a dignity that would remind this man of a time when they were family, of a kind. In her old voice, her tone of cool calm, she told the truth.

"I need your help."

7

The Bergers didn't hesitate. They discussed what was to be done, how they could protect Clara, starting with setting one of the boys as a guard. Frau Berger coaxed him out of bed, a scrawny thing whose clothes were too short at the legs and wrists. Clara tried to tell them he didn't have to do this, but his mother grasped his shoulders and forced him to stand taller. "Show Fräulein Falkenberg respect." She swatted his back, and he bowed like a puppet before scurrying up the cellar steps and out into the cold.

Solemnly, the old man fetched a neckerchief from a cigar box, unfolding the red-orange fabric on his palm. Clara recognized the symbol on the fabric, a bird's wing sweeping up like a stylized flame. The Falkenberg symbol, everywhere in her life since the day she was born and wrapped in swaddling clothes with that symbol stitched on the cotton. Only a hot iron could have branded her more clearly. The old man tied the kerchief around his neck, his chin up. It was done with such ceremony and Clara remembered the many acts of respect for her family over the years: the workers lining up like an honor guard, the bankers whispering on the way to the vault. None of that compared to this. None of them took the risk the Bergers were taking now, putting themselves in jeopardy to stand by her against Allied soldiers.

The loose skin of his jaw trembled as Herr Berger tied the knot. "Fräulein, in the name of my family—"

Embarrassed, she gestured for him to stop.

"—I want to say how honored we are to be of service. We'll do everything we can to help you."

She didn't know what to say in the face of his decency. On her own for so long, it had been some time since she had been truly grateful to anyone and here she was, her first day home, gratitude washing over her in waves. "Thank you," she said, shaking his hand, Frau Berger's hand, and then the children's, each bony hand raised out of the blankets. She wanted to do something for them—not solely to be a burden or a problem. She flourished a can of chopped pork and another of peas and carrots from her backpack, and the children chirped happily.

As Frau Berger busied herself with the soup, the old man admitted the family had been bombed out of their own house across the street. "Still can't believe it," he said. "Bombing us at the last minute. A disgrace. The whole western end of Sophienhof gone in one raid."

"When exactly?" Clara was rolling the meat into balls that would cook in the soup, and as she listened, she concentrated on rolling a perfect edible sphere.

"Eleventh of March forty-five. You must remember that one, fräulein. That was hell raining down from the sky."

She nodded, dropped the meat in the soup and then scrubbed her hands in the basin. Eleventh of March. The same day she left Essen. As soon as she had heard the sirens, she had known it might be her last chance to get away. For weeks she'd delayed the decision as the bombardments pounded them, news flooding in of lost battles, massive fatalities, and the Americans crossing the Rhine, the ultimate sign that the war would be over in days. She was too exhausted to be glad, too wrapped up in the questions: Should she flee? Should she stay and surrender? She had guessed what the Allies would do to people in high positions like hers or her father's. If she stayed in Essen, she would be arrested, and if she told them what she had done for the foreign workers in her care, they would think she was lying to save her skin. The thought of going to prison for the Nazis—the injustice of it had made her boil.

As the detonations grew closer, she had bent over the sink in the office and cut off her blond hair. The dark roots were coming through, but she couldn't be sure of the back of her head, and so, with shaking hands, she had shaved the rest. She hadn't been willing to look at herself too closely in the mirror, and had ended up dabbing blood from cuts all over her head. Her backpack had been packed weeks before and hidden in a cabinet she had emptied of papers. At the time, it had been a month since Clara had heard from Papa. She had known the Russians were flooding toward him in Berlin, and the Americans toward her, and she had hoped he would run.

Herr Berger fretted the corners of his handkerchief. "The British came at us with a thousand bombers. English bullies—" He stopped himself, looking penitent. "Sorry, fräulein. But what did they do? Pounded us to hell when the war was all but over. Know what I think? They had to use their bombs before it was too late. What's the point of having bombs once a war is over? So they dumped them. Killed a thousand people that day. Women and children and older folk too. For nothing."

"What happened to Elisa . . . Frau Sieland?"

"She got through the raid all right. I saw her outside with buckets trying to put out the flames. The house was still burning when . . ." He tossed a worried look at Frau Berger.

"The soup is ready, fräulein," she said too cheerfully.

"When what? What happened?" Clara asked.

The old man was dabbing his handkerchief at his lips again. "It was a bad time, fräulein. So much smoke. Was hard to see anything."

"See what?"

The old man lowered his handkerchief and studied whatever encrusted it. "Well, they . . . came for Frau Sieland. To be honest, I knew they'd come and get her eventually. She was always out of the house at all hours, as if curfew and raids didn't apply to her. Work, she'd say. But I ask you, what kind of work did she do that she'd slip in and out of the house in the middle of the night?"

Clara rubbed her neck, feeling the hard knot of anxiety lodged there. "Herr Berger, you're not making sense. Start at the beginning and tell me exactly what happened."

The Bergers couldn't agree on how to tell it. Frau Berger started with a car, a great black car, surprised anyone had the gasoline, she said. "Who cares about the car?" Herr Berger interrupted. "It was two men, big brutes. They went straight for Frau Sieland while she was hauling water to her house. They wouldn't even let her stay and see the fire put out."

"It wasn't put out," Frau Berger said, "it was impossible. Too big. And there were too many other fires. Now our house was—"

"She argued with them. One of them took her arm but she yanked it right back, threw down her bucket, and went with them, quickly into the car like she wanted to get it over with." Herr Berger shrugged. "That was it."

"Who were the men?" Clara demanded.

Herr Berger picked at his lip. "Looked like Gestapo to me."

She had guessed as much. In the war, they would show up at her office accusing her of violating a regulation someone in Berlin had thought up the day before. The Gestapo men she'd had the misfortune to meet were overworked and not the brightest and she had managed to ignore them a good deal. They could smell disdain, though. She'd had to watch her step. Fortunately, there were never many Gestapo men in the city. More dangerous were the informants, people around her who might talk, people she knew. It was hard to trust anyone, but she could talk to Elisa. Max too—for a time. No one else knew what Elisa was doing to help the foreign workers as head of Falkenberg's Housing Office. She had informed Clara about the inadequate food supply, the sanitary facilities in need of repair, the overcrowding in the labor camps, the epidemics of illness. Clara had made calls, demanding more resources from the government, more supplies, more medicines, and in the rare times she got them, it was Elisa who spirited them, secretly if necessary, to the workers in their barracks. Her arrest couldn't have been because of that, or had they made a mistake? Given themselves away? Clara pictured Galina eating bread on the dusty floor, the line of young women contentedly smacking their lips in the shadows while Clara reminded them in whispers to keep their heads down, to avoid the windows, to talk only at night, and always quietly.

At the oven, she rubbed her cold hands and tried to think of a likely explanation for what had happened to Elisa. "I'll tell you what that was all about," she said, thinking out loud. "Every time there was a bombardment, most of the foreign workers would stay at the Works or in their camps and help dig us out. But a few would take advantage of the chaos and go scavenging in the city or run off. Once the Gestapo got wind of that, they'd march over to my office and demand to know what we were going to do about our workers stealing food and whatnot. I'm sure the same thing happened after the raid that day. They couldn't find me or Max, so they picked up poor Elisa."

Everything she said had happened before. But she wasn't at all sure it was true this time. The coincidence of the date—the bombardment that day, the same day Clara left the city—it seemed to mean something.

"I'm sure she came back in a foul mood," she said, her tone more confident than she felt. "Elisa hated dealing with the Gestapo as much as I did."

Behind her, the silence thickened, and she turned to see Herr Berger and his daughter-in-law exchanging a glance. "What is it?" Clara asked.

The old man coughed into his handkerchief and Frau Berger began handing out soup to the children. "Fräulein, she never came back," she said.

Clara rustled the blankets on the empty bed, circled to the shelves where Elisa had stocked up for the raids, cans of everything imaginable, toilet paper, emergency flashlight and batteries. The shelves were nearly empty now, and there was nothing Clara remembered. "She must have come back. This is her house."

"We moved in as soon as the fires were out, fräulein. Been here ever since and haven't heard a thing from her."

"What about Willy?" Clara asked. "What happened to Elisa's son?"

"Didn't see him during the raid. I don't think he was here when they came for Frau Sieland. We got a few bits of her mail once the mail was running again." Frau Berger removed the envelopes from behind the rusted coffee can. "But it stopped soon after."

Chilled, Clara thought of Fenshaw, who had intercepted the letter she had written to Elisa. The letters that had reached Elisa didn't help at all: an appeal for money from a distant cousin in Hessen, an appeal for money from a charity. Clara tossed them aside and roamed the cellar again, trying to understand. The Gestapo had taken Elisa and she had never come home, and Clara had not been here to help. She had fled when Elisa needed her most. If the Gestapo had arrested her because of what they had done together for the workers, the punishment would have been swift and severe. Prison at the very least. In the war, there had been posters around the city warning people not to give food to the eastern crews, some of the hungriest and most miserable of the lot. Clara and Elisa had done so much more than feed them. They had known the risk, had discussed it, and Clara had always assured her that if they were caught, she would take responsibility. As head of the Works, she would shield Elisa as much as she could. But she had fled, and Elisa had vanished. A barren land unfolded inside her—the thought that maybe

Elisa hadn't survived. She stopped herself, pushed the thought away. It did her no good to think the worst before she had all the facts.

"I'll find her," she announced to the Bergers, who were exchanging worried looks. "I'll be careful. And I'll make sure you have somewhere else to go once she's back." Clara couldn't promise them anything more. She had nowhere to go herself, except perhaps home to her mother. Anne might know more about what had happened to Elisa. Once Clara found her, she would leave the city. She couldn't risk staying with Fenshaw on her trail. She wasn't even sure if she should stay with the Bergers, but she didn't see what choice she had. For now.

The Bergers looked doubtful. "If Frau Sieland survived, why hasn't she come back already? It's been over a year and a half."

"She must have thought the house a complete loss and moved in somewhere else. Or maybe she didn't see the point of evicting you."

"She's got something better, then? Not many options, fräulein, unless she found herself an Allied soldier as soon as they took over."

Clara shook her head—absolutely not, not Elisa—but then she remembered how her friend had been late in the war, a kind of glow in her as the Allies swept closer. Sometimes Elisa would sing at the top of her lungs as she ran errands at the iron works. At the time, Clara hadn't thought much of it. They were all going a little mad. Everyone felt the end coming. Max used to blare swing music on the old windup record player in his office. Clara took great care to tidy her desk even when the ceiling shed plaster after the bombardments. She roared at whatever staff she had left to clear the hallways, her father's voice ringing in her ears, reminding her to save the Works, preserve it, cherish it. She would have no chairs blocking the way, no rubbish, and no rubble. She would have a clean, orderly environment as the world turned to dust around her. Elisa's singing was no odder than that, a strange expression of joy as the Americans pressed toward them.

"Did she leave anything behind that might tell me where she went?"

"We salvaged some of her things," Frau Berger said, opening a battered suitcase in front of Clara. "It isn't much. Suppose it's no surprise she didn't bother to come for them."

It was a rummage sale of personal items. A tarnished compact mirror, broken. An address book once soaked by water, words illegible. Sunglasses, one lens missing. A pair of black shoes with holes where the big toe had chewed through.

Clara didn't touch these things. She felt around inside the suitcase and pulled out a notebook, also waterstained but still readable. It was Willy's from a time when he still wrote in all capitals. BIRDS, he'd printed on the first page. From there, he had noted the numbers of pigeons, sparrows, and other birds he'd seen in the city. He used to carry the book pinned under his arm, a serious-faced seven-year-old with his gaze on the treetops and the lampposts and the windowsills high over his head. Seeing his boyish handwriting made her remember his hand, her thumb stroking the soft pillow of his palm the many times she'd held it.

"What did Willy do when he came home after the fire and found his mother gone?"

"He never came back either, fräulein," the old man said softly. "We thought he'd been sent off to fight."

"He was just a boy," Clara snapped. "He didn't fight." She held his notebook tightly in her lap, thinking. At the end of the war, he was thirteen. She remembered how one day he had appeared in his Jungvolk uniform in Clara's office, asking for a job. He wanted to do something for the war effort. Her heart wasn't easily broken, but a little piece of her shattered deep inside, seeing a boy so desperate to work for a lost cause. Instead of sending him home, she gave him a crucial role. He was to mind the blackout at the iron works. From then on, when she could stomach looking out of her office window, she would often see him on his bicycle racing around the groups of foreign workers trudging through the ruined factories. Now and then he would stop and watch them go by. She had been too far away to see his face, if he felt horror or pity or fear at the sight of them.

She turned the pages of Willy's notebook again. BIRDS. And then she remembered what was missing from the cellar. "Where's Gertrud?"

The Bergers looked at one another. "Who?"

"Willy's canary."

"We didn't see any bird here." Frau Berger shrugged. "Maybe it died. Not like there wasn't enough of that going around."

In the corner of the cellar, she found the hook in the ceiling. "He kept her in a cage right here." Clara had given Gertrud to Willy for his twelfth birthday. She'd been nervous about it because the canary was damaged, a wing not quite right so that the little thing fluttered around instead of flying. But that was the very thing that won Willy's heart. He had taken one look at the clipped wing and the way Gertrud struggled in her fear of him, and this boy, Elisa's quiet boy, who rarely spoke to other children, had begun to whisper gentle words to the little yellow bird.

8

The boy soldier was a creature of habit. After Jakob slept off his exhaustion on an army bed, he awakened groaning and muttering about his pains while the kid paced back and forth in what Jakob began to think of as a camp. It was a wide tunnel reinforced with timber and steel beams. The dead end looked as though somebody had wanted to blast it and then changed his mind. Holes dotted the rock where the blaster had set the dynamite, then failed for whatever reason to push the plunger. There was no dynamite now. Jakob felt the weight of the earth over his head. He had been born to be a miner—the son following in the father's footsteps and all of that—and he'd thought himself a clever fellow to avoid these tunnels by going to war.

A war that was over a year and a half ago. The boy

in the uniform was playing a peculiar—if disturbing—
sort of game, acting as though it was still in full flow.
He paced from the crate he used as a table to the map
on the wall to the curtain that blocked the camp from
the main tunnel. His steel helmet cast a shadow on his
face, but Jakob saw his jaw well enough. So smooth, it
had never seen a razor. A rash of spots dotted the left
side of his mouth. And if Jakob squinted, he thought he
saw freckles on the tip of the boy's nose.

"How old are you, kid?"

"I'm not a kid. I'm thirteen." The boy frowned
down at Jakob as if he disapproved of him being half
naked—as if it was Jakob's fault. "Stay here," he said,
and vanished into the next tunnel.

Jakob heard a rustling and a series of irate peeps.
For the first time, he noticed a kind of shelf in the rock
wall at the foot of the bed. On it was a nest of twigs and
paper occupied by a yellow canary. She shivered her
wings and cocked her head and chirped at him for so
long, he got the impression she was trying to tell him
something important.

"Hello, sweetheart," he said, holding his hand out
to her. "Call me Jakob." She shrank back, still chirp-
ing, her tiny legs stomping her nest. He understood
her hesitation; he was a stranger after all, so he left
her alone. He was glad she was there. *A mine is a liv-*

ing thing, Papa used to say. *It breathes.* Noxious gases could come at any time, carbon dioxide hovering along the floor, methane floating odorless and invisible near the ceiling. As long as the canary lived and nobody lit a fire, the air was probably safe.

Soon the boy returned with gifts Jakob was only too glad to receive. Fresh army trousers, a sock, an army shoe that looked a size too small. It didn't matter. To get out of the mine, he needed clothes, his strength, and his prosthesis. The kid was also thoughtful enough to bring an aspirin. As it dissolved in a tin cup, Jakob said, "If you find my wooden leg, I'll owe you, kid. I'll light candles for you in church. I'll introduce you to my sisters. We'll go into business together. What do you say? Go out and search for me?"

The boy rotated on his heel, swept aside the curtain, and kept watch, one boot in the tunnel room, one outside it. His silence was unsettling, a kind of absence, as if he wasn't wholly there. Jakob tried a different tack.

"Met your canary, kid. What's her name?"

The boy let the curtain, a wool blanket spanning a rope, fall back into place. He scratched the eagle on his tunic. "Gertrud."

"She's sweet. What's your name, then?"

The boy paused as if thinking long and hard about this. Then he shook his head and again set about pacing—nest, table, map, curtain. This continued for what felt like hours. The kid rarely spoke or changed his route except to piss into a bucket or replace the spent lamps with full ones. Jakob began to think time moved in circles inside the mine. He had slept for at least a few hours, maybe the whole night, into the next day. He ate the meals the kid gave him, but Jakob couldn't guess the interval in between. He had no watch and the kid offered no information. Even the grumbling of his stomach didn't help Jakob measure time. He was permanently hungry like everyone else in the world. At every meal, the boy opened a can and handed it with a spoon to Jakob. Then he noted something in a leather-bound book he kept in the footlocker by the bed. Jakob longed to see what the boy was writing.

But mostly, he watched that uniform, the gray tunic coat and the helmet. At the end of the war, the Nazis tossed boys at the losing front. Cripples too, and old men. The Volkssturm, they called it, as if children and the dregs of the army would attack the Allies like a storm. The people called it the Cripple Guard. When Jakob first saw the big-eyed boys and trembling old geezers he was called up to train after his recovery, he'd nearly busted his teeth to keep from weeping.

"You a Werewolf?" he asked, trying for the tenth time to start a conversation.

Finally tired of pacing, the boy now sat at the crate table, sorting junk. Screws, wires, coils, nails dropped into tin cups. He had sorted them once already, then emptied the cups into a heap and started again for no clear purpose that Jakob could see. He repeated his question three times before the kid said, "A what?"

"A Werewolf. Partisan fighters. Fanatics. They murdered the mayor of Aachen a while back."

The kid dropped the last screw into its cup. Then he turned to the map of Europe on the wall.

Jakob snapped his fingers.

The boy didn't blink. Whatever he saw in that map, it absorbed him. Jakob took the opportunity to shimmy down the bed to Gertrud's nest, and this time, she let him stroke her head with his thumb.

"Stop that." The boy swept his bird out of her nest and set her on his shoulder. She tilted as she flapped her wings, the feathers clipped on one side.

"I got one leg, you got a bird on your shoulder," Jakob said. "Between the two of us, we'd make a nice pirate."

Nothing. Not even the hint of a smile from the boy. He pulled the curtain aside and stared into the tunnel in that expectant way he had. Jakob got the feeling he didn't exist for the boy just then.

Jakob braced himself on Gertrud's shelf and pulled up onto his good foot. No dizziness: a good sign. His leg wobbled, that stork feeling he always got when he stood without his prosthesis. Once steady, he did an experimental hop. It made his jaw rattle, and he let out a groan of pain. He glanced toward the curtain.

Boy and bird were gone. An opportunity Jakob couldn't pass up.

He hopped along the wall and leaned, panting, against the map. The German Reich and its conquests sprawled across Europe as if time had stopped in 1942. Writing covered the map, tiny notes that Jakob could make out only when he got close. Dates, units, troop movements, none of them within the borders of the old Reich, as if the two-front war that crushed Germany had never happened.

He eased himself back onto the bed and raided the kid's locker. He found a military identity card without a photograph made out to Wilhelm Sieland, born September 27, 1931. His father, Reinhard, was deceased, and his mother was named Elisabeth. Under the addendum, someone had penciled in what Jakob assumed was the boy's address in Sophienhof, a Falkenberg housing estate Jakob knew of but had never had cause to visit.

He set the card aside and picked up the notebook the kid had been writing in. A picture slid out, a family snap by a big house. The father was in uniform, puffed up like an ape in spectacles. The mother was a knockout in a white blouse and loose curls. Reinhard and Elisabeth, Jakob assumed. Between them, the boy soldier, midget version, held a toy train. On the back of the photograph: *Willy's 10th birthday, September 27, 1941.*

Jakob looked at the identity card again. He rubbed his forehead, slow at the math. If the kid was born in 1931, he'd be fifteen now. Didn't he say he was thirteen?

Back to the ledger. The first page was a list, an inventory of the supplies in the mine. Jakob couldn't believe this stuff existed all in one place. Fruit and soup, beans and sugar, fish and dried meat and on and on until he got the feeling he'd woken up in Schlaraffenland where wine flowed in the rivers and houses were made of cake.

After the inventory, a new list began.

1. 200g bread, 1 tsp each margarine and artificial honey, 150g canned ham.

It reminded Jakob of his mother's recipe book, but it was no recipe. It was breakfast. The numbered columns stretched down the page. And the next one. And the next. Jakob read at random.

298. 3 zwieback, 1 pellet Knorr pea soup (with bacon).
901. 3 slices bread, 1 sardines, 1 carrots.

Jakob flipped to the last written page.

1,932. 1 ham, 1 peas and carrots, 300g powdered potatoes. 1 tsp margarine. 150g powdered milk. 1 packet Dr. Oetker pudding (vanilla).

Willy was keeping track of the food he took out of the stores. Jakob assumed the food was for the kid's family, but—if so—why such small amounts? Why keep the ledger at all? He couldn't imagine the men who owned the supplies would care. When Jakob's old employer gave him a chicken leg, he sure as hell didn't write it down. On the other hand, two thousand meals was more than an occasional gift.

"Put that down." Willy snatched back the ledger. Gertrud tipped off his shoulder and fluttered back to her nest.

"What is this place?" Jakob asked. "You're sitting on a fortune in food and cigarettes. You're dressed like you want the Tommies to lock you up for good. What are you doing down here?"

"My duty."

"What duty?"

"Guarding the depot."

"Figured that out. But what for?"

"Ever heard of the End Push?"

"When we rise up against the Allies with our secret weapons and kick them out of the Reich forever? That End Push?" Jakob watched the kid tuck the ledger back into the locker, saw the gas mask, the ammunition pouch. He felt the first cold prick of a terrible, impossible thought. "The war is over. You do know that, right?"

Willy took off his helmet. He was the standard blond-blue combination, the face printed on the five Reichs-mark note, the Nordic boy, gaze fixed on his future of death and glory. That face got lost in a uniform. There were tens of thousands like it. Jakob had the same face. As a kid, he'd rubbed coal dust in his hair to be different for a day.

Willy did have something special. His eyes. Frosty blues that bulged enough to be striking. Without the helmet, he looked even younger than Jakob had thought. Thirteen? Fifteen?

"Victory," Willy said with awe. He splayed his hand on the map, Atlantic theater. "When the Tommies bowed to the superiority of our V-2 rockets, we swept the Western Front, didn't we? Our submarines shot missiles at the American coastline. The Americans withdrew from Europe to defend their country. That left us to turn against the Russians. The Bolshies are finished, right? Nobody would leave them standing. The führer never would. When did they surrender?"

"You think the Russians surrendered? They had thirty million men."

"One German soldier is worth five of them."

"You mean there were five of them for every German soldier. We lost, kid."

Willy turned abruptly from the map. "That's impossible. We can't lose. We . . . We'll fight until the last man." He was scratching his tunic again. "Until victory."

Jakob's head throbbed. One thousand nine hundred and thirty-two meals. If he calculated three meals a day for one person, how many days had the kid been down here? How many months? That is, if Willy didn't take food for his family and had been consuming it alone since . . . when?

After the war, the Americans had kicked over every rock and poked around in every cellar. They'd searched for weapons, Nazis, partisans, soldiers who refused to surrender. So many coal mines snaked under Essen, the city should have sunk by now. But still, wouldn't the Americans, or the British who came after them, have found this place? Could this kid really have been here alone all this time?

He looked around the room. The camp bed, the map, the table, the locker. They had the settled feel of a bunker for one on a front that hadn't moved in a long while.

"When did you come down here, kid?"

At the curtain, Willy watched the tunnel. Jakob repeated the question twice before the boy said, "March." His eyes bulged in the darkness. "The eleventh of March."

"It's the . . . sixth of December. Or the seventh. I don't know. Time is strange down here. But—all right, it's 1946. December 1946. You with me?"

Willy returned to the crate table. He poured nails and screws out of the cups into a heap.

"Don't drift away yet, kid. Tell me the year you came down here. The year."

The boy sorted the nails from the screws.

"Willy."

The boy dropped a screw and turned his big eyes on Jakob. "You know my name."

"It's 1946. You turned fifteen in September. You got to know that. You're not thirteen, Willy. You're fifteen."

"You're not making sense."

"*I'm* not—" Jakob pressed his temples. If, and it was a big if, the Allies had missed this mine after the war, maybe—just maybe—it was possible the supplies had

sat undiscovered for eighteen months. If a black marketeer had found the depot, he would have sold it immediately and retired to grow fat with a beautiful woman on
the island of Sylt.

"Listen to me. Listen, you poor idiot, you can forget
about all this. The war is over. Go home."

"I will stay at my post until victory when I'm relieved
of duty." Willy selected a nail. "I was warned about
people like you."

"Sane people?"

"Defeatists."

Jakob clawed his hair. "I'll say it slow so you understand. The. War. Is. Over. We lost."

Willy dropped a screw into one cup, a nail into the
other.

"Come back to me, kid." Jakob threw his empty meal
tin, and it glanced off the table. "Listen to me. US and
British forces encircled us in April '45, the whole Ruhr
area. If you been down here since"—he could barely say
it—"since the eleventh of March 1945, you came in before the pincer closed. But it did. The Allies squeezed
and we surrendered. Three hundred thousand of us
surrendered. It's over." He held out his hands in appeal.
"Understand?"

The last of the nails and screws clanged into the cups.

Willy wiped his hands on a cloth, folded it according to the rules of geometry, and faced Jakob.

"I can't let this stand. You're a thief and a defeatist." He drew his pistol. "Another traitor."

"Wait, listen—"

"The sentence for treason is death."

Jakob shook his head. This was a madhouse. Any minute now, Gertrud was going to start talking. Maybe his leg would grow back. If it did, he'd disarm Willy, the little prat, and throw him out of the mine by the seat of his pants.

"You know where my father died?" Jakob asked.

Confusion passed over Willy's face.

"Underground. Mining accident in the war. He was sent down to save the fellows who got buried and ended up dead himself. I was at the front. You know what I see, when I think about it? I see him wearing his Draeger on his back—it made him look like a beetle with a hose in its mouth—and he's crushed under a pit's worth of coal and rock. Most of us don't get to choose where we die, kid, but I am telling you right now: I am not dying in a hole in the ground like Papa did. If you want to shoot me, take me outside."

The dull look was back in Willy's eyes. "My papa fell in the war. For the Reich. But my mother . . ."

"I'm sorry about that, kid."

Willy blinked. "What did you say?"

"Nobody wants to die in the dark. Take me outside."

It was day. After the darkness in the mine, the gray sky beamed down on Jakob like a spotlight. He shaded his eyes with an arm, let the light in slowly. When he looked up, he saw for the first time where he'd landed.

Frost covered the valley and dusted the hills and brambles a gleaming white. Above him, the cliff jutted like the prow of some old sailing ship and curved away in both directions. The mine's entrance used to be a rounded portal, but the stone had eroded from the hill above and slid down, hiding the space.

In daylight, Willy's skin looked the color of spoiled milk. Jakob remembered men like that, hidden in cellars and bunkers too long. Years ago, he had looked like that himself.

"Down there." Willy motioned down the slope toward the marsh. The river was a silver line behind the weeds.

"Think about what you're doing, Willy." Jakob hopped toward him, one, two steps, and the shovel slipped. His good knee cracked on the ground as he went down on all fours, and he cried out.

Willy aimed at his head, and Jakob went still. He

didn't feel the pain in his knee anymore, only a cold spot where the bullet could enter his skull if he made a sudden move.

"Wait, kid. Listen." He eased himself slowly into a sitting position so he could see the pistol while looking Willy in the face. "The war is over. We're free to tend to our own business instead of bleeding for the Reich. Tend to our families. Our gardens. Some philosopher wrote that, right? Some Frenchman. Help me out." Jakob realized it wasn't the best moment to bring up the French to a Hitler Youth boy with a gun. "Nobody survives alone, Willy. You need your family. I guarantee they need you. You got brothers and sisters?"

The gun shook in Willy's hand. "No."

"All right, it's just you and your mother. Think about that. She needs you. Go home. Or wait, you know what? I'll go to your house for you. I know your address from your identity card. I'll break the good news to your mother. When she hears you're alive, she'll probably—"

The shot boomed through the valley, and Jakob was on the ground, body pressed into the cold grass. The echoes built in his head, rolling through him like machine-gun fire and artillery. When it faded, he moved his leg. He touched his chest. Nothing. He was okay.

The kid aimed again, muttering, "Concentrate, concentrate, concentrate."

Somewhere around the bend in the cliff, men were shouting. Jakob couldn't see them yet, but he guessed who they were.

"Miners, Willy. Lots of mines around here, you know that, right? They heard that shot of yours. They're coming. They're coming to raid your depot and there's nothing you or me can do about it."

Willy tripped backward and recovered his balance, swinging his pistol from the cliff and back to Jakob. The kid's hesitation, the miss at point-blank range, had to mean he wasn't a killer or a soldier, despite the uniform.

"Miners got big families," Jakob said, "lots of mouths to feed. They won't waste a thought on us. You're just a boy even with that gun and I'm just a cripple. Our kind always get the short straw in this world. If we work together, we got a chance. Not only to survive. There's enough in that mine for us both to really do something with."

"I won't desert my post."

"Leave me the gun, kid. Quick."

Willy swayed.

"No fainting." Jakob snapped at him in the voice he hadn't used since the war: "Achtung."

Willy straightened.

"Drop the gun."

It thudded to the grass.

"Run."

Willy scrambled up the slope and through the crevice in the rock as the miners rounded the bend, three men in baggy trousers and shirts streaked with black dust. They waved at Jakob and shouted *"glück auf."* They would have a horse-drawn cart, maybe. A way to get him home. It was only a question of explaining the shot.

He picked up Willy's gun. The Walther P38 reassured him because he was used to it, not because he liked it. He had fought in the war too long to be sentimental about weapons.

When the miners were close enough to see, he raised it to his temple and waited for them to run to him, trying not to tremble and blow his brains out in the meantime. He calmed himself by repeating the address of Willy's house in his head over and over. He thought about Elisabeth Sieland and what she would do when Jakob told her about Willy. He imagined she would fly down here to fetch her son out of the mine. In her gratitude, in all that motherly joy, she would leave the depot and all its delicacies to the good man who had helped bring her boy home.

9

The old man was sitting on the toilet in Elisa's yard—clear-as-glass proof to Clara that the order of things had been turned upside down.

Herr Berger didn't seem to notice. He sat with his back straight and hands clasped on his knees, his coat draping over the ground and his worn shoes planted in the brown grass. He used the toilet only to rest, so his trousers were where Clara preferred them to be, securely belted high on his waist. He was watching the street for her. In the days since she had arrived at the cellar, he'd insisted on guarding her himself. An honor, he said, and of course he was healthy enough to do this sacred duty. And truly, when he kept watch for her, his hands didn't shake and he dribbled a little less than usual. She didn't have the heart to tell him that he looked suspicious to anyone who might pass by. If Fenshaw saw him, that would be the end.

She was grateful for Herr Berger's dedication, but even the dignified way he sat couldn't erase the fact that the scene was ridiculous. Toilets were not to be in yards. Intimacies were not to be made public. Every time she left the cellar, poking her head out like a rabbit sniffing for a fox (or whatever ate rabbits; she was a city girl), she couldn't accept what she was seeing: the bomb-blasted street, her grandmother's beloved work destroyed, Elisa's ruined house.

"Why don't you go back inside, Herr Berger? You must be freezing."

He kept his face to the street, unbearably serious. "I won't leave my post, fräulein."

"Only fools stay at their post when they're sure to get frostbite or pneumonia, and you're no fool." She took his arm. "Come on. Up you go."

He was stubborn. He refused to be moved, and she was surprised by his weight, or her own weakness. "Please," she said, "even sentries take breaks sometime. I'll be fine alone for a little while. And if the enemy comes"—they'd taken to calling Fenshaw the enemy— "I'll hide in the ruins. All right? You'd really like a nice hot drink, wouldn't you? Come downstairs."

Finally he let her lead him to the cellar door. She

noticed him swallowing pain as he limped gingerly down the stairs, one step at a time, leaning against her. She deposited him next to the oven and went back outside to assess the ruined house.

There was nothing to be done about the toilet. It was too heavy for her to move to a less conspicuous spot. And so she began to do what the Bergers hadn't done, to tidy the house's frontage, which faced the public street. She lifted bricks from the rubble and stacked them as she'd seen the cleanup crews do, her banged-up hip and shoulder twinging as she stooped down. Once she had a small, wide wall of bricks, she paused with satisfaction at the bit of order she had wrestled from the chaos.

It wasn't enough. She climbed over the rubble, deeper into what used to be Elisa's foyer, and pulled out of the broken stones the mangled remains of Elisa's telephone. Altogether, they'd carried on years of conversation on this thing. When they were younger, they had telephoned so often that it had driven Papa to distraction. "Should I invite her over, then?" Clara had asked, knowing her mother wouldn't allow it, through maybe Papa? But he had poured himself a cognac to the top of the glass and drank it down in one swallow, then promised to have a private line installed for Clara at Falkenhorst.

She carried the telephone to the lawn and set it on the grass. She returned to the house, found the shattered frame of the foyer mirror, and remembered checking her hat and her face after a meal or a drink or an evening of games with Willy. She set the frame next to the telephone, and continued to salvage bits of furniture, a rusted iron, a cigarette case. The wind was creeping into her joints, and to keep warm, she kept rooting around in the debris. She was, as far as she could tell, in Elisa's bedroom, which had been upstairs but was now at ground level and part of the general destruction. She concentrated on a charred bit of the wardrobe, digging down under stones and plaster until she felt the slightly soggy yet firm form of a good-sized box. It took her a while to free it, but eventually she carried it out to the front lawn.

The box was light but not empty. The moment Clara lifted the lid and saw the snow-white silk, she knew what it was. Elisa's wedding dress, a summer frock she had altered to fit snugly under her bust and expand over her growing stomach. Now it was damp and smelled of lavender and mold. Elisa had insisted on white, which was a bit of a stretch, considering she'd been eight months' pregnant when she showed up with her groom at the registrar's office. Clara hadn't gone. She had been forced into visiting extended family in Vienna, a spur-of-the-moment trip she suspected her mother had arranged to stop her from attending the ceremony. Clara had only

seen a photograph of Elisa and Reinhard Sieland standing stiffly side by side. It had vanished from the house
as soon as he went to war.

She spread the dress next to the other things, and
waded through the rubble to what used to be the kitchen.
Searching on her knees, she found a piece of porcelain
in the debris—half a cake plate, blue flowers on a white
background. Elisa had used this set for her husband's
funeral coffee. Or tea, rather, since coffee wasn't to be
had near the end of the war. Elisa had made it out of
acorns and roots and it had tasted like mud, even with a
splash of precious canned milk.

It had been an odd gathering held in mid-February
of '45, a few weeks before she left Essen. When Clara
arrived, Elisa had thrown open the blue door dressed
in a delicate flower-print frock. Clara remembered the
shock of seeing Elisa's freckled arms in short sleeves
when she herself wore several layers and was still shivering in the cold. But then, these were the last mad
months of the war. Oddness was tolerated.

Still, Clara remembered turning in astonishment to
Max, who had arrived with her directly from the Works.
Max had been Reinhard's friend, and was shaken by his
death but not shattered. Too many had fallen already
for that. He gave Elisa a cold glance as he swept past her
into the house. Clara wasn't sure what his look meant,

if it was a continuation of the latest battle the two of them were fighting at work. Elisa was as determined as Clara to scavenge supplies for their workers, while Max now urged caution. As the Allies swept closer, the Nazis grew more violent, more out of control. If any of them wanted to survive, he said, they had to be sensible and keep their heads down. Sometimes Clara refereed shouting matches in her own office. This too she laid at the door of the defeat that was grinding swiftly toward them.

And so at the tea, Clara observed them carefully: Max avoiding Elisa yet watching her coolly over his cup; Elisa chatting and smiling as if this was a cocktail party.

"What is wrong with you?" Clara said, whispering.

Max shook his head, and she let him be. By then, things had changed between them too.

She tried to talk to Elisa, to warn her she was giving a bad impression.

"I'm just trying to lighten the mood," Elisa said.

"You don't lighten the mood at a funeral."

"This isn't a funeral. It's a remembrance." She chimed her spoon against her teacup. "I'd like to thank all of you for joining me to honor my beloved husband."

Max bristled on the other side of the room, a tiny twitch of the dueling scar on his cheek.

"Let's not be sad," Elisa said. "Let's remember Reinhard as the man he was"—she aimed her smile at Max—"in the good times. When he wasn't drunk, he was one of the best husbands a woman could have."

After the shock—and thank God Willy was outside kicking a ball around the garden—Clara steered Elisa into the kitchen. She'd known the marriage wasn't a happy one, Elisa had told her that for years, but airing it now, in front of the guests?

"What is going on?" she demanded.

"You don't expect me to put a halo on my dear departed husband, do you? It's a little late in the war for hypocrisy."

"All right, but you still have to keep up appearances."

Elisa leaned against the sink and put her face in her hands. Clara had rarely seen her cry, and it melted her instantly. She gathered her friend up in her arms. Elisa squeezed her back and gave a little sniffling laugh. "Do you know you're always right, Clara?"

"I am not."

"Most of the time. It's really annoying." Eyes wet, she primped Clara's hair as she had often done when they were younger. "Will you go out there and smooth things over for me? You're good at that kind of thing. Tell them I'm bad at mourning. You know."

Clara rejoined the guests to apologize on Elisa's behalf. Later, out of the window she saw Max in the garden showing Willy how to balance a ball on his shoe and kick it straight up in the air. Willy couldn't manage it, the ball always slipping off or bounding toward the shed. He kept trying, determined in his single-minded way, and she knew he would be out there until well after dark kicking that ball over and over. Max knew it too. He caught the ball and spoke to Willy as he always did, man to man, nodding toward the house. Willy followed Max to the back door without protest, a mix of adoration and something like caution on his face. Maybe he sensed the change in the old friendship between his mother and his beloved Uncle Max, as he called him.

Clara set the cake plate next to the other artifacts from the ruins. Laid out on the grass, everything she'd found looked like rubbish, nothing worth coming back for. Sighing, she held up the wedding dress, and the wind filled the wide skirt, revealing a square hole in the silk the size of a hand. The edges were clean, as if the square had been snipped away by sharp scissors.

A man's voice disturbed the quiet. "You're holding up about a thousand marks right there, liebling."

He was leaning on a crutch, his face crisscrossed with cuts as if he'd fallen into a rosebush. He had only one leg. Clara had been raised not to stare at infirmities, but she couldn't help locking her eyes on to the space where his other foot should have been. With his crutch, his whole body was unnaturally tilted. She wondered how much of his leg was missing under his long overcoat.

Then she flushed. "I'm sorry . . ."

"Everybody stares at first. Doesn't offend me. I stare at the guys with one arm." He was smiling at her, quite a feat. On his jaw was a bluish contusion the size of a small egg. Her jaw twinged in sympathy, and she touched it to see if she hadn't grown one of those eggs herself.

"Yeah, I know," he said, "I look like the morning after a pub brawl. It's all right. I'm harmless. Seems like you've gone a few rounds in the ring yourself. If a man did that, you got my permission to knife the coward in the back. You getting married?"

She had forgotten the dress over her arm and folded it back into the box. "God, no." She added the box to the rest of Elisa's things on the lawn. "Who are you?"

"Jakob Relling. Pleased to meet you." He touched the brim of his hat. "Can I rest here a minute? Haven't come a long way, but well, yeah, you saw the leg. My back is killing me, let me tell you." Before she could protest, he eased himself down on the toilet in the yard. "Better. This is practical. I like it. You happen to know where Elisabeth Sieland's house is?"

He spoke with the extra consonants and easy familiarity of a working-class man, probably a coal miner. She wasn't quite sure why she came to that conclusion. The war and his missing leg would have taken him out of the pits. But then she noticed a smear of black on the hem of his coat that could have been coal dust, and more shadows that looked like smears he had done a bad job of washing out.

"You know Elisa?" she asked.

"I'd like to know her." He lit a cigarette. "I'd like to know you too, liebling. What's your name?"

"Fräulein Müller."

"That's a beautiful name."

She didn't want to smile at such cheap flattery, but she did anyway. "You're laying on the charm rather thickly, don't you think? What do you want, Herr Relling?"

"I'm naturally charming, fräulein, and I want to pay a visit to Elisabeth Sieland."

"Her house is right behind you."

He swiveled, surveyed the destruction. "Did the cellar make it?"

"Yes, but it's fourteen steps down."

He flashed a grin that lit up his whole mangled face. "Could you do a fellow a favor? Go down for me and see if she's there? Tell her I got good news for her."

"She's not here at the moment. Give me the news and I'll be sure to pass it on."

"That's a nice idea, and I'd do it if I could, but this is something I have to talk to her about myself."

"Ooh, a secret."

"Jealous?" His grin again. It was contagious, though she knew he was manipulating her, or trying to, in the harmless, boyish way her brothers once did, especially Friedrich. When he strode into a restaurant—in a suit, dinner jacket, uniform, didn't matter—women twice his age would twist in their seats to get a look at him. And he knew it, smiling when he met someone's eye, gracious about the admiration and asking for it too.

Jakob Relling was gazing at her with bright interest. She tucked her hair behind her ear and tried to think of something to say. "Where did you fight, Herr Relling?" She hadn't wanted to ask that, such a stupid, unpleasant question. The war was on her mind far too much.

"I was in Russia mostly." Something flickered behind the charm. "You happen to know when Frau Sieland is coming back?"

"I'll tell you what I know if you tell me why you're looking for her."

"I just need her help with something."

"You said you had good news for her."

"That too. Come on, liebling." He fanned a half-dozen cigarettes at her. "I thought we'd manage to do this friendly, but I'll pay for help if I have to."

The idea of bribery shamed her. She was never the type of woman whose goodwill needed to be begged for or bought. After Elisa had told her that a worker had injured her hand in the stamping plant, Clara had immediately ordered her own doctor to treat her, and for the girl to be brought to her afterward to do lighter work at headquarters. That was how she had met Galina, how she had learned in Galina's broken German about their home far away in the Ukraine, and about the friends she had in Clara's factories.

She took the cigarettes Jakob was offering her and tucked them back into his coat pocket. He smelled of shaving soap. He'd cleaned himself up for Elisa. Why?

"She hasn't been back here since the war." She told him about the aftermath of the March 11 bombardment, and the glow dropped from his face.

"Gestapo, eh? You sure they let her go?"

"Yes." Doubt pricked her nerves, one small jab after another, all the way up her spine. "No—I mean, I'm almost certain it had something to do with her work. Something routine. She had to deal with them now and then."

"In the end, they could pull you in for forgetting to raise your arm, you know."

"She did everything that was expected of her." She gazed at him steadily, daring him to question her version of Elisa as a law-abiding citizen. An idea was growing slowly in her mind. She wanted to trust him, maybe because he felt familiar. She had worked with men like him at the family collieries. Local miners complained about everything, but were usually honest, upright, straight-talking men. She had never felt uncomfortable or threatened in a group of them, though Max had told her they were different once they went to the showers or the changing room, that as they plucked their street clothes from the baskets that hung from the ceiling, they traded theories about what she was like under her tailored suits. She hadn't minded that they talked in that way about her. She minded more that Max could hear about it without punching someone.

She wondered if Jakob Relling had ever worked for her family, if she could appeal to the same sentiment and loyalties as with the Bergers. But it was too soon to ask, too risky. If she wanted him on her side, she would have to make it worth his while.

"Maybe we could help each other, Herr Relling."

"I'd like that. I'd like that very much, liebling."

She doubted he would once he knew what she was thinking. She backed into it gently. "You are a black marketeer, am I right?"

"I never said that. Did I say that?"

"Sometimes I can read between the lines, especially when a man knows the cash value of a lady's dress. Tell me, what was your favorite deal?"

He blew a stream of white smoke at the sky. "It was the old egg racket. A classic. First, you need chickens. I organized mine from a farm in the Bergisches Land. Best chickens you could ever have. Averaged two eggs a day. Me and my family ate four eggs a week. That left ten to trade. Know what you get on the market for that?"

"Ten marks an egg?"

"Fifteen. At a hundred and fifty marks a week, I didn't have to work. I was a full-time chicken farmer."

"Was? What happened to them?"

"Somebody broke into the cellar and stole them."

She couldn't deny it. She loved the chicken story. True or not, it showed Jakob Relling had an inventive and enterprising mind. "I assume you know people in your line of work," she said. "A lot of different people."

"Sure."

"Do you know any policemen?"

"I avoid that kind of people."

"Ex-policemen, maybe? Ex-Gestapo?"

He snorted and puffed with amusement on his cigarette.

"I'd like you to find a policeman who was there

when Elisa was detained," she said. "I need someone
willing to talk to me."

"Can't be done."

"Why not?"

"You have to ask me that?" He lowered his voice.
"You think some fellow is going to raise his hand and
say: Yes, it was me, I was Gestapo and arrested your
friend in the war, let's talk?"

"You'd have to convince him."

"Oh, yeah, I would. And I thought you were sure
they released her."

With a shiver, Clara remembered the times she'd
had to enter the Gestapohaus on Kortumstrasse, an office that seemed like any other: desks, files, a map on
the wall. She had known what went on there, however.
Everyone knew. She had finally gone herself to complain about the treatment of factory workers who had
fallen into the hands of the Gestapo. She knew the line
she walked when she raised her voice just a little—they
should not think her a hysterical woman—borrowing its
icy edge from her mother, who was a master at it. Clara
had made it clear to those men that she was a Falkenberg. That they had no right to mishandle her people.
Each time she did her best to hide how she trembled
and sweated in her suit. They could smell fear. But now
and then, she succeeded in getting workers released

from custody. If she hadn't fled the city, she could have done the same for Elisa.

"I want to be absolutely certain what happened to her. Maybe it'll give me a clue as to where she is now."

"You're asking the impossible, fräulein. Forget it." With a groan, Jakob hefted himself onto his crutch.

"Herr Relling, wait." She entwined her arm in his. "I was wondering how much a one-carat diamond is worth on the markets."

It was a shot in the dark, but she saw it connect with him, the curiosity—greed, maybe?—sparking on his face.

"A carat gets you fifteen thousand marks in Munich. Maybe fifty in Berlin."

"And in Essen?" She took off her glove, and Jakob drew in a breath at the sight of her grandmother's diamond, those facets sparkling under the gray sky. "It's yours if you can get me what I asked. And if I find Elisa first, I'll let her know you want to talk to her. What do you think?"

Jakob had lost all of the glowing charm he'd worn when he first started talking to her. It had made way for something deeper and sharper. Calculations were ticking along in his head. She could almost see him selling the diamond, or trading it for something else he could sell for more profit, and on and on until he got the one thing that he really, truly wanted. Whatever that was. She didn't care. As long as he thought he was going to get it by helping her.

Her hand ached with cold, but she didn't put on her glove. She had to keep the incentive out in the open.

Finally, he closed her hand in his. "Have I seen you somewhere before, liebling?"

She pulled away. They had been standing too close and it was her fault. To distract him from her face, she went back to the box with the wedding dress. "Take this as down payment. Elisa won't mind. I'm surprised she kept it."

"I couldn't take that. Wouldn't be right." He said it as if her offer was indecent, as if he was having second thoughts about her, the diamond, their deal. But then he said, "Meet me a week from today at twenty-one hundred at the South Sea Club in Rüttenscheid. It's in a warehouse off the rail lines near the freight depot. You can't miss it."

"I'll be there." She stuck out her hand to shake. Like a gentleman, he bent over her fingers and kissed the diamond. As she watched him hopping away, she wondered what he had seen in her face—and if the ring was enough to make him forget.

Wood

The first thing Willy did was unwind the screws and dump them into the cup he'd labeled *screws* with ink he'd made from coal dust and spit. Without the screws, the leather straps came right off the wooden leg. He'd found it outside in a bramble at the bottom of the cliff. He assumed whoever had robbed Jakob Relling had cut the straps, and they'd been out in the wet cold ever since. Willy wasn't sure what was best. Repair or replace. He set the straps aside.

Next he turned his attention to the wood. He ran his hand over the foot, feeling a little wrong, a little disgusted at removing the damp and moldy sock and the brace that held it up. The brace was all right but the sock needed washing. He set that aside as well.

Naked, so to speak, the wood looked like a real leg,

at least until it reached the knee. Willy spent a long time examining the mechanism of springs that made up the joint. Somebody had really thought this through, somebody with a mechanical mind. Thankfully, the joint was still intact. Just needed a little oil.

The upper part of the leg interested him even more because of its strange shape, like a long narrow bucket. In a book, he'd once read about pirates smuggling things in their peg legs. Now he saw how that could happen.

Willy took a clean cloth and began to polish the prosthesis, starting at the toes—strange how they were stuck together—and down around the foot where he was ticklish, and up the ankle and the calf and over the joint to the upper leg. This was where Jakob Relling's flesh and bone fit into the wood. Obviously, losing his leg in battle had made Corporal Relling bitter and defeatist and more than a little delusional. It was disgusting, the lies people told, especially the ones they told him, as if he couldn't see the truth. There were traitors everywhere, on the streets, in the shops, even in his own home.

The war is over, Corporal Relling had said.

The war is lost.

Go home.

At home, Willy would lay on his bunk in the cellar, and late in the night, Mama would tiptoe down the stairs and quietly open the door. He tried to keep his breathing deep and regular as she leaned over him to be sure he wasn't awake. He shouldn't know she'd been out. There were so many things she hadn't wanted him to know.

Willy scrubbed the wood harder. He was going to get every bit of dirt out of the cracks. This wood was going to shine.

10

Fräulein." One of Frau Berger's girls had thrown open the cellar door and was calling down to Clara, panting. She had taken over guard duty from Herr Berger, and had been watching for police or the British in the street. "They're coming."

Clara had been warming herself by the oven, fretting about whether she had done the right thing in enlisting Jakob Relling's help. She rushed for her backpack stowed under the bed. In the cellar, she was trapped. "How far away are they?"

"At the entrance to Sophienhof. They're clearing the rubble we put in the street."

That had been Herr Berger's idea, and Clara was now hugely grateful for the precaution: anything to slow Captain Fenshaw. She said quick good-byes to everyone, no ceremony, no handshakes, and pounded after the girl up the stairs. "Thank you," she called down to the family.

Herr Berger waved. "Go, fräulein. They'll be here any minute."

Outside, dusk was closing in under a white sky that hadn't seen the sun since she returned to Sophienhof three days ago. The street was empty, but she thought she heard the sound of idling engines, the shouts of men. The girl darted across Elisa's old vegetable patch, leading Clara onto a footpath through overgrown gardens flanked by the rubble of bombed houses. They crossed Sophienhof along secret routes carved out by local children and emerged on a street of abandoned shops. Clara tucked a can of ham into the girl's hands as thanks.

Feeling shaken, Clara gasped for air, her hip aching again, and then began to walk, forcing herself to slow her pace. She should look like the people around her, moving slowly, weighed down by the packs on their backs or the bags over their arms containing valuables to exchange for food or something else they desperately needed. Knowing that she would feel safer in a crowd, she joined a group of people examining bits of paper on the wall of a shuttered house. *Christmas gifts for the whole family,* someone had written on a banner. The papers advertized what people wished to trade—a set of dishes, a grandmother's kitchen cupboard—and what they wanted—a baby pram, a pair of men's shoes, a camera. Clara pretended to read, glancing now and then over her shoulder. The wind was sharp against her cheeks, and she felt her nose starting to run in the cold. She didn't want to sleep in the ruins again if she could avoid it.

She had six days until Jakob Relling would be ready for her. In the meantime . . . She started as a black car turned at the end of the block. It slowed as the children who played in the street moved out of its way. Clara saw the British soldiers inside, and felt sick. As they rolled past, they glanced at the crowd, and several men around her saluted. The car continued on.

She waited, taking deep breaths, then set off again, feeling the pull of her family home, Falkenhorst, where it would be warm and safe, for a while at least. She didn't know if her mother was still there, or if she would even help her. Could she trust her mother to stand by her—finally?

Clara didn't see that she had much choice but to shelter at Falkenhorst and take her chances with Anne. She needed to be off the streets, to wash, to eat. And there was the possibility that her mother might know where Elisa was.

On the way, she passed burned-out houses that seemed on the point of collapse. A reconstruction crew, all women, passed stones from one to the other down a hill of debris. At the corner, an old woman sold chestnuts she was roasting in a dented pan over a fire she'd built on the pavement. Not far away, a girl of about ten squatted on a doorstep brushing the shoes of anyone who could pay her a chip of coal or a bit of bread. On the shutter of a shop was a poster of Christmas trees and angels the shopkeeper might have painted himself. Clara was glad to see such signs, even if small, of life and resilience. She had seen it in the worst of circumstances. During the war, one of Galina's friends had carved a little wooden box for Clara, and nailed a piece of tin to the lid in the shape of a daisy. She had kept it on her desk, another reminder, like the caricature from *Punch*, of what she was in the eyes of others.

As she approached Falkenhorst, the streets grew quiet and empty. She entered the estate from the back, pausing to listen for an engine, footsteps, whispers, any sign of Fenshaw or his men. A low wall was the only thing that signaled the line between the city and her family's grounds. It was hardly a barrier to keep anyone out, more a symbol of otherness. She lifted one leg over it, and then the other, and faced the trees of the family forest. No one had cut them down for firewood. That was the magic of this border, a sign people still respected the boundaries of Falkenhorst.

It had never been a thick forest, and since smog no longer penetrated from the nearby iron works, she could see deep into the trees. She took a meandering route, preparing herself for what she was about to con-front—Falkenhorst intact or destroyed, or some state in between. By the end of the war, it had become a kind of haunted place where the artwork and family valuables were in storage, the furniture draped with sheets. Once the power lines were destroyed, her mother rattled about alone in the halls by candlelight with an old ser-vant to see to her needs. By then Clara rarely went home. She preferred to sleep at the Works headquarters or in the bunker. They were better than Falkenhorst with her mother and the ghosts.

Soon the forest made way for the park. The smaller trees and bushes, now ragged, not sculpted as they once were, led to Falkenhorst's back lawn. At its edge, she stopped. The house was still there, sprawling on its heights. It rose up before her on land rumored to be waste rock from Falkenberg coal mines. The family denied they had built on an industrial dump site, but she quite liked the idea. When nobody else was around,

Friedrich claimed their family motto was *Falkenberg: Built on rubbish.* She used to hit him playfully for that.

The walls were the same soot-gray from the Works. She picked out her bedroom on the second floor, looked hard, and decided that, yes, a green plant was flourishing on the inside sill. In her mind, she left the room, tiptoed along the burgundy carpet past her brothers' doors, and descended the main staircase. The parquet cracked under her shoes. When her mother hosted a soiree, conversation and cigarette smoke would drift down the hall and curl in the parlor chandeliers and spill onto the terrace where stone falcons roosted on their pedestals. As a girl she would crouch behind them and watch her mother floating from guest to guest. Once when Papa lit his cigar on the terrace step, she caught him gazing at her mother the way he looked at an intricate piece of machinery.

She scanned Falkenhorst's roof for the family's red and orange banner that used to fly over the house. They had taken it down in the war, but it was still the first thing she looked for, that spot of flame in the sky. Sluggish, the flag stirred, unfurled for a moment, and when she saw the deep blue and bits of white and red, she slid to her knees behind a hedge. The Union Jack over Falkenhorst. The British had taken over the estate. Was her mother, her English mother, still there? She had to be. From the moment she married Papa, Anne Heath considered the house hers, and inviolable. Growing up, the experience was of living in a kind of stylish barracks run by her mother, the servants in fear, visitors in awe, the children taught to respect the house by speaking quietly, closing doors gently, and refraining from leaving scuffs, dents, or stains. If her mother had had her way, all of Falkenhorst would have been encased in glass to be admired, not touched. Clara was sure not even the surrender would drive Anne out of her beloved home.

So close to the house, Clara moved with more caution, tree to tree and bush to bush, aware of the crunch her shoes made on the dead grass, and the gasp of her own breaths in the silence. Figures were moving behind the glass terrace doors. Hunched, she approached on the flank and knelt behind a boxwood shrub. She had no idea how she would find out if her mother was inside. Maybe one of the old servants would show up, or even a new one who didn't know her but could say if Anne was there.

When the doors opened, Clara covered her mouth to keep her frosting breaths from betraying her. An officer, unmistakably British, stepped out. Besides the uniform, he had the mustache and a slightly bemused look as he flipped open a cigarette case and held it out to a second man. He was in civilian clothes, respectable but worn-looking, probably a German. His hat tilted at an angle that seemed familiar, as did his hand as he smoked, cigarette balancing between his fingers.

Even with his back to Clara, she knew him. She nearly called out his name. Max Hecht. Once her Max. Relief drowned out the pain of old grievances, the breakup of long ago. Max had survived. He was alive, and he was at Falkenhorst. But why? Did she really want to know? She couldn't decide if she wanted to throw her arms around him or sneak away in ignorance, nursing the old wounds he'd given her.

A second soldier came onto the terrace and lit a cigarette. After a respectful nod, Max moved away to smoke alone. One of the falcons blocked him somewhat from the soldiers, and he seemed to relax. His old posture came back, the one reserved for when he was not in uniform or around people in uniforms. He leaned a shoulder against the stone bird, his feet crossed and a hand in his pocket, every move like liquid, one step away from dancing. He had put himself through university charging ladies in spa towns three marks for a dance, sixty to have him as their partner for the night. He was in such demand, people began to suspect him of offering something beyond the ballroom, at which point he was thrown out of some of the best hotels and clubs in Baden. By the time Clara met him, he'd given up all that, but she knew he had made good money. Nobody danced like him, with his hips, his whole attention fixed on her. When she was younger, she had thought there must be something beautiful in the soul of a man who moved so beautifully. He'd wanted to be a professional dancer, but his father had condemned it as "womanly," and Max had read law instead, hating every moment, but strangely good at it too. As she had gotten to know him, she felt herself attune to his sense of inner rebellion, even as he walked, against his will, the sensible path his family expected of him.

She would speak to him after all. He would tell her why he was at Falkenhorst, and where her mother was. He might also know something about Elisa's fate.

So Clara waited, trying not to shiver or to let her breaths show. When the soldiers lit more cigarettes and Max didn't follow, she was afraid he would go back inside before she had her chance. But he was closer to her than the soldiers, and she decided to risk it. She shook the boxwood bush, rustling the leaves.

Max straightened, frowning out at the garden. She moved the bush again and he focused on it instantly. She raised her hand and waved.

The soldiers were deep in conversation. Max lit another cigarette and then strolled onto the lawn, not directly toward her, but meandering as if looking out over the park. The two British men glanced at him briefly, then turned back to each other. After a circuit of the garden, pausing a couple of times as if this tree or that interested him, he stopped near the bush. Without looking down, he dropped a cigarette nearby and whispered, "I don't have anything else. Clear off before the Tommies see you."

He was thinner than she remembered, his bones finer, and there was a dark bruise under each eye, just as there had been in the war when he wasn't sleeping.

"Max. It's me."

He stared down at her as if he didn't understand what he was seeing. "Clara?" He lit up, and she remembered him in his dinner jacket under crystal chandeliers. "Clara, treasure—"

"Can we talk somewhere?" She said it firmly, more a statement than a question. He shouldn't think she was begging him for help.

He glanced at the soldiers. "I'll be at least two more hours. There's a meeting."

"You work here?"

He knelt and made the motions of brushing dirt off his shoe. "The military government confiscated your house and turned it into offices. The carriage house should be safe. I'll meet you there." Before he left, he reached for her, and she drew back, afraid of what would happen if he touched her, the old buzz on her skin, that familiar need for him she had pushed out of herself long ago.

Hurt and disappointment stood out on his face. "You're still holding a grudge? After everything we went through?"

She almost answered him, wanted to say that some acts couldn't be forgiven, but she knew her silence would hurt him more. She backed into the bushes, angry that he was appealing to a history together that was long gone. Too much had changed since the night they had begun their life together. She had been a sheltered girl, just turned sixteen and as sure of herself and her place in the world as if it was engraved in stone. It was the same year she met Elisa, and she had been nagging her mother to let her go out dancing or to a film with her older, more experienced friend. To her surprise, her mother agreed on one condition: a mandatory stop at an address on a slip of paper that Clara was to memorize and then destroy. She burned it in an ashtray with some amusement, as if playing the spy. Then she took a cab with Elisa to the place in question, a newish block of flats in the Steele district.

Max waited for them on the doorstep, a finger to his lips. Clara had never seen him before, but Elisa greeted him without saying how she knew him. His dinner jacket hung open, bow tie undone. This was his gigolo attire. Only later did Clara learn he had dressed for a conquest. He held the door, Clara accidentally brushing against him on her way in. The contact made her hurry after Elisa up the stairs. He smelled like smoke back then, and the tiniest whiff of cologne. Clara sensed him behind her in the stairway, and she worried about how she looked to him from that angle, the drape of her gown in front of his eyes.

Music was playing low in the apartment. Six months' pregnant and feeling well again, Elisa swayed into the parlor and straight to a sturdy man with light hair and spectacles. Reinhard Sieland, an accountant in the office where Elisa worked, and the man she would marry, though Clara didn't know it yet. This was his flat, and he made a show of pointing out its highlights, especially the record player and music collection. It wasn't the kind of place Clara was used to visiting, and at first she stood stiffly to the side, unsure of what was appropriate behavior in the flat of a bachelor she didn't know. Elisa stuck by her, led her to the sofa, was the first to call the men by their first names as if she knew they'd all be friends. They drank beer out of water glasses, another new experience for Clara, who had only ever tried wine and champagne. She gradually relaxed, the beer tasting better the more she drank. After a little more chatter, Reinhard led Elisa to another room and closed the door behind them.

Clara was left by herself with Max. She opened the window and stayed standing before it, hoping for a breeze. She wasn't sure she wanted to be alone with him. So far, he had spent the evening gaping at her. "You look like a fish, Max," she said.

"Thank you, Clara. I make an effort. Could I offer you another drink?"

There was a thump from the other room, and laughter. For Elisa's sake, she had to stay alert. For her own sake. She waved away the glass.

Max was still looking at her with an intensity she would get to know well over the years. "You're *that* Clara, aren't you? Falkenberg."

She sighed at his awe. She'd lived with it long enough for it to bore her.

He started buttoning his jacket. "I'm a lawyer. In the Legal Office. At the Works."

So that was how Elisa knew him. Her first job at Falkenberg had been in the same office.

"You missed a button," Clara said.

He went to the mirror and corrected the jacket and tied the tie, starting again twice, looking at her reflection instead of at what he was doing.

From the other room, the sound of wood creaking and a gasp from Elisa made Clara gnash her teeth. She felt sluggish and hot. Dirty. She had brought Elisa here. She was no better than a . . . what were those people called? A pimp. A procuress. Her eyes watered with humiliation and shame.

"Would you like to dance, fräulein?" Max put on a new record. The music, a brisk tango, soothed her hammering pulse. It tuned out the noises from the other room.

"I don't know how to tango," she said.

He positioned himself in the center of the room and held his arms out to an imaginary partner. "The link is everything," he said. "Here"—he tapped his chest—"is the line between partners. Come here."

"Don't use that tone with me."

"What tone would you prefer? Servile? Groveling?"

She opened her mouth in shock. But she was drifting toward him, filling that space implied by his arms in the air. She wiped her hands on her skirt and touched his jacket. When their hands met, she feared he would feel the tremor rolling through her.

"The link," he said. A gentle tap at her neckline, and lower to where her heart rattled, and back to his own chest. "It never breaks. We sway, we turn, we dip. The line never breaks." Slowly, he showed her the first steps, and she listened to his voice instead of the cries from the other room. She concentrated on her feet, tried to get the technique, the correct turn, the precise angle of her body to his.

"You're too soft," he said, and tightened his hold on her hand. "Keep the tension in your body. Push me back."

She tried the step again, yielded to his pressure, and stumbled.

"This dance is a battle, fräulein. Push back."

"I am."

"Push me."

"I am."

"Harder."

Her forehead touched his chest and her arm trembled at the effort of holding her ground. Every bit of her was pushing against him until she didn't know whether the pounding in her ears was his heartbeat or her own.

The bedroom door opened. The scraping hinges seemed far away and insignificant compared to Max's next move. His body absorbed her.

"What a handsome pair." Reinhard was smoking against the doorway in his undershorts, the tails of his shirt to his thighs.

"For God's sake," Max said, "get dressed."

Clara pushed past them into the bedroom. Elisa was

snoring gently on the sheets, wearing only her heels and stockings. Her naked body shocked her, the misshapen bulge of her stomach.

"Wake up." Clara shook her by the arm. She pulled Elisa's gown over her friend's feet and up her legs little by little, Elisa a dead weight and immovable from the waist up. "Elisa." Clara slapped her cheek, and Elisa whimpered in her sleep. Clara cried, "Elisa, get up, get up. We're leaving right now."

Elisa stirred and leaned on Clara's shoulder. "Don't hate me. Reinhard is a good man. He is. We're getting married. Isn't that nice?" She burst into tears.

They staggered together to the bedroom door where Max caught Elisa's other arm and propped her up. "I'll help you."

"We don't need your help."

"Don't be silly," Max said, "you'll never find a cab to take her like that. I'll drive."

During the ride, Elisa dozed between them. Together they got her home, Max holding her outside the door while Clara searched her purse for the keys.

"Fräulein, this was a bad way to start. We can do this again properly. Dinner and—"

"I don't want to have dinner with you, I don't want to start anything with you, I want you to go away." Clara pushed open the door, coaxed Elisa up two flights of stairs, listening for Elisa's widowed mother, and managed to get her inside and to her room. She left her snoring, her arms tight around her stomach.

Outside, Max was waiting by the car. She marched away from him. Something horrible had been done tonight and she had done it. But what? Why had her mother wanted them to come here? How did she know Reinhard Sieland? And why would Elisa go straight to bed with him? Even knowing she was pregnant, it was a side of her Clara hadn't been able to imagine. In the two months they had known each other, Elisa had never said a word about him. And now she was marrying him? Just like that? Was he the baby's father, the man Elisa refused to name? The one time Clara had brought up the subject, Elisa had looked distressed and said, "If you're my friend, please don't ask me that again." If it was Reinhard, why not say?

She stopped in the street. Max was waiting a short distance away. He was only a shadow, but she knew it was him. She was already used to his intense way of watching her. There was something both soothing and unnerving about it, as if he wanted to protect her from dangers she couldn't yet imagine. Her palms were moist, and she wiped them on her skirt. She didn't want to go home, not yet, not when her nerves were bound up with the memory of her body pressed against his.

"Take me dancing," she said.

For a while, she forgot her anxieties in his arms. That was part of what would keep her with him for so many years. He knew how to make her forget the things that unsettled her. He found a club where they were playing swing, but she couldn't keep up with him, didn't understand yet what his body would do, where it would go. But she wanted to learn.

At the end of the night, at midnight sharp—the grandfather clock had boomed from the foyer of her house like a warning from her mother—he embraced her in Falkenhorst's drive and gave her a long, electric kiss. The kiss and the clock broke the spell. Deep down she knew she was not to speak of this night again. She couldn't be Elisa's friend and look too closely at the things she did. There were questions Clara shouldn't be asking herself or anyone else. It would be far better, she would be far happier, if she closed her eyes and kept her mouth shut and focused on the man who had given her music and dancing and her first kiss.

11

The carriage house was older than Falkenhorst, though Clara never knew if the stories her father used to tell about the place were true. He had shown the children the half-timbered structure and said it had once been a stable for some long-lost convent. She didn't know if her father believed this, but he did consider the carriage house to be holy ground. Her mother never dreamed of setting one of her slippered feet into the place. She always said it was too dirty, too smoky, "too manly, darling. Men are just boys in long trousers. Leave them to play in their dreck. They're happier that way." As a girl, most of Clara's experience of the place was peering into it secretly through one small window.

It was thick with grime now, impossible to see through, but Clara scratched at it gently with her thumbnail until she'd made a small circle on the glass. She didn't want to presume it was safe based on Max's word alone. He was working for the British, after all. She wondered how that had happened, what he had told them to wipe away enough of his "guilt" that they would hire him. Regardless, she didn't think his cooperation went so deep that he would turn her in.

Through the circle she had made on the window, she saw only darkness. She crept along the back wall and remembered Papa in the garage touching each car as he passed it—the armored Mercedes, his beloved Bugatti Royale, the Model T from Henry Ford himself—a gift from one engineer to another. The south end of the carriage house had been blocked off and reserved as his workshop.

She was relieved to see the narrow door to the back entrance was still there, not bricked up or shuttered. The weeds were overgrown and there was no sign anyone had entered this way since she had been here in the war. She pushed the handle, and it gave with a rusty shriek. Papa had never locked this door. Who was going to sneak in and meddle with his machines on the grounds of his own estate?

Inside, dust coated the workbenches and the tools that had fallen from their hooks or lay rusting in an open box. The smells of gasoline and oil still hung in the air and comforted her as they always had. She reached over her head and touched the model airplane dangling from a cord. This was Friedrich's, a Kondor E.3 he'd spent weeks if not months building, scaling down from the original blueprint, overseeing the sections stamped at one of the plants, welding it himself here in Papa's workshop while Papa looked on. She had hated that plane, how much of Friedrich's time and care it took from her, and Papa's obvious pride as it came together, this father-son project that excluded her so completely.

She crossed to the interior door and listened for anyone on the other side, then opened it enough to see into the dim length of the garage. There were army vehicles and crates and barrels. Papa's cars were gone now, but she remembered how Galina and the other young women had gasped when they first saw the few cars that hadn't been confiscated in the war. Galina had taken the kerchief from her hair and polished the mirrors in awe. The other women took turns fixing their hair or sadly checking their teeth. That first day, their energy gave out quickly, and they didn't dare sit inside the cars, but slumped against the garage wall, too weak to stand for any length of time.

Clara closed herself back into the workshop, feeling safer than she knew she should, being so close to the British. This was her father's place and she had the unreliable sense that nothing bad could happen to her here. She lifted the tarp on the engine he had been working on when he left, one of the many he'd designed, built, spent years improving little by little. When she was a girl, he'd spent Sundays on a long and loving tour of the insides of whatever contraption he happened to be constructing. Sometimes she was allowed to bring his supper.

"This one loves the cold," he told her, the soup spoon in his blackened hand. He sat beside the engine in overalls, a cloth of Falkenberg red around his neck as if he was any other worker. "Dry, moderate cold," he said between mouthfuls, "makes this machine breathe better, like you and me. Try it, Clärchen. Breathe on a cold, dry day."

"It's just a machine, Papa," she said, always a little jealous of the engine. "It doesn't breathe. It can't feel anything."

He scraped the last of his soup, not looking at her. In his workshop, he had eyes only for the things he could assemble. "Some machines are sensitive like people," he said, "and some people don't feel much at all, like machines." She didn't understand what he meant until the war.

She ran a finger over the workbench. He would be appalled at the condition of his workshop now, the dirt, the cobwebs, his tools scattered. He used to spend hours sorting them into his particular order. She got to work, hanging the hammers and saws first. Since she didn't know his old system, she arranged them by size. She scrubbed the counter with a rag moistened with frost, and she attacked the cobwebs with a broomstick. As she worked, an old anxiety crept over her, the same feeling she'd had when Galina and the women were here. To get them to the carriage house without arousing suspicion, Clara had overseen them sweeping the streets— a common sight, foreign workers bent over their brooms—and had led them, little by little, to Falkenhorst's low wall, the family forest, and the carriage house. At their barracks, they were reported missing, which Clara, back at the Works, duly noted in her files with a thrill of satisfaction and terror. She had stepped over a line she hadn't known she would ever cross.

When Max still hadn't come, Clara inspected the cupboards, setting aside old paint cans and jars of loose bolts and screws so she could free the shelves of droppings and dead spiders. She stood on a stool and reached to the back of the top shelf, wiping her rag blind over the surface. Her hand nudged something soft. She coaxed it down and turned it over in her palm. It was a rolled-up bit of silk, dark with grime and tied with a slender ribbon of faded scarlet. As she unrolled it, she glimpsed the pure white inside, and her heart clenched into a fist pounding at her ribs.

She dropped onto the stool and draped the silk square over her leg. It was the same fabric, the same shade of white, the same size as the square cut out of Elisa's wedding dress. It was impossible that it was here, and yet there it was on her knee. She wanted to roll it up again, put it back where she'd found it. She had disturbed something she wasn't meant to see. That much she knew. The rest—who put it there, and why—she couldn't fathom.

Elisa had never been in the carriage house, not even when Galina and the others were hiding here. Clara hadn't wanted Elisa involved, in case they were found. Years before the war, Elisa had visited Falkenhorst once after nagging Clara to smuggle her in. Clara had been petrified her mother would hear from the servants, and she did. Clara had been put under house arrest for a week, but it was worth the few minutes she spent escorting Elisa and little Willy through the ground-floor rooms. In the library, Elisa had gazed up at the family portrait of the Falkenbergs painted the year they met, the year Willy was born. She spent a long time at the painting, pinching her lip until it looked bruised. Willy was more interested in the golden glow the sun cast upon the family virtues stenciled on the wall in real gold: *Honor, Fidelity, Industry, Courage.* Clara lifted him in her arms and he rubbed the letters with both hands, gasping with delight. To her knowledge, that was the only time they had set foot in the house. She had definitely never shown them Papa's workshop.

Clara rolled up the silk and carefully tied the ribbon back into a bow. The scrap had been a gift. Some kind of memento. A memento for someone Elisa couldn't marry? When she was a teenager, Elisa used to devour cheap romances, books, films, magazines. This was the kind of idea she'd have found in one of those.

When she wore the wedding dress, Elisa was eighteen. At that time, Friedrich was nineteen. Finished with school, he was continuing his education with the engineers at the Works. When he wasn't doing that, he was here, in Papa's workshop, designing and building his plane. He could have tucked the silk far back in the cupboard where no one but him would ever see it. Least of all their mother. She or the servants controlled every space in Falkenhorst except for here.

"God, Friedrich." Clara carried the silk with her, looking at it again and again as she circled the workshop. If Friedrich had been alive, she would have punched him the way he had taught her, a fist in the kidney. She would have demanded an explanation, the whens and hows and, most important, the whys. Why did he never tell her? Why hadn't he trusted her? And Elisa. Why hadn't she said something? All those years and not a word.

Friedrich should have told her, given her some hint. He'd never been secretive; he didn't have that dark spot in him for deceit. He was golden, Friedrich. It was easy to see Elisa at seventeen dazzled by him. Clara didn't blame him; she didn't blame Elisa. She understood the fascination, the power of teenage desire. Hadn't she given herself to Max at almost the same age, just as reckless and passionate, willing to keep him a secret— hers and only hers—even from her parents?

And then there was Willy. All of this meant that Willy was her nephew. A Falkenberg. And in a way, Elisa was her sister. If only Mother had allowed Friedrich to marry her. They would've been sisters-in-law. Real sisters.

A soft knock on the door startled her.

She crushed the silk into her pocket as Max slipped into the workshop, kicked the door closed, and scooped her into his arms. One hug, the familiar feel of him around her, the warmth—one moment of it—she could allow that for both of them, but then she struggled away from him, looking at the door. "Did you bring someone?"

"Who would I bring?" His voice hardened. "You think I'd call in my new British overlords to catch you?"

"No. I don't know." Outside the window, it was turning dark. She found her flashlight in her backpack and shone it in his face. The lines cut deeper around his eyes and mouth, and there was something washed out about him that made her think of tarnished brass. "You look the same."

"Liar. I'm practically gray."

"I don't see it."

He turned the light on her. "I'm glad your hair's dark again. I always preferred you that way."

"How have you been?"

"Lost. Dead. I thought you were gone for good. Nobody knew what happened to you. I thought you'd died in that last bombardment."

"Did the Americans arrest you?"

"I turned myself in, and was interned. They broke my nose and my collarbone when they saw I was SS, but I can't blame them for that. When the British took over, they wanted to talk to me about Falkenberg. So few people left in the city knew it like I did. So we came to an agreement. They're not a bad bunch. I like pragmatic men."

"You work for them?"

"Oh, I'm still on a kind of probation, pending the result of my denazification proceedings. Don't worry, treasure, I might yet end up in prison again once I've stopped being useful. I suppose you think I deserve that."

Her light was trained on the floor, and on the edge of the glow, she saw graffiti scratched low on the wall. Cyrillic letters she couldn't read. "I don't know what we deserve, Max. I don't think anyone is holding a scale with our good and bad deeds on it. I doubt we could separate them out in that way. They're too entangled."

"What happened to your face? Somebody hit you?"

Clara told him about Captain Fenshaw and the train and the steel locker. By the end of it, Max was pacing the workshop, swearing softly. "What's he playing at? If he wanted to arrest you, why didn't he just pick you up in Hamelin?"

She switched off the flashlight, and the room fell into darkness. "Maybe I'm a very special kind of war criminal." She felt her father's engine against her leg, a comforting reminder of a different time. "God, it was a shock, hearing him call me that."

"Being born German is enough." Max paused. "He came to see me, you know."

"I was told he wanted you to identify me after my arrest."

"He talked to me months ago, but I don't mean that. You were still solidly missing then. No, he came a couple of days ago again, looking for you. Thought I'd hidden you in the attic or under the bed. He brought me the best news I'd had in years. Imagine it. This officer turning my house upside down, and I didn't care. I toddled after him asking, 'Are you sure? She's alive? She's really alive? You've seen her? How is she?' Annoyed him no end."

She smiled. "Good for you."

"Clara, we have a thousand things to sort out, but I have to ask you right now. Why did you leave? Why didn't you tell me what you planned to do?"

"You would have tried to stop me."

"I would have helped you. You know that. You caused a world of trouble, walking out. Did you think about what would happen to the rest of us?"

"The less you knew about my plans, the better. It was safer that way." She fingered the silk in her pocket. "The people in Elisa's house told me the Gestapo picked her up."

"What did you expect? As usual, some of the foreign workers were out scrounging around the city after the bombardments. The police came to headquarters wanting to know what *you* were going to do about it. We found your office empty and your hair in the basin with your identity papers, half burned. I was the first person they questioned. They wanted to know if you were a deserter and if I had helped you. They knew that you're half English. They asked me if you'd made a break for the British lines."

"Have you seen Elisa since the war?"

"Do you think I spared a thought for her? You were gone. I thought you were dead." He was holding her hand tightly. "I've had to try and live with that."

"I'm sorry, Max."

"Are you? Nearly two years and not a word from you. Not a whisper. What in God's name were you doing in Hamelin?"

Clara knew he was asking whether she had another man. She felt the heat rolling off him, feeding her old grievances. "How is your wife these days?" she asked. "Hannelore, was it? The perfect SS wife. Young, fertile, and stupid."

"Clara—"

"Oh, I forgot, and obedient. After all those years with me, I'm sure that was most refreshing. How are the children, by the way? How many do you have now?"

She heard the steady grind of his teeth. "Three."

"One came after the war. Congratulations."

"Don't do this, Clara. You left me."

"At the end of the war. You left me in 1943 when you married that empty-headed, big-breasted girl."

"For you. The SS wanted family men. I had to get promoted. For you. You agreed to it."

She drew back, not wanting to be reminded of that, the worst part of the whole sordid story. Max had come to her, outlining his plan—she remembered the coffee they were drinking in her office, as if this was a discussion between colleagues—and she had listened to the reasons he had to marry. It was expected of him. He had found a girl dull and obedient enough to do her duty, as he called it. Nothing would change between them; Clara was still everything and always would be. But alas, the world was as it was. In the SS, family men advanced. And he needed to advance to help her in her work and, maybe one day, to reach a level her family would accept.

She had viewed it as a temporary situation. She'd thought herself practical enough to see it through, even saw the benefits when it came to quietly helping the foreign workers. Max knew how to argue with the authorities. Improving worker conditions increased productivity. More food meant stronger backs, faster production, a boost for the war effort. This was a fine line he walked for her, a risk. He could have been accused of being soft on those people the SS called subhumans. Clara was immensely glad she didn't have to hear Max speak of them in this way. She knew it disgusted him as much as it did her.

But after he married, when she realized he went

home to another woman, and especially when she heard the woman was pregnant, she had begun to withdraw from him, to turn her cheek when he tried to kiss her, to make excuses when he wanted to meet her in private. She couldn't have a relationship with a married man.

The final break came in late '44. She had been carrying a bag of rations to the carriage house, and even before she went inside, she sensed the strange stillness from the building. Papa's cars were there, the bucket in the corner where Galina and the women would urinate, a head scarf one of them had left behind. They had been instructed never to leave the building, but Clara had gone out to look for them anyway, frantically searching the park and the forest. In the undergrowth, she had discovered another scarf. Galina's. She found no other trace of the women.

She'd gone back to Falkenberg headquarters anxious, confused, on the edge of looking for the women in their old barracks. Then Max had come into her office, grim, stiff with anger. She had met his gaze and instantly knew what had happened, what he had done. She flew at him, fists up, but he wrestled her to the wall, held her there as she struggled. Did she have any idea how stupid she'd been? How easy it was to follow her to the carriage house? He couldn't stand by and let her be caught, arrested, imprisoned, or worse, because of half a dozen Ukrainian women.

"Tell me—what happened to Galina and the others after you betrayed them?" she asked now.

He was breathing heavily in the dark of her father's workshop. "I told you at the time. They were sent back."

"To where?"

"Home. To their own people."

"And you believe that?"

"Clara, I don't know. I honestly don't. But you're not safe here, treasure. You've got to come home with me."

"No—"

"Fenshaw won't be coming back to my place. He knew it was over between us a long time ago. It was clear to him I hadn't even known you were alive. You'll be safe with me."

"What would your wife say?"

"What does she have to do with it?"

"A whole bloody lot if she finds me in her house."

"She'll come around."

"Max, you have children."

"They're too small to make a fuss. They'll love you. Clara . . ." He grasped her face, her cheeks in his palms. "We could disappear. Remember what we used to talk about? The dance school in Buenos Aires?"

Dreams from another life, fantasies they used to discuss curled up together in bed, knowing it would never happen. She pulled his hands from her face. "Max, that wasn't real. It was just talk."

"Before, yes. But now, why not? The world has changed. What we did in the past . . . it doesn't matter anymore. We could start again. Wine and music the rest of our lives. We'll be free. We didn't have a chance before, but now—"

"You're a father. A father doesn't abandon his children. What are you thinking?"

She heard him sniffling in the dark, bitter laughter he was trying not to show, and she snapped on the flashlight to catch him at it. "I'm not going to break up a family. Not even for you. I know you'd leave everything for me if you could. But I wouldn't respect you if you did. You know that because you know me. Better than almost anyone."

"I see your ironclad principles are alive and well."

She gave him a look, but decided not to let him bait her. "Did the British put my mother in the attic at Falkenhorst?"

"Worse. They evicted her."

It was such a horrendous thought, Clara had to fight the urge to laugh. "How did they get her out? With a bulldozer?"

"More or less. She's living in a flat in Bredeney."

"I need to see her. She'll know where Elisa is." She was aware again of the silk square in her pocket. "Do you know the street?"

"I know the exact house. After the Allies hired me, your mother stooped to talking to me now and then. She thinks I'm her spy."

That wasn't at all how Anne used to be. She would mumble and complain about the riffraff—Max and Elisa—who Papa and then Clara had allowed to rise at the Works. Outsiders were not to be trusted, Anne always said. Clara had ignored that. Her mother was the last person she looked to for advice about trust.

"Will you take me to her?"

"No." The flare of light as he lit a cigarette. "I don't think I will."

Clara knew Max too well to argue. There was no need. She clicked off her flashlight and waited for him to finish his smoke. When he did, he kissed her in the inky dark of the workshop, his fingers pressing her skull, his teeth rattling hers. She remembered this too, how he could funnel anger into his kisses, how submitting to them could calm him and get him to do what she wanted. They separated, her lips numb from his, and he led her outside to where his bicycle leaned against the carriage-house wall.

12

Jakob Relling got home a little drunk but contented, as he'd been most of the time since the miracle of Willy Sieland's depot dropped into his life. He deserved some luck—cripple's luck, as he wasn't afraid to call it—and since it had been a long time in coming, he was savoring it all the more. Even better, he was learning how one piece of luck could lead to another. Willy's delicious depot had led him to Willy's house, which had led him to the diamond ring worn by one Margarete Müller. Her mission to find an ex-Gestapo man was ridiculous, but his luck was holding out even there. He knew a fellow who knew a fellow who tonight had insisted he could set up a meeting with another fellow who might be the one. If that worked out, the diamond was his. Once he had the diamond, he'd have capital.

With that, he could do anything. Buy clothes for the baby, shoes for his sisters, a new suit and a gold-plated prosthesis for himself. He might even get a half-crazy kid out of the mine while taking the food for his growing family.

The only problem, or rather a pleasant concern that had been nagging at the back of Jakob's mind, was Margarete Müller. Talking to her, an odd feeling had nudged him toward . . . he wasn't sure what. Somehow he associated her with damp leather and straw and wood smoke, smells that were comforting and so intense he'd smelled them in the cold air at Sophienhof. And so, as he'd been out working on her behalf, Jakob carried around with him the memory of her gray eyes, drained of color except for the black pricks of the pupils. He thought of the graceful black curves of her eyebrows. He wasn't dumb. He knew an alias when he heard one. That woman was no Fräulein Müller. But if not her—then who?

Humming to himself, he hobbled into the dank foyer. His building had four walls and something like a roof and most of the time he could push away his fear of it collapsing. He lived with his sisters on the ground floor, which suited him, considering the upstairs neighbors had to climb a ladder. The Rellings had it easier, two rooms for three people, four until their mother passed on. The rest of what used to be their flat was occupied by the next-door neighbor and her daughters, whose apartment had collapsed in on itself. Their beds lined the narrow hallway, and as Jakob limped past them toward the kitchen—his sisters' room—he considered how living at such close quarters was going to be even more awkward once he got the food from Willy's mine. He wasn't about to feed the whole neighborhood.

He paused in the hallway. The beds were empty. Strange for this time of night. For weeks, the neighbor's girls had slept two to a bed, wearing wool hats and clutching each other for warmth.

He looked into the parlor, still and cold because it had no oven. He usually slept on the sofa, and his bedding was there, folded neatly. This alarmed him. If he was out late, his sister Dorrit made up his bed. He never asked her to do it. She'd taken over the task from their mother, just as she had taken over the household after her death.

"Dorrit?" He stumbled on his crutch to the kitchen. "Dorrit? Gabi?"

The heat in the kitchen surprised him, his face tingling. To conserve fuel, the girls usually didn't feed the oven quite so much. But it wasn't just the oven. Half a dozen thin girls occupied the bench and chairs at the table. These were the neighbor's daughters, who had no business being in the kitchen this time of night. Their mother, Frau Kreuz, sat on the bed Jakob had installed next to the oven for his sisters. Dorrit was there too, her hands writhing on Mama's old apron, a rose pattern that covered her bulging stomach. She was weeping in noisy gasps.

"Dorrit." Jakob dropped beside her, his balance slightly off from the schnapps he'd drunk. "Little mouse. What's wrong?"

"She's been crying for the better part of an hour," Frau Kreuz said with disapproval.

Dorrit wiped her sleeve over her nose. "That is a lie."

Affronted, Frau Kreuz gathered up her daughters and left the room. Jakob put his arm around Dorrit, and reached down to touch Gabi's head. She was kneeling on the floor, leaning against Dorrit's knee. With a familiar pang, he noticed how thin they were, how bony Dorrit's shoulders had become, how Gabi's hair wasn't growing as a girl's hair should.

"All right. What's going on? What happened?"

"Nothing." Dorrit wiped her face with the apron and struggled to calm herself, as he'd seen her do often the past few months. He didn't have the heart to tell her she shouldn't wear their mother's things. He suspected it made her sad but somehow brought her closer to Mama, though Dorrit wasn't about to admit it. She aimed her moist eyes at him and gave him a weak smile. She was seventeen and a soldier's dream, which was her downfall. Soft blond curls over her shoulders, honey-brown eyes like their mother's, a habit of smiling at strangers. All of that and a dash of poor judgment got her in the situation she was in now: her belly growing and the rest of her wasting away.

"Come on, you were crying about something. Does something hurt? The baby?"

"No, it's not that." She put her hands to her cheeks. "I forgot to make your bed."

"You don't have to make my bed." The blue veins under her skin seemed darker, more prominent. The pallor of her face was getting worse. She looked ghostly, and it scared him. The extra rations she was due as an expectant mother weren't enough. She was crying because she was hungry, but she would never tell him when she knew he was doing everything he could for her already. He kicked himself for leaving the mine without food, but what choice had he had with Willy pointing a gun at him?

"If you're hungry, eat. You can take some of my rations. You know that."

"I'm not hungry."

"Liar. You have to feed him too." He tapped her belly, and she smiled.

"He can feel that."

"Eat, Dorrit. We're going to be all right. I told you about the coal mine, didn't I?" He gathered his sisters in his arms and told the story of Willy's stash all over again. They listened with big eyes, as they'd done when they were little and he'd spun tales about princesses who lived in castles made of diamonds and coal and all the things you had to dig for.

"We aren't going to be hungry much longer," he said. "I'll take care of everything."

After he finally left his sisters, Jakob retired to the parlor. He was sober now, and exhausted. Three months ago, their mother had died of one of those summer colds that turned into pneumonia. She had left a hole in him he still didn't know how to fill, a silence in the room where she used to iron or sew at night when the electricity was on. She probably knew about the pregnancy before Dorrit did herself, but Mama took it in her stride, as she had everything else. Not much could shake her. And there was Dorrit, trying to walk in her footsteps, hungry all the time as they all were, and worried—

Jakob had overheard her anxiously telling Gabi—about the baby and how to get the simplest things like cloth diapers or a sweater. He was going to get her what he could, on the black market if necessary, but she needed so much. He had quietly traded Willy's gun for a pram, the little mattress and bedding to go with it, and the deal showed him that babies needed things he hadn't even dreamed of. He hardly knew where to begin, or how he would pay for it if he didn't get Margarete Müller's ring or the food from Willy's mine to trade soon.

He didn't bother to make his bed, just stretched out in his clothes, still wearing his coat, and piled on the blankets. "Good night, liebling," he said to the calendar on the wall. Miss December, a smiling American girl with a plump thigh displayed prominently under her short Christmassy skirt. Usually, she cheered him up. Tonight she was only paper.

Once the lamp was out, his mood darkened further. He wasn't high enough in the world of the black market to lay on a feast for his family whenever he wanted. Food was scarce, and winter had begun. The cold always made him think of Russia, of being wounded, of what it had been like when he finally came home, his leg left behind in a pile of amputated limbs in a field hospital he barely remembered. He used to think constantly of air bubbles and syringes, of throwing himself under a train or down a flight of steps. Eating poison, or a bullet. A merciful bullet.

He hadn't done any of these things because, once the surgeries were done and the pain bearable, he had woken up to find himself the last man in the house. His father was dead, his two brothers gone, Claus fallen on the Eastern Front, Hansi to follow soon after. As his mother had pointed out, Jakob could keep feeling sorry for himself, or get off his backside and do something useful instead of lying around being served like a prince. Didn't he know there was a war on?

That had shamed him enough to get out of bed. As soon as he was moving, as soon as he was useful to his family again, the darkest parts of him retreated. He was still a man. He would provide.

He turned to lighter, more pleasant thoughts, which took him back to Margarete Müller. She was a puzzle he longed to solve. Something about the way she carried herself, the way she talked, didn't fit her shabby clothes and the bruises on her face. Behind those bruises, he thought he'd seen . . . he wasn't sure what. Not a pretty face. It was too intense for that, battered and suspicious. But if he wiped those flaws away in his mind, if she healed, relaxed, cleaned herself up, and ate her fill, she would be something else altogether. A chilling beauty. It was her eyes. They reminded him of the winter sky over the Volga. They reminded him of frozen ponds, their sunken depths unknown. They reminded him once more of Russia.

Perhaps he had seen her in a photograph? On the front, the men passed pictures around, of wives, girl-friends, daughters, sisters, mothers. *This is Käthe. Married her right before I came here. Look, that's my littlest one, Ursula. Just turned two. Ever seen anything so sweet?* The front made them sentimental. They said things to each other they'd never have said at home.

Now and then, if they knew they'd be staying put awhile, the men tacked their photographs from home onto the wall of whatever house or shed or barn they happened to be sleeping in. Made for a homey feeling, all those women and girls—some film stars too—in a collage in front of them. There was one kid, maybe eighteen or nineteen. Everybody teased him for pinning up a picture he'd ripped from a women's magazine.

Jakob bolted upright. He tore away the blankets, knocked over the lamp in search of his crutch, and limped into the hall. He hammered on the neighbor's door.

"Herr Relling?" Frau Kreuz squinted in the light. "It's the middle of the night, are you mad?"

"Tell me you've still got that collection of the *NS-Frauen-Warte* you always displayed when you had visitors."

She peered at her bare wrist. "What time is it?"

"Those magazines. The ones you hid from the Tommies so you can use them as toilet paper. Any left?"

"You drunk? What do you want a women's magazine for?"

He searched his pockets for a cigarette and held it out to her. She stuck it behind her ear and lumbered into her bedroom, rummaging quietly under the bed where two of her daughters slept. She emerged with a moldy cardboard box full of the magazines. For another cigarette, she carried them into his parlor.

Quietly he inspected the *NS-Frauen-Warte*, the National Socialist women's magazine. A typical cover from the early years showed a fat-cheeked baby in the arms of a young woman in a field of daisies. Caption: *Mother, you carry the Fatherland.* He examined every picture, then shifted to the next one, and the next, sure that when he saw the woman he was looking for, he'd know her instantly.

In 1944, the propaganda machine was well into Total War mode. No plump baby now, but a girl in a bomb factory and not looking too happy about it. German women didn't exactly line up to build bombs. Jakob searched every page for Margarete Müller, then tossed the issue aside.

The cardboard box was nearly empty. He lifted out one of the remaining few, and there she was. On the cover, the last '44 issue. It wasn't the same photograph he'd seen in Russia, but it was the same woman. She posed at the open door of a Mercedes. The landscape behind her was smokestacks and brick factories. Her platinum-blond hair was straight out of a bottle and the wave from a Hollywood poster. Her eyes were as pale and hard as that diamond on her finger.

Caption: *Clara Falkenberg—the exceptional duties of the German woman at war.*

"Jesus, Maria, and Joseph." He stared at that picture. That name.

Clara Falkenberg, the Iron Fräulein, the former Reich's most eligible heiress.

13

The villa in Bredeney was a powder-blue confection, just the place for her mother, who was far too fine to share an attic room or a cellar. But then, in the doorway, Clara saw the list of names on bits of paper or scrawled directly on the wall. The villa had been divided into flats, and by the look of it, not enough to fit the number of families who lived inside it. Her mother's name wasn't there, but Max assured her they were in the right place. He pushed open the door without ringing, and she saw in the narrow foyer that someone had cut away the wires to the buzzer.

Max deposited his bicycle under the stairs and then led the way up, moving stiffly and gripping the banister. There was something alarming about seeing him like this, worn out after the frozen ride across the city.

Energy was the one thing he had always counted on, even in the war when they worked devilish hours and hardly slept.

"Are you eating enough?" she asked.

In the stairwell, he paused by the strip of painted flowers, chipped and worn, that ran along the wall. "I'm better off than most. They feed me at Falkenhorst, but I skipped it today."

Nobody skipped a warm meal. As she followed him up the next flight of stairs, she guessed what he hadn't told her. He had packed up his food to take home to his family.

He led her to the second floor, and they paused in the hallway to catch their breath. A bulb burned on the ceiling, shaded by a thick round of paper. The door on the right was badly scuffed at the bottom. Clara tried to imagine her mother kicking it open every time she went in. After knocking, she waited, feeling that this must all be a mistake. Her mother couldn't possibly live in a place like this.

Anne Heath Falkenberg opened the door, and then stood there as if frozen. Her face was pouched and sagging, the eyelids, the mouth, the chin. Clara didn't recognize the wattle of skin, and the creases in what used to be Anne's proud neck. She felt disoriented, as if she needed to eat something immediately, and then it passed and her mother was still standing there. She had opened the door with her own hands instead of waiting for a servant to do it for her. It was nighttime but she was still in her morning gown. A tear had been badly sewn at the shoulder.

"Darling," her mother said. She grasped Clara's arms, kissed the air at her cheeks—one side, the other—and then vanished in a cloud of perfume and blush tulle.

Clara felt a pressure on her arm, Max shoring her up. "I'll come by tomorrow to see how you're getting on."

"Where are you going?" She suddenly didn't want to be alone with this unfamiliar woman whom she hadn't spoken to in nearly two years. "Stay, Max."

"She won't want me here. You don't want me here either."

"Warm up a little. Maybe she has food."

They entered the small foyer where a coat and hat hung on the wardrobe, two pairs of shoes on a mat beneath. It was so common a scene, Clara assumed these were the servants' things. She doubted her mother had ever lived without one. But then she passed into the parlor, an impossible jumble of furniture no maid would tolerate. Her leg bumped the arm of a settee, teak, draped with indigo cloth. That was from the winter garden at Falkenhorst. The cloth and the fan on the wall were relics from Anne's childhood in India. Near the stove hung a picture that made Clara smile, the framed sketch of the bird Papa had drawn for her when she was a girl. By the settee was an ottoman, then a teak chair, and then the statue of Artemis Clara also recognized from the house's park. She wondered how on earth her mother had gotten it here, and why. Between all the furniture, there was hardly room to move.

"So it is true," Anne said. She faced the tall window—it had glass in it, a luxury—and her hands were flat on the sill. "You've come back, darling."

"It's good to see you too, Mother."

"Is it? Is it really?" Anne turned enough to show her profile, one of the over-the-shoulder looks that used to make young men shoot themselves to get her attention, or so her mother used to tell it. When Papa proposed to her, he'd set a pistol on the table between them and said he would point it at his heart and pull the trigger if she refused him. This was unacceptable to Anne, of course, until he admitted with one of his secret smiles that it had no bullets. This convinced her mother he was the one. Handsome men willing to maim themselves for love were ten a penny. But a man who wasn't a complete fool? Priceless.

"I know, darling. I'm an old hag."

"Of course not, Mother."

"You're a dear to say it, but don't lie to me. Herr Hecht brought you here, and for that I thank him"—she gave him a curt nod—"and now he may go."

"He needs to rest. He hasn't eaten."

"Clara," Max said, "it's all right."

"You see? He's got a home of his own, darling. He doesn't need to loiter in mine."

"He's a guest in your house, Mother. Where are your manners?"

"Where are yours? In the old days you wouldn't have dared to bring him home. You knew his place."

"Times have changed."

Max put his hat on. "I'm going. I'll check on you tomorrow, Clara."

"Don't bother, Herr Hecht. She's in good hands now."

Clara saw him to the door, a small gesture of thanks for his help. On the threshold, he took her hand. "I'll see you soon. There's so much I need to tell you." He glanced uneasily toward the room where her mother was. "Good luck. Don't let her get to you."

Back in the parlor, Anne was banging into the furniture, almost knocking over the potted palm on her way to the little burn-all stove. A hole had been knocked into the wall for the flue, and badly plastered. Anne glared at it, and then down at her hands. She rubbed them over the weak heat given off by the stove. The bucket on the floor was empty except for black dust and some splinters.

"Don't you have coal?" Clara asked.

"They'll deliver it tomorrow, darling. It's warm enough."

Clara noticed that Anne wore a thick sweater and trousers under the morning gown, which partly explained the clumsy way she moved, so different from her former grace. Clara moved the coal bucket, then looked around for something else to feed the flames. Behind the settee she found a pile of what looked like chair legs. One had been sawed halfway through.

"The servant hasn't finished that one," Anne said. "You can't find good help these days."

Clara sawed the leg and began another. "At least they let you have this flat to yourself. I haven't had a room of my own since the war."

Anne sank into the chair by the stove. "This place is unfit for human habitation, darling. One bedroom, one bathroom containing a lavatory that is practically in the bath itself. I have to eat in the kitchen. Can you imagine that? It's unhygienic." She clapped her hands, a dry, papery sound. "Times have changed, you said. Well, times are bloody awful. You have no idea."

"I think I do."

Her mother looked her over with disapproval. "Where have you been all this time?"

"In Hamelin."

"Good Lord, why there? Not for the rats, I assume."

"I just ended up there. I'd walked most of the way from here trying to avoid the Allies. By the time I reached Hamelin, I couldn't take another step. It was a quiet life. I almost married the local doctor until I found out some of the things he'd done in the war."

"You've become so judgmental, darling. It's not healthy, you know. Where did you get all those bruises on your face? You look like a battered wife."

"That," Clara said, ferociously sawing the wood, "was Captain Fenshaw."

She told her mother about the train, the steel locker, and the close escape from Elisa's house. Anne slapped the arm of her chair. "The cheek." She went to her secretaire and walked her fingers through a rosewood box Clara remembered from her childhood. Her mother's dossiers. Anne collected details about everyone she had ever met, likes and dislikes, secrets to use against them should she need to one day. She plucked out a card and settled her spectacles on her nose.

"Captain Thomas Fenshaw, born 1906 in London, family has been in Parliament for three hundred years.

Not one of my cousins"—she glanced over her lenses—
"I checked."

"How the bloody hell do you know him?"

"I have my sources, darling. He apparently galli-
vants around the British Zone arresting Nazis, which
makes him a throwback to the Stone Age. Someone
needs to slap him and tell him to arrest a communist.
Times have changed. Anyhow, he's a widower and has
one teenage son. He's considered a know-it-all who always gets his man. One of his successes, I've heard, is
that he supposedly tracked down the leader of one of
those Einsatzgruppen, wanted for doing terrible things
in Russia. He found him working as a carpenter in a
village in the Harz Mountains. Rumor has it he made
the fellow dig a grave and kneel at the edge, then held
a gun to his neck for several minutes before arresting
him properly. Apparently the man complained, but
it didn't come to anything. There was no proof, you
see, no witnesses. The captain seems to have a flair for
poetic justice."

Clara rested on her knees, worn out by the sawing.
If Fenshaw was looking for men who had committed
massacres, why was he so determined to find her?

"He said something to me about a BUF rally in London in '36. It was as if he was there. He claimed to have

a rather good opinion of me, but the next moment shut me in that locker."

"Bit of a sly fox, darling. On the whole, nobody in local military government likes him. Everyone claims he's an awful bore. I must say, I agree."

Clara climbed to her feet. "Wait—you met him?"

"He was here a couple of days ago. Left mud on the carpet. I had to have it scrubbed."

"What did he want?"

"What do you think, darling? He said there were rumors that you had surfaced. Nothing about you slipping through his fingers, though. He didn't strike me as the type to admit a mistake. He seemed very keen. Very keen indeed. He was determined to search my little hovel in case you were hiding in the kitchen cupboards. He would not be wrong, you know. He would find you, the bloodhound. How furious he was when he didn't. He hid it well, but one knows. He looked shattered with frustration and fatigue. Serves him right, going after you like that. I had my own brush with the Allies too, you know. A great brute of an American arrested me at the end of the war. The most embarrassing moment of my life."

"Why did they arrest you? You're English."

"Ask them how much they cared about that. I was the last Falkenberg left standing in Essen, so they took me in for questioning. They thought I must have dirtied my hands at the Works, but I assured them I was merely the social butterfly of our family, at least in Theodor's eyes. You were the one he trusted with the factories, and you were gone. They thought I would know where, but of course I had no idea. You didn't see fit to confide in your old mother. But would they listen to me? Now I ask you, how does one reason with an American? They're not equipped. They're like puppies with machine guns."

Clara added wood to the fire and fanned it with a piece of cardboard as her mother went on about the Americans, the endless interrogations, the offensive personal questions. The blockheads had to be told everything two or three times, Anne said, all the while writing notes with a pen in their meaty fists, and chewing their repulsive gum. There was something soothing about listening to her mother rant. Her body had changed, but her spirit was still indomitable.

"Now, listen, darling, it really is a sad story."

Clara knelt at the oven and let the fire warm her face. She was used to her mother's drama and was genuinely interested in what Anne had told the Americans to get herself freed. Anne had had very little to do with the Works—it was not prudent, her father had thought, to have an Englishwoman too deeply involved in an industry so crucial to the war effort. But she was still a Falkenberg, and Clara didn't doubt this was all that mattered to the Americans who'd arrested her.

"As a young woman," Anne said, "I fell in love with your father, the great Theodor Falkenberg. I was honored to become his wife only to find—to my dismay—that his political views were contrary to my own."

Clara shook her head in disbelief. Of course her mother hadn't mentioned that hers were the views that had aligned most closely with the Nazis'. Papa was a nationalist who thought Germany the light of civilization, but he had privately grumbled about the violence of the Brownshirts, the Reich's strict organization of society, the race theories, and, most of all, the control they exerted on the economy and on his business. When he spoke at government functions or addressed his personnel, he focused on Germany's cultural greatness and tried to avoid the other topics. When he worked in Berlin, he'd told her, he was doing his best to influence the regime's economic policies. It was Anne who applauded the Nazi severity, as she called it, their gift for organizing the rabble.

"Now, as a good and dutiful wife, I was obliged to follow my husband in all things," Anne said. "I told the Americans I was forced to socialize with those abominable people. To join the Women's League. To attend those

Fascist rallies. When the war began, I had to choose: my family or my country. As any wife and mother would do, I chose my family. With a heavy heart, I stayed here and watched as everything was taken from me. My husband imprisoned, all my sons fallen. My only daughter vanished, presumed dead." Anne spread her arms. "Has any mother suffered more?"

"I'm sure it was a fine performance."

"Of course it was. Playing the victim isn't difficult. Any sensible person would have done the same. You should give it a try, darling."

"I assume the Americans were too dense to believe you."

"Even my own people questioned it, those miserable little men. But I am not without resources. Thank God for Uncle Henry in Whitehall. Eventually, I was released, but evicted from Falkenhorst. Evicted. From my own house. By my own people." She lit a cigarette in the oven fire and sat back. "And that, darling, is why I'm reduced to living in a boxcar."

Clara didn't bother to point out that her mother was doing much better than most people, including her. "Are the Allies making you work for your ration like everyone else?"

"Yes, but actually I don't mind it, darling. I've been able to improve my standing with the local military government. I am now a kind of cultural ambassador. I host events that build understanding and sympathy between the victors and the defeated. Isn't that nice?" She patted her electric blond hair, the roots showing through, a white line along the parting.

"Have you heard from Papa?"

"Papa. Always Papa." Anne crushed the cigarette into her ebony holder. "He's hanging on in that horrid internment camp. The Americans aren't nearly as good-natured as they'd like people to think."

"I saw a photograph of him in a magazine. He's very ill."

"Poor Teddy. Takes everything to heart."

"Is he getting a defense?"

"We're a bit cash-strapped, darling, as you might imagine. But we've been calling in favors where we can. You know. Priests, nuns, orphans. Anyone who can testify to his good character. For goodness' sake, he founded a hospital and a library. He sponsored the brightest working-class children so the poor unfortunates could stay in school. If that doesn't melt the hearts of someone in his courtroom, I don't know what will." Anne gazed at the fire. "It's been hard, darling. He'll be so glad you're back. So glad. He probably won't believe me. He'll think I'm trying to buck him up ahead of the trial. Why don't you write him a letter? He'll know it's you when he sees those extravagant g's and f's of yours."

"You've been to see him?"

"They won't let me, and it may be a long time until he's with us again. I'm told he's likely to get ten years or more if he's convicted."

Ten years. For all his playacting the Nazi friend. Her father had been so deeply wrong about them pushing on through. They would have all been better off leaving, the whole family in exile. Clara remembered his distress as the war dragged on, tiny signs, the twitch of an eye, a hardened muscle in his face. The worn arms of his chair. "He told us to pretend with the government, with their followers. He took them all for fools, I suppose. 'Hold your nose, open your wallet, and shake their hands.' That's all it was supposed to take." Clara wiped hard at the soot on her fingers with a rag hanging on the edge of the coal bucket. "But even if we pretend to collaborate, we're still collaborators, aren't we?"

Anne gave her a confused look. "What do you mean, pretend?"

"You knew I hated all the Iron Fräulein nonsense but I went along with it. Maybe it helped protect me from the Nazis. I thought it did. I don't know. Papa was the same in Berlin, making those stupid speeches, working on Speer's committees. That was his way of cloaking himself. He didn't want to do any of it."

"Of course he did, darling."

She didn't expect her mother to understand. Anne had believed in Fascism, or so she'd said at the time. Clara wondered if that had been an act too, her mother riding the winds of power. In another age, she might have been a courtier devoted to her king no matter how mad or corrupt he might be.

"Papa confided in me, Mother. I know his conscience bothered him."

"I was married to him long before you were born, so I think I might have a few more insights into Papa than you do, my girl. You're right, he had a conscience, but he correctly decided that other things were more important than those few little pangs."

"The family, the Works, the legacy, and so on. What's left of it now? The whole system—the forced labor—was criminal. We went along with it thinking we were going to save Falkenberg for future generations. Well, how did that work out?"

Her attention on the fire, Anne took a long drag of her cigarette.

"At least a few of us tried to help people," Clara said,

trying to goad her mother into saying something. "Did you know about that too?"

Anne looked sour. "Herr Hecht informed me after the war. It was extremely foolish of you, you know." She sat up straighter and said with indignation, "You endangered all of us with your little schemes. Did you think about that? Hm?"

"All the time. I never said anything to Papa but I think he guessed. He was doing what he could as well. He tried to convince those scoundrels in Berlin to make things more bearable for the workers."

"What in the world makes you think he was doing that?"

"He told me. He talked to Speer, he talked to Sauckel, he—"

"He talked to them all the time, of course, but he wasn't on a crusade to save anyone, darling. He told you such things to make you feel better. He was always very concerned about your well-being. You had to be pacified so that you would carry on doing the work he set for you."

Clara took a couple of breaths before speaking, careful, afraid of the raw cracks in her voice. "Are you saying that he was perfectly fine with what we did? The transports, the labor camps, all of it?"

"Clara. Do you have any idea how much money we

were making? What plans we had? Papa wanted to buy you a castle if you ever managed to marry a suitable man, preferably a nobleman."

Clara collided with a chair on her way to the wall. Hanging there was Papa's sketch of the bird. She had thought it some kind of a sign, something that might help her remember who he was before all of this. But now . . . "You didn't answer my question, Mother. Did he or did he not care about the terrible things that happened on our watch?"

"Oh, darling, Papa would lay waste to continents for his family. Especially for you, his baby girl. You do know that?"

Something splintered in Clara's chest, a cherished truth about her father she wasn't willing to see destroyed. "I didn't want any of it. I went along with it because he explained to me, he assured me, there was no alternative."

"Quite so. Why are you tearing yourself up about it now? The family was of the utmost importance to you too, as it should be. It mattered more than the foolish little voices in your head—or a few silly girls in the carriage house. Now I want you to stop all this nonsense about conscience. You and Papa did the right and proper thing in the war. A few foreigners might have benefited from your softer nature, but that's neither here nor there. You served the family and the Reich well. We were all very proud of you."

Clara snatched the sketch off the wall and flung it down, wanting the glass to smash, but the frame merely cracked on the rug and then tipped against her mother's sideboard. The drawing was as cheerful and whimsical as ever. Her father's little bird for his little girl. If he had been here, if he had been sitting in his old armchair, she would have . . . she didn't know. Screamed at him for the first time in her life. Demanded he explain himself. Called him filthy names, every one of them true, because he hadn't playacted with the world, he had done it with her, in their closest moments, for years. Stupid as she was, needy, starved of his love, guilty about the danger she'd put her family in, she had wanted to believe what he told her, against the evidence of her own eyes and heart.

Anne stooped painfully and picked up the sketch. "You might have smashed it, girl, what is wrong with you?"

Clara's fury ebbed to a steady pulse at her temples. She approached the warmth of the stove's fire and watched the shadows flicker on her mother's face. Anne had talked about Papa as if he had calculated what his conscience could bear, and it was almost anything. Where did that leave her? What had been her line in the sand? She had thought they were so close. That they had been walking that line together.

She took the scrap of silk out of her coat pocket and crushed it in her fist. She needed to talk to Elisa about all of this, about what they had done and hadn't done and tried to do and why. About the man she had always thought her father to be. And the man she was being confronted with now. Her friend would understand. Clara balled up her rage as she had learned to do as a child, and set it aside for later. She needed a clear head.

"Do you know where Elisa is?" she asked, dampening the anger in her voice.

"No, darling, I don't. Why should I?"

Clara spread the piece of silk on the coffee table. Anne used the end of her cigarette holder to lift a corner. "What's this? A handkerchief?"

"It's a piece of Elisa's wedding dress. I found it high up in a cupboard in the workshop at Falkenhorst."

"Well. That's odd."

"Very odd, I'd say. It was Papa's place. And Friedrich's."

"I'm sure there's a simple explanation."

"Oh, yes, I'm assuming that, Mother. I'd like to hear yours."

"I really have no idea, and that's the truth. Now,

why don't you have something to eat and then a bath. You know how grumpy you get when you're hungry. Even as a girl. What a little beast you were."

Clara was not going to let her off that easily. She followed her mother into the kitchen, little more than a cooktop and a table with four chairs, two Clara recognized from home, slender and regal, two Anne must have found in the ruins, scraped up and patched. Anne began opening cupboards and slamming them quickly shut after she'd snatched this can or that plate. Clara caught glimpses of empty space, a single package on a shelf, a cracked cup. She didn't offer to help her mother perform this unnatural act—providing food for her daughter, a thing she had never done before. Watching her do it was sadly fulfilling, as if she finally had a loving mother.

"We can talk now, can't we?" Clara asked. "We're the only two left in the family who are alive and free. We don't have to pretend anymore."

Anne speared a can with an opener. "I have no idea what you're talking about, darling."

"It's like me and Max. Too many years have gone by to keep pretending we weren't together. We were, and you knew it. We don't have to talk about that. But Elisa's dress in the workshop. That's different. There's a reason it was there, and I think you know what it is."

"Honestly, darling," Anne said tightly, "I don't know anything about a silly dress."

Clara let out a frustrated breath. Her mother was going to make her build the case. "The first time I met Elisa, at that café over the river, you arranged it. Why?"

"Because I felt sorry for her, darling. She was a bit of an outcast, you know. Disgraced. I thought you two had something in common after that sordid episode at your school."

Clara let that pass. "The night Elisa met her husband. It was also the night I met Max. You sent us to that flat. Elisa had never mentioned Reinhard before, but that night, she said she was going to marry him. Just like that. What did you have to do with it?"

"Why would I go around arranging marriages for our employees? Do you think I didn't have better things to do?"

"We gave them a villa at Sophienhof as a wedding gift. We could have given them a set of crystal, but we gave them a house. That wasn't just generosity. You aren't going to go on pretending you did all this for Elisa because you felt sorry for her."

"Darling, you're really making no sense." Anne slapped a tiny sliver of margarine onto a slice of bread and dropped the plate on the table. "Eat. Bathe. Sleep. You'll feel better, and then you'll see how muddled you are."

"I'm thinking clearly, Mother. Really thinking about things for the first time. You always asked me about them, remember? You wanted to know what Elisa was doing. You wanted to know what kind of boy Willy was shaping up to be." She wanted Anne to look at her, to take the conversation seriously. She grasped her mother's arm. "You wanted them close. You were watching them. All those years. And it suits you now that they're gone. They haven't been home since the war. Did you know that?"

Anne's lips formed a flat red line. "You'd do better to calm down, darling."

"When you introduced me to Elisa, she was pregnant and alone. You knew who the father was."

"Aside from your infatuation with Herr Hecht, you were a very dutiful daughter, Clara. Don't start a rebellion now. It's no use to anyone."

"I want to know the truth."

"If you really wanted to know, you would have demanded answers from that girl years ago. But you were sensible. You minded your own business. It's one of your virtues."

"It is my business. Elisa is my oldest friend. We both

know that she was pregnant before she married Reinhard. I think she gave a piece of her wedding dress to a man she couldn't marry. The man who was Willy's father."

Anne set her cigarette case, holder, and lighter in a row on the table and then folded her hands on the walnut.

"First of all, I do know that woman and her boy are missing. But I had nothing to do with it, if that's what you are implying. My contacts tried to find them, but it seems they've covered their tracks well. We found no registration for them in the city since the war. They haven't drawn ration books."

"Did Willy fight?"

"If he did, there's no record of it. No death certificates either. I assume they left for parts unknown as soon as they got the chance."

"That wasn't easy. I got out on foot like a refugee with a bundle on my back. For all I knew, I was walking straight into Allied lines. If Elisa and Willy left even a day later, they'd have found it almost impossible to get out before the Allies closed in."

"Maybe they left after the Americans came. Or in the transition to the British. Maybe your Elisa found herself an Allied officer. She was good at that kind of thing. I don't know, Clara." Anne tapped her cigarette holder near Clara's plate. "You do realize I occasionally don't know things."

"The people in Elisa's house told me the Gestapo came for her. Maybe you know something about that?"

"My contacts heard the same thing, but they found no documentation to support it. Hardly surprising, considering the whole world was on fire. If she was taken in at all, she was probably questioned and let go. It happened to Herr Hecht and he's still alive and well."

Quickly, before she lost her courage, Clara said, "Willy is one of us, isn't he? He's a Falkenberg. I'm right about that."

Anne lit another cigarette and snapped the lighter onto the walnut. A single blue vein pulsed at her temple. "Yes, darling. You're right about that."

Bats

The bats were sleeping. Willy couldn't see them, but he sensed them rustling in the tunnel over his head. The bats and him, they had an understanding. They left their droppings in the tunnels he rarely went into, and he never disturbed them with light or noise. They were his ears, so to speak. They flew out into the night and over the world and listened—blind, like him, in the dark. Sometimes when they flew back, when they swept into the tunnels, he heard a kind of chatter and clatter and he understood it. They were bringing him news from the outside world.

The war is over.

The war is lost.

If he closed his eyes and thought hard, he was home, in Mama's kitchen. He was eating a thin potato soup.

It was dark, the blackout curtains all around them and the lantern burning because the electricity was gone. Mama ate nothing. She watched him with her knuckles on each side of her face. She almost always had red welts on her cheeks and around her eyes and a little downturned curl on the left side of her mouth. Whatever was wrong with her was his fault. It always was, or why else did she look at him like that?

He squatted in the tunnel as the bats breathed in the dark, their hearts beating in their furry chests. He wished he could be like them. He wished he could sleep.

14

Early morning, long before dawn, Clara was trudging up Alfredstrasse, the wide street named after the patriarch of the Krupp Steel family. As a young man, Clara's grandfather used to ride here just like old Alfred, but Heinrich Falkenberg had kept a leisurely pace so that his horse had time to relieve itself somewhere along the route of the family rivals. Remembering that made her smile, though the wind was so cold, her teeth ached. The street was now silent, empty, a layer of glittering frost on the pavement. No soldiers, no Fenshaw.

She hadn't expected to sleep at her mother's, but Anne had left the flat abruptly after cutting off their conversation about Willy and Elisa. She'd quickly changed into a deep blue evening gown, insisting she had an urgent social engagement. After she'd gone, Clara had the flat all to herself. It contained so many things she had missed—privacy, heat, running water, clean clothes— she luxuriated in it all. After dozing in the bath and changing into her mother's trousers, blouse, and jacket, she had filled her backpack with tins from the kitchen cupboard and clean clothing from her mother's dresser, along with a new matchbox, candles, batteries, even toilet paper. Lastly, she'd rolled up a blanket and then hesitated at the door, regretting that she'd no longer have the comforts of this place. She had been happy to leave, though, disturbed by the knowledge of how rotten the core of her family had been all these years.

At the last moment, she had written a note on light blue paper and left it on the secretaire. *Thank you for the food and supplies, Mother. —C.*

As she walked, she kept her head down and avoided the main streets when she could. In five days, she would meet Jakob Relling as arranged. She was looking forward to seeing him more than she expected. She still longed to speak to Elisa, of course, but there was an allure to a clean start with a person who had no idea who she really was. But until then, she would hide out in a place so large and deserted and full of chaos that even Fenshaw couldn't find her there—the iron works.

At daybreak, she was still crossing the city, hours

when the cold wind and the exertion scoured all thoughts from her mind. To be on the cautious side, she stayed away from Falkenbergstrasse, though it would have been a more direct path to the Works. She detoured around whole blocks of rubble and streets barricaded for safety. When she reached the western gate, she knew it instantly. The black iron, the beauty of the work, arabesques entangled in the family symbol: the wing and the flame.

The gate was padlocked. She pulled at the chain with numb hands, but this was good weighty iron and it would not give. She rattled the gate and the sound echoed in the empty street. She had the vague image of some Allied lackey locking her out on purpose. This was her place. She had run it in the war, her father had run it before her, and his father before that. She would not be kept out.

There was no one else around. She followed the wall, whole sections of it crumbled, but she didn't try climbing; she couldn't feel her toes and, after the long walk from her mother's flat, she didn't have the energy to get over that mountain. Eventually she came to a section of the wall which had been blasted away, automatically adding it to the list she used to keep in her mind of what needed to be done to keep this place going.

On the other side of the wall she recognized the locomotive shed. The ceiling had collapsed and the blasts had tossed the trains around like toys. She remembered that bombardment, the dismay she'd felt when she saw the damage, the chaos. They had tried to clean it up, and now she saw how badly they had failed. All of that work—she had even gotten herself a shovel and joined the men and women forced to clear the rubble—for nothing. At the time, she had thought her father would have wanted her to do it. Preserve the Falkenberg legacy at all costs. Preserve the family. She had taken that duty as seriously as he did.

She left the shed and wandered the deserted factory roads, some blocked, the pipes down, the power lines snaking in the frost. She was too far past the western gate to see headquarters, that tower of her pride. Ten stories and she'd felt as if she was flying, hovering high over their domain. During the war, she'd looked down on it thinking she could be everything at once: the loving daughter conscious of her duty, the director of the Works with an iron spine, and the most secret part of her, the dissenter who listened to her conscience. As if it was possible to be all of these things, and still hold herself together.

She came to one of the older factories, a real beauty, blond and dark brick in patterns up the walls, a great entrance sealed with iron doors. Again they were padlocked, so she circled the building until she found a gap in the wall—what a rat she'd become, scurrying through holes—and she entered the factory floor. This would do. It had a roof and the window spaces were high enough that no one would see her light. The floor was swept, leaving only the tracks in the concrete where the machines had been bolted down. In the war, the foreigners had worked here with sheets of iron and steel. They had done it without gloves or safety glasses, items that were scarce later in the war, though she had plundered the supply depots at the Works looking for more and finding none. She crossed the factory floor aware of the workers accusing her from the shadows. What a slippery thing conscience could be. It had driven her in two directions. To her father, with all the duties of family and work. She could have refused this, lived out the war in comfort abroad, but what kind of guilt would she have carried for abandoning everyone and everything she knew? And then she had been driven to help the workers, an act that put everything else at risk. One side of her conscience undermining the other. And still she had listened to both. She had thought she could do justice to both.

Clara settled herself into the corner of the factory where the walls looked most solid and intact. It was dim enough inside that she needed her flashlight to find materials for a fire: brittle scraps of paper, a wooden crate. On her knees, she balled up the paper and built a little pile of it on the floor. She was not her father. She had helped those she could, but did it really matter compared to the crimes she had allowed to happen? She looked up at the great spaces of the factory windows. Right here, thousands of men and women from many nations had worked for her against their will. They had crowded into camps and barracks. After the worst bombardments, they had lived in trash bins, under bridges, in filth. They had begged for food and worked to the limits of endurance. They were forced to live without dignity. She remembered Galina eyeing Clara's food with longing, like a dog. What Clara had to give was a tiny drop in the sea of human misery that she had helped build and maintain right here. She had feared the consequences of speaking out. Accusations and arrest, imprisonment or exile. Betraying the family. Disappointing her father.

Back at the crate, she raised her foot as high as she could and stomped, enjoying the noise of splitting wood so much, she stomped on it again and again and again, thinking of her father, the greatest actor she knew. So perceptive, so sure of how to handle her, to tame her. He was a complicated man, she'd always known that. A hard man to understand. Loving, warm, generous, indulgent with her and her brothers. But also set in his ways, in his beliefs, with iron-edged clear-sightedness. Now she knew just how ruthless he was. Two-faced. Morally corrupt. As the wood split under her feet, she felt something splinter at her core. She didn't know who or what she was anymore. Her father had built the foundations of her world, and they were crumbling away within.

She stopped, panting, and then bent to collect the slats of wood. Her hands were still numb, and something, a noise, rumbled deep inside her—or from far away. She knelt to arrange the wood with the paper, the noise growing louder in her head until she paused to look up at the empty windows, listening. A thick silence lay over the factory hall. But the rumbling sound was real, its echoes penetrating the brick walls from somewhere outside. It was an engine.

She kicked the wood, scattering it quickly, randomly. She stowed her pack under a pile of debris and then scurried through the factory looking for a hiding place.

The engine was close, and she heard a man shout. She scrambled into the nearest place, a crack in the wall just big enough to squeeze into. Crouching, she had a view of the entire hall, her only advantage, but it was too late to find anything better. She doused her light.

Outside, men were talking softly in English. Someone rattled the padlock, and she recognized the voice of

Fenshaw's officer, Reynolds. "Over here, sir. There's a hole."

Their flashlight beams crossed the factory floor, and she drew back. She pinpointed Fenshaw only from his voice. "Jennings, you're skin and bones. That ladder should take your weight. See what's up on that landing." His light swung past her hiding place, and she flinched. Scuffling sounds, the whine of iron, and a man—presumably Jennings—called from above her head. "She's not up here, sir. Nothing but rubbish." Men were emerging from farther away, the offices and break rooms, she assumed. They each reported the same thing. She's not there.

"Right. Move on to the next quadrant."

She dared peek out of the hole. Fenshaw deployed his men, pointing to areas on what she assumed was a plan of the Works. She tried to remember if she'd left some clue, had said something to the Bergers or her mother about where she might hide. Then again, maybe Fenshaw was simply relying on instinct, searching all the places from her old life.

When the soldiers left, he stayed.

He was so close.

He fumbled with the plan, pinning it under his arm as he took a pen out of his pocket. He looked around, presumably for a table, and finding nothing, he spread the plan on the floor. He stretched out on his stomach, the light angled into the paper, and began to write, annotating the layout before him. All he had to do was shine his light at a different angle and he'd see her instantly.

But he didn't, too busy with the energetic scratches of his pen, too focused on his mission. This was a man who knew what he was about. Single-minded, blessed with authority, chock-full of convictions. She envied him all that. If she could somehow take half of the self-assurance he showed in the tilt of his head, she would. Gladly. His task was clear and easy. He was hunting a war criminal.

He truly was.

And it was her.

Her sight blurred. A pressure built up inside her, a need to cry out, and she struggled to keep it in, to keep quiet. She saw her father in his internment camp, and there was no injustice in him being there, no over-zealousness on the part of the Allies. The camp was precisely where he was supposed to be. And what did she deserve? Was she as guilty as him, in her own way? She had the sudden urge to stop all of this right now, the running, the hiding. All she had to do was move. Cough. Fenshaw would look up, and all of this would be over. And yet a sense of self-preservation held her back. And fear. It quaked deep in her gut at the thought of what Fenshaw would have in store for her.

He folded his plan, a complex undertaking he did perfectly. Then he took a swig from his flask, set it on the floor, and lit a cigarette. He sat cross-legged, smoking, looking at nothing in particular, close enough for her to see in his flashlight beam the well-rubbed plating on his flask. After a while he took something out of his pocket and angled it to the light, a small paper she instinctively knew was a photograph—her. Next he drew out another paper, light blue—the note she'd written her mother. Clara imagined he'd dropped in on Anne this morning unannounced and had seen it before she did. He studied the note, then the photograph as he finished his cigarette.

He packed up his things and, after sweeping his flashlight beam across the factory floor one final time, he went to join his men. Clara crouched in the wall until she was sure they had gone, long minutes when the cold wind drifted into the factory and numbed her bones. Later, as she huddled by the miserable fire she had coaxed out of the debris, she remembered the poor falcon, that proud creature her father had blinded to protect it from the world it couldn't bear to see.

15

Clara arrived at the South Sea Club limping, her face a mask of cold, a dull ache behind her eyes. The blue neon sign flashed over the door, and the faint sound of music felt like an echo from long ago. The doorman, a wide fellow in earmuffs and mittens, glared down at her, daring her not to laugh, she supposed. She wasn't in the mood to poke fun, or be detained. The club glowed behind him, and a delicious heat seeped out of the doorway.

"I don't know you, sweetheart," he said.

"Do you know Jakob Relling?"

"What's it to you?"

She let out a long breath into the scarf knotted at her chin. It seemed the doorman had been instructed not to let in the riffraff, the common folk looking for a little warmth and light. All he saw was her dirty coat and her chapped lips, the result of a week sleeping rough, like half the rest of the city. The shelter she had built in an office of the factory was not much different from a cellar or a bomb-damaged flat.

"Jakob Relling," she repeated. "I have an appointment."

"I'm not his secretary."

She understood then. The bruiser wanted a bribe. She felt around in her pockets for something he might want. She'd scoured the Works for useful items to trade on the black market, and came up with a coil of electrical cord. "Well?" she asked as he stuffed it into his coat.

"What's Relling want with you?"

"Let's go and ask him."

He shrugged, held open the door, and, as she passed, swatted her backside with his mittened paw. There was no hallway and no curtain. She was there in the bar with its smoke and noise and moist warmth. Suddenly she wanted to make an entrance, to let the world know she was alive. A woman, not a rat in hiding, not a timid thing who allowed herself to be insulted.

She rounded on the doorman and slapped him so hard, his earmuffs popped off his head. He roared at her, more surprised than angry. He rubbed his cheek and looked confused. The room had gone quiet, mostly men around little tables and lining up for drinks, who then burst out laughing.

They let Clara through. She draped her coat over her arm and pretended to ignore the stares and the greetings. *Hello, sweetheart. Got a temper on you, don't you? Not seen you around before.* She made her way to the bar and while she waited for her drink, she took in the place, its scuffed floor and cracked ceiling hidden by a mad mix of tropical and Christmas decorations. Girls in grass skirts served drinks at tables decorated with coconuts and sprigs of fir. Tinsel glittered on the paper palm trees flanking the bar. She loved it. Loved the unapologetic campiness, the poverty it wouldn't succumb to. This club worked hard to be cheerful, and she wanted—needed—to be cheered.

She raised her glass to the men and drank the schnapps without a cough. That got her some admiring comments and offers to pay, which was her object to begin with. She couldn't afford black-market prices. "Is Jakob Relling here tonight?"

The man who paid for her drink had the bland face of a crooked bureaucrat. "You can do better than a cripple, fräulein."

"Oh, but I love cripples." She took her drink into the next room.

Someone had tried to bring a cosmopolitan flair to the second bar, with its worn leather armchairs and the prints of skyscrapers framed on the wall, apparently cut out of magazines. She loved this place too, quiet, less garish, the men doing their old boys act, pushing cigarettes across cocktail tables or counting wads of money. She saw Jakob at a table by the wall and withdrew to a quiet corner to observe him.

He'd polished himself for tonight, she saw that right away. The slick hair, the perfect tie, the trim suit coat. Sitting there, he looked like any other man, his crutch nowhere to be seen. He talked and joked, his cigarette bobbing in his mouth. He called to everyone who walked by, knew their names, shook hands, shared a laugh. It was a revelation to see what he could do with a smile and a handshake. Everybody played along, but she sensed the wariness behind the smiles. Nobody in that room trusted anyone else.

She waited until his table was full and then sauntered up. "Gentlemen." She settled down on the arm of Jakob's chair and raised her drink to him. "Don't let me interrupt you."

"There you are, liebling." He insisted on standing like a gentleman, a struggle on his crutch but one she wouldn't dream of helping him with. He was glowing at her, gleaming. An old feeling flooded her then, ancient, something like the early days with Max. It made her want to unpin her hair and kick off her shoes.

The men excused themselves in a way she recognized, giving Jakob space as if she was his conquest and they wouldn't interfere. She stayed where she sat, her arm draped over the back of his chair and her drink on her thigh. She was wearing a green dress she had taken from her mother, saved all week for the occasion. She was going to look decent at a club, her hair up, a dab of lipstick, good stockings. Her footwear didn't match the dress, and the only thing to do about that was to flaunt it, her legs crossed, her clunky winter shoes bobbing as if they were the finest heels.

"Do you have good news for me, Herr Relling?"

"I most certainly do, fräulein." His hand hovered near her knee—in her head, she dared him to touch her, not knowing what she would do in response—but instead he reached for his drink. "I contacted an ex-cop who knows a thing or two about your friend. He'll be here later tonight."

A knot tightened in her chest. "I haven't found her yet. Maybe he can tell me something useful."

A thoughtful look on his face quickly transformed into another smile. "You look good, liebling. All healed up."

"You too. Almost."

He touched the fading bruise on his jaw. "I put on my best suit for you. Paid 1,190 marks for it."

She made impressed noises and stroked the fabric at his shoulder. "You're not spending my ring already, are you?"

He covered her hand, his warm and clammy. "No need to flash that around."

She slid off the arm of his chair. The drinks made her feel dangerously reckless. "Could you show me the rest of the club? Is there a dance floor?"

"We got a nice little ballroom. But maybe we should keep it quiet, you know? I got a room reserved just for us. You hungry?"

She handed him his crutch. "Show me the dance floor first."

To get there, they had to go through the first bar. The doorman wasn't there, perhaps nursing his wounded pride outdoors. Men called after her, telling Jakob to be careful, that she was fast with the flat of her hand.

"You slapped Günther? You nuts?" Jakob asked as they made their way down the hall.

"He should've kept his hands to himself."

"You can't go around slapping fellows in here. People remember that. You got to be more careful."

She thought of Fenshaw gazing at her photograph in the factory, how close he'd been, how close she'd been to giving herself up. "I'm tired of being careful, Herr Relling."

Guests were scattered around the tables in the ballroom—another attempt at a tropical scene, palm trees and birds-of-paradise painted on the walls. Silver tinsel fluttered over the edge of the bar. A three-piece band played a light jazz number, and a few couples danced to it, halfheartedly. Clara recognized the professional dancers, paid to keep the floor occupied, as Max had done before figuring out he could maximize his income as a gigolo.

"Watch my coat," she said to Jakob as she kicked off her shoes and padded onto the dance floor. Her presence confused the professionals. They swirled to a stop, and then one of the men—very much like Max, painfully polished, self-consciously so—asked her to dance. For the next few minutes, the world was light and music and cold parquet under the soles of her feet. The dancer was nowhere near as good as Max, but better than she was now, and he tried out increasingly intricate moves that took most of her concentration. Now and then she looked to see if Jakob was watching her, what effect she was having on him. Seated at the bar, he was taking nervous puffs of his cigarette, his gaze roaming the room. His mind seemed far away and it irritated her. She wanted him to look at her just as he had when he first saw her tonight.

She returned to him, breathless. "Would you like to dance?"

"Don't think I've done that since 1942. For obvious reasons." He adjusted his crutch leaning against the bar.

"Move your stool around. Like this." She turned him herself, grasping his arms, good thick arms. He took her hand and her waist, a light yet confident touch, just as she liked it.

"That was the easy part," he said, his face close to hers. He was sweating a little at his hairline. "What's next? The Lindy Hop?"

The best they could manage was swaying, him on the stool side to side to the music. The longer they did it, the wider they smiled at each other, and then the giggles came, contagious, until they were both laughing at how ridiculous they looked.

The dancers cleared the floor and a singer in red velvet began to croon "Irgendwo auf der Welt" into her microphone. Jakob's mood instantly changed. He listened with a sad vacancy on his face, as if he too was waiting for happiness somewhere in the world.

Clara leaned close. "May I ask who you're thinking about?"

"Nothing, really. Nobody."

"This song reminds you of someone, I can tell. Wife?" She was being bold and maybe even rude. It was the drink he kept motioning the bartender to refill at her elbow.

"Never been married."

"Girlfriend?"

"You'll laugh. Or you'll think I'm—I don't know— strange."

She held up her hand as if taking an oath. "I will not laugh or think you strange."

"All right." He took a drink—didn't seem to realize it was out of her glass. "My mother died in September. She loved this song. If it was on the radio and she was ironing or something, she'd stop and listen. I think it reminded her of my father."

She didn't have to ask to know his father was gone too. "I'm sorry."

He brightened, but it was a struggle in his eyes. "Enough of this old stuff, liebling. It's a beautiful night."

But she didn't want to let the moment go. She had almost reached something beneath the surface of him, something real and warm and deep. "Do you think about the past a lot?"

"Not often. What good would that do? We can't change any of it."

"I think about it more now than I did a year ago. A month ago, even."

"It doesn't matter now."

"Maybe it does."

"It's over. Look at us. We got a roof over our heads, enough to drink and the company is nice. What more could we want?"

"It's not like we were born in 1945. I was . . . different back then." She hated that she had to be vague with him. "Or maybe I wasn't. That's the issue. I was her, and I'm me now, and what I did or thought or felt back then still matters. I can't pretend it doesn't."

"You're making things hard on yourself. In the war I had some bad luck and now I use a crutch. Who cares? We got out alive. Hell, do you remember what it felt like when you heard it was over and you realized you'd made it?"

She couldn't remember a single moment when that had dawned on her. Maybe somewhere on her trek to Hamelin, or in a cinema with Dr. Blum, but she couldn't recall.

"You made it," Jakob said. "If you messed up in the past, do better from now on. If you didn't kiss your man enough back then, you can make up for it now."

"He's not here."

"I am."

For a few exquisite moments she imagined the room empty except for the two of them and the song. She picked up his cigarette to have something to do with her fingers, tapping the ash into the tray for him. "I think I'd like to eat something now, Herr Relling."

The private room was full of mirrors and fake gold carvings, gaudy as a girl's jewelry box. Clara circled the room, her image fractured, light sparkling all around her. She rustled the organza curtains on a window that was painted onto the wall, no real view to the outside world. Plush chairs and a rose-patterned sofa formed a half-circle that gave at least a partial view of the door. This was a room for people who wanted to keep an eye on the escape route. Perfect.

"What's that panel on the wall?" Clara asked, sitting down on the sofa.

Jakob pressed a button. Music and conversation from the dance floor hummed out of the speakers. "What do you want to eat? I can get you anything you'd like. Lobster? You want oysters? I can get you caviar."

"I really have a taste for pork. Potatoes. A butter parsley sauce. White wine. I like it dry as a bone."

"Anything you want." He pressed another button on the panel, a buzzer sounded, and a few moments later, a woman came in to take their order. There was some argument about how he'd pay for the meal, and he glanced at Clara with a smile of embarrassment as he argued about a tab that didn't seem to exist. She liked the front he was putting up for her, the nice suit, the drinks, the food, this dollhouse of a room. It was costing him, and she showed her appreciation by assuming he could pay.

"When is the policeman coming?" she asked.

"He'll be here soon." Jakob sat beside her, an awkward fall into the cushions. "Are you in a hurry?"

"No, actually, I suppose I'm not." She slid closer on the sofa, not close enough to touch him, but close enough to feel his heat. "So, Jakob Relling, who are you?"

"What do you mean?"

"Who are you really? I know the unimportant things. You're a black marketeer, one of those scoundrels who takes advantage of normal people by funneling goods out of the shops and driving up prices. People talk about hanging men in your profession."

"I could be an unemployed cripple with my hat on the pavement, if you prefer."

She shook her head. "I know you loved your mother. That's important."

"You know a lot about me already, liebling. Tell me about yourself."

"Your story first."

A sly smile. "All right, then you."

She paid attention to how he began, a technique she had learned from her father when she sat in on interviews of potential employees at the Works. Jakob began where people usually did, said he was born in Essen, had never been anywhere else until he was drafted and went off to war. His father had worked in mine rescue. With a trace of pride, he told her he had died rescuing other miners in a collapse. Jakob spoke at length about this, longer than he talked about himself. She was instantly more comfortable with him. He was a grown man who thought his father a hero. She envied him that.

"It was his idea to leave me in school," he said, "instead of sending me down into the mines. Thought I had some talent up here." Jakob tapped his head. "With numbers mostly. He said I was too clever to hammer rock all day. We didn't have a lot of money—there were five of us kids by then—so Papa hit on the notion of getting me sponsored to stay on. You know, pay for my shoes and books and things so I could pass some exams and become something that didn't get my shirt dirty." He paused as a girl brought the food and wine and then vanished with a rustle of her grass skirt. "So one day, my papa gave me a good spit and polish and took me up to the Falkenberg Iron Works for an interview with

Herr Falkenberg himself. He was known for his charity, you know."

Clara's fork, loaded with pork, stopped midway to her mouth. "Oh? When was this?"

"Spring of '33. I was thirteen."

She tried to remember if she'd ever seen him at the Works. At the time, she was enamored of Max and unlikely to notice a miner's son five years younger than herself. She could imagine what Jakob had been like back then. One of those cocky golden boys she thought she would dislike but who always charmed her in the end.

"We presented ourselves to Herr Falkenberg," he said. "Me, I was struck dumb. You know, awed. My father twisted his cap in his hands. Our priest looked like he'd raise the dead if Herr Falkenberg ordered him to. Herr Falkenberg asked me questions. My favorite subjects at school, if I got into fights, that kind of thing. Then he turned to my papa and asked, 'What are your hopes for your son?' Now Papa didn't have a big mouth like I do. He thought about it for a while and he said—and I'll never forget this—he said, 'This boy has a future, sir. He shouldn't live his life down in the dark. He deserves to live in the light.'"

"Your father sounds like a good man."

"He was."

She waited for Jakob to say if her father had granted the sponsorship he'd given to dozens of boys and girls over the years. "Well? Did you stay in school?"

"Sure did. Every year I had to write a grateful letter to Herr Falkenberg. He even wrote back to me once. In his own hand and everything. Said I was going to be a credit to my family one day." Jakob's voice trailed off. He seemed to have forgotten his cigarette. The ashes dusted the sofa cushion, and he quickly brushed them away. "Now it's your turn, liebling. Who are you?"

She shoved a forkful of potato into her mouth, chewing slowly. Her father had taken pride in his generosity, his charity, his hospital and library, his support of needy children. Considering what her mother had told her about the ease with which he put his conscience aside in the war, she wondered if all this generosity had been just as calculated, improving the family image, making him feel noble. Maybe he hadn't cared about the children he helped, only the advantages he could get from helping them. Her father, a carefully constructed mirage.

Jakob was watching her, and she remembered he'd asked her a question. "Who am I? Damned if I know."

"Come on. You walk like there's a vase on your head. You dance like a dream. I bet you can talk circles around everybody in this place. Except me."

She humored him, spinning the tale of Margarete Müller as she had with Dr. Blum and Frau Hermann. She was the simple secretary who'd lost everything in the war. Jakob looked mildly skeptical so she embroidered, adding parents who had ambitions for her, raising her for poise and all that, but what good did it do to walk like a queen when the ground was crumbling under your feet, courtesy of Allied bombers? She played the universal sport of blaming the war for everything; it was the safest excuse there was for anything he might feel was odd about her.

"Do me a favor, will you, liebling? Could you bring me the magazine in that drawer over there?"

She was handing it to him when she noticed the title. The *NS-Frauen-Warte*, the rag her mother had ordered to be displayed in the foyer at Falkenhorst when she expected visitors from the Party. On the cover, a woman climbed out of an armored Mercedes, her chin turned up, as if the taking of the picture was an unwelcome interruption of more important things. The Iron Fräulein. Clara felt a gap of distance and time opening up in her mind as she looked at that face as if it wasn't her own. It was like seeing an old friend who had once betrayed her.

Carefully, she said, "If you want to read a ladies' magazine, Herr Relling, try *Die Frau*."

"You're on the cover of that too, are you?"

For a moment, she couldn't find the right words. "I don't know what you're talking about."

"That's you."

She forced a little laugh—not convincing, she knew—scooped up the last bit of butter sauce from her plate, and sucked it from her fingers. "This has happened to me before, you know. It's a mistake, Herr Relling. A resemblance."

"In the war, a fellow had a portrait of you up on the wall. In Russia. Back then I spent a few weeks falling asleep looking at that girl. It was the kind of thing that kept me going. I know it's you. I know those eyes of yours. Eyes don't change."

Her resistance crumbled, just as it had with the Bergers in Elisa's cellar. Jakob knew who she was. He knew, and it was as if he had stepped closer to her in the knowing. She wasn't alone anymore.

In the mirrors on the walls, she saw her pale cheeks and slumped shoulders, and with a flush of embarrassment—he knew her, and she looked like this?—she sat up straighter, chin up. "Who have you told? The policeman—"

"He doesn't know. I haven't told anyone."

"The British would pay a lot for this information. How do I know I can trust you?"

"I guess you can't."

The disappointment drove her to stand up, look for her coat.

"Come on, liebling. I meant you can't know you can trust me, you just have to do it. Take a leap of faith."

"You're a black marketeer, not a priest."

"I'm on your side. I want to help you."

"Why? Because my father sent you to school?"

"He saw I had a head on my shoulders and he saw I could be more than what I was born to be. That's worth something. You could say I owe him."

It wasn't enough. She was hugging her coat, wanting more from him.

"Do you respect oaths, Herr Relling?"

"God, no, I was in the army."

"I'm not asking you to swear to the führer and the fatherland. I need to know I can trust you. There must be something you'd take an oath on."

"What's the point? We're all out for ourselves. Alliances are temporary. They last only as long as we got a mutual advantage. No sense in taking oaths we're not going to keep in the long run."

"You just said you owe my father."

"Same as saying I owe him a thousand marks. It's not honor. It's business."

She understood now. "You're hoping to call in a

favor someday if you help me. You want my family in your debt."

"What's wrong with that?" By the look on his face, he honestly didn't understand why she was upset.

"You talked about mutual advantage." She sat on the opposite end of the sofa, a gaping space between them. "What's in all this for me?"

"Glad you're back to talking sense, fräulein. I got you the information you need tonight. That's a start. I can help you find your friend. More important, I can help keep you on your feet."

"What do you mean?"

"You're thinner than you were last week. That dress and the makeup can't hide that. You haven't been sleeping either. You need more than powder to hide those circles under your eyes. You been living rough. In the ruins."

"How do you know?"

"Your shoes. No offense, but they're filthy. I grew up poor, and we clean our shoes. It's a matter of pride. If you don't even have the means to do that, things are really bad. I'm not sure about my house, but I can find you somewhere safe to live. I can even feed you." He paused, and she sensed him holding back some excitement. "Not so much now, but things are going to get a lot better soon. It's winter. You aren't going to survive on your own." He took her hand. "Let me help you."

For a man like him, it was a lot to offer. The skin of his hands was hot, and his breaths were shallow. She wanted to keep being a part of whatever was moving him so deeply. But there was still the question of trust.

"Did anyone in your family survive?" she asked.

"Two kid sisters. Gabi is thirteen, Dorrit is seventeen. She's got a baby on the way. Hope it's a boy. Need to balance things out at home."

Right then and there, he had her. Jakob Relling was a man who took responsibility for his family. That trumped everything else he was, or might be.

"All right," she said. "I'm going to trust you. Please don't disappoint me."

"I won't, liebling. I promise. Promises are better than oaths. A promise is just between you and me. No flags or führers needed." He held up the magazine. "Should I get rid of this?"

She'd never read the article. It was something her mother had cooked up, Clara as the face of the last-ditch effort. She skimmed the pictures, landing on one of her and her father, their heads together in his office. It was from earlier in the war, before her brothers fell. Her father still had a full head of hair. A couple of years later, he had called her into his office, and his hair was so thin, the scalp glowed under the strands. As he talked, he had looked out of the open space that used to be his office window, shattered in the last bombardment. "I've been called to Berlin permanently. You will direct the Works here. All of it. The mines, the plants, logistics, contracts, labor. Can you do it?"

There was something in her father's voice she'd never heard from him before, not with her. Doubt. It was unbearable he should doubt her.

"Of course, Papa." And then she said the words that had burdened her ever since. "I'll never let you down."

She closed the magazine. "Let's burn it."

Water

Nighttime, and Willy was squatting by the river filling the ten-liter jug. He'd rolled up the arms of his coat and thrust his hands under the water and held them there as the jug bubbled and blubbered, filling up. He wanted it done fast. He wasn't afraid of the dark, it was the air. It felt as though something was coming, a hard, sharp wind that stung his ears and made his nose drip.

He dragged the jug out of the flow and then dried his hands on his coat. They felt stiff, and the wind made them worse. It hurt when he bent his fingers. It was like the drills in winter. Boys lined up outdoors, at attention. He was just a *Pimpf*, a measly little kid, back then, and the group leader had it in for him.

All together, they had to chant in the cold: *Boys of*

the Jungvolk are hard, silent, and true. Boys of the Jungvolk are comrades. The highest virtue of Jungvolk boys is honor.

Over and over again, shouting it into the freezing mist around them while his toes went numb and then the tip of his nose and then everything else. He'd had a sore throat and a cough and he couldn't shout like the others. The group leader didn't like that at all. He stopped in front of Willy and screamed at him.

"A soldier doesn't cough!"

Willy had tried to swallow the tickling in his throat, but he was shaking, his nose blocked. The longer he tried to shout, the more he lost his voice until the group leader motioned for everybody else to be quiet.

"Listen to him," he said with a smirk.

Willy chanted as best he could, but he sounded like a croaking frog. The group leader laughed, and that was the signal for the other boys to laugh too.

They were always laughing at him. Pointing at him. Willy is small. Willy is weak. Willy is a mama's boy—because he liked to go to the shops with her and carry her packages and stand in the lines alongside her. Sometimes she had things on her mind and seemed to barely know he was there. But sometimes she chatted with him and asked his opinion about what she should cook. Sometimes she smiled at him in a warm, easy way. It was worth hours at the hair salon or the grocer's for the chance that she would smile at him like that.

When he got home from the drill, she had wrapped him in blankets and sat him by the stove and fixed him tea and soup. He didn't tell her what had happened but she seemed to sense it. She kept running her fingers through his hair, the warm tips along his skull. She was there beside him, asking him what he needed, but she kept looking at her watch, and again, worriedly, at the clock on the wall. Because she had to go out. Just for a while. "Will you be all right, little one?"

She shouldn't have called him that. What did she think he was? A boy? A snot-nosed child?

He wanted her to stay. He wanted her to go, to leave him alone, because she didn't understand a thing about him. When she did go, he hated her for leaving. What was she doing that was so much more important than him?

Willy slapped himself now, a dull pressure on his jaw.

He was outside, at night, down by the river. He turned up his face, and the lightest, coldest flake landed on his cheek. The wind whistled around the cliffs and battered his coat, and the snowflakes were racing around him. He hauled the strap of the water jug over his shoulder and scrambled up the slope, back to the mine.

16

Clara ripped the magazine a page at a time, enjoying the tearing sound, taking it slowly. Jakob lit the scraps. He juggled them between his hands, lit one torn page, touched it to another, and there it went, her old life up in smoke. The fire consumed her blond hairdo and the fake smile. It crawled over her old desk and the files and reports and the papers she'd signed. All that work. The vows, the duty, the sacrifice, the anguish, the feeble attempts to help. It all came to nothing.

She carefully swept the ashes with the edge of her palm into a decorative bowl, dipped her handkerchief into her wine, and then scrubbed the last of the gray smudges off her hands. Jakob had lit another cigarette in the last flames and now he relaxed with it, an arm stretched along the sofa back. His hand was so close to her shoulder, if he wriggled his fingers, she'd feel the tickle.

"Now," he said, "you can tell me what the hell I've got myself into. Why were you all beaten up when I first saw you? Why are you living in the ruins?"

She told him about Captain Fenshaw, his mission to hunt down war criminals, his disturbing sense of poetic justice. Jakob surprised her by flicking away the butt of his cigarette in the arrogant way the Allied soldiers did. "I like this, liebling. I get to piss on a Brit? Love it."

"What about the risk?"

"Remember I said my sister's pregnant? I never did get my hands on the Tommy that did that and then ran off, the cowardly son of a bitch. Your captain is going to have to stand in for him." He was rubbing the thigh of his amputated leg. She didn't think he knew.

"Are you going to tell me why you're looking for Elisa? Jakob?"

He was still somewhere else in his head, and she touched his leg to bring him back. His attention snapped to her, and she snatched her hand away, kicking herself inside. She shouldn't have touched him there. She'd gone too far. Offended him, maybe. "I'm sorry. I shouldn't have—"

"It just means I get to touch your leg too. Fair is fair."

He held up his hand for her inspection, and then placed it snugly on her knee. "Very nice."

She put her hand on his so he wouldn't get the idea he could work his way up her thigh. "I barely know you. I only met you last week."

"That's what's so amazing about life. Think what great things are going to happen tomorrow."

"You're the last living optimist."

"I have to be. The alternative is no fun at all."

The girl in the grass skirt looked in and said his visitor was here. Jakob removed his hand from Clara's leg, and she was sorry about that. She felt a surge of anxiety and needed his support. "Who is it?" she asked.

"His name is Peter Konstantin. He was criminal police at the end of the war. He knows what happened to your friend."

"Did he already tell you?"

"Fräulein."

The way he said it, the gentle preparation for bad news, rattled her. All she wanted, all she was hoping for, was a hint as to where Elisa had gone in the last weeks of the war. That information might lead her to where she and Willy lived now, if they'd survived at all. "What did he say?"

"It's a little . . . complicated. Let him tell it, all right?"

Needing to move, she circled the sofa and faced the door as it opened. The policeman ducked inside and then paused to admire himself in the mirrored walls, turning his bulk this way and that with a look of deep satisfaction. His fur hat had shed crystals of snow as it brushed the lintel. He didn't remove the hat during the introductions and handshakes, and when he threw himself into the armchair, the fur flaps batted his shoulders like bear's paws. His nose had been broken at least once and healed off-center. She kept wanting to follow the tip to his left eye.

"You're a policeman?" she asked.

"Used to be. I got fired for doing my job in the war."

Jakob passed Konstantin a cigarette in an easy fashion, as though they'd done it before. Of course they had to have met, but their familiarity unnerved her.

"What did Herr Relling offer you to come talk to me?" she asked.

"Free drinks and a girl wearing coconuts." Konstantin said it to Jakob, and Jakob glanced up at Clara, and she knew there was something he hadn't told her. She would learn it soon enough.

"You were Gestapo?" she asked.

Konstantin held up a thick finger. "Kripo. Criminal police. We had to do the legwork for those Gestapo shits often enough."

"Weren't you the same in the end? Police is police."

"Says you. Not all of us saw it that way. You think we liked being drafted for Gestapo duties? As if we didn't have enough to do."

"Weren't you on the front in '45?"

"Had my fill of that earlier in the war." He took a savage puff from his cigarette. "What's all this? You think I'm some fellow off the street come to lie to you?"

"It crossed my mind."

"Best thing for a woman is to not think. Hurts the old brain." He tapped his hat. She cringed, hoping he was bald under there or had lice or some horrific skin disease.

She sat on the sofa and took a breath. "Elisabeth Sieland."

"Yeah. Brown curls, freckles, big blue eyes. Arrested eleventh of March 1945 after the bombardments."

"Herr Relling told you that."

"Jogged my memory, yeah, but I remember her. We always made arrests after the bombs dropped. Had a lot of plundering, mostly the eastern workers, POWs, some Germans too."

"She wasn't plundering. Her house was burning down."

"That's why I remember her. Back then I thought: Why the devil are we called out to Sophienhof in a firestorm to arrest some bird in her own house when we got people thieving all over the city? But orders are orders."

"Who ordered it?"

"No idea. We just made the arrest, all right? Went in, got her, took her for questioning."

"About what?"

Jakob shifted in his seat, watching her with a hint of anxiety. Konstantin was taking his time, torturing her as he pinched out his cigarette and tucked it into his pocket. He brushed the ash from his fingers. "Rassenschande."

"I beg your pardon?"

"I wasn't the investigator on the case, but I heard they got her for fucking a Russian."

She grasped the arm of the sofa, ready to get up, face him, tell him exactly what she thought of his lies. But her legs wouldn't do it. The shock made her breathless. She didn't believe a word he said. Did not. In the war, Elisa inspected the barracks and camps of the Russian civilians for her. Sometimes she would go at night to slip food, soap, and other small but precious goods to the workers. Not once did Clara see a hint of inappropriate behavior. Max, her eyes and ears at the Works, hadn't seen a thing, hadn't heard a whisper. He would have told her, without a doubt.

"Who accused her of such a thing? Somebody must have."

"I told you, I wasn't on the case. The usual way it went, we get a tip, or they're seen with their pants down, whatever. We pull in the happy couple. We do the interrogation, get a confession, and we pass the case over to the Gestapo. They dealt with the Russians." Konstantin crooked his neck and yanked at the invisible rope over his head.

"Did you arrest a Russian that day?"

"A cartload of them. Don't know if any of them was the one giving it to the Sieland woman." He snorted. "Good German men dying on the front, and here the women at home bent over for the lowest scum."

"There's scum everywhere, Herr Konstantin." She poured her-self another drink. She'd lost track of the number and didn't care. Who could have possibly hated Elisa enough to shop her to the police with such a lie? In the war, sleeping with an eastern worker was a blood crime. To the Nazis, it was treason. "I want to be clear about this. Your people interrogated her, not the Gestapo?"

"Things were a little chaotic by the end, sweetheart. You wouldn't believe the workload. We ignored the usual process and handed her over to them directly."

"Without talking to her?"

"She wasn't in a talking mood and neither were we. We drove her across the city and it was worse than a goddamn battlefield."

"What about her son, Willy? Where was he?"

"Wouldn't know. Never saw him."

"Nobody's seen him. A boy can't just vanish." Clara looked to Jakob for sympathy, and was surprised when he turned away. In the mirrored wall, she saw him chewing an unlit cigarette. "Theoretically," she said, trying to be factual to calm herself, "if Elisabeth Sieland was accused of a sex crime, what would have happened to her?"

"Depends," Konstantin said. "She'd have been in jail awhile till she was tried. Lucky for her the war ended a couple weeks later. She wouldn't have had to sit long."

"What if she was convicted?"

"Prison. KZ maybe."

She didn't believe it, refused to imagine Elisa in a concentration camp. "The war was ending. There wasn't time to transport her anywhere, was there?"

"If they were in a hurry, they could've put a bullet in the back of her neck."

A block of ice dropped into her stomach. Jakob touched her arm, and it woke her, a comfort, a reminder that the worst might not have happened. "Do you have proof for anything you've told me?"

"Sure, sweetheart, I carry around all the old Gestapo files," Konstantin said.

"Then how do I know you're not lying to get your free drinks and your girl in coconuts? It's an easy night's work."

"So she does think I'm lying. That's the thanks I get."

Jakob said, "Shut it, will you?" To Clara, "Liebling, if he told you what you wanted to hear, the story would sound a lot different. A lie would have explained things tidily and made you walk out of here happy. A lie would've been easier on all of us. But I thought you wanted the truth."

As if the truth was that easy to see or believe. "Is it possible Elisa was let go after questioning?"

Konstantin examined his chapped knuckles. "Not too likely with that kind of accusation, but who knows? If she was nice to them, maybe they were nice to her. It was clear she wasn't picky, eh?"

"Thank you for coming, Herr Konstantin."

He grumbled at being dismissed, as he called it, but at least he left without her having to shake his hand. At the control panel, she turned up the volume on the speaker. In the ballroom, a man was mangling "Five Minutes More" as if he'd never heard of Sinatra, the English language, or the concept of being in love. A tiny doubt nagged at the back of Clara's mind: Elisa years ago when they first met, pregnant and unmarried. She had thrown herself into an affair back then. Had it happened again? In her work, had she grown so deeply attached to one of the Russians that she had thrown caution to the wind to be with him without telling her best friend?

She sat beside Jakob and wrenched the diamond off her finger. "You held up your end of the deal."

Instead of taking the ring, he cradled her hand in his, warm, gentle, and admired the ring pinched between her index finger and thumb. "A beautiful thing. Where'd you get it?"

"It was my grandmother's." The longer he held her hand, the more it relaxed, a weight she didn't have to carry herself. The effect spread through her, the soothing support of his body. She didn't want him to let go.

"We'll think of some other payment," he said, his look so intense, she felt herself blushing.

"I'm afraid that I don't use my body as currency, Herr Relling."

"I didn't mean that."

"Come on. I'm Clara Falkenberg, the great fräulein and so on and so forth. In the war, you used to fall asleep gazing into my eyes. We've heard about my dear old friend and her supposed crime. What other payment did you have in mind?"

"You don't have to snap at me because you're angry."

The singer finished, and the band started up a schmaltzy number with far too much muted trumpet. Through the speakers, she heard the dancers return to the floor, the scuff of their shoes, the rise of conversation. She was ashamed at how easily she felt attacked and offended, and she rested her hand lightly on Jakob's sleeve.

"I'm sorry," she said. "I don't know what to think about anything anymore. I guess it's possible Elisa did this. Slept with a Russian. But why the risk? Did she think about the consequences for her son?"

"You're really worried about him. You know him well?"

She picked at her skirt. "I did before the war, but after it started, there was so little time." She'd ignored her own nephew. She hadn't known what he was to her at the time, but the guilt stung her now. "Wherever Elisa is, so is he. Maybe she was in a Gestapo jail and then the Americans freed her. She would have tracked him down, and now they're both . . . somewhere." Even to her, this explanation sounded far-fetched. She was trying hard to stay hopeful, but nothing she'd found out so far was helping her.

Jakob cupped his hand over his mouth and massaged it as if he was trying to keep something from slipping out. Then he turned the knob on the panel. Music flooded the room, so loud she had to lean close to hear what he said. "We talked about trust, remember? Can I trust you?"

She tightened her hold on his arm. He was about to tell her something important, perhaps the reason he had been looking for Elisa too. She dreaded what it might be—another crack in the ground beneath her feet. "Of course you can. What is it?"

The music suddenly cut off in a jangle of cymbals, shattering glass, pounding shoes. Someone shouted in English, "Over there, behind that curtain," and someone else—she recognized the voice of her old friend, Reynolds—"She won't be hiding under a table, you idiot." Suddenly, quite close, as if he was leaning into the speaker, Captain Fenshaw said in German, "Line up in an orderly manner, ladies and gentlemen. Orderly."

"His timing is getting better," she said. She didn't know why that pleased her so much. In a detached way, she wondered if she was drunk.

Jakob shoved her coat into her arms. "If that's your

English captain, he was called, and I bet I know who called him. Slapping Günther was a really, really bad idea. He'd sell out his grandma for a cigarette. But getting the Brits to raid his own club? That's low."

"How could he possibly know to call Fenshaw?"

"Wouldn't cost him much to buy a few informants in the underworld. I wouldn't trust a single one of the fellows around here in the dark."

"They can't hear us, can they?" She adjusted the sound on the panel. The panic was gone, and there was only the hum of whispered conversation. Now and then, she could hear snatches of bad German as soldiers demanded papers.

"Liebling, we need to go. Now."

"We've got a little time. Captain Fenshaw will tear apart the ballroom, the bars, and the ladies. I'm most likely to be in those. He thinks he knows me." She was smiling, maybe at the foolish idea that one person could ever really know another.

"Did you tell Günther you were looking for me? Because he sure as hell knows I'm here. And if they catch Konstantin, he'll tell them where we are."

That cut through the warm fog in her head. She pulled on her coat and stumbled against the furniture on her way out. Jakob checked the hallway, then led her to the door at the end. Beyond was a cold corridor lit by bare bulbs. It reminded her of the servants' hall at Falkenhorst, the space behind the ovens that warmed the family's rooms. The corridor went on and on. Jakob muttered to himself, counting the doors as they passed. On the other side of the wall, policemen and soldiers were giving orders. *Don't move. Block the doors. Papers at the ready, please.* After a while, she didn't hear them anymore, only the thump-tap of Jakob lurching on his crutch.

Through a door into a dim hallway. "No light," Jakob whispered, and pressed on to still another door. A bolt pulled back. Then complete darkness and stinging cold. The air smelled of grease and gasoline.

"Got a flashlight?" he said.

She fumbled it out of her coat. The light caught a wing, a wheel, moved across the hood of a car. Next to it, a flat wagon stood on a strip of rail track. "What is all this?"

"Transport for the racketeers who run this place. Shine that light over here, will you?"

It illuminated a box on the wall. He pawed through keys on little hooks, selected one, and led her to a small-wheeled contraption that looked like a shrunken armored vehicle. "Can you drive?"

"This thing?"

He pressed the key into her hand and hopped to the garage door. "Get her started."

"We could drive right into a police blockade."

"We're on the other side of the warehouse. If there's a blockade, hopefully it's behind us." Grunting, he bent for the door handle. "Hurry up, liebling. No headlights."

She started the engine, and it puttered like a small motorcycle. A car with that weak a motor couldn't possibly move.

Jakob hauled up the garage door. She looked out into the night with dismay. The street and buildings had vanished behind a curtain of snow.

17

The snow fell heavily onto the windshield and seeped into the cracks of the car—a tin can, Clara thought, that smelled of wet dog. The snow and their breaths condensed on the windows. The engine was better than she'd thought, though, and the tires had some traction. When she saw herself heading straight for a streetlamp, she jerked the wheel, and the car reacted, sketching a wide arc in the snow, one complete turn before straightening enough for her to regain control. Thankfully, there were no other cars on the road.

"You're doing fine, liebling." Jakob rolled down his window. Snow pelted him as he leaned out to look behind them. "Nobody is following us."

"You're sure?" She could see nothing through the

frosted rear window, but imagined Fenshaw pursuing them in his vehicle.

Jakob pulled himself back inside, closed the window, and then brushed the frozen crystals off his hair and clothes. "It's dark behind us. I doubt even the Tommies are crazy enough to drive in this weather with their headlights off. We're good, liebling. Keep her steady."

Her hands were sweating and her arms ached but at least she was thinking clearly despite all the alcohol in the club. She drove on instinct, concentrating on the tunnels of light her car cast in front of her. "I'll get us to the Falkenberg Works," she said. "We can wait out the storm in the camp I pitched in one of the abandoned factories."

"In this weather, we need four solid walls and a stove. We can go to my house."

"If Fenshaw finds out I met you, he might look for me there."

"He won't look for you at the iron works?"

"He already did and he didn't find me." She swiped her glove over the windshield. "There. That's the main station." She eased them over the Freiheit, the crossroads transformed into a wide field of snow. After a right turn, they passed snow-blown buildings and white mounds she took to be abandoned streetcars. She prayed that she and Jakob wouldn't end up in a snowdrift, trapped. Their car might get them where they needed to go, but it would make a rotten shelter from the storm.

Jakob helped her navigate, pointing out buildings he said he knew by shape alone even if they were nothing but dark lumps under the accumulating snow. He insisted it was possible to orient yourself in a storm like this by instinct. He'd done it often enough in Russia, hauling supplies air-dropped to their lines, dragging the sled through drifts up to his thighs, every bit of him bundled up except for the slits around his eyes. Even then, when he was blind from blowing snow, he made it. He made it every time.

She sensed he was telling her this to make her feel better, and it did, against all logic. "Thank you," she said. "For getting me out of that raid."

"For a minute there, I wasn't sure you wanted out."

She kept her eyes on the road, what little she could see, but felt him looking at her in the dark. "I don't know what you mean."

"I mean you and your English captain. I promised to help you, but I won't be dragged into a game. You were teasing him, right? All night. You wanted him to show up."

It shocked her to hear it said so clearly, an idea that up until that moment had been a tiny voice in her mind. "That's ridiculous."

"Then why were you the woman everybody was supposed to remember? Slapping the doorman, flashing her diamond, dancing barefoot."

"I was just having some fun."

"A peculiar kind of fun if you ask me." The angry flicks of a lighter, a brief flame on his cigarette. "I'm not playing along. I can't afford jail right now."

She concentrated on the road, aware of him smoking, disgruntled, beside her in the dark. She'd thought they were friends, or at least heading in that direction. She didn't want to lose him already. "May I call you Jakob?"

He didn't reply, and she chose to interpret that as consent. "Before the raid, you wanted to tell me something. What was it?"

"Nothing."

"It must've been important, Jakob. You said something about trust."

He blew out a stream of smoke, long and slow. "Yeah, I sure did."

They were chugging along a wide boulevard when the engine began to cough and gasp, unsettling noises she associated with ailing machines from her childhood, living things that her father had said could grow ill or fail if they were not cared for. Clara changed gear, and the whole car shuddered. Jakob thumped the fuel gauge and then sat back cursing.

A few minutes later, the engine gave out with a disconcerting suddenness. They drifted, Clara working the brakes and steering them gently into a snowdrift. She recognized nothing outside the windows; all she could see was the driving snow and the white bulk of the ruins all around. "Stay here. I'll go and see where we are."

"Fräulein, wait—"

The wind nearly blew her back into the car. She stabilized, pushed against it, angry now at the storm, one more thing in her life trying to knock her off her feet. She wasn't going to stand for it, not tonight. She trudged one slow step at a time toward the rear, her feet sinking in the snow up to her ankles, until she reached the trunk. There was no miraculous can of gas inside, but she did find a blanket and a flashlight without batteries. She wrapped the blanket around herself, tucked the flashlight down her coat, and struggled through the snow to a junction. Someone had planted a sign on a post with arrows pointing in all directions. They were in English, and directed the Allies toward the collieries and factories in the area. She recognized the names, knew them all, and cried out in triumph when she saw *Falkenberg Iron Works, 1km.*

She threw herself back into the driver's seat. "We're a kilometer from the Works. We can walk it."

"No we can't."

"I have supplies. We can make a fire, and—"

"This storm is going to get worse before it gets better. I can smell it. A kilometer is too far."

"We have to try." Their breaths were clouding. "We can't stay here. We'll freeze to death."

"And how fast do you think that's going to happen out there? Listen to me. In the war, I had to live for weeks, months, in weather like this. Worse than this. You want to know what the cold can do to you? I'm not talking about frostbite. I'm talking about your body shutting down so gently you don't even notice. You cool till your muscles and joints don't work, and you're drifting in your head. Sleeping, dreaming, gone. You're like a corpse. But you're still alive, you know? Alive, but your heart slows down. It keeps slowing until it stops. I've seen it happen. I've felt the White Death creeping up on me more than once and I am not going through that again."

She hadn't expected him to show his fear, but she understood it. For him, it wasn't a matter of walking a kilometer. His crutch was jammed the full length of the car. He had no coat, no hat, no gloves, and, of course, no left leg. She suddenly guessed how he'd lost it. Frostbite in Russia. It had eaten away at his toes and his foot and the doctors had taken his leg to be sure. This kind of weather was an old enemy that had already won as far as he was concerned. She didn't know how to motivate him without showing she knew this, that she'd guessed what lay behind his fear. She didn't want to damage his pride when that was the only thing that would get him onto his good foot and out of there.

"One kilometer," she said. "A straight shot. No hills."

"It's not about hills. It's the cold, the wind. One false step—"

"We're going to make it and I'll tell you why. This is my territory. This is my street. We are heading for my iron works, and I'm telling you right now we are going to beat this storm."

Her old arrogance could be persuasive, she knew that, and in the moment of silence after she was done, she sensed it had impressed Jakob. "What's your plan if I fall on my ass and break the only leg I still have?" he asked.

"I'll carry you, of course."

He sighed back into his seat, murmuring a prayer. After the amen, he said, "Okay. I'll try."

"No, you're going to do it. I don't have any use for a man who only tries." She carried his crutch with her around the car and opened his door. "Ready?"

It took two attempts to haul him out of the car. He was heavier than she'd expected, but the main problem was his height as he tried to unfold himself from such a small vehicle. His crutch under his arm, he needed a moment to catch his balance, to test the wind and the ground. The snow quickly whitened his clothes, a danger she hadn't thought about. Without a coat, he would be damp to the skin within minutes. She wrapped the blanket around him like a toga, tucking in the ends to keep it snug. She knew he was ready to go when he gave her hand a strong squeeze.

They struggled against the sharp chips of snow the wind blasted into their eyes, Jakob's head down, concentrating on where his crutch hit the ground. She tried to help how she could, shining her flashlight in his path, searching for ice or deeper patches of snow or debris that could trip him up in the road. They oriented themselves by what little light penetrated the storm— a streetlamp, the glow of a lantern in a window—and focused on the road and the wall of blowing snow in front of them.

"How much farther?" Jakob called suddenly, and it scared her, the winter expert asking her to orient him.

"We have to be close."

They both stepped into a rut in the road at the same time; the snow was deeper there, her foot sinking to the slick and uneven bricks that paved the road. She grasped at Jakob to regain her balance, but he was off-kilter too. She felt him keeling over, pulling her with him, and she dug in as best she could, hugging him and shifting her weight until he could use his crutch to right himself again.

"Are you all right?" She didn't know what they'd do if he fell, or hurt his ankle, or any of the hundred other things that could go wrong.

"We need to get there, liebling."

She held his hand tightly as they set off again. Finally, when she looked up, blinking the flakes from her eyes, she saw the end of the street blocked by something large and black. "It's the southern gate," she called.

Padlocked, of course. They groped along the wall until it ended at a wide space Clara didn't recognize. She dug down into the snow with her heel and hit the slick rail of a train track. They followed it to the locomotive shed, and from there, Clara led the way across the Works, her flashlight little help on the treacherous ground: bomb craters, pipes, and rubble, and all of it invisible under the snow.

Finally, they made it to the factory, and stumbled in

through the crack in the wall, shaking and crying out with relief. Snowflakes billowed through the window spaces, but there was a roof over their heads at last.

"I told you we'd make it," she said, brushing the snow from her coat.

"Nobody likes a gloater, liebling." She heard the smile in his voice, though it was too dark to see for sure.

He followed her to the office where she'd built her camp, a kind of lean-to made of a large desk and an empty bookcase tilted on its side. The window was missing here as well, but she'd done her best to nail up shutters over the space. The room was free of snow, and the only wind blew through the open doorway to the factory floor.

Trembling, they threw themselves into the shelter. She wiped the snow off him, and rubbed his arms and hands. Eventually, he swatted her away, and shuffled on his backside out of the shelter to the unhinged door leaning against the wall. She understood what he wanted, or thought she did. They lifted the door together, and as she tried to tilt it into the doorway to the factory floor, he said, "No, we need it over here. Let's close up this shelter of yours." After they crawled back inside, he pulled the door against the entrance.

It felt like being in a cave. In the dark, she groped for her flashlight and illuminated Jakob fumbling to cover them with the blankets she had been using the past week. "We'll build a fire after the storm passes," he said. "And kill that light. Save the batteries."

He cradled her back, his arm tight over her chest, and they shivered together. It had been a long time since she'd lain with a man in the dark. She had forgotten how comforting it could be.

With Jakob's breath warming the back of her head, she fell into an exhausted sleep.

The storm raged all night, and when morning broke, the winds had died but the snowfall continued, wet and heavy and endless. She did her best to fight it, shoveling the drifts that formed on the factory floor, clearing the hole in the wall over and over again. Jakob did the tasks he could without moving around too much: heating up the tins, tidying their camp, keeping the fire going. They hadn't needed to negotiate who did what. The division was natural, and a little unexpected, him so domestic, her out scavenging for anything they could add to the fire. He seemed to accept the limitations of his missing leg.

The fire was small, barely enough to heat what was left of the food she had brought from her mother's house. She choked down some dried bread while he ate lukewarm carrots in the can. He kept gazing around him, at the hole in the wall, the empty window spaces, the roof. "Reminds me of Russia, camping out in a damaged building. All that's missing is artillery, a few snipers, and it should be about twenty degrees colder."

"At least nobody is shooting at us."

"I could handle being shot at. Could shoot back until we ran out of ammo. But the cold. We couldn't do anything about that except crawl into a hole and try to survive. We had a saying: 'Patient with our fate we sit, for we got ourselves into this shit.'"

She laughed, wanting something to laugh about to keep back the cold and the creeping despair as the snow kept falling. They started trading wartime jokes, the things people told in secret, or when they were drunk, or more openly later when they were fed up.

"You know the most useless thing that was ever air-lifted into Stalingrad?" Jakob asked.

"Is this a joke?"

"One of the biggest. Guess."

"No idea."

"Condoms." He lit his cigarette in the fire. "I mean, what the hell did Berlin think we were doing out there?"

She was laughing again, this time with regret. It brought back all the futility of her own acts in the war, trying to help but doing the wrong things, or not enough. "I don't know. What were you doing out there?"

"Eating our boots. I mean, we were living like this"—he gestured at the hall—"worse than this. We were living in cellars and bunkers, holes in the ground, right? Now, if you could eat a condom . . ."

"No, you didn't—"

"Why not? You can boil up pretty much anything if you put your mind to it. Add a pinch of salt. A touch of marjoram. And let me tell you what you can do with nutmeg. A fellow in my unit dragged a supply of kernels all the way to Russia. He grated a big mound of it, mixed it with whatever we had on hand—lemon is best, but it's not like we had that, so we just choked it down with the last of our schnapps."

"Why?"

"For the high, to escape reality. At least, that's what my mate told us. It worked for him, I guess, but the rest of us just got sleepy or were sick to our stomach. And we stunk like nutmeg, but hey, it was better than how we usually smelled."

She was laughing more than was called for, given the deep tragedy of all of this. She looked at Jakob sitting on the opposite side of the fire, the flames lighting his face as he talked. He'd lost the polish he'd shown in the

South Sea Club, his hair over his forehead and his jaw prickly. He needed a wash—as did she—and the cold had given him patches of red around his nose and the edges of his eyes. His manner was easygoing, yes, he was enjoying the stories he was telling, but there was something a little distant in him. He'd be better off if he sat closer to her. It had been almost warm in their shelter when they had lain chaste and close in the dark.

"Do you believe what that magazine said about me?" she asked. "Clara Falkenberg, the Iron Fräulein?"

"I know propaganda when I see it."

"But . . . you do know I ran this place. I was director of the Works for two years."

"Keeping the chair warm for your father." He said it warily, looking at the fire. The topic was making him uncomfortable, and she felt the same, but she suddenly needed to know who he thought he was dealing with.

"You think I was following my father's orders? That he was telling me what to do all the time? Like I was his little poodle?"

He was looking at her curiously now. "Were you?"

"It would've been easier if I was. I really wish I was the type of person who pushes responsibility on to other people." She thought about that. "Maybe I am like that, a little. When it comes to my father, anyway. It's very easy to blame him for . . . most things. He was always a difficult man to understand. His motives weren't so clear to me. When it suited me, I could always say, well, he wanted me to do this or that. The things I did in the war."

A troubled look had settled onto Jakob's face, but he didn't say a word. She rushed to fill the silence, compelled to tell him about the moment the transports of human freight had begun to arrive. The train doors rolling open, releasing a stench so overpowering, her eyes had watered. Gray, shriveled faces squinting out at her from the cars. Dozens of faces, hundreds, an impossible number in so small a space, as if the people had forgotten their bodies in the occupied lands. They were corralled into lines so they could be examined and allotted work assignments in the factories and mines. She told Jakob how she had watched, stiff with horror, unable to look away, stunned by her own failure. She knew the Nazi goal to enslave the Slavic people. She had never wanted to be a part of that. But as her father had pointed out, Falkenberg needed men to fulfill the government contracts and quotas. Staying in production was not a choice, it was a matter of survival. And so she had stayed on the platform as the trains rolled in, watching what she hadn't been able to prevent.

She gestured at the factory walls. "Once my father handed the Works to me, it wasn't his sin anymore, it was mine. I let it happen."

She studied Jakob's face in the firelight. His war stories had been peppered with black humor, avoiding the difficult truths. Some of the POWs who had worked for her might have been men Jakob had captured in battle. He on one end of the system, she on the other. Did he think about that?

She didn't linger on the things she and Elisa and even Max, for a time, had tried to do to help these people. It was such a small part of the larger, grimmer picture of her past. But she told Jakob some of it. She wanted him to know she had tried.

His troubled look had deepened into what she sensed was pain at some terrible memory of his own. She wanted him to know she of all people would not judge, and scooted around the fire to sit next to him, to show him she was there to listen if he wanted to speak. But he flinched away, silent.

Clara rested against the wall, its smell of damp concrete mixing with her body odor, so strong it wafted from her scarf and coat and embarrassed her, even if Jakob was in the same condition. "I'm sorry. You don't want to talk about all this." She smiled thinly. "Nobody does. But I can't help it. I keep trying to find that one turning point in my life when I could have changed things. One moment where I could say: There, if I'd done the exact opposite, everything would have been better. I wouldn't have hurt people."

Her legs were cold and stiff, and she tucked them under her blanket. "I don't know what that moment was. I might have listened to my mother and married a nobleman and had babies all through the war. That's nothing to feel guilty about, is it? Having babies, even if the Reich would have sent them away." She sadly remembered Willy in his Jungvolk uniform, so proud of the tie and the sig rune on his sleeve. "I was nineteen when I started working for my father. Maybe that was the moment. I shouldn't have been so interested in production schedules or logistics. Should have kept up my ballet lessons instead. Or run off to Paris to be an artist. Something harmless . . ."

Jakob smiled faintly, the first sign he'd been listening to her. "We all think about this, you know, about what might have been."

"I could have emigrated when the war started. I could have gone to England and written pamphlets to be dropped over Germany. Resist the Reich. Sue for peace. Why didn't I do that? What's the sorrow and anger and guilt about abandoning your family compared to a clean conscience?"

"Nobody gives up their life so easily. We put up with a lot to try to keep it going how it always did."

"I'm not talking about what I put up with. I'm talking about what I did. Or didn't do." She looked up at the new snow drifting from the windows. "I could stand up and tell everyone how I resisted the regime; I could make it sound like I was some kind of a hero. What risks I took. How courageous I was. I might even fool some people. But I'd know. I'd know how utterly inadequate I was."

"Come on, liebling. You tried. That's more than most of us can say. It's all right to acknowledge that. You're not a devil just because you could've done more."

She wasn't so sure. It was hard to know how to weigh the contradictions inside her. She reached for his hand and he let her take it. "You said yourself, the Collapse is the chance for us to be someone new." She thought of Blum and her life in Hamelin. "You have no idea how long I've wanted that."

He smiled, wide, spontaneous, warm. And something kindled inside her, deep, where the fire couldn't reach.

Air

Finally.

Willy poked his fist through the hole he had made in the snow. He wiggled his arm around until the hole was the size of a ship's porthole. He put his eye to the hole and his eye watered and the water turned to ice. It felt as though somebody was piercing needles into his eyeball. His head was aching, his hands were cold—the mine had everything but gloves, imagine that—but he had to ventilate. With a shovel, he made the hole bigger and the light became sharper and whiter and brighter until it cut into the tunnel. The wind swept in—at last! The tunnel was windy again. This was a good thing, a very good thing, and he sucked in breaths of fresh air. But the odd, cloudy feeling in his head didn't go away.

He jabbed the shovel at the snow again and pushed it outward, and when the hole was the right size, he climbed out of the mine. His lungs swelled up. He dropped the shovel and grasped his knees. Every breath hurt, and the light, the hot light in his head . . .

And there was snow. Snow all the way down the slope and over the marsh and onto the river over the still, flat surface of the river, and out to the opposite bank and over the hills way over there. Snow on the tall grasses and hanging from the trees, on the cliffs, clumped in the rock and on the clean, flat ground at his feet. It shone like a mirror, all that snow.

If he went home, he could build a snow fort in the garden. If he went home, he could make a tiny ball of snow and melt it in Gertrud's bowl. He could drink something warm at the window and look at the snowy world, if he went home.

But he couldn't go. Not after what he'd done.

He scrambled back into the mine, the soothing dark of the mine, and when his eyes adjusted, he went to Gertrud who was waiting for him on the footlocker. He was shaking with cold and didn't lift her up because he didn't want her to freeze in his palm. He knelt and let her flutter onto his shoulder and then he went to the weather board, the slate and chalk the miners left behind. He was going to note the weather conditions and air quality. This was useful information.

He began to note the date: *March 11.*

He wiped it out, wrote: *March 12.*

Which was it? His aching brain didn't know. He couldn't remember. March? It couldn't be March. Not with all that snow. There could be some snow in March sometimes, but that much? What was it Corporal Relling had said?

Willy rubbed out March and wrote: *December.*

He sat back. What day in December? He tried to remember how many days it had been since Jakob Relling was there. He was tingling, sweating, hot now but still cold. If Jakob Relling told the truth, it was the middle of December. Maybe.

And the year?

The tingles were jolts now, thunderbolts straight through his temples. Corporal Relling had said it was 1946.

Willy couldn't believe it was true. He hadn't been down here that long.

Had he?

18

On their third day at the Works, Jakob got it into his head that he would make himself ski poles. Clara supposed he was inspired by her stories of Winterberg and the Swiss Alps, though as Jakob pointed out, ski trips were not the kind of thing people like him went on. But she had, and for lack of any other entertainment, she and Jakob had been talking about everything they could think of that might amuse the other. If most of her stories were about her privileged upbringing and his about scrounging in the shadow of a pit tower, then so be it. That was who they had been. His stories interested her, and hers seemed to interest him, and if that time she nearly burned down the ski lodge inspired Jakob to make his poles, she was glad. She was even more grateful for the break from the serious things they had talked about yesterday. She felt lighter, as if some of what had been weighing her down had floated away.

He worked on the factory floor, a wonderland since the storm had stopped and the temperatures plummeted even further. Every surface shimmered with ice and snow. Frost swirled on the walls, and when Jakob exhaled, his breaths glistened and curled away. Two broom handles he'd scavenged lay beside him next to several foraged nails. He was musing out loud about the best way to attach them when she remembered seeing a hand borer somewhere. When she gave the rusted thing to Jakob, he smiled up at her—his lips chapped, his face pale, and his eyes deeply tired—and whatever had been cracking up in her cracked some more. She was letting new things in.

She wanted to help him, knowing how hard it was going to be for him to make it back to his house in the frozen wastes the whole city had become. As he got to work boring a hole in the end of a broomstick, she kicked aside the snow on the factory floor until she found an iron rail where one of the machines used to be. It took her ages to prize it up, and then she tried to fashion a kind of ski using wicker from a battered office chair.

"Best I can do," Jakob said when the poles were finished. "What you got there?"

"I'm not sure." She had been trying to weave the wicker through holes in the iron rail. "It looks like a cross between a snowshoe and a ski."

He looked doubtful. "Let's try it out."

At the edge of the factory floor, she attached the ski to his shoe with extra wire. He wavered, ski poles stuck in the snow for balance. As he practiced, he fell over several times, but soon he was pulling himself over the snow more or less securely.

"I'll need to oil that ski before I go anywhere, Clara."

"I looked but couldn't find any machine or lamp oil. We don't have much left to eat either, so I think I'll go out and see what I can find on the markets. No one will recognize me if I'm wrapped up against the cold."

"Nobody'll be out in this weather. And anyway, I'm not letting you go alone."

She didn't argue with him. She acknowledged his expertise when it came to the tricks used to survive in Russia. He was serious about them, even waking her overnight several times so that she would move her hands and legs, get her blood pumping. He didn't want her to lose any fingers or toes.

She supposed that was why he watched her as he did. He hardly allowed her out of his sight, studying her as she walked to see if she limped, or if she'd gone too stiff, showing signs of anything worrisome. He made her swear to tell him about any pains or numbness that didn't go away once she warmed up by the fire or curled up at night with him.

Nights were her favorite times when they settled in their shelter to sleep or to talk if they couldn't sleep. He'd said he would help her look for Elisa, but when she lay in the dark on the fourth night making plans about where they might look, and whether the things the policeman had told them were true and what they could mean, Jakob didn't respond.

"What is it?" she asked.

"What?"

"Is something on your mind? It feels like I've been talking to myself the past half hour."

His arm moved over her shoulder—he was careful to avoid any intimate parts of her—and he rested his hand on the crook of her neck between her scarf and her skin. She didn't move. She didn't want to scare him away.

He didn't say anything for a while, his palm on her neck, not caressing it, just there.

"Are you worried about your sisters?" she asked to get him to say something.

"Always. I was like that on the front too. All that flag and country stuff. What good is it? I wanted my family to live and to hell with everybody else."

"Everybody? Even girls?"

"Had my share till my leg. I slowed down after that. I needed to get myself together. Some fellows, they have a girl for that. But when you lost so much, you got to rely on yourself, you know, build yourself back up."

It was more than he'd ever said about his leg, and she was curious about the emotional wound, what happened inside him when he realized what he'd lost. "I imagine it's like having a core inside of you made of glass, and it begins to splinter and crack. You don't know who or what you are anymore. At least, it feels like that to me."

After a long pause, he said, "It wasn't that gentle or gradual. One day I woke up and knew and it blew me to bits. Honest, if it wasn't for my mama and sisters, I would've blown my brains out. A cripple? Me? No way in heaven or hell. I was going to be something. Run a big department store. Play midfield for Rot-Weiss Essen. I was going to be a credit to my family."

"You are."

"I'm just getting by. If I can see Gabi and Dorrit fed, that is a good day. It isn't much in the world, but it's everything too. I have to see they get through. It's how I finally got off my backside and stopped feeling sorry for myself. Got tired of that. Being angry about stuff I can't change."

"You're still angry?"

His fingers moved, a tender touch that made her shiver. "This one night in Russia," he said, "we were sleeping in one of those log cabins they have, you know, in the villages. All of us packed into this one room. The family that lived there was just women and kids. They crawled up into a kind of loft above us to sleep. I don't know how long we'd been on the move. We were a motorized unit, but try getting armored cars and trucks through that mud. I'd never been that exhausted in my life. I was glad of a roof even if I had to share it with ten other fellows. All I wanted to do was sleep."

He shifted against her a little, and she felt how fast he was breathing. "There were children up in the loft, like I said. I don't know how many. They kept sniffling and whining. I didn't understand what they were saying, but kids—you know? Hungry, cold, scared. Scared of us." His voice tightened, as if he was struggling to get the words out. "We told them to be quiet, we needed to sleep. But the kids, they started crying. 'Shut up,' we said. We could hear the women trying to shush them, but they were children. They cried. And then"—he took a stuttering breath—"we said to hell with it, pulled out our pistols, and shot at the loft. It was quiet the rest of the night."

Clara's throat felt too thick to say anything. She pulled his arm closer around her. He had listened to her talk. She would listen to him.

"I did that," he said. "I thought I'd never, ever hurt a child, and I did that. Sometimes I think . . . I think it was worth losing my leg to be pulled off the front. I couldn't do something like that again." He tugged at the blanket, and she imagined him wiping his eyes. "I never told anybody that before. I'm the nice guy, right?"

"I'm the last person to judge you, Jakob."

He rested his cheek on her head. She thought he'd had enough of talking, but then he sighed into her hair. "Don't be angry with me, Clara."

She shifted in his arms. "At least you realize what you did. You regret it, and—"

"I don't mean that."

She waited for him to say more, then wriggled out of his arms and switched on the flashlight. When she blinked the sparks out of her eyes, she saw how deep the grooves in his forehead had become.

"What's happened?" she asked.

"I should've told you earlier but I wasn't sure about you after the club. You know. Trust."

She sat up on her elbow, forcing her voice to stay calm. "You can trust me."

He gave her a look full of hope and doubt. "You've been searching for your friend, and I've been keeping back a fact or two that might have helped you."

"What fact?"

"It's not so easy to explain. I don't know where to start."

He'd worried she would be angry with him and, in a flash, she was. "Were you Elisa's lover? Is that what you're trying to tell me? Is that why you're looking for her?"

"No—"

"You miss her? She owes you money?"

"No. Hey, Clara—" He caught her arms and pulled her back onto the blanket, and he swore on Jesus, Maria, Joseph, and all the saints that he had never met Elisabeth Sieland in his life.

She stopped struggling, prepared to hear him out, but only just. "Then why are you looking for her? Why would I be angry at you?"

"Listen till the end, all right? You can scratch my eyes out after I'm done." He began to talk. At first about meat from a pig at a black-market slaughter, a deal he'd made with a farmer in the southern district of Heisingen. Then a mugging on the hills overlooking the Ruhr.

She had no idea where he was going with this, why it should upset her. She stayed tense under his hands.

He talked about seeking shelter in an abandoned coal mine, and as he described in detail the food he'd found there, she began to think he was making it all up.

"Jakob, this is a dream, a bedtime story for hungry children."

"It's true. Every bit of it. If I could give you a quarter of what's down there, you'd be fat in a year."

"I don't believe a word of it. But we've only got two tins of beans left, so let's go to this magical coal mine and stuff ourselves until Christmas."

"Sounds like a good plan to me." He fell quiet, his face filled with apprehension. "Willy is down there."

"Who?"

"Willy. Your friend's boy."

Snow shifted on the factory roof, sliding from the eaves and pounding the ground outside. When the echo died, she said, "What on earth are you talking about?"

"Willy Sieland, born on the twenty-seventh of September 1931. I saw his military identity card, or one he took from somebody else and filled out himself. Had his address on it. That's how I knew his mother's name and where they lived in Sophienhof. That's why I was trying to find your Elisa. She's supposed to convince him to leave the mine."

He was going too fast. She needed to know what this Willy looked like, and Jakob's description was perfect, right down to the freckles and the bulging blue eyes. And he had his birth date. Who else could it be?

"Willy?"

"That's what I've been trying to tell you. He won't come out of the mine. Got it into his head the war is still on. He's guarding the place—"

"Wait." She sat up, close to him in their shelter, and grasped the ends of the tie he'd wrapped around his neck as a kind of scarf. "You know where he is. You knew I was looking for his mother and him too and you didn't tell me?"

"I couldn't."

"Why not?"

"Trust, Clara. There's a fortune down in that mine. Enough food to feed an army. Look at us. In a few days we won't be good for anything if we don't eat. Food is life."

"This isn't about the food. It's about a teenage boy living . . . is that what you mean? Living in an abandoned coal mine? And you just left him there?"

"Your friend's precious boy is armed. He's not right in the head." Jakob told her how Willy talked, wolfish and crazed, delusional, the conflict still raging in his mind, the Reich preparing for the last great victory.

"He shot at me. Sentenced me to death because I told him we'd lost the war. I told him the truth and he answered with a bullet."

It was impossible. Willy had such a gentle nature: the other boys heckled him and punished him because he was small and shy and clumsy. When doing marching drills he would turn the wrong way. "I can't believe this. It's really him? Willy Sieland?"

"It's really him."

"Is Elisa down there too?"

"I don't know. I didn't see her."

"So he's alone?"

"He has a bird. A canary."

"Gertrud." Clara's eyes grew moist. On his birthday, when Willy had removed the cover from Gertrud's cage and saw her for the first time, Clara had known she'd given him something he would never willingly be parted from. Whatever the Hitler Youth had been teaching him, whatever the war had forced upon him, dissolved from his posture and his face. He was a boy again, looking in wonder at a small, vulnerable creature, something he could love and protect. That boy did not long for the war, talk of treason, or shoot at men. It was impossible.

She pushed Jakob onto his back. "You should have told me. How could you know all this time and not tell me?" She was balancing on his chest, her hands knotted in his hair. She hoped she was hurting him.

"I'm sorry, Clara. I wanted to, but I had to keep the mine secret. It could mean everything to my family. Survival."

"And Willy doesn't matter?"

"He wouldn't listen to me. What was I supposed to do? Carry him out of there?"

"You should have told me before."

"Well, I'm telling you now. And I'm going to take you down there. First thing tomorrow, no matter how cold it is."

She heard the edge of the same fear he'd had after they'd left the club in the storm. Her anger drained away, replaced by the first prickles of happiness. Willy was alive. Her nephew, Friedrich's son, was alive and she would see him tomorrow.

Jakob shut off the flashlight and tentatively wrapped his arm around her. "It's going to be all right. You'll see."

Clara lay awake most of the night, trying to make sense of it. Who could have put Willy in an abandoned mine—and why? How could he still be down there after all this time? When she finally did sleep, it was with an image of him from long ago, tenderly cradling the bird in his hands for the first time, its tiny heart beating in his palm.

19

They rested on the remains of a wooden fence over-grown with snowy brambles. She was afraid it wouldn't take Jakob's weight, and the wood creaked when he eased himself down with a groan she knew she wasn't supposed to hear. The snow had stopped for good, but it lay with a slick crust on the ground. It had taken most of the day to cross the city; the long route along the river to avoid some of the steeper hills and cliffs was now at their back. Jakob had preferred the security of his crutch along with the support of one ski pole, but she'd had to hold on to him to keep him from losing his footing on the hills. His nose ran and his face was chapped but he'd cracked jokes all the way, things that were only funny in the war, and maybe not even then. She guessed his chatter was supposed to distract her from thinking about what she'd find in Willy's mine.

They were everywhere, the mines. She had seen the mouths of some, filled in or overgrown. She had seen the land dented where some tunnels must have collapsed. That worried her, though Jakob had said Willy's mine was reinforced. She'd never been inside one like Friedrich had—down underground—but knew enough to know these were old, these black mouths in the hills and cliffs. There were no pit towers, just rusted rail tracks showing here and there through the snow.

"You got your breath back?" Jakob asked. They had rested at least half a dozen times on the trek south, and he always made it seem as though it was her needing the break more than he did.

"Are we almost there?"

"So close that if Willy was outside and you shouted his name, he'd hear you. But let's keep this quiet." He began to lay down the rules of entering an abandoned mine, the dangers piling one on top of the other in her imagination. The dark like no dark she'd ever known. The unreliable ground that could give way at any moment. The uniformity of the tunnels that fooled you into thinking you knew where you were. Most of all, the "weather." She knew how important this was, and what miners meant by it, from her time working at a Falkenberg shaft. The air quality, the gases, the signs that the weather was good or bad. No fire, Jakob told her. No wandering off without him. Did her light still work?

She tested her flashlight, shining it in his face, and only then did he gather his crutch and ski pole and lead her the rest of the way to Willy's mine.

"Good boy," Jakob said, poking his pole at the snow packed into an orderly drift outside the entrance. "He ventilated."

At the cliff face, she felt a sensation of weight, of what was straining down on the tunnels Willy lived in. She still couldn't believe he was in that crack in the earth, hidden by folds of rock. Nobody could live there. "You're sure this is the right place?"

"He's here. Glück auf, Clara. For luck."

"Glück auf."

Also for luck, she assumed—miners needed lots of it—he gave her a peck on the cheek. She barely felt it on her skin, but the kiss set off tiny explosions in her chest.

Since Clara had the light, she went in first. Timbered walls, damp but somehow tidy. She'd expected cobwebs, grime, insects, and rodents bedded down for the winter, but the timbers looked scrubbed clean. An electrical cord spanned the wall near the ceiling. She stood upright and felt a little more space over her head. She hadn't expected that.

"The older tunnels have lower clearance," Jakob said.

"Which way?"

"To the dead end, then take a right. That's the reinforced side."

Deeper in the tunnel, the natural light failed completely, and she knew why Jakob had been so anxious about her flashlight. She held it high so he would see the light too. The air seemed thick with particles in the beam.

"Is that normal?" she asked.

"We're still getting fresh air from outside. Keep going. To the right."

Since he'd warned her about the ground she took careful steps even here, when she saw the concrete all around. The corridor was wide enough for Jakob to hop beside her as he told her what was behind each door. Coffee, sugar, chocolate. She thought she heard sounds from beyond the light, scratching noises that sent a chill through her. "Rats?"

"Probably. There's bread in there."

She couldn't stand the thought of Willy with the rats. She headed toward the sound, turned a corner, entered the first room she came to. Paper packages were stacked on top of a row of crates, a small path cutting between them. Something crunched under her shoe. Her flashlight found white grains, and she dropped to her knees, peeled off her glove, and poked a hole in one of the packets. She licked the grains off her fingers. Sugar. Packets and packets of sugar. She had never tasted anything so good.

"Where's that bread?" she asked as she cupped her hand under Jakob's mouth. He lapped the sugar out of her palm like a puppy.

She cried out in delight at the boxes of dark bread stacked wall-to-wall. She tore open the nearest one, pulled out a fat can, dug in the box for an opener. Her hands were too numb and sticky to use it. She threw everything down in frustration and looked in the next room. Packets of dried bread. She tore one open with her teeth and ate the whole thing. The edge taken off her hunger, she went back into the corridor. Jakob stood in tense silence.

"Where's Willy?" she asked.

"His camp is in a short tunnel not far from here." His voice sounded strange.

"What's wrong?"

"I don't know. Just feels . . . quiet. It was quiet before, but this is different."

She rubbed her throat. He had said bad air hit quickly and if it was really bad, the earliest symptoms meant it was too late. Dizziness, queasy stomach, trouble breathing. She had them all. She couldn't decide if it was bad weather or fear or both. She picked up a chunk of coal, and as Jakob led her down the corridors, she numbered and labeled the doors and marked the turns they took in the passage. She was putting her stamp on this place, establishing some kind of order she could understand.

He stopped at a blanket hanging from the ceiling and spoke in a whisper. "Take it easy. Let's not startle him. He can be a little jumpy."

She eased the curtain aside. "Willy? Anyone home? It's your mother's old friend Clara, remember me?"

Darkness, a rasping breath. The first thing her light hit was the row of tin cups sitting on a crate. Moving the beam slightly higher, she found a map she recognized instantly. She had pored over an identical one in the war, the Reich a nightmare of logistics, crisscrossed in her mind with rail lines stretching east and then farther east into occupied territory where the gauges were different. Closer to the map, she saw Willy's tiny notes and arrows: troop movements.

"Willy?"

From her left, a soft cheep.

"Gertrud!" Carefully, she touched the canary's head. Since the episode with the falcon, she had always been a little nervous around birds.

"Bring that light over here, liebling."

On the way, her foot grazed something large on the ground—her flashlight found a footlocker—and then she saw the bed. Her beam moved over the crumpled blankets and stopped at the leather sheen of a boot. She peeled the blanket aside and saw matted blond hair, then the whole boy balled up like a baby.

"Willy . . ." She dropped to her knees and touched his forehead. Damp, warm. He was only sleeping, curled into himself, conserving heat. He was alive, and he was here; he was really here.

She didn't like the sour odor in the air: sweat and urine. She patted the bed—dry—and then her leg brushed a bucket. It sloshed a little, the smell pungent. "He's been ill." She knew nothing about nursing, and regretted she hadn't picked up any experience in the war. "Is there water?"

Suddenly, there was light. Jakob hung a lantern on a wall hook and then hopped to an army jug where he tapped water into a cup. She tried it—stale, but it would do—before dribbling some onto Willy's lips. His brow wrinkled, and he puckered his mouth, a glimpse of the little boy he had once been.

"Hello, Willy." She dampened the end of his blanket and rubbed his cheek firmly, as she had seen Elisa do when he was younger.

He surfaced, his limbs moving slowly on the bed.

Weakly, he said, "Stop."

"So you are awake."

His eyes opened. Wide, wider. They were pale and unfocused.

"You're not dreaming," she said. "It's me. Clara. Clara Falkenberg."

A slow blink, his tongue wetting his lips, then each word forced out of his mouth. "No, you're not. She's blond."

"I dyed my hair all those years. Shocking, I know. How are you feeling?"

He touched his forehead and glanced at his fingers as if they belonged to someone else. Then: "You." He looked past her at Jakob, who was stroking Gertrud's back.

"Yes, me. Good to see you alive, kid. Bet you didn't expect me back, eh? Good thing I came. Not nice being sick when there's nobody around to care for you. We all got to watch ourselves this winter."

Willy struggled onto his elbow. "It snowed. I have to ventilate. Clear the air shafts—"

Gently, Clara put the water cup to his lips again.

"You cleared the entrance to the mine already. The air is fine. Look at Gertrud."

As if she had heard her name, Gertrud chirped. Willy immediately relaxed and closed his eyes. When she was sure he had gone back to sleep, Clara left his bed and threw her arms around Jakob. "I owe you so much. You have no idea."

He had stumbled against the wall and clutched her to keep his balance. "I like you being in my debt. Let's start with . . ." He pretended to think about it. ". . . a coat. Willy had one the first time I was here. Army, but I can't be picky. I could sure do with one if you could find it."

While he rested on a stool and rubbed his back, Clara searched gladly. The footlocker first, setting aside the blanket, folded neatly, the gas mask with its regulation pamphlet, the military identity card Jakob had mentioned, Elisa's name and address there as he'd said. The ledger was next. She set it on the crate and leafed through, Jakob pointing out the inventory, the list of meals, his calculation about just how long Willy had been using the supplies. There were no dates, but the sheer number of meals convinced her Jakob told the truth.

"God," she said. "Almost two years. Who ordered him down here? What demented Hitler Youth leader? I'll skin him alive."

"Willy acted like he was waiting for somebody. He said he had to be relieved of duty."

She slammed shut the ledger, and the corner of a photograph slid out from between the pages: Elisa, Willy, and Reinhard at Sophienhof. She took the picture to the lantern, tried to see something in Elisa's face. She didn't know what. Happiness. Misery. A sign of the secrets she had kept so deep inside not even Clara had seen them.

"Elisa isn't here." Clara replaced the photograph and put Willy's things back in the footlocker. "Maybe Willy has some idea where she is."

"He came down here when she was arrested. The same day."

That fact unsettled her. It raised the possibility that Elisa had told him to come here, but Clara couldn't imagine her wanting her son to live underground like this even given the alternatives. She concentrated on her search for Willy's coat, tearing through crates filled mostly with tins and cutlery. Everything was stacked and dusted. The tins, she noticed, were in alphabetical order. She approved and would have done something similar in his situation.

She looked under Willy's bed and spotted a bundle of field-gray wool. Tugging it out, the coat seemed heavier than it should. Unfolding it, she found something wrapped up inside.

"Jakob, look." The wooden leg gleamed, polished, and so precious it was something only Jakob should touch now.

"Holy Mother of God." He ran his fingers down the wood and tugged gently at the straps. "The kid fixed it."

He began to wriggle out of his trousers, and she felt an odd sense of unreality when she saw his bandaged leg stop at the knee. Embarrassed, she turned her back, and he said, "Yeah, it's still strange to me too. I don't blame you for looking away." The comment offended her. She wasn't so delicate as to recoil at what the war had done to him. But she caught only a glimpse of Jakob's pale thigh and the brownish scars before he re-wrapped the bandage quickly up his leg, bending over as he did so, blocking her view. Then he pulled on the prosthesis and busied himself with the straps. When he was finished and dressed, he held out his hands to her. She hauled him onto his two feet.

"My shoes don't match," he said. One slow step at a time, he hobbled to the opposite wall.

"Does it hurt?" she asked.

"Chafes. I've lost weight. But it'll do." Once Jakob had found his sea legs, as he called them, he began to hum a tune she didn't know, held out his hand to her and they did a lurching dance in the corridor to a waltz beat—one-two-three, one-two-three. She was proud of Willy. Proud he'd done this kindness for a good man.

For the rest of the day and into the next, she cared for Willy as best she could, never leaving his side except when Jakob took over the more intimate tasks involving what he called man stuff. Willy was fifteen and she didn't want to embarrass him. She waited outside the curtain, hearing Jakob say, "Come on, kid, you'll feel better after a good piss." Listening to them reminded her painfully of her brothers.

Once he was on his feet again, his head brushing the ceiling, Willy was as cautious and reserved with her as he used to be. Hat in hand, little bows of respect. Yes, fräulein. No, fräulein. I'll get that for you, fräulein. Not servile exactly, but the well-mannered boy Elisa had raised. Now Clara noticed it for what it was: a reflection of the distance between them. It was as if Willy still saw her as some kind of a princess up in her tower at the Works. She didn't want that. He was her nephew. By the way he treated her, it was clear he had no idea.

"Willy, I think you're well enough to leave now," she said on her second morning in the mine.

"I won't desert my post."

"You're not deserting. The war is over, remember?

Jakob—Herr Relling—explained it to you already. I've explained it. We can walk out of here right now."

His respectful demeanor cracked a little. "You never neglected your duty, did you, fräulein?"

"Nobody ever asked me to live in a coal mine."

"You lived at the Works."

"That was different."

"How? You slept in the bunker under headquarters, didn't you?"

Now he was annoying her. She wished Jakob was there to support her, to help cajole Willy into action, but he was somewhere in the mine stuffing an army bag full of goods to take home to his sisters. "The war is over, Willy. There is nothing keeping you down here. No one is going to punish you for neglecting your duty. It's over."

He shook his head as if she was one of those poor people who had lost their minds. At his crate table, he dumped out the screws and nails from several cups and began to sort them. She recognized the boy who used to play quietly alone sorting blades of grass by length. In a few moments, he'd be far away, unable to hear any more from her.

She clapped her hands close to his ear as she had seen Elisa do sometimes when he was little. "I've been looking for your mother. Do you have any idea where she is?"

He dropped a screw, bent to pick it up. He blew off the dust, set it on the table.

"She was arrested in the war and nobody's seen her since," Clara said. "I know you came down here at the same time they took her away. Did she tell you to come here?"

He continued to sort, dropping the nails and screws into their cups. She had lost him for now. She would wait him out, wear him down with patience. She busied herself making his bed, folding the blanket with precise creases. After a while, he began to talk.

"Have you ever felt like things are planned for you, fräulein?" Willy was on round two of his sorting now, the nails and screws poured out of their cups again. "Like the whole universe or a god or something planned everything before you were born? That it was all decided for you? And that you don't have a say in any of it?"

This was a delicate moment. What she said next might tip him back into silence or allow him to open up to her. She picked up the folded blanket, shook it out gently, and began to fold it again. Maybe her movements soothed him as much as they did her.

"It seems like a lot is planned for us, yes." Thinking of her father, she added, "But not by gods."

He held a screw up to the light and scraped it with his

fingernail. "I happened to be on my bicycle at a certain time of night, checking the blackout. I was supposed to pass by her window at the warehouse at the docks, that little office she used when there were shipments coming in on the canal. Except there weren't any. I knew that. You didn't have any more ships, fräulein. In fact, Mama had said she was working at headquarters that night. So what was a light doing on in an empty warehouse when there was no work to do?"

She hadn't heard Willy say so many words at once . . . ever. "I'm not exactly following. What night do you mean?"

"The night I saw them. In January." Smiling strangely, he dropped another nail onto the pile.

January 1945. It had to be. She wiped her clammy hands on the blanket and began again, edge to edge, fold, crease. "Who did you see?"

"The warehouse at the docks was this big empty space. Sound traveled. Echoed loudly. I followed it all the way down the empty hallway to the door. Maybe she was only whimpering a little, but it really carried. I heard something creaking, someone breathing. Everybody has lungs and throats and we're all basically the same, so how did I know that it was her in there? I knew it was. I knew it here." He tapped a screw at his chest.

She sat listening, without moving.

"I opened the office door," he said. "Wide open. They didn't even notice. He was sitting in the chair and she was on his lap. He had his hands all over her. It was disgusting." Now he was scratching the crate table with a nail, little scratches over and over. "Disgusting."

"They?" Her throat was clogged. Dust. Words. "Your mother. And who else?"

He kept scratching, scratching.

"Willy, who was she with? Someone you'd seen before at the Works? A Russian?" She was ready to hear about Elisa's Russian lover and yet she still couldn't actually believe it.

Willy was looking at her sideways, cautious. "He was old. Barely any hair left. My father was away fighting and Mama was at home betraying him with an old man."

Old? It wasn't possible. Clara hadn't employed old men, not the Russians anyway—she had needed strong backs. Willy had to be mistaken.

"What was he wearing? Did he have the badge on his shirt, the one for eastern workers, or POWs? Do you remember?"

Willy was gouging the wooden crate with the nail. "A tie."

"What?"

"He wore a tie. A suit and tie."

Impossible. An old man in a suit and tie was not possible. She got up and grasped the table, rattling the cups, his orderly sorting ruined. "Who was it?"

Willy started, and she fought to calm her voice. "Willy, please tell me who the man was."

He shook his head. The knot of panic in her grew.

"I think you knew him. Why won't you tell me?"

He wouldn't look at her, focusing instead on his screws and his nails as they rolled out of their cups and onto the table. She thought of late January '45, the last time she saw her father. He was in his fifties and still a handsome man even if his skin sagged and the lines around his eyes and mouth were deeper than they had once been. He'd lost his secret smile. He didn't smile at all in the three days he was in Essen for meetings. He sat like an immovable pillar and spoke little, giving instructions in a weary tone. Before he left for Berlin, he didn't touch her, no hug or kiss on the cheek. Not even a handshake. He had unmoored himself from the world, and from her.

"Was it my father, Willy? Was it Theodor Falkenberg?"

Abruptly, Willy fetched his steel helmet from the shelf. "The door," he said. "When I left the warehouse, I didn't shut the door. What do you suppose they thought after they were done? Did they think they had left it open? Or it was a draft? A spy?"

Her father. And Elisa. She had worked for the family for fifteen years, she had been Clara's friend, and not once did her father so much as mention her unless Clara had done so first. In the rare times when they had been in the same room—an assembly of headquarters staff, for instance—he had never spoken to Elisa or even looked at her. Clara had always had the impression he was embarrassed about their friendship, yet tolerated it, knowing the good it did her. During the war, he and Elisa would not have had the time to develop a relationship. She had been in Essen; he had worked mostly in Berlin. And Elisa? She wouldn't have slept with her best friend's father. That was out of the question.

"Willy, it couldn't have been my father. It was a Russian after all, wasn't it? It shocked you; maybe you were ashamed. They taught you so many terrible things in the Hitler Youth. But, Willy, you've got to tell me the truth about this."

He was rubbing the helmet, polishing it with the palm of his hand. In a small voice, he said, "I did."

In her coat pocket, Clara grasped the soft roll of Elisa's silk. The wedding dress, the white square hidden far back on a shelf in the workshop, a place her mother would never go. Only Father.

But Friedrich too. Maybe all of this was a mistake;

it was Friedrich whom Elisa had loved, who got her pregnant, who stayed away from her all of those years, keeping the secret as she did, while she married another and claimed legitimacy for Willy. Friedrich. Not her father.

But the chain of reason collapsed in the face of what Willy had seen. If she had really loved Friedrich, Elisa would never have had an affair with his father. Even at the end of the war, in the madness and chaos—the Americans coming, the Russians coming—she wouldn't have done that.

And so. It was her father all along. All those years ago when Elisa was practically still a girl . . .

Clara groped along the timber walls to Willy's bed and sat heavily. She remembered Elisa at the café over the river when they had first met, how vulnerable and lonely she had been. Had he taken advantage of her? It was despicable. It was filthy. He was married with four children and he was old enough to be Elisa's father. How could he have put his hands on a teenage girl, get her pregnant, and then deny the child? But of course he could. Her dear, beloved papa. Of course he could have done this. He was morally bankrupt, through and through.

Willy cradled his helmet in his arms, watching Clara with wide and wary eyes. He had the same powder-blond hair as her father and brothers in photographs of them at the same age. His eyes were his mother's, but Clara saw something familiar when he turned away from her gaze, something in his profile that reminded her so much of her father, it cut her in two.

"Oh, Willy. Willy, I'm so sorry. I didn't know."

Still hugging the helmet, he backed away from her to the map. He looked frightened, confused. He must have no idea what she was talking about, what he'd truly seen in the warehouse that night. If Elisa had never given him so much as a clue to his parentage, Willy could not have guessed who his real father was. She must have kept the secret all his life.

"We need to find your mother, Willy. She has a lot of explaining to do to the both of us. Do you have any idea where she could be?"

"At home."

"She's not there."

"She has to be." He fetched a rag and began to polish his helmet properly, scrubbing furiously. "They said they'd take her home when they were done."

She knelt beside him in the dirt. It was the only way to see his face and, besides, her knees had turned to water. "Who's they?"

"She couldn't get away with it. Betraying my father like that. He made the ultimate sacrifice for the Reich.

After he died, she didn't even try to act like she was sad. She was glad he was gone. But she had no right to be glad."

His father. He was talking about Reinhard Sieland. Willy saw his mother and Theodor Falkenberg together in late January. They got word that Reinhard had fallen just a few weeks later, and Elisa had been torn with relief—and guilt?—at the funeral tea. The Allies were sweeping toward them. The war was in its last months, the last bloody crescendo. They were all going mad one way or another. And Willy, nursing his confusion and anger at what he had seen at the Works, and now racked with grief . . .

"Willy, what did you do?"

"I'm a soldier like my father. I had to do my duty. I had to, fräulein."

Clara stood abruptly. "What did you do?"

"You saw her at the funeral. She deserved it. She shamed my father. She shamed me. She deserved to . . . to be punished. I had to tell them what she did." He seemed barely able to summon the next words, but once he succeeded, they tumbled out. "They listened to me. The Gestapo. They didn't laugh at me or send me away. They believed me. I had to tell them something so they'd come for her. Tell them it was a Russian instead of—"

"You betrayed your own mother?"

"She's the one who betrayed—"

"It doesn't matter what she did. You were only thirteen, but you weren't stupid, Willy. You were never
stupid. You were old enough to know what would
happen next. You brought the Gestapo down on your
own mother? How could you do something so low, you
miserable—"

He swept the cups off the crate, the nails and screws
scraping her hand and thudding against her coat. Then
he drew his gun, and for a mad moment, Clara saw
sparks in her eyes, thought she had been hit, felt the pain
of it in her chest. But he hadn't fired; he was shouting:
"Get out! Get out! Out-out-out-out-out—" On and on,
the gun at her back as she tripped down the tunnels in
the dark, and then the strip of light, the mine's entrance,
Willy behind her crying out-out-out-out—

—until she climbed into searing daylight. She felt
arms catching her, Jakob smelling of fresh smoke, a
bulging sack at his feet. "Clara, what happened?"

She told him, the horror swirling inside her—Willy
with a gun, a gun at her back—and then she pulled away
from Jakob, stumbling down the snowy slope to the riv-
erside. She kept going, stepping into the river, her feet
cracking through the ice sheet. The cold bit her ankles
and she gasped at the sharp pain as Jakob pulled her out
of the water and into the weeds.

"What the devil are you doing? He put a gun on you?"

"It wasn't his fault." She hugged Jakob tightly so she wouldn't fall. "He doesn't know who he is."

"What are you talking about?"

Jakob's coat, his heartbeat, his closeness, began to soothe her. "He's my brother."

"What?" He was holding Clara, turning her face up to look at him. "I thought he was Elisa's son."

"He is. And my father's." She told him what she knew, what she'd pieced together, and even after she had told it, she still felt that she had been spinning a tale, that none of this could be real.

Gently, Jakob turned her toward the mine. "Come on, Clara. We need to get you warm and dry."

"I'm not going back in there. I just can't. Not yet."

"Your legs are wet. In this cold—"

She pulled away from him. His reaction left her in despair. He didn't understand. The cold didn't matter. Willy was her brother, and he had betrayed her oldest friend, his own mother. Clara could understand Willy's shock at seeing her father and Elisa together. She understood his grief at the death of the man he'd thought was his father. He'd felt wronged, ashamed, angry. He was just a boy. But what kind of boy walks into Gestapo headquarters and reports his mother and lies because he's angry with her?

"I think you should take what you can from the mine and go home, Jakob. Be careful. He's—" She couldn't admit that Jakob had been right. Willy was more unstable and dangerous than she'd ever thought possible. The quiet, gentle boy she had known had been twisted into someone new. "I think it's best if he calms down alone."

"Come home with me, Clara."

A flare of gratitude cut through the turmoil inside her. "Thank you, but I need to think some things through on my own. Besides, Fenshaw might come looking for me there. Meet me at the Works tomorrow."

She could see the indecision in his face, the anxiety. "I'm all right. I really am. I'll keep warm on the way back and you'll see me tomorrow. Bring me some food."

"You're sure?"

He was squeezing her hand, and though she was already pulling away, she held on to him too, their fingers linking until the last moment.

Dark

Willy cradled his head in his hands as if she had hit him. Pounded him over and over. She'd called him a low, miserable . . . what? What was he? A boy? A man? A soldier? A dirty rat?

He stumbled to the crate table, to the map on the wall, that stupid map. All of his stupid little notes about stupid armies moving from one stupid battlefield to the next. What did it matter? He was in a hole in the ground alone.

He scooped up a handful of dirt and spat on it and rubbed his hands until they were good and black and then he smeared the muck across the map, soiling it.

He dropped onto his bed, and Gertrud fluttered to his leg, rustling her wings and peeping.

"I'm all right," he said. It wasn't true, but he didn't want to worry her. For her sake, he pushed away his anger. For her sake, he took long and dusty breaths.

He allowed ten minutes to compose himself, counting the time in his head, every one of those six hundred seconds. By then, he wasn't shaking anymore. He washed his hands and opened his footlocker, mumbling, and took out his ledger. Just as he suspected, nobody had recorded the food taken from the stores the past few days. He would have to correct this. There was a proper way to do these things.

The ledger under his arm, he went into the corridor and noticed charcoal marks where there weren't any before: arrows, numbers on the doors, and sometimes labels—bread, sugar, cigarettes. She did this. He didn't know how he knew. It didn't matter; he wanted no reminders of that woman. He rubbed out the marks, uneasy because he was destroying something that made sense, something he should have done himself.

In the room with the canned bread, he sighed at the chaos, the open boxes, the dented cans, the opener on the floor. Then he began the long, soothing task of stacking them as high as he could, one can on top of the other, a shining tower.

20

Jakob limped to the street corner and paused to catch his breath, leaning against a lamppost that had lost its lamp. He needed the rest. He wasn't about to stumble into his own home and collapse from the walk, several hours, maybe more, from Willy's mine. He didn't want to scare Dorrit and Gabi like that. They were probably scared enough. By his reckoning he'd spent three days snowed in at the Works and almost two days in the mine, and he was anxious to show them he was all right, to see that they were all right. He laced his thumbs under the straps of the pack on his back, shifting the weight from his aching shoulders. The girls were going to forgive him for being gone so long when they saw the delicious feast he was bringing them.

The food should have put him in a good mood, but as he smoked a cigarette from the mine, he couldn't stop thinking about Clara. He still felt the pressure of her head on his chest as the words flooded out of her—Willy, her brother, his mother, her father, the Gestapo—a rambling story he didn't understand except for one major fact. Willy was Theodor Falkenberg's son. Clara's brother. If Jakob had known, he wouldn't have kept the kid a secret for so long. But then, she clearly hadn't known either. Her story had been hard to follow when she was clinging to him, needing his comfort, his support, and he was still stunned by it. Amazed by the wound she had shown to a fellow like him. He should have done more, should have helped her, but he hadn't known how at the time—and now she was gone.

He hoped she had had the sense to find a public hall on the way back to the Works, somewhere to dry off, to thaw her feet. He knew what the winter could do, what a slip in a frozen river could do. He shivered at the thought of her curled up in her camp, a victim of the White Death. He wouldn't wait until tomorrow. As soon as he had checked on his sisters and warmed up, he was going back for her. He shouldn't have let her go alone.

The snow was piled all along the curbs, dirty and trampled, formed into snowmen with bits of rubble for eyes. The neighborhood kids went scurrying around him, kids he knew by sight. He followed them onto his street as they streaked in one direction, toward the army vehicle parked near his house. A British officer sat on the hood, arm deep in a cardboard box. He was rummaging around, taking his time, teasing the kids swarming around him.

In German, he said, "I think it's empty."

The kids shouted, "No! No! Chocolate, Tommy! Biscuits, please!" They pressed in, the younger ones hopping and squealing.

Jakob was stiff with cold, his back a roar of pain that started at his prosthesis and licked like a flame up his spine. All he wanted was to get home, to sit by the oven, to see how his sisters had done in the blizzard. But the officer stood between him and his front door and it was no coincidence. Jakob had no illusions. This was Clara's English captain.

The sadistic son of a bitch. What kind of a louse put a woman in a locker? And there he was, torturing the kids, playing games when they were literally starving for whatever he had in that box.

"Biscuits," Fenshaw called, flourishing a packet over his head. "Who likes biscuits?"

Two dozen kids bellowed, "I do, sir! Me, sir!"

"They go to whoever can guess my favorite color."

The kids screamed colors while, all around, women

swept snow off the pavement or hung out of the windows dislodging icicles from the drains. Jakob's sisters weren't in the crowd, but he thought he saw a movement behind the dirty cellophane that formed their parlor window. He would have to risk it, and why not? Fenshaw had probably tracked him down after talking to people at the South Sea, but he had nothing on Jakob. Not really. Besides, Jakob wanted a closer look at the bastard.

He limped past the crowd toward his door.

"Jakob Relling?" As he handed the biscuit packet to a screaming toddler, Fenshaw flashed Jakob a cold smile that reminded him he was wearing the army-issue gray overcoat from the mine.

"Is this about the coat, sir? I meant to dye it, just haven't gotten around to it yet."

Fenshaw answered in German dominated by a strong English accent. "It's too cold to talk outside. Maybe you could invite me in? Looks like you've been walking a lot today, and in this weather. I'm sure you need to warm up. Have a wash, maybe?" Fenshaw rubbed his clean-shaven chin, and Jakob resisted the urge to scratch the stubble on his own. Fenshaw's mustache looked as though he trimmed it under a microscope. His coat was spotless, his trousers pleated. His cuffs—you could tell everything from cuffs and hems, Jakob's mama used to say—were good as new. His shoes were wet from snow but had the clean gleam of leather polished that morning. Compared to Fenshaw, Jakob felt like a grimy, hairy creature recently rolled in out of the jungle.

On the doorstep, Fenshaw noticed the broken brick keeping the door ajar. In the hallway, he rattled the stairway balustrade. Splinters of wood fluttered to the steps.

"Wouldn't go up there if I was you, sir," Jakob said, wishing Fenshaw would do just that, step onto the landing that no longer existed and plunge through the ceiling of what used to be his neighbor's flat, now a rubbish heap.

Dorrit was waiting for them in the hallway. She wore their mother's apron and held a wooden spoon upright as though she was about to thwack someone with it. "Oh, Jakob, you're back! Where have you been?"

He forced himself around Fenshaw and clamped his free arm around her waist, careful about it, not wanting to squeeze too hard. "You got through the storm all right, little mouse? Where's Gabi?" He led her into the kitchen where Gabi was cutting a turnip into transparent slices. She flew at him, so excited and relieved, she forgot about the knife in her hand. He snatched it away as she threw herself into his arms. That's how Fenshaw found them when he looked in on the kitchen. He was decent enough to touch his cap and withdraw.

"He's come every day since the storm blew over," Dorrit said, whispering. "I don't like him. He's too nice. He brought us chocolate and coffee. Nobody does that for nothing. What does he want from you?"

Jakob wrestled the pack off his back, and when the girls saw the tins and packets, they gasped with delight. "Don't eat it all at once," he said, kissing both on the head. "Make some coffee, will you? We have to show some hospitality, whether we want to or not."

"Are you in trouble?"

"You know me. I can talk myself out of anything." He waited by the stove for the coffee and then took it into the sitting room. Fenshaw was browsing through the ladies on the American calendar, lingering on sweet-faced Miss December, and then he turned his attention to a group photo on the wall, the one Jakob had hung low enough to see when he lay on the sofa at night. The Rellings before the war, twelve including grandparents, all tangled elbows and grins and giggles as they huddled together to fit in one picture.

"You have a large family," Fenshaw said.

"There's just the three of us left." In Jakob's mind, he heard the questions Fenshaw didn't ask and didn't really want to know the answer to. Nobody wanted to hear about other people's tragedies. Everybody had their own.

The next few minutes were strange. An exchange of courtesies, Fenshaw wishing he'd brought in some biscuits to go with the coffee, Jakob getting up for milk, Fenshaw waving him back to his seat. Fenshaw supplied the cigarettes, leaving a full packet on the table between them. He talked about the weather, that dreadful storm. Jakob compared it to winter in Russia, though there was no comparison, the whole time wondering why Fenshaw was being so damned friendly. If he wanted to know about Clara, why not demand the information? In Jakob's experience, you had to watch the Tommies when they were being too nice. You never knew when they'd turn on you, remind you of what a Nazi you'd been, regardless of the truth. The Tommies would call you a lowly foreigner in your own country. Fenshaw looked the type.

Fenshaw steered the chitchat toward Jakob himself, his history. He seemed to know exactly who Jakob was, where he went to school, that he had finished his exams before the war. "I hear you were a scholarship boy," he said, sipping his coffee.

"Sure."

"Falkenberg, wasn't it?"

"Sure."

"Met the great man himself before the war. What did you think of him?"

"I was just a kid at the time, sir. Herr Falkenberg seemed like the chancellor, the president, and the pope all rolled into one."

"You'd be amazed how many people thought that. Would you say you're an ambitious man?"

The new direction threw Jakob off. At the mention of Falkenberg, he'd been preparing himself for an assault on Clara, a battery of questions about her.

"Suppose so, sir."

"What do you want to do with your life now the war is behind you?"

"Start an import-export business. American goods to and from Europe, you know? Buy cigarettes there, sell them here for a massive profit. Use that to buy a camera here, sell it over there. Profits like you wouldn't believe. Soldiers are cashing in. Why not me?"

"That's what interests you? Profit?"

"Just trying to take care of my family, sir." Jakob's hands shook slightly as he raised his mug to his lips. He wanted Fenshaw to get to the point but didn't know how to force it without exposing himself.

Fenshaw sat back and touched the satchel he'd brought in with him. "Why do you think I'm here?"

"No idea, sir."

"Come on."

Jakob lit a cigarette, automatic motions that covered

up his nerves. "You don't want to marry my sister, do you?"

"I like to see people in their own homes. Drag someone to a police station and it's harder to see what kind of chap you're dealing with. At home, he shows a different side."

"Nobody acts normal with an Allied officer in the house, sir."

"We're not enemies, Herr Relling. I'm here to help you if you're willing to be helped." Fenshaw took a portrait-sized photograph out of his satchel and set it on the table between the coffee things. "Recognize her?"

In the picture, Clara must have been twenty or so, and if Jakob had known her at that age, he would have melted into a puddle at her feet. Her blond bob swung close to one eye, giving her a peekaboo look. At the same time, she was trying to look regal, her nose up. What got him, what really tore him up inside, was the freshness in her face, the innocence winning out over the sophisticated look she was aiming for. Back then, she wasn't disillusioned. He supposed that was true of everybody since the war, but it still hurt to see how far she had come from this: portrait-sized, with dramatic lighting.

"Never seen her before and I'm sorry about that, sir, believe me."

"She's a brunette now, much thinner, a bit worn down by the war. She's thirty-one years old. She tells people she's twenty-five."

"Vain, is she?"

"In her way, yes."

Jakob studied the photograph a little longer. Clara's shoulder was bare, reminding him of his nightly dreams at the Works, in the mine; she'd been right there beside him, curled in his arms, but he dreamed of her anyway. In an evening gown and pearls striding toward him, white silk hushing across the dance floor, her saying, "I'd love to."

He pushed the picture away. "I don't know her, sir."

"A dozen witnesses claim you were with a woman fitting this description at the South Sea Club the night the storm hit." Fenshaw set an identity card on the table, the photograph smaller and smudged but definitely Clara as she was now. Darker, edgier, more guarded. "She calls herself Margarete Müller."

The whole club had seen her, she'd made sure of that with her antics with Günther and her barefoot dancing. There was no sense in denying it.

"I didn't know that was the same woman, sir. She looks different."

"Did she tell you who she was?"

"Margarete Müller, just like you said. A secretary or something."

"What else did she tell you?"

"Sob story. Typical stuff. Homeless. Man dead. That kind of thing."

"You took pity on her, wined and dined her, took her to a private room in a black-market club. Was she prostituting herself?"

"No, are you crazy? Her?"

"What's so special about her if she was only a widowed secretary?"

"I don't know. Must be some reason you're looking for her."

"We found some ashes in the private room, some scraps of paper that didn't burn very well. They're from one of my favorite articles about her." Fenshaw pulled the familiar magazine out of his satchel, and Jakob tried to look interested, as though he was seeing it for the first time, even as his throat was tightening with dread.

"It was clear to me she didn't say one damn word attributed to her in this article," Fenshaw said as he turned the pages. "For the führer and Reich. Victory for the people. Words put in her mouth. I wonder if she knew, if she wanted to be used. Did she happen to say anything to you about that?"

He tossed the magazine onto the table between

them, but Jakob didn't touch it. He looked at what she called the old her, the Iron Fräulein, the cover picture of Clara looking competent, in control, which of course was a lie that late in the war. An intact silhouette of the Falkenberg Iron Works spread behind her as if the place wasn't bombed to bits. Willy's delusion that all was going exactly as planned? It had started a long time ago and God knew he wasn't the only one who'd had it.

"I've never seen this magazine in my life, sir."

"Herr Relling, could we please stop wasting time? You know who she is. And I believe you know where she is now."

Jakob dug the heels of his mismatched shoes into the warped parquet. An odd thing, feeling the floor even with the wooden foot, the ghost leg.

"I know this is hard for you," Fenshaw said. Jakob had to hold back from saying something he'd regret in the face of that fatherly, understanding tone Fenshaw was trying to sell him. Well, Jakob wasn't buying. Fenshaw didn't understand a thing.

"You're a young man," Fenshaw said. "You're intrigued. An heiress has walked into your life. She's in need, and you have the chance to help her. If I were you, I'd find that almost irresistible too." He was touching the portrait of Clara, stroking it with his thumb. "But she's wanted by the military government. It's your duty to help Allied authorities. Where can I find her?"

Jakob didn't like how Fenshaw handled the photograph, his delicate touch, Clara's face hidden in his palm. Fenshaw must have noticed what he was doing. He colored, and quickly tucked it into his satchel. "You want payment, I suppose. Food. Cigarettes."

"No, sir."

"What do you want then? Profit? There's no profit in this if you don't cooperate."

"I don't know how I can help you, sir. I've said all I know."

"Right." Fenshaw tapped his cigarette on the tabletop, a thoughtful look on his face. "Let's go back to the night of the raid at the South Sea Club. Why did you and your Fräulein Müller run if you had nothing to hide?"

"I don't know about you, sir, but if I'm in a black-market club and the police arrive, I run."

"Guilty conscience?"

"Common sense."

Fenshaw smiled thinly. "Tell me again how you met her. At the club? Somewhere else?"

Jakob had to think fast, stitch together an easy story in his mind. "At the club."

Fenshaw motioned for him to go on.

"She showed up in the lounge and sat on the arm of my chair. I was as surprised as the next fellow. I mean, I'm not a bad catch, but things like that don't happen to me too often."

"It's a nice fantasy. A lovely woman strolls into the room and lands in your lap."

"She didn't sit in my—"

"The problem is, I have a witness who insists you convinced him to go to the club that night to speak to the fräulein about an incident in the war. To sum up, you enlisted an ex-policeman to talk about Fräulein Falkenberg's oldest friend to a woman who happens to look very much like her. In the room where that happened, we found evidence of a wartime article that also happens to be about Clara Falkenberg. The coincidences are rather adding up, Herr Relling, don't you think?"

The nerves in Jakob's bad leg were sparking like electric wires, and he rubbed it to stave off the pain. "What would you do, sir? I mean, if we switched places and you were in my position. Would you give her up?"

"I can have food delivered. Coal. It's a bad winter."

"Would you give up a woman like her for a sack of coal?"

"Herr Relling, I understand your hesitation—"

"No, you don't. You have no idea, sir, so stop trying

to be my friend or my father or to buy me off. I got nothing more to say."

Fenshaw leaned back in his chair, arms folded. "I see she's been very nice to you. Charming? Just the right amount of naughty to keep you interested? Or maybe she's been playing up her downfall. The heroine in her own tragedy. Don't let yourself be fooled, Herr Relling. I've been studying her for years. She's excellent at manipulating how others see her. I'll wager you think you've been dealing with an heiress down on her luck. Faded glory and all that. Repentant, even. She might seem within your reach. She might have even let you touch her. But it's to her advantage, not yours. You'll get nothing by protecting her."

"You didn't answer my question, sir. Would you turn her in?"

"Of course."

Jakob hated the bland ease of Fenshaw's lie. Because it was a lie. He saw it on Fenshaw's face, that he'd answered out of irritation, to keep things moving.

"I'm not so quick to stab a woman in the back, sir."

"She didn't milk cows in the war, Relling. She ran the Falkenberg Iron Works."

"A figurehead. A stand-in for her father. You got him already. What do you need her for?"

"She managed her family's factories at the expense

of human beings who worked themselves to exhaustion and death to meet her quotas."

"She did what she could for those people."

"Is that what she said?"

Jakob didn't want Fenshaw to know everything Clara had told him. He wasn't about to share that intimacy just because he was in trouble. He tried a different argument. "She didn't have any real power. She's a woman. Nazis didn't listen to women."

"Normally, you'd be right, but most women aren't named Falkenberg. The SS loved her. Himmler thought she was some kind of princess of iron and fire. All her brothers were SS. And she had a long love affair with an SS officer who moved heaven and earth in her interests."

Jakob slapped his lighter onto the table. "She wasn't like them. She's got to be the only person in this whole country who voluntarily thinks about what she did in the war. You got any idea how disgusted she is? She's sorry."

"You think it's enough to be sorry? She's not a child. Being sorry doesn't wipe the slate clean. There are still consequences to what she did."

"Why are you after her like this, sir? All that stuff about the war, come on. Is it really that straightforward? She thinks you're playing some game of your own."

Fenshaw looked interested. "What exactly did she say?"

"Not much more than that. And I think she wanted you to raid the South Sea. She wouldn't admit it, but it was pretty clear to me."

"Why would she want that?"

"She thinks you know her. Well, she said you think you know her."

Fenshaw shaved a match on the box with a sharp flick of his wrist and watched the flame. He was looking thoughtful and a little pleased with himself, a good moment for Jakob to press his advantage.

"Look, sir, come on. You know she's not a war criminal, right?"

"Her father will go on trial for war crimes. Some people think she deserves to be there next to him."

"Is that what you think?"

The match was burning in Fenshaw's fingers. He winced and shook it out.

"You're a British officer. Your people are running things around here. If you wanted, you could decide her future yourself. You know more about her than anybody. I can tell. If you have doubts, why not let her go?"

"I don't have—" Fenshaw stopped himself. "For the last time, Herr Relling, where is she?"

Jakob knew things were about to get a lot worse for

him. But what could he do? What kind of man would he be if he turned her in? What would she think of him then?

"As I said before, sir, I don't know."

Fenshaw went still, and his face unnerved Jakob, the struggle in the muscles to stay composed. In Russia, Jakob had seen officers look like that before giving orders they wished they didn't have to give.

"How far along is your sister?" Fenshaw asked.

Jakob's heart contracted, as if Fenshaw had turned some screw inside it. "About seven months."

"Where's the father?"

"Went back to his rat hole in England, I guess."

"Do you have any aunts, uncles, cousins? Anyone who could help her out when you're in jail?"

There was a creaking sound from the hallway. Jakob pictured Gabi listening at the keyhole, Dorrit behind, her ear pressed against the glass she held to the door. Ever since they were little girls, they had eavesdropped on him like that. They were trying to be quiet, but he heard them clearly now, the gasping breaths Dorrit couldn't hide, the hush of Gabi's knees on the floor as she adjusted how she knelt. For their sake, he answered Fenshaw calmly.

"You can't arrest me, sir. I haven't done anything."

Fenshaw folded his hands in front of his lips, his eyes closed for a second, two, three. "You're a black marketeer. The Allied government is committed to fighting the black market. It's my duty to take you off the streets, and I will. If I have to."

Behind the door, a new sound. Dorrit was sniffling quietly. If Jakob was arrested, she would think it was her fault, that he'd worked on the black market to get the baby what it needed. He wanted to tell her it wasn't her fault. Whatever happened was his choice. She should know he would never do anything that would hurt her or the baby. When she first admitted she was pregnant, she had stared at him with big eyes full of dread as she braced herself for his fury. But he hadn't been furious. He had known she was pregnant weeks before she said anything. He knew what it meant when a girl knelt at the pail every day. He'd worked through his anger long before she knew it was there, and when she finally told him the truth, he hugged her and said if it was a boy, she should name him after one of their brothers taken in the war.

The family portrait was hanging crookedly, and Jakob tapped it straight on the wall. His sisters, the baby, they mattered more than a promise and even a woman like Clara. He had to believe she would understand what he was about to do.

21

Clara began to think her mother would never come home. She huddled on a patch of snow by an ornate iron fence, her scarf wrapped around nose and mouth, only her eyes exposed, watching the street and Anne's house. She had been waiting for . . . she wasn't sure how long. On the trek up the slick slopes from Willy's mine, her toes had lost their feeling first, then her fingertips. She peeled off her glove, and the skin on her fingers was an odd white. She pressed her neck and couldn't feel the warmth. She registered this with a strange detachment.

The few people who walked by in the street paid her no attention, even the men in uniform who rushed into their houses or cars. She knew she looked like one of the women who had run out of whatever reserves of

energy had once kept them going, thin creatures waiting for the line to move or the train to arrive at the station. She didn't know if it was shock at what Willy had
told her, or what he had done to her. She thought of him
jabbing his pistol into her back, at that iron rod she'd
never had in her spine. There was a knot of pain where
she'd recoiled from him. Willy. Who had informed on
his mother. For sleeping with his father.

Her father.

Their father.

A shadow crossed into her line of sight, and Clara,
hunched at the fence, tried to shake herself awake. She
saw leather boots spotted with damp, a coat hemmed
with silver fox fur.

"Darling?" Anne was holding the fur at her neck,
looking down at her in horror. Clara couldn't help
smiling. She must look worse than she suspected.

"Mother."

"God in heaven, what are you doing sitting out here?
You'll catch your death." Anne hauled Clara to her feet
and helped her limp across the street and into the house.
The stairs were difficult, Clara couldn't quite get her
knees to bend how they should, and she misjudged the
height of every step. Anne held on to her the entire way,
coaxing her forward to get her blood moving. The wall of
heat inside the flat made Clara gasp, and she had trouble

breathing as Anne stripped her of her coat and wet shoes. Her mother vanished for a while, leaving Clara on the divan acclimatizing herself to the bright light, the thick air, the clutter of things from Falkenhorst. Her life had become a museum already, her past a collection of artifacts preserved or ignored. She was feeling drowsy, but roused herself enough to look at her father's bird sketch, back in its place on the wall. She pressed her lips tightly to keep back the sadness welling up inside her.

Anne returned with hot tea and a bucket of snow. To Clara's surprise, her mother knelt at her feet, rolled down Clara's woolen stocking, and began rubbing the snow on her leg, a common if questionable method of thawing frostbitten skin. Clara was so shocked at her mother's gentle care, she let her do it.

"Where have you been, darling? Why are you so filthy?"

Clara noticed the coal dust that had left black streaks on her coat. "I've been to see Willy."

No change in her mother's face, only a cold neutrality. "He's alive, then."

"It would've suited you if he wasn't."

"What kind of thing is that to say? I hardly know the boy." Anne started rubbing snow on Clara's other leg and added in a light tone, "Where's he been keeping himself, then?"

Clara didn't want to tell her. She needed to protect Willy from the woman Clara was sure had already got her manicured claws into his life. "He's not too far away. But Elisa isn't with him."

"Oh? Abandoned him, did she?"

Clara pushed her back onto the carpet. Her hands burned, her feet, her whole body, life rushing back into them at last. "Tell me, Mother. Who is Willy's father?"

Anne went rigid, the creases deepening in her face. When she began to move, it was slowly, grasping the arm of the divan and pulling herself with a gasp onto one foot, then the other. She found her cigarettes and a lighter, and sat in the armchair next to the pencil sketch. "You do realize talking about this is a great humiliation. I have no intention of sparing your delicate feelings." She smoked with a grim and absent look on her face. "I'm curious. Who did you think the father was?"

Clara felt a tremor under her feet, a memory of the bombardments, the ground trembling slightly. "I never knew. Elisa refused to speak about it. When I found that piece of her dress, I thought Friedrich. But I was wrong, wasn't I?"

"Our dear, handsome, sparkling Friedrich. My darling boy." Anne was silent a moment. "Yes, you were wrong about him. We count backward from Willy's birth and we come to late December 1930. Friedrich wasn't home for Christmas that year. He spent it in Berlin with your great-uncle Alfred studying the airplanes of the Lufthansa. He didn't come home until late January. By then, that girl—"

"You mean Elisa."

"She was already pregnant even if she wouldn't know it for some weeks yet."

Clara tried to remember that time sixteen years ago, but the years of childhood Christmases blended together—the tree in Falkenhorst's foyer, the candles in the windows, her brothers singing carols. Her father presiding over the festivities, smoking his cigar, a red carnation in his lapel, contentment glowing on his face. But that year, that special year, he had left the warmth and comfort of his family to see one of his office girls in secret.

"Where did they meet? At the Works, I assume?"

"So you have figured it out."

There it was. The truth admitted in so few words. The last bit of hope that her father might have been innocent—of this, at least—crumbled. She wanted to strike out at them all—her father, Elisa, her mother—for the secrets they'd kept from her. "They met at the end of the war, you know," Clara said. "Rekindled their old romance, I suppose. For one night, anyway. Maybe there were others before that when he was in town. I don't know." It wounded her to say it as much as it wounded Anne to hear it. Her mother's face seemed to wither.

"Now you're just being hurtful, darling."

"We're telling the truth now, Mother. Let's look at Papa as he really was. How did you find out about the original affair?"

"Theodor told me. He had the decency not to lie. You see, a wife knows when her husband is straying. I knew, but I did not expect it to be a freckle-faced teenager in a repulsive office romance. To add insult to injury, the blasted girl had to get pregnant. Theodor is not the type of man to have his mistakes running around in short trousers. He came to an arrangement with her. If she played along, so to speak, she got her house, a suitable husband to shield her reputation, a job for as long as she wanted it."

More playacting, her father arranging another grand bit of theater in his life, in the lives of others. "You bullied Elisa into agreeing to it, didn't you?"

"I didn't need to. Theodor negotiated most of the conditions. The impulse to be generous came from him."

"Generosity. Is that what you call it?"

"It's what he called it. I would have liked to drown that girl in the Ruhr. I would have sent her so far away no one here would know she existed. It was he who insisted on taking care of her and the child. In return, I set the condition that the affair was over right then and there. We both agreed—all three of us, actually—that no one else should ever know the identity of the child's real father."

"Why on earth did you introduce her to me, then? She might have told me."

"If she had, our little agreement would have been null and void. She would have lost everything. And, of course, if it ever did get out that the boy was a Falkenberg, it would have been the family's duty to take the child into our bosom." She folded her hands on her chest. "And there would have been no place for a girl like her in our circle."

"You threatened to take Willy away from her if she told?"

"I did no such thing. She understood the stakes and the rewards too. That girl knew exactly what she was getting out of the whole business. Everything she had—*everything*—was from us. She was a stone around our necks."

Clara couldn't believe it: Elisa so calculating—and little more than a child herself. But this was, after all, only her mother's version of events. "I think you wanted to keep her close, Mother. You introduced us. You wanted us to be friends. You used me so you could watch her. And the closer we became, the more tempted she was to tell me and go back on your agreement. How excruciating it must have been for her. And what exquisite torture for you. Papa must have squirmed. When he was being difficult, did you remind him he had a little bastard son?"

"Our sons are dead. *My* sons."

"Don't go wailing about your sons. You only loved Friedrich. We all knew it. And it embarrassed him. Mummy's boy."

Anne bolted toward her, and Clara grasped her mother's sharp and bony hands and pushed her onto the divan. Anne had the nerve to stare at her with wounded astonishment. "What's happened to you, Clara? You've become rough. Common. You've forgotten who you are."

Clara pulled on her cold and damp shoes. She fetched her coat.

"Where are you running off to again?" Anne spread her arms. "This is your home. Your family. You can't just leave it all behind."

Clara took a last look at the artifacts from a life that was long past. She looked at her mother, the crust of makeup cracking around her eyes, the skin trembling at her neck. There was a slight tremor in her left hand, something Clara had never noticed before. With sadness, she turned away. "Good-bye, Mother."

It took several hours for Clara to trudge back to the Works. The wind swept across the junctions where people moved, hunched and slowly, choosing each careful step on the slick pavement. She joined them, staring at the ground as she walked. The core of her had gone cold—a numb emptiness now that she finally understood just how far her father had been willing to go to preserve his precious ideal of the family, and himself. He could compromise anything—his conscience, his political views, even his morals—if he was left intact as a shining idol. He had wanted to take care of Elisa and Willy for his own ends, to keep his secret, and it seemed like a plaster put on a vast wound, a small act of decency within the larger dishonesty, baseness, and corruption. Her father was a selfish man. He was full of his own vanity. He disgusted her.

She entered the Works through the crumbled wall and followed the trail she and Jakob had made in the frozen snow when they left two days before to see Willy. The track from Jakob's homemade ski pole made her smile, but only a little. She was trembling again, and the muscles of her face were stiff even in her scarf. She kept walking because she ordered herself to, and her body obeyed because she had no choice but to keep moving or collapse. As soon as she reached her camp, she tore down the wooden slats she'd nailed over the window space. After the mine, she needed light and air even if it let in the cold.

In the shelter she and Jakob had made, she swaddled herself in the remaining blankets. She was still shivering, but not as much as before. She didn't know if this was good or bad, and strangely, she didn't care.

He would be here soon—Jakob. He'd said he would come, and she had no doubt he would do as he promised. She slipped away, half-asleep, aware of her and Jakob's musty smell in the blankets. It felt like the war, a night in the bomb shelter, and her head filled with a film reel. Her father young again in a dinner jacket and tinkering with an engine, his hands oily and black. Her mother trying to scrub them with a brush that had needles instead of bristles. Elisa over to dinner at Falkenhorst picking at the bones of a falcon and sucking her fingers. She was nude. Everyone was pretending not to notice. Clara was dancing with Max around the table, their tango odd and jerky because of the rope he'd tied to their ankles. Willy was older, a young man in a Luftwaffe uniform, identical to Friedrich, who sat beside him. They were going over the details of their last mission. Jakob wasn't there. How odd, she thought as she danced, that Jakob wasn't there when she had invited him for all the world to see. She didn't care about his leg or his birth. Didn't he know that?

The voices changed, lost their dreamy quality, became sharp and urgent. Her head was touched lightly, then her neck, and under the blanket she felt a gentle hand on her chest. Some irresistible force pulled her by the feet. She felt herself lifted, settled, lifted again, rocking slightly as she floated on air before she was lowered for good. A pressure on her face, her eyelid eased back. Light.

"Miss Falkenberg." He was shaking her shoulder. It was very irritating. "Miss Falkenberg. Come on, girl. Wake up." She must still be dreaming. It was Captain Fenshaw's voice.

She struggled to open her eyes and he was there, unbuttoning his tunic, saying something else. She tried to focus. Thought he said, "Cough." But why?

He was really making no sense. But she ordered her lungs to take a breath, and she coughed.

Behind him, there was an open cabinet with rolled bandages inside. It occurred to her she might be in an ambulance. The light was strange, glaringly white somewhere behind her head. Fenshaw looked pale and unreal, his tunic off, face white against his white collar. Hands lifted her again gently, and Fenshaw wrapped her in his warm tunic, and then his coat.

"Keep shivering," he said, another bit of nonsense from him. As if she could stop. "You still with us?"

He was patting her cheek and she ordered her voice to say, "Get your hands off me."

Over her head, he barked, "Where's the bloody tea?"

He put the cup to her lips. Her fingertips and toes slowly began to tingle, and the pain radiated through her body with a single thought: Captain Fenshaw is here. Not Jakob.

No one told her where they were going and she didn't care. Prison was prison. They rode silently with her in the ambulance, Fenshaw and a medic who kept checking her pulse. She drank from the thermos cup and ate the chocolate Fenshaw gave her, breaking off the wedges one at a time, rationing them. The chocolate helped. She began to see the irony in her situation, her arrest. She was wearing her captor's clothes, drinking his tea, eating his chocolate, while he served her looking disheveled but triumphant in his shirtsleeves.

She was reclining on a stretcher, but that was just her body. If the body was weak, the spirit could be strong. She imagined herself like Grandmother Sophia upright on her deathbed, refusing to be caught lying down even at the end. Clara's head was swimming, but she was fighting it, trying to sit up.

"Lie down. Rest." Fenshaw's voice, all of him, was wrapped in a cocoon of certainty and self-satisfaction. She wanted to puncture it. She wanted to hurl abuse at Jakob for betraying her, for who else could it have been? Even if he had been forced to do it, he had hurt her deeply, and she aimed her anger and pain at Fenshaw, the man who had caused it all.

"Feeling virtuous, Captain? Heroic? You've got your war criminal and the world is safe. You're the chap who caught the Iron Fräulein. Bravo. I hope they give you a nice pat on the head."

He smiled at her just as he had after pulling her off the train. Knowing, indulgent. "You're going down fighting, are you? I'd expect nothing less."

"And it's such a fair fight, isn't it? Me against the army or the military government or whoever will be interrogating me. Well, that's fine. You can tell them I won't say a word about the war to anyone. You must have threatened Jakob or his family, and for that, I am not cooperating with you, Captain."

"Don't act against your own interests just because you're angry at me."

"My interests are my business. Tell them they can starve me or keep me out in the cold. It won't bother me. I've had all of that lately and I'm still here. I'm not afraid of prison."

The ambulance slowed, and everything she had said, her bravado, was gone. Out of the window she saw a squat building that looked like a barracks dropped onto a snowy field. She'd imagined prison to have barbed wire and watchtowers, but she couldn't see any of that. She was breathing so hard that the window kept fogging over. As the ambulance doors opened, the wind blew snow crystals into her eyes. British soldiers peered inside. "Mind your own business," she said, and they snapped back in surprise.

She kept her head up as she limped on Fenshaw's arm to the barracks. There were no guards. No fences. No matron telling her to disrobe. Just an empty hallway that smelled of damp leather and fried onions.

At a door, Fenshaw said, "I'll give you fifteen minutes. Everything you need should be in there. I'll be out here until time is up." He opened the door to a row of sinks and mirrors. She ignored those—she hardly wanted to see the state she was in—and picked up the things laid neatly on the bench. Soap, clean towel, hairbrush. An army shirt and trousers were folded nearby.

She spent a good ten minutes under the shower, soaping herself until she finally felt clean and warm, a grand waste of what had become precious to her, simple things like hot water and soap. But who knew when she'd next be offered such luxury. After dressing, she brushed her hair back like a man's and then presented herself to Fenshaw as a girl soldier in British Army togs. She saluted him and declared herself ready for duty, *sah*, just as she'd seen in war films. He seemed too preoccupied to notice her disrespect. He waved at her to follow him to an unused office. Her dinner was laid out on the desk, one set of dishes but two teacups by the pot. The food was plain and plentiful, some meat in a bland sauce and heavenly mashed potatoes that warmed her stomach. She ate quickly and when she had finished, Fenshaw poured the tea.

"Remember that BUF rally we talked about after we took you off that train? London, 1936?"

The food had mellowed her. She wore fresh clothes and had eaten a hearty meal. She expected prison was going to be much worse than this. She guessed she was being prepared for the real thing, and she wanted this comfort to last as long as possible. "My mother dragged me to a lot of rallies, sir."

"You still don't remember me, do you?" He was fiddling with his teacup, his ears flushed red. It triggered something in her, a memory she couldn't quite reach.

"You were in the cloakroom," he said. "I hadn't planned to talk to you. You'd left the stage and when you didn't come back, I thought to look for you. I might have walked right past if I hadn't noticed your shoe sticking out from behind someone's rain cape. You seemed very alone in there with all those coats."

She drew a breath. She remembered now. She'd paid the cloakroom attendant to leave her alone while she hid out where her mother would never think to look for her. A young man had greeted her shyly from the other side of the counter. He'd been squeezing his cap, awed like most men who had any idea what her family was worth. She remembered his ears flushed red, as if speaking to her embarrassed him immensely. She couldn't quite believe that painfully shy man had been Fenshaw.

"You didn't have a mustache back then."

"You invited me to sit with you and we talked. Must have been an hour or more. I claimed I was a voter from Shoreditch, and you told me I was too sensible a chap to vote for the Fascists. You had solid arguments about how they would botch things up if they ever got hold of real power. A roomful of Fascists next door, your own mother onstage, and you were determined to rob them of my vote."

"I'm afraid I don't remember a word of that conversation."

"Well, we did empty our flasks. There was a lot of cognac and whisky." He looked at her steadily over his cup. "You seemed completely different from your mother and the rest of your family as we knew them.

We were keeping an eye on the Falkenbergs, but no-body looked into the baby girl until I did. We watched your career with much interest. Once the war broke out, we thought you might be of some use to our side. You're half English, after all. It was possible you'd feel squeezed from both sides of the family. A conflict of loyalty. But there was no conflict. When the führer called, you be-came one of them."

"I was never one of them."

"Then what were you? The generous, sensible, in-dependent-minded woman I met before the war? She wouldn't have served them."

He sounded disappointed in her. He had met her so long ago, but back then he seemed to have seen more of what she was and could be than she had known herself. Everything he'd done since pulling her off the train—the hunt for her in the ruins, pressuring Jakob to betray her—perhaps it was really a search for that woman. The one who had once impressed him, surprised him, maybe touched him somehow, but in the end was a great disappointment. He didn't know what she had tried to do in the war. He couldn't see her conscience.

"Sir, I tried to help people. You have all those files about me. Do you have the letters I wrote to Berlin, anyone who'd listen, begging for higher rations for the foreign workers?"

"You wrote letters," Fenshaw said, leaning back in his chair. "Very heroic."

"I wasn't trying to be a hero. I was trying to get people fed. I harassed the construction companies to build decent housing, I forbade mistreatment of any kind in my factories, I gave the foreign workers space in our air-raid bunkers, I sent medical personnel into the camps to treat people. Is any of that in your files?"

Fenshaw set a cup in the middle of the table between them, then balanced a spoon lengthwise on top of it. "You wrote letters." He pinched sugar from the bowl and dropped a few grains into the spoon. "You tried to improve housing"—a few more grains—"medical care"—still more—"and the general treatment of the workers." A dusting of sugar was in the bowl of the spoon. "But here"—he picked up the sugar bowl—"is where you imported and used at least twenty thousand workers over the entire war." He overturned the bowl. Sugar spilled across the table. "In the end," he said, "you did very little good compared to the harm you inflicted."

"Do you think I don't know that? But what more could I do? Close the Works? Walk away? Do you think my father or my mother or some other director would have treated the workers better than I did? All I could do was try." She thought of Galina and her friends, almost told Fenshaw that she had hidden people, tried to keep them safe. But her riskiest act was also her biggest failure, and it shamed her. Besides, it seemed wrong to use Galina and the others to try to impress Fenshaw now, their lives the price for setting her free. She put her fist to her mouth and looked around the sparse office. "Where are we?"

"This is just a way station."

"On the way to where exactly?"

"An interrogation center. We'll be moving there shortly."

There was a draft coming from somewhere, a cold she felt in the oddest places: behind her ears, between each of her fingers. She couldn't disappear into an Allied facility. Willy was out there alone, with a gun. And Elisa? Was she even alive? If the Gestapo had released her and she had survived, if she was out there somewhere, she had no idea Willy was in the mine or she would have already talked him out of it somehow. Clara had to let her know where he was. But how?

Fenshaw was stacking the dishes onto a tray. Her time here was nearly up. She assumed if Elisa was still alive, Fenshaw knew where she was. His files went back years. He'd searched for her at Elisa's house. He had to know what happened to her.

"Sir, I know I'm in no position to ask a favor, but I'm going to ask for one anyway."

He listened, cautious.

"I urgently need to see my friend Elisabeth Sieland. I've found no trace of her in the city. You know everything about me. You've spoken to everyone who knew me. Did you speak to her?"

"What could possibly be so urgent?"

"She's my oldest friend, you must know that. I need to know if she's alive. I don't have anyone else."

"That's not altogether true." He seemed about to say something else—about Jakob, maybe?—but then he shook his head. "It's not possible. I'm not arranging a meeting of any kind."

"Please, sir. I'll go to prison without giving you any more trouble, but let me see Elisa before I go."

"No, Miss Falkenberg."

"Why not?"

"You're delaying the inevitable." He opened the door and spoke quietly to the soldier outside.

She desperately tried to think of something that would change Fenshaw's mind. Something he could possibly want. The mine? She thought of Willy in his army uniform, the rooms full of army food, and finally the army gun he had threatened her with. Fenshaw would want a wartime depot of the German Army, especially one with weapons.

"Sir, I have information for you. Something you'll be very interested in."

He motioned for her to come with him, but she grasped the back of her chair, standing her ground.

"You remember how the Wehrmacht hid supply depots all over the place so that your lot wouldn't bomb them? There's one still out there. One you didn't find."

Fenshaw closed the door, looking skeptical. "And where is this long-lost cache of the German Army?"

"I'll tell you if you arrange a meeting with Elisabeth Sieland."

He shook his head, his hand on the door again.

"It's in an abandoned coal mine. Underground, but it's a surface mine, not deep."

He turned back to her. Reserved, but listening.

"The army put all sorts of things down there. Boxes and boxes, tunnels full of canned food, coffee, sugar, cigarettes. There are uniforms. And weapons."

"How do you know?"

"I was there."

"When?"

"Arrange a meeting with Elisabeth Sieland. Afterward, I'll tell you everything. I'll draw you a map. I'll take you there myself if that's what you want. But let me see Elisa first."

Without saying anything, Fenshaw left the room. Clara dropped into her chair. She was shaking, and she poured the last of the tea, lukewarm now, to calm herself. The timing was so important. When she told Elisa where her son was, Elisa had to try to get to the mine before Fenshaw. Somehow. She had to get Willy out before Fenshaw saw him in his Wehrmacht uniform, with his gun. If he was caught as he was now, he'd be arrested. If he was disturbed enough to fight . . . Clara didn't want to think about that, just as she didn't want to think about the possibility that Elisa hadn't survived the war. And Jakob—Clara was robbing him of his dream to take the depot for his family. His betrayal still wounded her, but she had no desire to seek revenge, or make him or his sisters suffer. She didn't know what else to do.

She tried the door, found it locked. At the window, she could see soldiers carrying boxes and crates to a lorry. With a chill, she remembered Fenshaw's steel locker, the complete darkness, the blindness like needles pricking the skin of her eyelids.

Finally, he returned carrying a coat for her, army and a man's; the shoulders were practically up to her ears. Then he led her outside and to the back of the truck.

"Let me help you up, miss?" On the truck bed, Reynolds held his hand out to her.

She turned on Fenshaw. "What is this?"

"Transport."

"To where?"

"Another way station. Safer than this one."

She wasn't sure if he was telling the truth. Maybe he was taking her to the interrogation center after all. "Do we have a deal?"

His nod was slight, but it was there and, with hope sparking inside her, she climbed onto the back of the truck. Fenshaw touched his cap and returned to the barracks.

"Looks like it's just you and me, miss," Reynolds said with a grim smile, a pair of handcuffs swinging from his finger. "You're not slipping away from me this time."

During the journey, she crouched between the boxes, her hands bound in her lap. Reynolds was nearby, clutching his rifle. The truck meandered through the countryside, stopping only when she had to stretch her legs or squat on the side of the road. The flat landscape could have been the Niederrhein to the west or Münsterland in the north. Eventually she saw hills in the hazy distance, felt the elevation as the air grew colder. Perhaps they were going east after all? The Sauerland? There were no stars in the night sky to orient by. The soldiers only stopped near wide and empty fields. If she ran, a rifle would soon find her—a dark spot moving across the white land.

They halted for good at the edge of a forest where snow hung heavy in the trees. Nearby was a crude cabin of warped, dark wood. Two horse head carvings faced away from each other over the door.

As the soldiers carried supplies inside, she shivered in the ruts the truck had made in the snow. All around her, there were only trees and hills and the lonely ribbon of the road. She was alone, so far from help, the soldiers probably had no fear of her escaping.

On the doorstep of the cabin, she looked up. "Oh, God."

Over her head, cobwebs hung in the corners of a peaked ceiling crisscrossed by sagging beams. Snow from a hole in the roof dusted her hair. The floorboards creaked and bent under her feet as she turned from the stack of camp beds to the empty shelves, taking in the dirt, the decay. She didn't want to know what little creatures crept and slithered in the dark corners of the room.

The seclusion of this place was disturbing, certainly, but maybe it was a good sign. Tomorrow, or perhaps the next day, Fenshaw would drive up in the snow. Beside him, in the passenger seat, behind the damp windshield, would be the pale, freckled, anxious, and then joyful face of Elisa.

22

"W here do you want this?" The British soldier had stopped in the kitchen doorway, his chin resting on top of the box he was trying not to drop. He was being polite, but it was the last thing Jakob wanted from one of them. They could all go to hell. Soldiers, Allied, German, he didn't care. He'd had enough of them for a lifetime.

The soldier touched his cap to Dorrit—polite boys, these Tommies. "Compliments of Captain Fenshaw."

This was the second time Fenshaw had sent them, along with food and coal, and Jakob didn't want the man's compliments now any more than he did before. "Tell the captain we wish him the plague and cholera."

The soldier looked confused, then withdrew, and

not a moment too soon. Jakob had been squeezing his lighter in his fist. He wanted to burn something down.

"Cadbury's Fruit and Nut bars," Dorrit said, reading the label. She looked at Jakob with a longing and guilt he could barely stand to see. She knew what he'd done for her, the baby, the family, and she blamed herself, as he'd known she would. Blamed herself for his scowls and his silence and the fact that he couldn't sleep. He had betrayed Clara, and it didn't matter that Dorrit understood why he'd done it. Did Clara? That was the poison he ate every day now—the idea that she might never forgive him.

He nodded at Dorrit, and she tore open the package with her teeth and managed to get the whole bar into her mouth at once. Gabi came in bundled up from the cold and dug into the box too, going straight for the chocolate. The girls put the food in the cupboards, their shelves no longer bare. This was the trade-off for betraying Clara's trust. Fenshaw had paid him well for it. So well, Jakob could almost think Fenshaw was feeling guilty for threatening Jakob's family to get his way. Not that it mattered. The bastard had won. Clara was gone. Just gone.

Jakob had returned to the Works to see for himself. There in the snow were the footprints of the soldiers who had taken her away. There, in their old shelter, were her blankets, the ones they had slept on together.

There, on the factory floor, were the remains of their fire. He'd nearly crushed his own teeth looking at those ashes. He and Clara, they had had so little time and he'd wasted it.

She was gone, yet there was no news about her arrest. Not in the newspapers. Not in the gossip at the markets. If a Falkenberg was arrested in this town, people would talk. He could only conclude that nobody knew, and something cold hardened inside him. A woman couldn't just vanish, not a woman like her. Jakob had spent the past two nights tossing in his bed trying to decide what he could do to help her, whom he might appeal to. It had to be someone with access to the Allies, someone with influence who could find her and make sure she was all right.

The solution came to him suddenly as Dorrit began ripping the box the soldier had brought them into pieces that would fit in the oven. Tearing, burning paper. The magazine he had burned with Clara at the club. The article had mentioned her mother: an Englishwoman.

Finding her was easy enough. He knew some English fellows who supplied him from the British stores when they could get away with it. One of them got him an address in Bredeney, a district he hadn't had much cause to go to, seeing as he didn't know any rich people, at least not until Clara. Her mother's place was powder blue and there were stucco grapes over the door. As he staked out the house, he saw British officers come and go through the front door, men with good instincts. A few stared at him as they passed, and one told him to move along.

"Yes, sir," Jakob said with mock respect, but he didn't move from the pavement opposite Anne Falkenberg's doorstep.

He had been worried that he'd fail to recognize the right woman, but there was no mistaking her. The moment she stepped out of the house, wrapped in gray fur, he knew her face. This was Clara but older, blond, and painted, sly around the eyes. Anne was beautiful, no doubt about it, but he hoped Clara wouldn't look that stiff and proud and spoiled in thirty years' time.

"Good day to you, Frau Falkenberg," he said, touching his hat.

Anne adjusted the furs around her neck. With the fur hat, it seemed her head nestled in the paws of some sleek animal. "Do I know you, young man?" She looked pleased and curious, and he took his cue from there.

"My name is Jakob Relling and it's an honor to meet you."

"Is it, now." Her gray gloves slid through the fur at her collar. "Why is that, then?"

He told her about his scholarship, that he owed his education to the Falkenbergs, that he wasn't a complete dimwit wasting his talents in the mines because her great husband had supported him. The longer he spun the story, the brighter her face became and, by the end, she was holding his arm. "My boy, it's delightful to meet such an admirer of my husband, and such a grateful one too. The world is full of ingratitude these days."

"It certainly is."

A car arrived at the curb and the driver leaped out to open the back passenger door. Anne gave Jakob a long, appraising look, then asked him if he needed a lift somewhere.

"Wherever you're going is fine with me," he said.

"Just the sort of man I like." She allowed him to help her into the car and had the grace to say nothing about the clumsy way he climbed in, or his needing to rub his bad leg afterward. During the ride, they chatted while the ruins slid past the window. He couldn't quite believe he'd talked himself into a car with Frau Falkenberg, and it made him feel dizzy, as if the world was moving too fast.

"I'm having a lovely time, darling"—Anne brushed the back of his hand playfully—"but I'm afraid I do have to ask what you want from me."

"Nothing. I just wanted to express my support for your family."

"Very dutiful of you, but also unlikely. It's a cold world we live in now. People only think of themselves. We used to live in a society, a great web of relationships"—she spread her hands—"linking the highest to the lowest as one people, helping each other, there for one another. Now"—she dropped her hands—"we're reduced to fighting each other for edibles in the rubbish bins."

"I doubt you'd ever do that, Frau Falkenberg."

"You're a good boy. Now tell me what you want." She fit her cigarette into an ebony holder. He lit it with his lighter, her face illuminated behind the flame.

"Did you hear what happened to your daughter?"

There was the slightest shift in her face. A hardening around the eyes. "My daughter?"

"Clara."

"I know my daughter's name, darling. How do you know her?"

"We're just . . ." He was about to say friends, thought he should dampen it to acquaintances, felt cowardly and said, "We're good friends."

"Really. And what happened to this good friend of yours?"

"She was arrested two days ago, and—"

Anne pressed her fingers to her lips and nodded

toward the driver. He looked as though he was concentrating on the road, but Jakob got the message and kept his mouth shut.

"There's really no time to talk now, darling. Why don't you come with me to the party? We can speak afterward."

"Anytime you want."

His charm wasn't having the same effect as before. Anne had stiffened beside him, and something sharp edged her voice. "Do you have any children? It might look awfully odd if you don't. It's a children's party."

He told her about Gabi, thirteen, but looking more like eleven. Anne said she would have to do. They stopped at his house, him praying Gabi was at home. He explained everything to her as quickly and simply as he could manage and she agreed, reluctantly, to join him. She didn't like parties, but maybe there would be sweets?

The party was at a hall in the Fürstinstrasse. In the doorway, a cheerful soldier with a silver ribbon pinned to his tunic consulted his clipboard before anyone could go in. Jakob held Gabi's hand, expecting to have to wait with the crowd of children and adults ahead of them, but Anne forged a path to the soldier, announced she had special guests, and escorted them into the hall. To Gabi's delight, there were vanilla crescents and cinnamon stars. Butter biscuits dented with anise. Chocolates in sparkling paper. A boy split a walnut in a nutcracker soldier. Another peeled an orange and mashed it into his face. Bewildered girls picked at Christmas crackers until a soldier showed them how to pull the ends. The girls jumped and screamed and one burst into tears. Carols were blaring from the speakers. Jakob hadn't heard this kind of din since the Battle of the Ruhr. Maybe this was louder.

Anne was quickly surrounded by women and officers, but she eventually broke away from them, taking him by the elbow. "You're looking lost, darling. I am dying to speak with you, but unfortunately I can't get away quite yet. Maybe you could have a little chat with . . ." She brightened and waved at a family that had just arrived, a plump woman with ringlets carrying a baby, her husband sleek and elegant, a strange match. He was holding the hands of two blond toddlers who looked exactly like him. Anne showered the family with greetings that seemed overly gracious. The woman looked stunned and pleased, and the man, introduced as Max Hecht, greeted them coldly but politely. His wife herded the children toward the food while he hung back.

"Talk about man things while I'm gone, hm?" Anne said, and strolled to the Christmas tree on the stage.

"I suppose she means the war," Jakob said as he offered Max a cigarette.

"Where did you serve?"

Turned out they had both been in the first thrust into Russia, and they had wintered a few kilometers from each other. But while Jakob stayed in the east, Max had gotten a ticket home. Declared too valuable to be cannon fodder, he had spent the rest of the war at the Falkenberg Iron Works. "I'm a lawyer."

"Gesundheit."

Max had the grace to smile, and that was a surprise. He was the kind of oily fellow Jakob had never liked—too handsome, too polished. A university man, he had the dueling scar he'd earned in one of the student clubs. When sober, those types usually had no sense of humor.

"What do you do, Herr Relling?"

"I'm a wholesaler."

"Black market, then."

"I didn't say that."

"Don't worry, I'm a realist. The black market is the only functioning economy we have right now. If a man makes some money off it, I don't hold it against him. How do you know Frau Falkenberg?"

"I was a scholarship boy. I'm grateful to the family."

Max snorted. "Aren't we all."

The music cut off, and a soldier announced their hostess as Anne Heath. Jakob guessed the name Falkenberg wasn't popular with so many Allied soldiers in the room.

"Children," Anne said in German, "welcome to our Christmas party. Everything here is just for you, for this wonderful season of peace and harmony." She addressed the adults, a line of drab and fatigued women and men sitting at the wall. "All of us in the British community would like to welcome you. We're happy to give your children a carefree moment of joy. Before you go, you'll be given one present for each child to take home." She gestured at the boxes under the tree. "Please accept some refreshment, and enjoy the celebration."

The soldier choir struck up "God Rest Ye Merry, Gentlemen." A woman held a tray of steaming punch in front of Jakob. As he sipped, he watched Anne go down the rows of children, shaking hands, patting heads, squeezing shoulders. She greeted the adults with the same grace and cheer. She'd been an early convert to the Nazi Party, according to the magazine, a British Fascist and Germanophile. Now here she was, the benevolent Englishwoman who had put aside her German name.

By the time Anne got to him, Jakob's head was aching from the electric lights blazing against the silver and gold decorations. He wasn't used to so much color and brightness, so much noise. The children were scurrying around with odd jerking motions, fired up from the calories and the glitter. It felt as though the party was on the edge of hysteria.

"Oh, darling"—Anne held his arm—"you look a little overwhelmed. I can't have that. No good friend of my daughter should suffer for my sake. Herr Hecht"—she turned an odd smile on Max—"take care of Herr Relling, will you? I'll have a moment to talk very soon."

After she weaved away into the crowd, Max said casually, "You're a friend of her daughter?"

As much as Jakob wanted to deny it—his relationship with Clara seemed too tender and vulnerable to discuss with just anyone—he also wanted to admit it, this secret about her identity he couldn't tell anyone about except his sisters. And Fenshaw.

"We're good friends, sure."

"What's that mean?"

Around the room, people began shushing each other and calming the children. The soldier choir began to sing "O Tannenbaum" in German. Jakob joined in but Max didn't. He stared at Jakob while the rest of the room sang.

When the noise of the party began again, Max said, "You haven't answered my question, Herr Relling."

Jakob didn't like his tone: the hostility, the suspicion. "Sorry, what question?"

"About Clara. What do you mean you're good friends?"

That little slip—Clara, not Fräulein Falkenberg—

was enough proof that Max had once known her well too, maybe something beyond being a friend of the family. Captain Fenshaw had mentioned an SS boyfriend. Was this him? This slick type who made Jakob want to bloody his nose to soil his collar?

"If you want to know, we got pretty close recently."

"In what way?"

"Oh, I don't talk about that stuff. Not in detail. I'll only say the cold nights are a little warmer when she's around."

The color emptied from Max's face, and he took a step toward Jakob, who stood his ground. He had grown up on the streets. He and the neighborhood boys used to beat up Hitler Youth, boys like Max had been and still was: spit-polished, arrogant, thinking they were better than everybody else.

"Where is she?" Max asked through gritted teeth.

"I don't know."

They held one another's gaze in a silent challenge. Max was the first to take a breath, collect himself. "I've been looking for her. If you know where she could be, if you have any idea, tell me."

"Herr Relling?" The girl with the punch tray seemed reluctant to get too close. "Frau Heath is ready to see you."

"Was a pleasure to meet you, Herr Hecht." Jakob

followed the girl out of the hall. He passed from dream-land back to reality. Under broken ceiling lights, he limped down a cold, stained hallway to an office where Anne, in her furs again, sat in a battered chair. She motioned for him to sit beside her.

"You've been limping," she said.

He tapped his thigh. "Wood."

"Light my cigarette, darling." To do it, he rolled his chair close to hers, leaned into her perfume. She exhaled at the ceiling. "Now, tell me what happened to her. Every detail."

He told her as much of the story as he could without incriminating himself, the fury on Anne's face alarming him. If she didn't know what had happened to her own daughter, could that mean that Fenshaw was acting alone? "Nobody told you?" he asked.

Her perfect white teeth clenched the cigarette holder. "I haven't heard a whisper, and I know all the important men in the military government."

"Fenshaw can't just arrest people and make them vanish."

"It looks as though he has. I should have had him dealt with after he came to search my house as though I was a common criminal."

"Could you ask around? Make sure she's all right?"

"I will find her and I will get her back, darling. Nobody kidnaps a Falkenberg without consequences." She picked up the telephone on the desk. He was surprised it worked, listening with admiration as she barked for a line to Glückaufhaus, British headquarters. After that, her English was so rapid, he didn't understand a word. Several minutes later, she banged the receiver back in the cradle. "Try getting anybody to actually do any work at Christmas. I'll have to nudge an officer or two at the party." She stood up, straightening her coat, a woman who was going to get things done. She would find Clara, he had no doubt about that. Anne seemed capable of charming or badgering anyone in her path until she got exactly what she needed.

Jakob thanked her and put on his hat, but he still had a niggling feeling in his gut. He hadn't yet done everything he could for Clara. She might be found, and Fenshaw punished somehow, but it didn't feel enough to erase his betrayal. He rubbed his hands, remembering her fingers entwined with his outside the mine, and the look she gave him: tender, full of needs and regrets. That was the woman he'd betrayed. She was opening up old wounds, trying to understand parts of herself and her past that most people would firmly ignore. He wasn't sure about her guilt or innocence. He'd seen enough in the war to know how close the two could be in one person. But her conscience was real and deep, and that had

to count for something, even if Fenshaw believed other-
wise. Jakob couldn't sit back and wait for news that she
was free.

"One moment, darling." Anne was watching him
the way Clara had, still and inquisitive. "I was wondering, did you recognize my daughter or did she admit
who she was?"

"I recognized her. It's not a face a man forgets."

"Did she tell you what she was doing in Essen?"

He sensed the real question behind her question.
She wanted to know if he knew about any of the family's sordid little secrets. "She told me she was looking
for an old friend. Elisabeth something."

"Did Clara talk about her much?"

"Some." He couldn't resist probing. Clara hadn't
known Willy was her brother, but he'd bet a thousand
marks Anne did; that was the kind of secret she'd have
kept from her own daughter. "I think her friend was
pregnant, and there was something about the kid's
father—"

"A very gifted accountant named Reinhard. Good
Nordic stock. I saw his skull measurements once. Di-
vine." Her lips hardened into a line the color of blood.
"I'm curious, what did Captain Fenshaw give you when
you betrayed my daughter? How low was your price?
Hm? Some coffee and a can of ham?"

"I didn't—"

She wiped her hand across his forehead. "You did. The guilt is oozing from your pores. A Falkenberg tolerates no treason. We expect nothing less than total loyalty."

"You're a Falkenberg again, are you? I thought you were an Englishwoman named Heath."

"You've done me a service telling me about my daughter. I will take over from here. But remember, if I ever trace one bit of slander about my family back to you, I will crush you, darling. Don't forget that. Oh, and have a very happy Christmas." She dismissed him with a pat on the cheek as if he were a boy at the party stuffing walnuts into his pockets.

It made him burn, but he'd done what he'd come to do. Jakob limped quickly back to the party to collect Gabi. Her cheeks inflated like a squirrel's, she looked up at him with big eyes and mumbled with her mouth full: "I don't want to go."

"Sorry, little mouse." As he was helping her with her coat, he glanced into the hallway. Anne was hissing at Max Hecht, who was listening with sharp attention and a readiness Jakob remembered having himself when he was a soldier ready to go to war.

Cracks

He was lying on his bed, staring at the ceiling, when he saw it. Right there, in his line of sight, was the black rock and the beam, and a fresh white jagged crack running through it.

He got up for a closer look, ran his hand along the crack, the splinters prickling his skin. It was a deep cut. If the beam were an arm, it would have bled, dripping down on him while he slept. He couldn't tolerate the idea of blood. Anything but that.

Squatting on the ground and sweeping the black dust with the edge of his hand into a little pile at his feet, he added a few drops of water from his canteen, mixing it to a paste with a spoon and transferring it onto a tin plate. He slathered it onto the cracked beam. "That ought to do it." Mama used to say, "You're the most resourceful boy I know."

Gertrud hopped onto his bed and cocked her head, assessing his work. Right behind her, not a hand's width away from her nest, was a split in the timber. That couldn't be. Lantern up, he searched for more and found them on the tunnel walls, on the ceiling, everywhere. Had the cracks always been there and he hadn't seen them?

He smeared thick slabs of moist black dirt on the walls, on the ceiling, on the beams, on the timbers. The more he repaired, the more chinks he saw. He couldn't get them all, couldn't possibly. They were everywhere.

He threw himself onto his bed. It felt as though his heart had shrunk and was rattling around in the cold empty cavity behind his ribs. "Gertrud, what's happening?" He wiped his mouth and there was moist black dirt between his teeth. In the thick air, his eyes watered, and he chewed the grit in his mouth, a paste collecting on his tongue that he spat out. Spat and spat. And everywhere he looked, the cracks.

23

The parlor had no stove, only a broken radiator that seemed to pump cold into the room, but it was Jakob's space and he chose it as the place to have a serious talk with his sisters. He didn't want Dorrit tidying up while he spoke, so he did it himself, hefting boxes of wire and scrap metal organized from the ruins, sniffing the clothes on the worn armchair, tossing the rank ones into the basket and folding the cleaner ones into the suitcase he used as a dresser. He rearranged the furniture too, angling the chair so that he could sit in it while his sisters had the sofa. If they all sat side by side, the girls could turn away from him too easily. He wouldn't know what they were really thinking.

Seeing them on the sofa now, hand in hand, faces closed with uneasiness and suspicion, Jakob's courage almost left him. Dorrit's belly was a constant reminder of what he had to protect at all costs. And Gabi, her hair over her forehead like the forelock of a pony, was too small, too fragile, a teenager who looked like a little girl. The pain he felt when he looked at them was love, he knew that. Seeing their mother die a few months ago had taught him how much love could hurt. But the rawest place inside him belonged to Clara. Wherever she was, whatever was happening to her, he was partly responsible. The pain of his guilt kept him up at night, his leg pulsing and enflamed: his own body punishing him for betraying her.

"I've decided." He cleared his throat, wishing he'd brought a flask of schnapps. "I'm going back to the mine."

"We have food," Dorrit said quickly. "What you brought from the mine, and what the Englishman gave us. It's enough for a few weeks if we're careful. You don't have to go back so soon."

He'd known she would say exactly this. He knew how scared she was of him leaving again and not coming back. It made what he was about to say even harder. "I'm going back for Willy."

"But the first time you were in that mine, he shot at you. The second time, he threatened Fräulein Falkenberg. He's dangerous. You said so yourself."

"He won't pull that kind of thing in this house. I'll see to that."

The girls looked at one another, and at him, incredulously. "You're bringing him here?"

"If I can get him out—"

"Why? Why here?"

"It's the mine that's making him crazy. I mean, he's been there almost two years. Once he's out and living in a normal family, he'll get better."

"He's not your responsibility, Jakob," Dorrit said.

He slumped back in the chair. He wasn't being all that convincing because he wasn't convinced himself that this was the right thing to do. For his family, it was a potential catastrophe. But for Clara, it was right. If Elisa couldn't be found, maybe helping Willy was the only thing Jakob could do to make up for his betrayal. It was an act almost large enough to erase what he'd done. He would show her what kind of man he really was.

"I'm going to tell you a secret and you got to swear not to say a word to anybody, all right?" After the girls crossed themselves, he said, "Willy is Clara's little brother. I'm not going to tell you the details because we are not a family that's interested in the personal business of others." Dorrit had bowed her head, and he put a warm hand on her arm. "I don't judge you, little mouse, and we're not going to judge Willy's mother either. The kid doesn't have anybody right now. We can help him until he finds his own way."

"What if he doesn't want to be helped?"

"I can only offer him a home. A temporary home until he gets used to how things are out in the real world. I know it's a lot to ask of you. We don't have much space and there's the cooking and cleaning and he's a stranger. But he's fifteen, right between you two. Gabi, you could take him to school, maybe. Oh, and Gertrud, his bird, would come too. She could be free here in the parlor."

Gabi's face brightened as she looked around, imagining, he assumed, the yellow canary hopping across the sofa back. Dorrit was unimpressed. "Where's he supposed to sleep?"

"In here. On the floor or in this chair, I don't know. But he won't go near you at night."

"He better not."

"And I'll put him to work. We got repairs needed all over the house. We can string some electrics, we got to do something about the water pipes, there's that hole in the kitchen wall . . ." He went on, detailing the chores he'd put off, wanting the girls to imagine Willy hammering down loose floorboards or up on a ladder funneling wire through a hole in the ceiling. If they could envision Willy being useful—and sane—Jakob had all but won.

Dorrit was stroking the dark blue wool stretched over her belly. Jakob squeezed onto the sofa between her and Gabi and put his arms around them.

"I have to do this." He stopped, his words lost, too twisted up as he pictured Clara in the bare cell of an Allied prison or the rough barracks of an internment camp. "I have to do this for Clara. She'd want to know her brother is safe until she comes back."

He didn't say the next bit. That if she came back and Willy was living in this house, he knew that she would come here, right here to this parlor, looking for him. If that was the only way Jakob could see her again, so be it. If she stormed at him or turned away from him in disgust, he could live with that if he had to, but at least he'd see with his own eyes that she was all right. And she would see that he had tried to help her, in the end, the only way he could.

"All right," Dorrit said, sighing, "he can come. For a little while. As long as he does his own laundry. I'll have enough to do when the baby comes."

They shook on it, and then he pulled her into as tight a hug as he could manage with her belly between them. Gabi joined in, the three of them—four, actually—wrapped in a warm embrace that Jakob tried to imprint in his memory just as he had years ago when he was about to leave for the front.

After the girls left the parlor, Jakob switched on the lamp and began packing the things he would take to Willy's mine. First, his beloved calendar. The American girl smiled at him as always, but she bored him now. Compared to Clara, she was as sticky sweet as an old toffee. Just the thing for a fifteen-year-old boy who hadn't seen a girl his age since the war. The year was printed in bold next to each month. Crazy as he was, even Willy couldn't think Jakob had somehow manufactured a 1946 calendar to fool him into believing that time had passed.

Next, Jakob carefully tore off the front pages of the newspapers he'd kept to use as toilet paper or to light fires. He looked for dates, headlines, photos, news of Allied conferences. If Willy had any sense left in him, he couldn't read them and think the war was still on.

The last thing Jakob had to do was the hardest. His family didn't have much that anybody else would call precious, but the wooden trunk his mother had brought into her marriage had always seemed so to him. It was good German oak, and that meant it would last forever. Jakob hadn't so much as opened it since she died. Gently, he lifted the lid, and a musty smell rose from his mother's dresses. He didn't have the heart to sell them right now, but he knew he would if he was hungry enough. Beneath them was his photograph album from the war. In gold engraving: *My Adventures on the Front*. He browsed the pictures, warm with shame, but longing too for the man he had once been, the one who strutted down the street in his uniform, enjoying the looks thrown his way. The one who danced. Who kicked a ball around in the alley behind his house. In one photograph from early in the war, he posed on the edge of a French forest, cigarette in his mouth, cap slanted at an angle to show what a saucy bastard he was. He looked like a soldier who knew only victory. He stood on his own flesh and bone feet.

He closed the album quickly. There was nothing left in the trunk but the false bottom his mother had installed toward the end of the war. He prized it up and, underneath, the bundle was still there. Nobody wanted to touch this, including him. But he had no choice.

The first thing he unfolded was the gray tunic, all Nazi symbols and signs of rank cut away. There was no sign he'd been wearing this when he was wounded. After the Americans demobilized him, his mother had scrubbed the uniform, repaired it, preserved it. She'd told him it was the sensible thing to do with a perfectly good uniform. Who knew when he might need it again?

He put on a clean white shirt, then pulled on the tunic. His muscles recoiled from the weight of it, the old, familiar sensation of his arms sheathed in army wool. A sense of dread descended, the same feeling he'd had the last time he wore this as a soldier in a losing army. The tunic's gray was washed out in places, like a rainy sky seen through cataracts. Out of the pocket, he took a wrap of cotton. Inside was his Iron Cross, earned for whatever they were calling valor back when he was in the army. He pinned it on and rooted in the bundle of paper where his tattered trousers lay. His cap was underneath. Jakob fitted it on his head in a gesture that was natural, something he'd done all his life. Feeling a fraud, he checked himself in the mirror. On the outside, he was a soldier again, the wrong kind. If the British caught him like this, he wouldn't be around to see Dorrit's baby born. It was a risk, but he had no doubt Willy would listen to him dressed like this.

Here and there, public transport was running again. Jakob rode on whatever streetcars or omnibuses he could find heading south, his army tunic hidden under a borrowed civilian overcoat. He was relieved when he left the more crowded districts of the city for the quiet meadows along the bank of the river. Almost all of the snow had melted, leaving wet soil and grasses that had immediately frozen. Each step crunched under Jakob's feet, and he chose his steps as carefully as when he had only one leg and a crutch. He reached Willy's mine exhausted, and rested on a flat stone on the slope. The only sound in the valley was his own breathing, the exhalations he made when he blew smoke from his cigarette. The clouds hung low and dark in the early twilight.

Ready, he stowed his coat in the brambles outside the entrance.

In the first tunnel, he paused where the daylight suddenly ended. He was shivering and his nose was running, and when he went back out to piss, he realized he wasn't just cold, he was nervous. The uniform, the damned uniform, reminding him of the old fears.

Back inside the mine, he entered the concrete corridor. He took down the burning lantern from its hook, and the shadows shifted around him.

"Hey, kid, it's me. I know you're here." As he went deeper into the mine, he glanced into each room, raising his lantern, seeing only the tidy boxes and packets his light could reach.

"Halt, thief." The command ricocheted off the tunnel walls.

Willy's voice was as rasping and wolfish as the first time Jakob had come to the mine. The voice was a sign. Willy moved backward in time instead of forward like everybody else.

Jakob tried to locate him in the deep dark outside the

glow of his lamp. Two tunnels, one broad and straight, the other jagged rock barely broader than his shoulders. Willy's order had come from one of them. He was hiding in the dark, the special, total dark of the mine that Papa had whispered about under the covers when Jakob and his brothers were boys huddled together, flashlight off. Nothing but their excited breathing and their papa's voice. *Retrace your steps in the dark. Go on and try. You can, but did you pay attention to all the side tunnels? One wrong turn leads to another. And another.*

"Willy? You still there? I'm not a thief. We went through that already, right? I'm here to help you."

"Where's the fräulein?"

"I don't know."

Willy was still keeping himself hidden, but he had moved closer. Not into Jakob's light, but near. "Why don't you know?"

"The British arrested her."

A long pause. "That isn't possible."

"I brought some presents for you, Willy. Christmas presents. Want to see?"

The silence lasted so long, Jakob finally swung the lantern into the next tunnel. Empty. The next, empty. He backtracked to his favorite room, the cigarettes, and discovered the packs newly stacked into a pyramid that reached the ceiling. He didn't know if it was a bad sign, if Willy had lost his mind for good.

Willy wasn't in his camp, but Gertrud peeped a greeting from her nest. "Glad to see you too, sweetheart," Jakob said. Propped up on an iron stand was a piece of metal bent into something almost like a star. A boxwood shrub stood on the crate table where Willy's nails and screws used to be. Stars cut from the lids of food tins hung from what Jakob assumed was the boy's version of a Christmas tree. Small packages wrapped in paper were stacked underneath. Jakob shook one, then peeled back the paper. It was a can of ham.

He recognized all of this. Christmas at the front. No Yuletide joy, only quiet, melancholy rest. His last Christmas in Russia, soldiers from around Europe had sung carols on the radio. When the opening notes of "Silent Night" began softly, it was the only time in three years of war that Jakob cried.

He pulled his own gifts for Willy out of his bag and laid them under the tree. These were the things that would convince the kid the world had changed. Between putting on his uniform and getting to the mine Jakob had been inspired, borrowing one of Dorrit's beloved books, with her permission, of course, and a promise to bring it back. He'd collected Allied forms, even a partially filled-out Fragebogen that his mother had abandoned when she fell sick. Her illness had made it irrelevant, and she hadn't belonged to any of the Nazi organizations anyway. On the way to the mine, he had peeled a military government notice off the wall of a building. He spread the poster out on Willy's bed, and Gertrud hopped around it, her head cocked as if she was reading what it had to say. The best for last, Jakob found a nail in the timber wall and hung up his calendar. The December girl smiled out, wholesome and inviting.

He withdrew to the dead end to watch and wait and guess what the kid would look at first. If Jakob had been cooped up in a mine for two years, the first thing he'd look at was the calendar. It had to be the girl or the kid had no warm blood in him.

But when Willy returned to his camp, he looked around, startled at the new things under his tree, on the wall and the bed. He picked up Dorrit's book and held it like a precious thing, angling it to the lantern.

"It was one of the first things published after the war," Jakob said. "Look at the copyright: 1946. A woman wrote it secretly when she was in prison near the end."

Willy set the book on the table, then shook out his hands as though he'd been burned. He stared at Jakob as if noticing him for the first time, his mouth open. "You're wearing . . . that."

"You should know I'm not just some fellow off the street. I was a soldier. I fought."

Willy swiveled away from Jakob's gaze and picked up the Allied forms, frowning deeply the longer he browsed them. "What is this? Why is it partly in English?"

"That's a Fragebogen, a form we use to summarize our lives and war and to see if we were political. It's a way for the Allies to ferret out just how Nazi each of us was. They want to know everything. Where we went to school. What kind of toothpaste we used."

Willy examined the half-dozen pages in his hand. "It doesn't say anything here about toothpaste."

"I was exaggerating. But they use it for what they call denazification. Sounds like disinfection, right? No coincidence. Anyway, you want a job as a teacher or something, they ask you: Have you been fragebogenized?"

Willy pulled a face. "That's a strange word."

"It's a strange world. To be honest, the world has been like that one way or another my whole life. It's even more true for you, kid. Just have to accept it and move on."

Willy let the forms spill to the ground. He walked over them, tracing black prints on the paper, and stopped at the government poster. Gertrud hopped across it, out of his way. He blinked down at the words, then put his hands to his face.

"Don't look away, kid. The truth isn't going to change just because you cover your eyes." When Willy didn't move, Jakob snapped, "Look at me, soldier."

Instantly, Willy dropped his hands and came to attention. His eyes shimmered. His whole body was like a twanging wire, vibrating with an anxiety Jakob could sense. He felt disgusted with himself for speaking to the boy like this, a reminder of how one man could stomp on the will of another with his voice alone.

"Do you respect this uniform?"

"Yes, sir."

"Look. This tunic doesn't have the Reich's eagle. You see? Look. No swastika." He emptied his wallet and showed his papers. "This is my identity card. Nineteen forty-six. And not a swastika anywhere on it. My ration card. Same thing. Look at them."

Willy did, glancing at the papers, breathing hard.

"I know you've got nowhere to go, and that's why I'm offering you a little help, kid. You can come home with me. I don't have much, just my sisters and a couple of rooms. You're welcome to stay with us, but you got to come out of here peacefully."

Willy pivoted away and stopped at the timber wall. The December girl and her cheerful smile. Nineteen forty-six.

"A lot of pretty girls out there," Jakob said. "I don't know if you realize it, but you're a handsome fellow. You'll be even better when you get some color back in your face, eat some fresh fruit and vegetables. There's a man shortage out in the world. You're going to get a lot of attention. Ever thought of that?"

"She's all made up. She looks like a tart."

"Nice to look at, though, hey? Why don't I take you to an American film? What was the last one you saw?" Jakob swerved away from reminding Willy of the past. "Doesn't matter. Pack up some stuff, we can take off these uniforms and be at the Atrium by eight o'clock. What do you say?"

Willy gave him a look of despair. And then he lowered his head like a bull's and charged straight into the wall.

24

At the sound of the motor outside, Clara ran to the window and wiped the glass with her palm. The soldiers went to meet Captain Fenshaw, and as she watched him get out of the car, she saw the empty passenger seat beside him. Her stomach tightened with anxiety and dread. Where was Elisa?

Fenshaw came in stomping his boots, trailing in snow. "How have you been getting on?"

"Sir, where is Elisabeth Sieland? You said you'd bring her."

He hung up his hat and began to unbutton his coat. "I don't think I said that."

"We had a deal. About the mine, remember?"

He rubbed his hands at the weak fire in the hearth, and checked the kettle had water. The soldiers Jennings and Dwight carried in boxes and unpacked them on the table. Fenshaw's files thudded one after the other onto the wood like the booming of her own heartbeat. He waved for her to take a seat opposite him, and opened the top file to a stack of blank paper. He sat back with it, a black pen with a flashing golden nib at the ready. "Tell me how you escaped from custody the first time, and your whereabouts and activities up to when we found you at the iron works."

"Why does any of that matter now? Why are you doing this? For your files? It's just paper." She picked up one of them, thinking she would hurl it at the flames, but he gave her such a sharp look of warning she immediately set it back on the table. "You know what's happened to Elisa, don't you? Why won't you tell me?"

"Why is it so important to talk to her now?"

She let out a sound of frustration and paced to the fire. She couldn't tell him about Willy yet. She had to protect him as long as possible and, besides, she didn't know how to begin to explain his situation.

"I can't say. You'd draw the wrong conclusions. About all of us. Why would you even try to understand? You've made up your mind about me already."

He slapped his papers onto the stack of files and got up abruptly, ruffling his hands through his hair as he stalked away from her to the cabin door.

"I've been trying to make up my mind about you since 1936." He turned back to her, a collision of anger and uncertainty in his face. "I've tried to be impartial, to approach your case like any other, a matter of gathering information, constructing a complete picture of who you are. But I could never quite"—he curled his fingers as if trying to grasp something invisible—"reach down far enough. Most people aren't that hard to understand, actually, but with you it's like trying to read a spinning compass. At that BUF rally, you were wonderful. You were courageous, independent, disrespectful, all the things the Fascists hate. You had me convinced"—he gestured as if he was alone, talking to himself—"you had me hooked, really. It was only after the war started that I wondered if you were as brilliant an actress as your mother, as the rest of your family. If you truly have any convictions at all. If maybe you had been playing with me to amuse yourself. If it was all a game."

She watched him pace, fascinated by how raw he seemed when he let his composure fall away. It amazed her that she had affected him so deeply, that such a brief encounter had fed something inside him for years. The young heiress had broken the professionalism of the government man, but how? She remembered her mother's dossier on Fenshaw, that he was a widower with a son. She wondered if he had been a single father grieving for his wife a decade ago, finding in Clara a woman who could replace something of what he'd lost, if only from afar. He would not be the first man to project onto her his own ideas of who and what he wanted her to be.

"I wasn't playing back then, sir. What you saw of me was real. What I thought and felt. Convictions . . . yes, I always had them, even in the war. I just . . ." She was rubbing her arms, cold suddenly. "Oh, if only you were in my family, you'd know. My father used to say, 'Kaisers and chancellors come and go. The family stays.' The foundation of everything. I thought the Nazis, the war, it was all temporary. It was only a matter of getting through, holding on, doing what I could." She stopped herself, sensing the old slip into excuses. She was on the verge of blaming her father, that anger pulsing in her again, but she was a grown woman. She couldn't push her guilt on to him as if she were a child.

Fenshaw sat again, his hair smoothed back, the color still high in his face. "For a long time, I've wondered—if I'd approached you more openly back then at the rally, in that cloakroom, if I'd told you who I was, established that contact early on, would that have affected what you did in the war?"

She tried to imagine it: a kind of lifeline to a different set of choices. With a little more encouragement, she might have passed on production schedules or weapons specifications to the Allies, sabotage on a grander scale than what she'd attempted with Elisa and Max. "I don't know if I would've done things any differently if you'd tried to recruit me. Back then, I would probably have felt like I was betraying my family."

"You're half English."

"Yes, but as you're well aware, my mother wasn't exactly the best representative of that side of me. Growing up, my aunts and uncles and even my grandparents in England were always a little distant as well. I was convinced they thought I wasn't really one of them—too German. Only my German family accepted me completely."

"Perhaps you're right," Fenshaw said, subdued. "Maybe there was nothing I could have done to change things." He fetched her coat from the wall. "I'd like you to wait outside for a few minutes."

"Why?"

He didn't answer, and she slipped her arms into the sleeves. His motives reached deeper than she'd thought. Underneath the layers of fascination, curiosity, and duty was a sense of his own missed opportunity to influence what he thought she'd become.

She buckled the coat's belt tightly, but she couldn't stop shivering as she waited in the snowy field behind the cabin. Reynolds was indoors with Fenshaw, leaving

Jennings and Dwight outside to guard her. They were young, barely older than Willy, and they'd treated her with distant politeness in her three days in captivity. She asked what was happening, but they just shrugged. Soon Reynolds came out with his rifle over his shoulder—nothing unusual. She assumed he was going on patrol as the soldiers did several times a day, but he stopped and stared at her.

"Go on in, miss." Still staring, he mumbled something to Dwight and Jennings, and then they started for the trees on the path they'd forged through the snow on past patrols.

After a few breaths to gather her composure, she went back inside.

A dozen portrait-sized photographs were hanging on the wall. The beds had been pushed back and a chair set in the middle of the room. Fenshaw was at the table with his files again, smoking as he read. "Please, sit down."

Instead she approached a random picture and recoiled at the bombed landscape, the wet ditch, the hand reaching out of the soil. Photograph after photograph showed men digging in the mud with shovels, with their hands, revealing a bare foot in the soil, an arm, a head full of matted, filthy hair. She pressed a hand to her throat. A knot was growing there, obstructing her breaths. Why was he showing her these things? She had nothing to do with those people. Nothing. Her head felt heavy, and she sat after all.

"Where do you think these photographs were taken?" Fenshaw asked.

She didn't like the position of the chair alone in the center of the room. She felt like the accused at a trial. "I have no idea."

"Not in Russia. Not in Poland."

"I said I don't know."

"In Essen, not far from the Grugapark."

She wanted to swallow but couldn't. The knot in her throat had grown hard and sharp.

"In the last months of the war," Fenshaw said, "foreign workers who escaped their labor camps formed gangs and lived in the ruins. Some joined forces with German criminals, thieves, black marketeers, and the like. The Gestapo had their hands full, as you can imagine. The jails overflowed."

She turned away from the images, but there was nowhere to look but the windows—and they were a disorienting white, as if nothing was anchoring the cabin to the earth.

"Let's think like the Essen Gestapo for a moment," he said, pulling a bottle of whisky and two glasses from his bag. "The Allies are closing in. Communications with Berlin are patchy. Local and district security have to decide for themselves what to do with the foreigners in their jails. Many of them were people who had once been forced to work for you, Miss Falkenberg."

She resisted the urge to get up, staying seated, hugging herself in the center of the room.

"The Gestapo had to act. But they weren't used to thinking for themselves. What do they do?"

"Why are you asking me this?"

"You know why."

"I don't. I had nothing to do with these photographs."

"Look closer."

She shook her head.

"You'll have to look at them sometime."

She realized he was going to keep the pictures on the wall for days if necessary. He would tell the soldiers to guard them until she did all that he wanted. She couldn't bear the thought of falling asleep with the corpses, of waking with them all around her. So she approached the wall again.

The first row of photographs hung directly in her line of sight. If she looked below them, there were more. If she looked above them, there was the timbered wall. She began counting the gouges in it, the images swimming on the edge of her vision.

"Come on, Miss Falkenberg. You must have an idea what the Gestapo decided to do. That was your world."

"When our people ended up in jail, we always tried to find out what had happened, what they were accused of, and to get them back if we could. We knew they'd be better off with us than with them. But it wasn't always possible. There were laws. We couldn't do a lot if the worker broke them." She cringed inside, aware of the excuses, the things she'd told herself in the war, told herself since—when maybe, just maybe, she could have done more.

Fenshaw stood behind her, not touching her, but close enough to force her to take a step closer to the photographs. "A special police court," he said. "That's the favorite solution of every police state that ever was. It's efficient. Men and women were condemned on the spot."

Directly at eye level was a picture of two men, one in a hat, braces, and a tie, the other in the shirt of a workman. Together they were dragging a corpse out of the mud. She couldn't tell if it was a man or a woman, saw only the wet and muddy bundle the men held, the lolling head. She was grateful she couldn't see the face. Spread behind the men were other people stooped over the soil, digging.

She covered her mouth, swallowed the sour taste,

but she couldn't look away now. The next image. More bent backs, a dozen men excavating in the mud, their faces turned away or hidden under their hats. Another image, a man in filthy boots looking wearily at the work going on around him. The next image, a close-up. An old man in a wrinkled coat was bending over a body slumped on the ground. The body wore a shoe of scuffed black leather. It hung from the foot. Clara saw the curve of a heel, a fallen stocking ruffled at the ankle. That shoe, the shape of that leg, somehow seemed familiar. The floorboards shifted, hollows under her feet.

"I didn't know about this."

"No?"

"How could I? I couldn't know about everything happening those last months. It was chaos. Do you think I wanted any of it?"

"When you fled Essen, what did you think would happen to the people you left behind?"

"I didn't think—"

"You didn't care?"

"I did care. I did. I'm sorry. I'm sorry about all of it."

"That's not good enough." He grasped her arms and it was a shock, him laying his hands on her. He turned her to face the wall again.

The crumpled stocking on the familiar leg. More than once she'd envied the shape of Elisa's calves and ankles as they flashed under her hem. And hated them too. Men had openly admired her in the streets. Clara had felt silly for being jealous of such a stupid thing. A leg. An ankle.

She had to be wrong. She was dreaming up similarities when there were none. "Who are these people? What are their names?"

"Based on the badges on their clothing, most are believed to have been Russian. A few people had no patches, different clothes. We assume they were Germans."

She let her gaze continue up the body, over the dirty knee and past the crumpled skirt. She reached the white blouse, its lace trim, its white buttons, the pocket at the breast and all of it spoiled by dark smears and splatters. Fenshaw was still holding her arms, the weight of his hands keeping her in this moment. "What are their names?" she asked again. "You have to know their names."

"One or two. Most of them haven't been identified. We do know when they were executed."

"When? What day?"

"The twelfth of March 1945. The day after you left."

Finally, she let herself look at the face in the photograph. Dark, like smoke in the air, was a curl of Elisa's hair. There was a wash of dark pigment where Elisa's nose and mouth had been, lighter around her eyes. The last thing Elisa had seen in her life was the gray sky above her, the barren field, the ditch. Her eyes were just the same as when they first met as girls, full of need and fear.

Clara tore herself away from Fenshaw and ran outside, gulping the cold air as she passed the truck and his car and kept running down the road, slipping and sliding in the snow. She missed her step and landed on her back. The shock of falling, the breath knocked out of her, the wet cold, and then stillness. The sky was white and empty and vast.

She could have prevented what happened to Elisa, to all of those people. She tried to think of how, how far back she'd have to go. The things she should have noticed, done, or said to prevent Willy from doing what he did later. As a girl, she should have shaken Elisa by the shoulders, demanded to know who the baby's father was. She should have done more for her son. She'd watched Willy drift through his childhood with parents who didn't love each other. He'd tried to sort and organize his world, moving through it quietly and alone. She could have been a kind of bridge for him to his mother and his real father. If she had known. If she had pushed Elisa to reveal her secret. If things had been different, maybe, after he saw his parents together at the Works, instead of going to the Gestapo, Willy would have come to Clara.

She could have confronted her father too. Instead of privately voicing her concerns about the workers and the regime, she could have stood up and declared her views in public, knowing the consequences and taking them. Perhaps her family would have lost the factories, would have been forced to leave the country. Perhaps she would have been silenced in some other, terrible way, but at least she would have spoken the truth. Maybe there would have been fewer transports, fewer people buried in the ditches.

Fenshaw stooped beside her in the snow, his face troubled and gray. She let him help her to her feet, and she held on to him as she swayed. The world was capsizing around her, filled with images of her father, Elisa, Willy, Galina, Max, the columns of workers trudging to her factories, the corpses in the photographs. In the long, twisted ribbon of actions and consequences, private corruption could lead to the biggest crimes. She hadn't wanted to believe how short the distance was between her labor camps and the death camps, the indignity of slave labor and a massacre. She had played a part in the greater crimes after all. Her. Not just her father. She wouldn't run away from that anymore.

Jennings and Dwight moved around the cabin lighting the lamps. She didn't know how long she had sat
in the dark, was surprised to look up and see the black
window. When she stood, the world tilted and her foot
banged against the half-empty bottle on the floor. She
was holding a glass, and vaguely remembered Fenshaw
pouring the full measure for her.

He was taking the photographs off the wall and
tucking them into a file with careful respect. It wasn't
until he eased the photograph of Elisa out of her hand
that Clara realized she'd been holding that too. He replaced it with another. "We found this in one of your
albums at Falkenhorst."

Her and Elisa with their heads together, smiling into
the camera. She wasn't yet twenty. They both looked
ready for a warmer, fuller life than either of them had
been able to live.

Fenshaw set a chair opposite her and sat, his back
bent, his elbows on his knees. His hair was thinning,
and it made her think of what time had done to all of
them, how vulnerable they were. How fragile their lives.

"Miss Falkenberg, where is the army depot?"

She ran her hands down her face. It felt strange, as
though it belonged to someone else. She tucked the

photograph in her pocket and thought of Willy, how he would react to the news. She would have to tell him. He had to know the truth of what happened to his mother even if he had already guessed. He deserved to know the whole story of who he was and where he came from and what it had led all of them to do.

"I need to go with you to the mine, Captain."

"Out of the question."

"Captain, Willy is there. In the mine. Elisa is dead and someone has to tell him."

"Willy?" He frowned, thinking. "Elisabeth Sieland's boy."

So Willy was in his files as Elisa's son just as Elisa was in them as Clara's friend. She took comfort in that, the link of relationships written down in ink. Fenshaw knew so much, she would not be surprised if he'd somehow worked out who Willy's father really was.

"Why on earth would he be in a coal mine?" Fenshaw asked.

"It's a long story, but—"

"Miss Falkenberg, I've been patient enough with you."

"I'll tell you everything, and you can send me to prison. But I need you to promise you'll help Willy. Don't arrest him or hurt him. He's been down there a very long time, and it's made him . . . sick."

Still cautious, Fenshaw sat back and lit a cigarette. "Tell me all of it." He exhaled a cloud. "And it had better be true."

The story was so extraordinary, she didn't know how to begin. "Willy Sieland is my father's son," she said in one gusting breath. "He doesn't know. Willy, I mean."

Fenshaw looked at her in surprise. "Theodor Falkenberg's illegitimate son. Your younger brother."

So he hadn't known. Suddenly she was certain she'd revealed too much, that Fenshaw would somehow use this information in ways she couldn't foresee. But it was too late to change that now. "He's been hiding in the mine since the war. He's convinced himself it's his duty to guard it, but that's not really why he's there."

Fenshaw held up a hand. "He's lived in this coal mine since—"

"—I left Essen at the end of the war. March '45."

"Almost two years?"

The horror in his voice fueled her anger at what Willy had gone through. "Two years."

"He must've gone mad."

"A little." She held that in. She refused to accept Willy was completely lost. "He believes the war is still going on and he won't leave the mine until it's over. But that's just the reason he's telling himself he can't leave. The real reason is that he turned Elisa in to the

Gestapo after he saw her with my . . . our father. He was confused. Angry. I think he suspects she's dead and it's his fault. That's why he won't come out."

Fenshaw was opening and closing his files as if looking for something to help him understand what she'd told him. These things were missing from all that he had gathered about Clara over the years, and she saw how he was trying to sort it out, if not in his mind, then in his papers. But there was nothing, and he sat back again, his composure cracked. "Bloody hell. It's madness."

"It's true. All of it." Her hands writhed in her lap. It was time for the direct appeal. "He needs help, Captain. I can't give it to him. I'll be in prison. I accept that. But he still needs help. I think he needs to surrender to an Ally so he sees once and for all that the war really is over."

Fenshaw was shaking his head in disbelief.

"It'll be a shock to him," she pressed on, "but it'll shake him out of his delusion. And after that . . . Isn't there a way you could do something for him?"

"What do you have in mind?"

"He'll need . . ." She hadn't thought through what Willy would need when he entered the world again. "Well, he'll need fresh food. He'll need to move around in the open air and daylight. He'll need someone to talk to. And practical things. He'll need papers—"

"If he leaves that mine with me, it sounds like I'll have a boy Nazi on my hands."

"He's not a Nazi!"

"Let's be charitable and call him an overzealous soldier. Those were the worst kind. Fanatics."

"I told you why he's there."

"Do you expect me to just turn him loose? His mother is dead. The man he took to be his father is dead. His real father denies him and is in an internment camp. You're captured. Where is he supposed to go? To his dear Fascist grandmother?"

"Never. She would ruin him. Worse than he already is. Please, Captain. You can find a place for him. You have the resources."

"You think I've got more power than I have."

"You stopped my train. You talked to everybody I ever knew in Essen. You brought me here. Don't tell me all of that was aboveboard." She spread her arms. "This is you. You do have power. You know the whole story now. You could go and tell Willy the truth and help him. I'll cooperate. I'll confess to whatever you want. But please . . . please, Captain, help him."

She reached out to Fenshaw, her hand close to his. If he understood anything she had told him, he would recognize that Willy was a part of the larger story. What Willy had done to Elisa was a part of the same twisting path that linked Clara to the massacre Fenshaw had showed her, and the suffering she and her father had caused. If Fenshaw felt a trace of regret at what he didn't say or do when he knew her as a younger woman, he might act now.

He sighed, looking down at his cigarette; then he stubbed it out in a dish. "It can't be done. Not like that. I'm sorry, Clara." He said her first name easily, as if he was comfortable saying it in his head and had been for a long while. She grasped at this sign of intimacy.

"Think about it. You could justify it to your superiors. Not only will you have captured the Iron Fräulein, you'll be the man who found the last big depot of the defeated German Army. Isn't that worth bending the rules a little, Thomas?"

He'd been packing away the bottle and glasses, and turned back to her, startled. The muscles in his face tensed, a moment when she couldn't decide if he was surprised at hearing her use his first name, or offended that she had dared.

"Tell me exactly where this mine is supposed to be. If the boy is there, I'll deal with the situation as I see fit."

"That's not good enough. Captain—"

He moved his files back into the boxes, and set a sheet of paper and a pencil on the table. "You said you'd draw a map."

"If you promise to help Willy."

"No conditions."

"He's just a boy. He's been suffering terribly."

He put on his coat. "If you truly want to help him, you'll draw that map. I'll give you one more night to consider. If everything you told me is true, every day you delay keeps him down there alone."

She followed him as he carried his files outside and stowed them in his car. The snow glowed in the yard. "Captain, try to understand my position. He's my brother."

He climbed behind the steering wheel. "I'll be back first thing in the morning. Whether I have a map to that mine or not, I'll have to turn you over to my colleagues for further questioning, and then internment. That's how this is going to end."

25

Clara watched until she no longer saw Fenshaw's lights in the dark, and then, in a dreamlike state, walked back to the cabin. She sat on her bed in a haze, her eyes wandering back to the wall where the photographs had been, the space where she had seen Elisa. She wanted to be mistaken about the body in the ditch. Maybe it hadn't been her. And then with a swift pang of nausea, she knew that it was far too late to deny the truth. She looked at the table where Fenshaw's paper and pencil lay. She didn't know what to do. Draw a map to the mine and potentially send Willy into catastrophe with the British soldiers? Or keep that piece of paper blank, leaving Willy safe but alone with his suffering? She thought of other possibilities. Max, whom Willy had loved and respected, but she couldn't bring herself to entrust her brother to him. Jakob was the only other person who might help. If he cared about her at all, he had to feel something for her brother. But the wound Jakob had given her had settled into a dull ache in her chest. Maybe he didn't care as much as she'd hoped.

Around her, the soldiers mumbled about the less than merry Christmas they were spending in that godforsaken cabin. She looked up at them. Christmas already?

Jennings said, "Let's take the lorry to Paris."

"Christmas in Paris." Dwight sighed.

Reynolds clapped his hands. "Enough. We'll stay as long as we're needed."

"He's about to say orders are orders."

"They are. If you were going to drop out of the army because the orders don't please you, you should've done it long ago."

Jennings hummed "God Save the King." Dwight stretched out on his bed. Reynolds glowered around the room and picked up the half-empty bottle of whisky. "He could've at least brought us another bottle."

She longed for it, another drink, something more to dull the sharp grief that coursed through her. Rummaging in the supplies for another bottle, she set aside the tins of bully beef and condensed milk, the packets of oatmeal and hard biscuits. One crate contained bottles of beer, but she needed something much stronger than that. In another crate, mixed in with blocks of chocolate and sachets of boiled sweets, were a couple of slightly shriveled apples and also lemons for tea. A pleasant aroma wafted from a tin container, and she opened it to find someone's muddled collection of spices—cloves, nutmeg, peppercorns, caraway seeds, even a broken stick of cinnamon. The cloves and nutmeg penetrated some deep memory, her mother in winter smelling just like this, wrapped in a blanket by the fire.

"Hot toddy," Clara said, and held out the spices to Reynolds.

He sniffed and passed the tin to Jennings, who inhaled and smiled.

"All we need are a pot, water, and fire," said Dwight.

They all turned to the hearth.

"We're on duty," Reynolds said.

"Come on, sir. What's the harm? The girl can fill the pot with snow. And there's more wood stacked under the tarp around the corner."

"It'll be wet."

"Some will be dry enough. What else are we supposed to burn?"

Reynolds turned a thoughtful look at the chimney. Then he helped Jennings clean the hearth. Dwight escorted Clara outside where she ladled snow into the pot. It did her good to dig down, hit hard ground. The cold sharpened her mind, and she thought of the truck parked at the front.

She carried the pot back inside the cabin and saw that Jennings had taken off his tunic and hung it on the back of a chair. The keys to the truck, she recalled, were in one of its pockets. The men ordered her to kneel at the hearth and blow at the flames. She wanted to touch the fire, light her finger and watch the flame spread over her hand, bite her sleeve and roar up her arm toward her heart. There lay the remains of her father's image, the half-woman, half-machine she'd become in the war, the last terrible moments of Elisa's life, the trust she had put in Jakob, shaken but not gone entirely.

Hot toddies. All of the men wanted a part in the making of this small cup of comfort, a taste of home. Dwight got to work cutting and squeezing the lemons, catching the juice in a cup. Reynolds searched for an extra bottle of whisky he could have sworn he'd seen when they packed the truck. Jennings tended the pot that hung over the fire, stirring in the cinnamon and cloves, not sure how many to put in and so adding them all. He gave Clara the tin and told her to grate the nutmeg. The repetitive, thoughtless work comforted her somewhat. She was rubbing the second nut against the grater when she vaguely recalled Jakob talking about nutmeg, what seemed like such a long time ago. It had been one of his war stories, someone in Russia taking it like a drug, hoping to escape reality when there was no other way out. Jakob had tried it for the promised high, she remembered, but he had only felt sick. She looked at the three soldiers, then at the dusting of nutmeg on the table. How much would it take to affect them? How would it taste?

She dabbed a bit of the powder onto her finger and touched it to her tongue. She immediately made a face, and her mouth watered to push the intensity away. The whisky and the lemon would harmonize with it, she hoped. She finished grinding all the nutmeg from the tin. When she tried to pour it into the pot, Jennings waved her away. "We'll add it to the cups," he said.

With a cry of triumph, Reynolds produced another bottle of whisky from the bottom of a box. This threw the men into a fit of merriment. They began singing Christmas carols while warming the teacups near the fire. Whisky was poured into each and then the hot brew of water and spices was ladled in. Dwight spooned in the lemon juice. By then, they were cheerful enough to allow Clara a cup, and so four of them were set out on the table. Clara had placed the bowl of nutmeg in the middle, and the men took a pinch each. It would hardly be enough to affect them the way Jakob had described. He'd given her the impression it took spoonfuls of the stuff. She could get the keys to the truck only if the men were sufficiently distracted—drowsy, drunk, or nauseated. For that, she needed them to dose themselves up. She would have to lead the way.

Sighing, she scooped up a heaped teaspoonful and stirred it into her steaming cup.

"What are you doing that for?" Reynolds asked. "It'll spoil the taste."

"It might," she said, stirring, "but I don't care. I heard a lot of nutmeg all at once can make you feel good."

"What do you mean, good?"

"I don't know. I've never tried it. I was told it can give you a kind of . . . high. I could use one right now." She set down her spoon. If the men didn't follow her example, the worst that could happen was that she felt better. Or sick to her stomach. Anything was an improvement on how she felt in her head and her heart right now. "Cheers, lads." She took a sip, made a face at the grit in her mouth as she forced it down. After one swallow, most of her drink was still left in the cup, nutmeg skimming the top.

The men were watching her closely, and she shrugged. "Taste does take some getting used to. More lemon juice would be nice."

Dwight spooned more into her cup, and then, at a

nod from them, did the same for the others. Jennings was the first to reach for the teaspoon and dump in a healthy heap of nutmeg. Dwight followed suit. Reynolds was cautious, adding only another pinch.

"Right," Jennings said cheerfully, "a happy Christmas to all."

Clara raised her cup to her lips and watched the others drink. They were, she saw, used to drinking quickly, their cups empty after several swallows as if they truly were taking a medicine. They portioned out the next round of whisky, talking loudly about home, about mothers and sisters and girlfriends and what they might be doing right now. Clara rested her chin on her hands and let the fatigue she felt show in her whole body, her hand on her half-full cup. They didn't ask why she wasn't drinking.

After the second round, the nutmeg bowl was empty. She still didn't see any effect on the men beyond the fact that even Reynolds—who'd had very little extra spice—was in a better mood. Jennings had the excellent idea to go out into the woods and find a little tree to bring inside and decorate, which he promptly went off to do with Dwight in tow. Reynolds stayed inside, smoking a pipe and watching Clara as she took a sip now and then from her cold cup.

She had moved Fenshaw's paper and pencil onto her bed, and she fetched them, still unsure if she should draw the map to the mine. She needed to get to Willy, but she had no intention of avoiding whatever punishment Fenshaw had in store for her. If she escaped the cabin, it would be a temporary freedom. After she helped Willy, she would willingly return to Fenshaw's custody. She could wait for him in the mine if there was a way to get her brother out first, and to safety. Somewhere.

Deflated, she thought longingly back to the nights spent sleeping with Jakob's arms around her, holding her together. She wondered where he was right now, if he was worried about her at all. What would he recommend she do? Draw the map? She didn't suppose he would. He wouldn't want the British to get all the food in the mine. She looked at the fire and imagined her head on his chest, his voice rumbling inside her as he talked. "Do what you think is best, liebling." That's what he would say. And she did know what was best. She wasn't her father. She didn't blind her conscience for her own ends.

As she was finishing the map, Reynolds watching over her shoulder, Jennings stumbled through the back door with Dwight sagging against him, deadly pale, holding his chest. "Something's wrong with him."

Dwight was gasping, breathing quickly. "My heart's racing."

Together Jennings and Reynolds helped him to his bed. Reynolds put his hand on Dwight's chest and ordered Jennings to bring the first aid kit. He tore through it, finding aspirin, bandages, but nothing that would help. Clara watched anxiously from the corner, thinking of the nutmeg. She hadn't intended for anything serious to happen.

"We have to prop his feet up," Reynolds said, rolling a blanket. "Go on, get another."

Jennings stumbled to his bed, reached for his own blanket and dropped it, holding his stomach.

"What's wrong?" Clara asked.

He shook his head. Sweat moistened his face.

Reynolds called to him with irritation, then noticed him leaning against the wall. "What's the matter?"

"I'm feeling . . ." Jennings tugged at his tie, breathing hard, then peeled off his tunic and dropped it on the floor. He was sweating badly. He staggered along the wall and rushed out of the back door into the snow.

"Help him," Reynolds told her, pointing at Dwight. He went outside after Jennings.

Quickly, Clara put on her coat and felt in the pockets of the tunic Jennings had thrown on the floor. The keys to the truck were not in the first, but her fingers closed around them in the second. She touched Dwight's shoulder, and his eyes fluttered open.

"Tell the captain there's a map. I'll surrender, but I have to do something first. He can come and find me. Tell him that."

Dwight didn't answer, didn't appear to understand what she was saying. She hesitated, not knowing what she might do for him, but Reynolds would be back any moment. "I'm sorry."

She paused in the snow outside the front door. Faintly, the voices of Reynolds and Jennings floated to her from behind the cabin. She swung into the cab of the truck, and after several tries, it roared to life. She was reversing toward the snowy track when she saw Reynolds dashing around the cabin. She had no choice but to keep reversing as he ran directly toward her in the light of the front headlamps, slipping, recovering, shouting at her. Afraid of veering off into a ditch or a tree, she split her attention between the side-view mirror and the windshield, which fogged in her quick breaths. She was focused on the land behind her when she heard a crack-crack, and the splinter of glass. A gunshot—she saw Reynolds still running, but slower, arm extended, trying to aim again. The windshield was all right, but only one headlight now cast its beam over the snow.

She braked slowly, and then struggled to turn the truck. Reynolds had stopped, panting hard but still aiming. She knew he was shooting for a tire, and that would be the end of her. As she gently revved the engine, she saw out of the passenger window that Reynolds was now very close, had decided to reach the truck himself rather than shoot again. She changed gear, hit the accelerator, and he was obscured in exhaust. The next time she looked in the mirror, he was farther away, and then farther, until he vanished in the dark.

The road continued down a gentle slope, and then forked, and it was here that she guessed from the complete blackness on either side that these hills fell away into deep valleys. The darkness dismayed her, the lack of signs or other buildings. She tried to remember the land from her journey to the cabin, but she had been in the back and had seen very little. To orient herself, she drove slowly, looking for a sign of any kind. She found some at a junction, but for towns or villages that meant nothing to her. For now, she wanted to avoid people, and drove almost blindly through the hills.

When she reached another junction, she followed a sign that felt as though it might be the right way, since she had little else to go on. She was feeling horribly drowsy, the effects of the whisky she had drunk, and perhaps a little of the nutmeg too. She rolled down the window for a while and let the cold air snap her awake.

Even if she could get Willy out, she didn't know what she could offer him in the real world that was any better than the delusional one he'd created for himself underground. It was no great honor to be connected to the Falkenbergs anymore. Only the Bergers and people like them believed that. At the thought of the people living in Elisa's cellar, Clara wondered if they were the solution, at least temporarily. If she told them Willy was Theodor's son and her brother, they would take him in out of loyalty to the family. Willy could live in his own home—his cellar at least—and stay with them until . . . what? But then, she wasn't sure Willy could live in a normal family, with other children, after what he had gone through.

Cold and quite awake again, she rolled the window back up. Willy was too damaged to live with Jakob's family either, even if she could convince him to take her brother in. She couldn't place such a risk in Jakob's home.

Lights were glowing and twinkling in the distance. The road was too long to double back and look for another route, and so she continued, rolling slowly into what looked like a town. It was more civilization than she'd seen in days—rows of houses along a street slick with stamped snow and ice. There were candles or lanterns in many of the windows, and here and there, people walked the pavements. She gasped with fear when she saw that some were British soldiers in groups, or with a girl on their arm. As she passed, a few waved at her and called, "Happy Christmas!"

She reached a central square with a church, lit up, and a bright building on the corner she assumed was a pub or restaurant, people stumbling in and out, smoke pouring from the chimney. A soldier in a greatcoat waved her down, and she had no choice but to stop.

"Where are you off to?" he asked. Silver tinsel hung from the lapel of his coat.

She hadn't thought of what she'd say if she was caught. But she remembered that she too was in army clothing, driving an army truck, and realized she was about to add impersonating Allied personnel to her other crimes. It was a small thing in comparison.

She exaggerated the English accent of her mother and said, "I'm to drive this thing from Minden back to Essen of all places, tonight of all nights. And no map. I got lost. I'm probably nowhere near, am I?".

He laughed. "You're in the Sauerland, lass. Where's your orders?"

"Don't have any."

He sobered a little, walked the length of the truck, took some time looking in the back, then circled to her window again. "It's empty, and one of your lights is out."

"I know."

"You're driving an empty vehicle on Christmas night and you don't have any orders. Sorry, but that sounds like a load of—" He seemed to change his mind about his language. "Right, what's your name?"

"Anne Heath," she said without hesitation.

"You're going to have to come down out of there while I call this in, Miss Heath."

He opened the door for her and she allowed him to help her out of the cab. The cold instantly cut into her, and she held her coat closed at the collar, trying to think of how to talk her way out of this. It seemed the sort of thing Jakob could do, and she thought of what it would be like if he was at the end of her journey. Maybe that was a story the soldier would believe.

"All right, sir. I wasn't quite ordered to drive to Essen. I had that idea on my own. It's Christmas, you see, and I haven't seen my fella in months. I thought I could drive the truck—nobody would miss it—and pop down to surprise him. Just for tonight. I was going to take it back."

"What's his name?"

"Jakob," she said in the English way.

The soldier stared hard at her, and then a smile

played on the corners of his mouth. "I'll regret this, but what the hell. It's Christmas. Peace on earth, goodwill toward men, eh? Wait here."

He vanished into the pub while she stamped her feet in the snow. If he radioed someone in Minden after all, she would be arrested on the spot. The soldier returned, crossing the snow with brisk steps. "Here you are." He spread a map in front of her and pointed out where they were, and what roads she would have to find to get her back to the Ruhr area and eventually to Essen. "It'll be tricky in the dark, but love finds a way, eh?"

"You're an angel, mate." She kissed him on the cold cheek, and he beamed.

"You tell your Jakob what a lucky man he is." He helped her back into the truck. "And remember. I never saw you, eh?"

The map spread out on the bench beside her, she started the engine.

26

Jakob didn't like it when Willy sat so close to the Christmas tree. The edges of the tin stars hanging from it reminded him of teeth, of knives, of the jagged edge of pain. He couldn't see the bump on Willy's head, but it was there, under the kid's hair. He winced when he rubbed the place with the flat of his hand. Willy hadn't managed to give himself a concussion, or at least show any signs of it, yet Jakob had watched him walk to see if he wavered, served him up a can of ham to see if he could eat, sat up as he slept fitfully on his bed to see if the kid might sneak in the night to his tree, take down one of the stars, and use it on his own throat.

"You thought about my proposal, kid? Coming out with Gertrud and staying for a while at my house?"

Willy hadn't slept for long. He got up and went to

the curtain. Jakob felt disoriented suddenly, as if time had shifted and they were back to when he first came down here.

"What is it?"

Willy shushed him. Jakob recognized his taut body, the sense of anticipation and caution. He joined Willy at the entrance to the tunnel. There was nothing to see in the lantern hanging from the wall and no sound.

"Someone coming?" Jakob whispered.

After an anxious glance at Gertrud, Willy stepped into the tunnel. Jakob followed him, not liking this situation at all. Willy wasn't acting as he would have before, the firm steps of a soldier on patrol, a guard doing his duty. He crept along the tunnel wall, eyes bulging. He still wore his tunic, but unbuttoned, black stains on the sleeves, his shirt half hanging out of his sagging trousers. He'd left his beloved steel helmet in the camp. And strangest of all, he'd left his belt with holster and pistol. Jakob considered fetching the gun himself, but he was not going to be the one to endanger them all by discharging it inside the mine.

Outside the room that contained marmalade and honey, Willy stiffened. He was listening, intense, as though he could hear frequencies beyond Jakob's capacities. All Jakob could hear was their nervous breathing and a ringing in his ears that came from inside his own head, a reaction to the deep silence of the mine. They waited, both of them straining to listen. Cold drops of sweat began to gather at Jakob's hairline and the back of his neck, an old reaction from the war, a sign of danger, a warning.

He grasped Willy's arm and tried to pull him away, back into the tunnel. Willy shook him off and, in a fit of recklessness, rushed into the next corridor.

"Willy?" The voice, vaguely familiar, reached Jakob weakly, as if the man had spoken from a high mountain, one of the odd effects of how sound traveled in the tunnels. Jakob crept along the wall and then looked cautiously around the corner.

The man was hugging a package in his arms as he stood half blocking the lantern on the wall behind him. His gaze was fixed on Willy, who had stopped close by, slightly crouched in surprise or fear, Jakob wasn't sure.

"Willy, I've been calling for you. I thought you'd gone." The light caught more of his face, and Jakob recognized the man he had met at Anne Heath's Christmas party.

Jakob immediately slid back into his own corridor so he wouldn't be seen. The alarm inside him was blaring now, pushing the sweat from his pores, winding up his muscles. All along, Willy had been waiting for someone to come back to the mine for him. If it was that man—

Max Hecht, was it?—likely Clara's old lover, who'd known the kid was down here, Jakob just might have to break a bone or two in the bastard. No decent human being would leave a boy here for two years, even a kid as stubborn and difficult as Willy.

Slowly, silently, Jakob put out the lantern in his corridor. He backtracked quietly to the next and darkened that lantern too. Then he slid along the tunnels again, and peeked into the corridor where Max was talking to the boy.

"It's for you," Max was saying, holding out the package. "It's Christmas." He took a step toward Willy, who scrambled back. "There's nothing to be scared of. My wife made it for you."

"I don't want it."

"Look." Max peeled away the colorful paper aside and pulled out a dark red knitted cloth. "It's a scarf. We thought you'd like something warm and homemade." He tossed the paper aside and shook out the scarf, displaying it to Willy. "Go on. It's yours."

"Thank you, but I said I don't want it."

"Well, what do you want, then?" When Willy said nothing, Max went on, reining in his tone. "Willy. You need to stop the nonsense and come with me. If you'd come out the last time I was here, you'd be opening presents and eating sweets with my family right now."

It was a variation of the promises Jakob had used to try to lure the kid out of the mine. He was ashamed to hear Max Hecht using the same arguments.

Willy was scratching his shirt where his heart was. "Do you know what happened to my mother?"

"She's still missing," Max said. "No news since the last time. But people are still looking for her. Once she's found, she'll be glad you're safe with me."

"I think you should go home, Uncle Max."

"Tell me what will make you leave this place. Whatever it is. I can help you."

"No, you can't."

"Willy." A snap of frustration. Max quickly smoothed it over, his voice honey again. "Let's go and find Gertrud. See what she has to say about all this."

Willy blocked his way. "No."

"This is madness, Willy. We're good friends. We've known each other your whole life. Why don't you trust me?"

Jakob stepped into the dim light of the corridor. "He's got good instincts. That's my guess."

Max jerked back, and Jakob smiled at the blaze of fear and confusion on his face. He straightened the army tunic he still wore, clasped his hands behind his back, and said, "Sorry to interrupt. I stumbled upon this place, this wonderful place full of delicious food, and every time I come down here, something interesting happens. So I'm curious, Max. Are you really the person who put the kid down here to begin with?"

"I recognize you. Relling." Max knotted the scarf in his hands. "You're the one who turned Clara in to Fenshaw."

Hearing it said aloud stung Jakob like a needle in the throat. He swallowed and kept up his smile.

"I did that, yes, and I'll regret it till my dying day. She's a much better woman than she thinks she is, and she deserved better from me. From you too, I bet. Does she know you put Willy down here? No, I didn't think so. She doesn't know about any of this."

Max stepped toward Jakob. "If Fenshaw hurts her, it will be on your head. I'll see to that."

"I'd watch my step if I was you. She promised to skin alive whoever did this to Willy."

"You don't have any idea, Relling. I've known Clara half her life."

"You might've known her back then, but I know who she is now. She's not going to accept what you did because there was a war on. She knows better than that. You wanted to save the boy at the center of the family secrets."

Willy backed up against the wall, his big eyes on Max. "What is he talking about?"

"I'll explain everything when you're out of here," Max said.

"Explain what?" Willy was sliding along the wall away from them. "What secrets?"

Jakob felt for the boy, but it wasn't his place to explain to him what he knew. "Go on, Uncle Max. Are you going to be the one to tell Willy what everybody kept from him all these years?"

"You don't care about the boy. You're a greedy opportunist, down here to steal the food. Well, it's yours. All of it. Take it away and mind your own damn business." Max stepped back, spreading his arms as if offering Jakob all the prosperity and good fortune in this world. But there was a catch, a sheen of malice in Max's smile as he added, "It's the best deal a cripple could ever hope for."

At that, Jakob punched him in the face. Max bellowed, holding his hands over his bloodied nose, a sight that made Jakob feel even better about what he'd done, at least until he noticed Willy staring at him, appalled.

"Willy—"

But the boy was stumbling into the next tunnel, fleeing as if terrified. Holding the scarf to his face, Max went after him, calling his name.

Jakob flexed his stiff hand as he limped into the room with the sugar, then the one with the canned bread. The plans he had for this food, the ambition, the raw desire—all of that had somehow evaporated. He wouldn't take a thing, not with Max Hecht dictating the terms. He knew now that the mine was too good to be true. It had been so from the very beginning. The only good thing to come of this place was Clara. He leaned against the wall and tried to imagine how she would want him to deal with Max and Willy. For her sake, if there was any more he could do, he would.

Clara parked the truck in a field of frosty brambles off a dirt road by the river. The silence over the still water chilled her more than the wind. Behind her, the cliffs rose up, one of them holding the entrance to Willy's mine. In the beam of her flashlight, she picked her way carefully up the slope and shone her light on the rock; seeing no dark crack in the cliff, she moved on. Unlike in the Sauerland, the snow had melted here. The last of it clumped in the folds of rock. On the ground, the slush had frozen, dirty and slick. She swung her flashlight from her path to the cliff and back again, uncertain how long it was going to take her to find the right mine.

Finally, she recognized the shape of a rock and the vines and moss covering it. She hesitated outside the black hole that led to the mine, remembering both the gun Willy had pressed to her back, but also the kiss Jakob had given her the last time she was here, for luck. "Glück auf," she whispered, warming a little.

She climbed into the first tunnel, the dread mounting as the opaque darkness closed around the light beam. The flashlight flickered—a moment of panic—and then the light steadied. At the dead end, she remembered to turn right into the concrete corridor.

"Willy?"

The lamps were dark. Willy would never let the lamps go out, would he? Unless he was ill again. Or gone. She thought of the river, of him walking into it and sinking without protest.

She looked for the marks she'd left in the tunnels, the labels and arrows she had scrawled on the walls and doors the last time she was here, her guide to the labyrinth. There was no trace. Even with her flashlight, the dark was too thick, too all-consuming. The air was damp and cold. She took a turn, then another, opened a door. A room with a row of stained toilets and chipped stalls. She didn't remember this from last time. She backed out, took another turn, another door. The stench from inside drove her back into the corridor—feces and urine and rotted food.

"Willy? Where are you?"

The walls narrowed, no longer concrete but stone

and timber. Willy's camp was partly timber, she re-membered that. Maybe she was close. Nervously, she swung her light along the tunnel, but could see noth-ing that would identify where she was: this tunnel was the same as the next one, and the next. She spotted the electrical cord overhead and began to follow it. Maybe it would lead to some kind of utilities room, or a genera-tor. As she turned yet another dark corner, her breaths gusted in her ears and she felt the pressure in her chest. If she was panicking, she could control that, she could calm her heart with the right thoughts, the right breath-ing, but if it wasn't panic, if it was bad air, it was already too late.

A rough hand closed over her mouth, and she cried out, swinging her flashlight at his head. He caught her wrist, turned the flashlight on his own face.

"Jakob?"

"Clara?" His hug crushed the air out of her and she didn't care. Her blood thawed immediately and was pumping through her veins again. "Clara, I am so sorry. I told Fenshaw—"

"I know." Inside her, the wound from his betrayal healed instantly. "You'll have to make that up to me someday."

"That's what I was trying to do. I couldn't leave Willy alone. I knew you wouldn't want that. It's why

I'm here. But where have you been? How did you get here? Did Fenshaw—?"

"He showed me . . ." She couldn't express it, not the detail of the horrors she had seen in his photographs. "I was in the Sauerland. I'm fine. But . . . Elisa is dead, Jakob. I saw proof."

"I'm so sorry. What happened?" When she let out a stuttering breath, he answered for her. "Gestapo."

She nodded, and he held her close for a few moments. "How did you get away from Fenshaw?"

"I hurt my guards and stole their truck. I don't have much time. Where's Willy?"

"In his camp, I think." Jakob was caressing the back of her neck. "But Max Hecht is here too."

"Max? How can he be here?" Not how. The question was why, and she drew back slowly from Jakob, working it out. "Max knew. He knew Willy was here all along."

The heat in her stomach was boiling over, shifting between nausea and pain as Jakob told her more. Max had tried to convince Willy to leave, had promised a warm family life, and Willy wouldn't go with him.

"Take me to them."

"I don't want to. If we could just . . ." He was holding her face in his hands, and she knew he meant go away. If only they could just go away. She wanted it too, more than almost anything. But for Elisa and Willy, and for herself, she couldn't leave her brother to Max. And she couldn't run from Fenshaw any longer.

She almost told Jakob about the map, that Fenshaw was coming, that she would surrender even if Willy didn't. Though he would. She was almost certain of it. But she didn't want to argue with Jakob about her plan. He would find out soon enough. She kissed him, one long warm kiss that tasted of the earth over their heads and under their feet. She was still scared of what she would find in the mine, Willy lost to madness and beyond help, and she clutched Jakob, held on to their kiss, as long as she could.

His optimism hummed inside her, something warm and magical from the core of him passed on to her. In prison, she would remember him and everything he had given her, and it would keep her alive.

He led her by the hand through the dark tunnels, and as her anxiety grew, she was glad to hold on to him for a little while longer. They reached a lighted corridor and paused to blink the spots out of their eyes. It shocked her all over again to see Jakob in uniform. "Why are you wearing that?"

"Willy respects it. At least, he used to." Jakob pulled the tunic over his shoulders, down his arms, and flung it onto the ground. For good measure, he stomped on it with his wooden foot.

Farther down the tunnel, Clara recognized the curtain blocking off Willy's camp. Closer, she heard a labored, nasal voice from the other side, Max trying to talk reason. "This place isn't going to stay secret forever, Willy. Relling found it. You think no one else will? He's going to go in and out carrying supplies. Do you think someone isn't going to notice that? You have to leave now."

Jakob gave her hand a last squeeze, and she moved the curtain aside.

Willy was on his bed, wearing his steel helmet, his knees under his chin and his arms wrapped tightly around his legs. He reminded her of the little boy she used to know. She wanted to rush over and hug him, but of course he was too old for that now. Besides, there was something feral in his eyes. He might lash out at any moment, and might have done so already if it wasn't for the soothing peeps of Gertrud shifting uneasily in her nest.

Max was a shock, his nose swollen, blood encrusted on his lips. "Clara, treasure. How—?" He touched her hair, and the gesture detonated the fury inside her.

"You knew." She pushed him hard, and he was surprised enough to stumble back into the crate, rattling the tree with its tin stars. "You knew Willy was here. How could you do this to him?" She pushed him again, but this time he stood his ground.

"Clara, listen, I did this for you. Did you want him thrown at the front? Cannon fodder? Elisa didn't know what to do."

Clara hesitated. "Elisa knew? I don't believe it. She would never have wanted him in a place like this."

"She knew I was going to help him. We'd agreed on that, but I had to keep the details quiet. It was dangerous enough to talk about hiding a boy from the army, let alone doing it. Once the Americans came, I was going to tell her about the mine—but she vanished."

"So you don't know what happened to her?"

"No. Willy was never supposed to be down here this long. But he refuses to come out." Max turned back to Willy, who was still hugging himself on his bed. "I've tried over and over to take him home with me."

Clara couldn't stand him talking as if his motives had been so pure, his generous act spoiled by circumstance and a stubborn boy. "Did my mother tell you to do this?"

"Damn it, Clara, listen to me. I wanted to protect him. You remember how chaotic everything was at the end of the war. He was safe here."

"You didn't do this for Elisa or even for Willy. You

said it yourself. You did it for me." She backed up to the timbered wall, its cracks smeared with black dust. "Why? What made you think I would want Willy hidden away like this?"

"He's your best friend's son." The discomfort in his eyes, how his gaze shifted away from her—they told her everything. She looked at Willy, the dismay on his face, and imagined the possibility that she wasn't the first person he had told about what he saw in that warehouse in January 1945.

"How long have you known about Elisa and my father?"

Max let out a long sigh. "So you do know."

"How long, Max?"

His nose had begun to bleed again and he pressed his scarf to it, muffling his words. "Since the night we met. Reinhard was drunk, and when you'd gone, he told me about the arrangements with your family. He'd been forbidden to talk but he was proud of himself. Getting a pretty girl and a career in the bargain. All he had to do was—" He glanced at Willy, who watched them with wide eyes, and said, "Keep everything secret."

She forced herself to go closer to Max, to see this man in the light of the lantern, a completely new light, after all these years. "This is why my mother tolerated us being together, why my father let you rise at the

Works. Because you knew everything. In exchange for your silence, you got a bargain too, didn't you?"

"It wasn't like that. It never was, Clara. I always loved you."

And she believed him. Late in the war, after months and months of estrangement from her, Max had decided to redeem himself by offering something valuable to Clara—her brother, even if she didn't know it then. He made sure to stash him away so that he, Max, would be the one presenting the boy to her after the war—in triumph. In love.

She saw all of it in Max's mangled face. It disturbed her. Even his affection. It was pitiful, desperate, repulsive, using a child in this way. She shook her head at him, and went to sit next to Willy. He was taking gulping breaths with his mouth open, as if the three other people in his camp were suffocating him.

"Mama is dead, isn't she?"

He took off his helmet, and something rigid in his face melted. He wasn't playing soldier anymore. He had fought the battles and was dirty and crumpled and she had to believe that, like all soldiers, he wanted to go home. She didn't know where that was, for her or for him. Now she was here, she didn't know what to say to convince him that anywhere in this world was better than this. He would recognize the chaos outside, the feeling of oblivion, everything they'd known buried under the rubble.

"I'm so sorry, Willy."

He turned the helmet upside down like a bowl, gazing at it as if he'd left some crucial thought inside. "I killed her."

"A Gestapo bullet killed her. It's done. Hiding down here won't change it. Willy, we can leave together. There's so much to talk about."

"I'll never leave. Never."

Max interrupted. "I told him I'll take him in, and I'll stand by that, Clara. Come with me, both of you—"

She snapped at him, "Get out, Max. You're not wanted here. Go."

"You're angry, I can understand that, but—"

From where he leaned against the wall, Jakob spoke up. "I think you're not hearing right, Hecht. She said get the hell out of here."

Max planted himself in front of Jakob. "This is none of your business."

"I'd be happy to discuss that outside."

"Stop!" Willy was clutching his head between his hands as if to keep it from cracking in half. "Go away! All of you!" He blundered off the bed, colliding with the table, and ended at the map smeared with mud. "What am I supposed to do? Everybody's dead. Everything's gone."

"I know," Clara said. "Everything has gone. So many are dead, but not everyone. We're still here," she added softly. "You and I."

He hiccoughed, close to a sob. He was so young. He was the same age she was when she first met Elisa that day over the Ruhr, the proud young heiress, safe in the cradle of her family. Willy had likely never felt so certain about who he was or about his place in the world. At the very least, she could give him some of what she used to have, the truth of where he came from.

"Willy, listen to me. Your father is alive."

"He fell in the war."

"I mean your father by blood."

"No." Willy backed up to the wall. "No."

"Listen." She told him everything slowly so that he would understand. She started with his mother, seventeen and—Clara knew now—in love with her employer.

"Theodor Falkenberg," she said. "My father. And yours too. He's alive. In an internment camp, but alive. In his way, he tried to take care of you. Your mother did her best for you. But there was always love, Willy.

It got buried under other things, pride and fear, but there was also love."

The anguish in Willy's face disappeared. His blankness terrified her more than his anger ever could. He was thinking deeply, and she suddenly knew he was remembering that night at the Works when he saw his mother and father together. He was thinking about the terrible mistake he had made. His mouth opened, a long struggle before he said, "You're lying."

"I'm done with lies. They were your parents, Willy—"

He covered his ears.

"Why would I lie about this? Do you think I wanted things this way?"

"My parents?" He dropped his hands; there was something wild in his eyes. "My mother, do you know how she used to look at me? Like she was seeing somebody else. She never saw me."

"That's not true."

"And my father. Herr Falkenberg? Smiles and a pat on the shoulder, that's all I ever had from him, and he's supposed to be my father?"

"He should have been honest with you. With all of us, about so many things. But it's done. We can't change what we did in the past. We can only act differently now."

He was shaking his head.

Clara had so little time until Fenshaw came. She was desperate to leave her brother with something that would help him. "You did what you did and you're going to have to accept it. You can't punish yourself forever. Nobody can live like that, Willy." She could see he didn't understand, that what she was trying to say wasn't getting through to him. "I can't explain it in here. Please come outside."

"Why? Why should I?"

"Because you're my brother and I'll drag you out if I have to. I won't let you die in here."

Willy let out a cry and plowed into her. They fell together to the floor, Willy striking out with his fists. Jakob caught hold of his arm, but Max seemed determined to be the one to save her. He pushed Jakob aside and the two of them were soon wrestling at the wall. Clara blocked Willy any way she could, her arms up, twisting from his blows. She had grown up with brothers; she had done this before. Soon she was kicking him, clawing his scalp, taking punches and giving them too, wrestling in the dirt. His fist hit the ground and came back smeared and wet. And then he was clinging to her, his face in her chest, her arms tight around him, holding him together before he broke apart for good.

Suddenly, men flooded the tunnel, flashlights and

lanterns swirling around them. The lights settled on her face. Blinded, she tucked her nose into Willy's hair. They stayed together on the ground while the men cried out in surprised English. Even when she felt a gentle tug at her arm, she didn't let Willy go.

"Don't take him away." She felt him quaking with panic. "Don't lock him away—"

"Fräulein, it's all right." Captain Fenshaw was kneeling beside them. "And you must be Willy." She saw the pity and horror behind the smile Fenshaw was struggling to maintain. "Everything is all right, lad. Up you get. Come on."

Willy's body relaxed, a long sigh of fatigue. He faced Fenshaw and raised his hands.

"I surrender." He hiccoughed, and sobs flooded out of him, his mouth wide open like a child's. She couldn't stand to see him so lost, and she wrapped her arms around him again, keeping him on his feet.

Max and Jakob both stood at the wall, their hands up. It was Max who said, "Captain, may I speak? I have very important information that proves that Clara, Fräulein Falkenberg, was an enemy of the Nazi regime. I have evidence, documentation, and I'm willing to cooperate fully even if"—he took a shaky breath—"I incriminate myself."

His words left her indifferent. She wanted no help

from him, no sacrifices. Captain Fenshaw was holding the ledger where Willy had kept his statistics about the supplies, listening to Max without glancing up from it. When he finally did, he looked not at him but at her, his face thoughtful.

"Right, I'll talk to you first, Herr Hecht." He issued orders to his men to lead the rest of them to separate rooms. Clara refused to leave Willy, and a soldier escorted them both to the one full of cigarettes. Under guard, they waited in silence, Clara too exhausted to do more than touch Willy's arm now and then. She didn't know what to say to comfort him. She was going to prison and she regretted all she couldn't do. Find him a room with a window, a proper bed. See that he finished school. Help him get a job or an apprenticeship. Elisa would have wanted that, and Clara had so much experience that she could share.

Once the practical things were taken care of—food and work, a routine—he might be ready to turn inward again. Not to punish himself this time, but to understand what he'd done and why. She wanted him to be able to accept it, so he might become the kind of man who could forgive himself—and others.

Fenshaw appeared in the doorway rubbing his forehead. "Fräulein, this way, please. I'll talk to the boy now."

"Let me stay. He's still upset. He's—"

"It's all right," he said more gently than she expected. "Come along."

She didn't know how to say good-bye to Willy and so she kissed him on the top of the head as her father used to do to her when she was a girl.

She expected Fenshaw to take her out of the mine, to whisk her away to prison, but instead he led her by the arm to a room where Jakob was eating dark bread scooped out of a can with his hand. When he saw her, he struggled to get up, spilling the boxes around him. Fenshaw left them alone, with the guard just outside the room.

She hugged Jakob for a long time, and there were kisses, slow and regretful. It would be the last time she held him like this, and she wanted to remember everything about it. How solidly he stood on his two feet, how straight his back was as she ran her hands up his shirt. He smelled of dust and faint cigarette smoke and she even detected the lightest trace of cologne. When he held her, his nose rested a few moments on her brow, his breaths warming her eyelids and gently moving her lashes.

In prison, years were going to pass. She felt them already stretching in front of her; how she would grow old in there; how he would marry and start a family.

He should live life, just as Willy should. That was what she wished for both of them.

"Clara, there are enough people walking around here without a shred of remorse for the things they did in the war and you're going to prison? It's not right."

"It's what I deserve."

He held her tightly, another thing she'd remember when she was gone. "I'll write to you," he said.

"I'm glad."

"I'll send you packages. Chocolates and sausages and bread and marmalade and honey."

"From the mine? You think Fenshaw will let you have some of it?"

"I'll organize it for you. I'm done with this place."

"Please don't break any laws."

He rested his forehead against hers, grinning. "Wouldn't be so bad. Maybe they'd put us in the same cell."

Fenshaw appeared in the doorway and gestured for her to follow. A hundred things she wanted to tell Jakob flooded her mind, but their time was up. The last kiss was short. She had to leave quickly or she wouldn't be able to leave him at all.

Fenshaw escorted her back to Willy's camp. They were alone except for Gertrud, who shivered in her nest. Fenshaw gently touched the canary's head, then sat on one of two stools at the crate table. Clara took the second. The Christmas tree was on the floor, and on the table were the same thick files that Fenshaw seemed to take with him everywhere. She wondered what kind of comfort he found in them.

"Are your men all right?" she asked. "I didn't mean to hurt them."

"They're being treated, but yes, they should be fine."

In her pocket, she touched the photograph of Elisa that Fenshaw had given her, and the silk scrap of her wedding dress. Clara hoped she could keep them with her in prison. "Thank you for letting me say good-bye to Willy and Jakob."

He opened the top file to a blank sheet of paper and unscrewed his pen. "Tell me everything that happened after I left the cabin last night."

He noted what she said, his script small and cryptic as far as she could see from across the table. It was almost as if he wrote in some secret alphabet of his own. By the time she finished, he had filled several pages front and back. He tucked them into the file, and again, she had the sudden feeling of time running out.

"You're going to help Willy, aren't you?"

"I told you. I can't."

"You saw him. He just needs time and someone to guide him."

He spread his hands on his files as if to keep them from flying away in a stiff wind. In the lantern light, he seemed younger and far less certain than he had even moments ago. He was more like the young man she had first met, struggling to understand the woman in front of him.

Finally, he stood up, and she knew she had lost. She would have to leave Willy to his fate. It was in Fenshaw's hands. She rose to face him. "Just . . . try to understand what he went through," she said. "He's still a boy."

Fenshaw reached into his coat—for handcuffs, she assumed. She expected to be taken out of the mine as the prisoner she was. So be it. She would face whatever he had in store for her: the interrogations, indictments, imprisonment. She would be honest about her father and what they both did and thought. Her father wouldn't understand why. He would see it as a personal betrayal. But she would show him what it was to have some integrity.

Fenshaw bent close to her as if he was about to whisper a secret into her ear. Instead, he slipped something into her coat pocket. She drew a surprised breath as she felt the familiar edge of her old identity card.

"Fräulein Müller," he said in a formal tone, "in the future, you will not use your old name under any circumstances. You will not settle inside the Essen city limits. Once a month, you will report to me in the form of a letter with your current address and activities. If you violate any of these conditions, if your name comes up in a police report for any reason anywhere in this zone, our agreement is at an end. I will come for you. Understood?"

She held the card in her palm, the photograph of another her, the hunted woman, hiding from herself.

"In addition," he said, "if I need assistance acquiring information about wanted war criminals, you will give it without question."

She thought of Herr Doctor Blum. "For instance, a camp doctor?"

"For instance."

He was giving her a chance, showing her a way to try to make things right. At least a little. It was so unexpected, it winded her. She sat heavily on a crate. "Are you sure about this?"

"I think you have it in you to do what's right." A brief smile. "I'd like you to prove it."

She didn't know if she could. Prison would feel like justice to others and to her too. In prison, she could believe she was really paying for what she'd done. If she stayed free, she couldn't live her life as if nothing had happened. She had to pay the debt she owed. But helping Fenshaw might be the beginning of things, a new start far different than she had ever imagined.

"Thank you, Captain." She touched his hand, and he waved her away in embarrassment.

"We'll get the boy some temporary papers, and off you go. Both of you." He pointed at her. "And I want a report about that doctor."

"I won't forget."

She tenderly lifted Gertrud out of her nest and carried her to the room with the cigarettes. Jakob was there now, sitting next to Willy, who was still slumped on the packets, sunk into himself. Gertrud began to chirp and wriggle in her hands, and Willy slowly awakened, reaching for his pet. A familiar feeling swept through Clara, the same rush of affection she'd had years ago when she first saw his mother.

They waited together in silence until a guard brought the papers from Fenshaw. Then he escorted them all to the entrance to the mine, where the last long tunnel ended in the pale light of morning.

Acknowledgments

My deepest gratitude to my agent, Laetitia Ruth-
erford. Her patience, honesty, editorial insight,
and faith in me went above and beyond the call of
duty. I imagine her on a skyscraper with her cape bil-
lowing behind her. A huge thanks to my editors, Sarah
Rigby at Hutchinson and Liz Stein at William Morrow,
for guiding me through the exciting and daunting process of getting a first book ready for publication. I'm
also indebted to Jocasta Hamilton for steadying the ship
when the publishing waters got a little choppy. Much
thanks to Molly Gendell and Rose Waddilove for their
help. Thanks also to the many friends and critique partners who gave new perspectives and impulses to early
versions of this book. To my parents—thank you for
your support over the years, and your absolute belief in

my talents. To my daughters, Olivia and Amelia—thank you for being patient with me. It's not easy to have a writer mom. Finally, to my husband, Jürgen—thanks for enduring my questions about all things German, and for being there every step of the way.

HARPER
LARGE PRINT

We hope you enjoyed reading
our new, comfortable print size and found it
an experience you would like to repeat.

Well – you're in luck!

Harper Large Print offers the finest in
fiction and nonfiction books in this same larger
print size and paperback format. Light and easy to read,
Harper Large Print paperbacks are for the book lovers
who want to see what they are reading without strain.

For a full listing of titles and
new releases to come, please visit our website:
www.hc.com

HARPER LARGE PRINT

SEEING IS BELIEVING!